A FANCY

TO KILL FOR

In the stinking darkness of the Waterloo underpass Ruth Macintosh wished she had dodged the traffic at ground level – anything would be better than this. She thought she heard a footstep close behind her and turned to see a rat scurrying into the gloom. She shuddered.

She was surrounded by smelly murkiness. Something moved behind an upturned iron bedstead obscurely tipped on end against the side of the tunnel. Ruth looked across, unable to see properly. The lights were on, but not all of them were working, and some parts of the tunnel seemed quite dark. Then close behind her she heard a sound. She turned quickly, swinging on her heels, alarmed. But as she did so, peering intently through the gloom, her fearful expression faded. Her lips parted in a tentative smile.

Ten seconds later Ruth Macintosh was dead.

Hilary Bonner is a former Showbusiness Editor of the *Mail on Sunday* and the *Daily Mirror*. She now works as a freelance journalist, covering film, television and theatre. She lives in Somerset. Her first novel, *The Cruelty of Morning*, was published in 1995.

HILARY BONNER

A FANCY *to* KILL FOR

Mandarin

First published in the United Kingdom
by Mandarin Paperbacks and William Heinemann 1997

3 5 7 9 10 8 6 4 2

Mandarin Books
Random House UK Ltd, 20 Vauxhall Bridge Road, SW1V 2SA

Random House Australia (Pty) Limited
20 Alfred Street, Milsons Point, Sydney,
New South Wales 2061, Australia

Random House New Zealand Limited
18 Poland Road, Glenfield
Auckland 10, New Zealand

Random House South Africa (Pty) Limited
Endulini, 11a Jubilee Road,
Parktown 2193, South Africa

Random House UK Limited Reg. No. 954009

A CIP catalogue record for this title
is available from the British Library
ISBN 0 7493 1973 9

Typeset in 11 on 12.5 point Plantin
by Avon Dataset Ltd, Bidford on Avon, Warks
Printed and bound in Great Britain
by Cox & Wyman Ltd, Reading, Berkshire

This book is dedicated to actors everywhere, bless them, without whom the world would be a saner place – but so much more dull.

With special thanks to Sergeant Frank Waghorn of the Avon and Somerset Constabulary, and Detective Constable Phil Diss of the Devon and Cornwall Constabulary.

PART ONE

Where death is
Elegant in flight
He sweeps by it
Knowingly.

Where life is
Like a rocket
He swoops on to it
Mercilessly.

Beautiful bird
seen but not heard
power in precision
creature with a mission
older than earth
destined from birth
to be a torpedo
of destruction.

Hawk on the wing
Hawk on the hunt
Hawk on the trail
of oblivion.

One

His hands rested possessively on her bare shoulders. She leaned back against him and smiled a silly smile which carried all the message of her sexual arousal. In turn his eyes were dark with desire and he moved his fingers sensuously, deliciously exploring the burning smoothness of her flesh. Oh how he loved this. To know they were both pretending. The best game of all.

She was stark naked sitting on the gold velvet bedroom stool. A woman past her prime in life, but with a body painstakingly well-preserved. He stood behind her still wearing the navy-blue pin-striped trousers of his immaculate city suit – jacket and shirt cast aside on the bed. The buckle to his trousers and the top button of his flies – always buttons for him, never a zip – were undone where she had grappled earlier in her uncontrolled hunger for him. He had told her not to be in such a hurry and had made her undress before him, then sit exactly how he wanted her to.

He returned her smile and screwed up his eyes so that they crinkled in the way he knew women found so attractive. He could feel the warmth of her breath, of her eager panting breath. The raven black halo of her hair was against his upper belly and as he glanced downward he automatically noticed how good it looked against his deep tan, just where the line of soft body hair trailed tantalisingly into his trousers. He checked that he was standing in the manner which best emphasised the clean hard contours of his body.

Fleetingly he moved his hands down to her breasts, so that his fingertips just touched her nipples, and pinched each one between thumb and forefinger, sharply, almost harshly. Before she could react he brought his hands up again across her collar bone and over her shoulders and, without warning, grasped her neck, squeezing, squeezing. Those long fingers, so delicately caressing just seconds ago, felt like the steel talons of a mechanical grip.

There was only alarm now in her fading blue eyes. She clawed ineffectively at his wrists, and with her little fists tapped against his back and chest using all that was left of her ebbing strength. It was useless. He was a professional. He knew what he was doing. With the last of her consciousness she searched his face for reassurance, for a sign that she was mistaken, that this was just another game. There was none. His lips were curled back in a snarl, revealing two immaculate rows of teeth, clenched together, and his eyes, too, were pressed tightly shut.

He did not want to see her die.

There was no need. He could do this blindfolded. He did not have to look. He raised a knee against the small of her back and deftly snapped her half-strangled neck backwards. There was a loud crack. He let go of her neck and she fell heavily to the ground – just a broken twisted thing now.

With care he stepped over her and reached for his shirt and jacket.

'I'm sorry, Maria,' he murmured.

Motionless for a moment he stood above her, looking down sadly at her crooked body. He was, as ever, controlled – but, none the less, not unmoved by what he had done.

When the shout came it was a shock, just like always for him at these moments. Half forgotten. No longer expected. Startling him back into reality.

'Cut!' yelled the director.

'Well done everybody, that was a good one. Wonderful, Ricky darling. Perfect as always. Belle – lovely, sweetheart.'

Richard Corrington, the most successful actor in British television, raised one hand rather limply in acknowledgement. He not only assumed this kind of gushing admiration from his directors to be his right, he had come to demand it.

After all, the Richard Corrington TV series, *Sparrow-Hawk*, was the biggest show in the world, selling to 140 countries.

A minder had already helped Ricky into a tracksuit top and Arabella Parker was eventually passed a towelling robe.

'That's it, folks,' called the director. 'It's a wrap. Another one in the can . . .'

There was a small outbreak of applause and even a cheer or two from crew and cast. Richard smiled benignly. He glanced briefly at Arabella.

'Splendid, darling, you died beautifully, thank you so much,' he murmured. The smile was a toothpaste commercial. The dark brown eyes – or 'come-to-bed brown eyes' as they were frequently described in feature articles in women's magazines – were all crinkly again. Just an extension of his performance for camera really.

He leaned forward, he a very tall man and she

rather short in stature, and brushed his lips against her forehead before making a somewhat majestic exit in the direction of his dressing room.

Belle did not trust herself to speak. She stiffened and headed for the exit, forcing herself not to run. Once outside the studio door she paused and almost fell against the wall. Tears shone in her eyes.

'The bastard, the utter bastard,' she said to herself.

The door burst open again. 'The bastard, the rotten bastard,' she heard. It was the veteran dresser, a woman Belle had first known many years ago in different better times, who had been looking after her all week.

In spite of herself Belle smiled.

'You noticed, I gather?'

'The times I've seen him do it, dear. The old nipple squeeze. Not in the script, eh?'

'I hate nude scenes,' said Arabella.

'Don't know why a woman like you puts up with his behaviour,' said the dresser.

'Yes you do,' replied Belle. 'I'll earn more from one appearance in *Sparrow-Hawk* than I have out of this rotten business in the whole of the last year.'

'You're a star you are,' the dresser told her. 'You shouldn't have to do this kind of stuff.'

Belle laughed hollowly. 'Those were the days,' she said. 'God, the man makes me feel like a whore.'

'Don't lose any sleep, dear,' said the dresser. 'He'll get his. You'll see . . .'

When he reached his dressing room Richard Corrington waved away the team of hovering sycophants and shut the door in their faces.

He knew he had given another cracking performance

– not just today but throughout the filming of the latest series. The grander of Britain's theatre actors and even many of the film boys might scorn what he had to do in *Sparrow-Hawk*, but it wasn't as easy as it looked.

His entire body and soul had gone into that last scene with Belle Parker. She had indeed been a star – once. Now it was his turn, and he couldn't resist making his position crystal clear.

As always he was experiencing the familiar tingling sensation in his fingers and toes, the slightly nauseous feeling in the pit of his stomach. It was like coming down after a terrific high. He knew that when he saw the rushes the next morning – he had complete control over *Sparrow-Hawk* and anything he didn't like was either cut or reshot – he would not remember much of what he had done on camera.

He held his hands before his face. They were trembling. He remembered pinching the woman's nipples. Never in the script, yet he often did it. It built the scene. It spoke volumes of humiliation, of contempt. There were all these little things he did which gave his show, his performance, the edge, the reality others sought and rarely found.

The one thing even those who decried Ricky's acting talent could never fail to admit was that he really *was* the vigilante hitman Jack Sparrow. And as such he had been almost personally responsible for taking British television into a whole new sphere. *Sparrow-Hawk*, twelve years old in the UK, had been on the American network for almost six years. That meant big money and massive exposure – Richard's only regret being that he knew American TV could never put him quite on a level with the Hollywood film stars he secretly yearned to join.

He took two steps forwards and lowered himself with a bump on to the swivel chair which stood before the big mirror surrounded by bright lights – just like a theatre dressing room. He switched on the lights. They were indeed startlingly bright. They took no prisoners, did nobody any favours, but when it came to looks Richard needed few favours. He stared at his reflection, with professional distraction he studied his face. Yes; still as handsome as ever at forty-nine. He was one of those men who seemed to be growing more attractive with age, which was fortunate indeed for an actor. His hair remained abundantly wavy. He wore it slightly longer than was fashionable and swept back in a distinctive quiff. Its rich brownness needed only the slightest touching up around the temples where the brown had turned very slightly to grey. He didn't mind the grey, as it happened. He had found all the wealth and fame he could possibly aspire to and about the only thing he still longed for was to be regarded as a distinguished actor. He was clever and able at what he did, but the adulation he received allowed him to nurture all kinds of misconceptions about his cleverness and ability in other directions. The truth was that, like many actors, Richard was a man of very average intelligence who had come to believe that he was exceptional because people kept telling him so. And in an alarmingly simplistic fashion he secretly believed that greying temples might change his image, that he might appear more distinguished and indeed more important. But the studio bosses didn't want Jack Sparrow grey. *Sparrow-Hawk* was immortal. Indestructible.

Richard smiled at his reflection. The big slightly

crooked grin came naturally now. He remembered how, as a young actor, he had spent hours before the mirror practising the facial expressions which made him look the most attractive.

His skin was good. The tan slap applied just an hour or so ago looked harsh and over-the-top in real life, but on the TV screen he would appear totally flawless and all the more handsome for it.

Only those who knew him very well would have been able to detect the signs of strain.

Two hundred miles away Richard Corrington's wife, the actress Amanda Lane, was in full flight. The windows of their grand old manor house, set deep in the heart of Exmoor, had not been cleaned properly. So she telephoned the window cleaner.

'One tiny little thing. You couldn't possibly pop around and just go into one or two corners you missed, could you? The rest of them look so splendid any weeny flaw stands out a mile . . . Oh that would be absolutely wonderful. And if you could tomorrow morning . . . Ricky's finished filming and I do like to have the house perfect . . . you're a marvel. What would we do without you?'

She replaced the telephone receiver. She had not been trained in the Rank starlets' charm school for nothing. Among her many other skills, she excelled in man management. She had never been all that interested in woman management. Her carefully contrived style left the Corrington household always wonderfully served and the Corringtons themselves in high repute locally where not a tradesman would hear a word against the golden couple. Not in public, anyhow, not while big bills were paid so promptly and all requests made with such unfailing courtesy.

Amanda had also, of course, first been schooled in the marketplaces of the East End of London where her father had juggled a succession of street stalls according to the level of interest in each currently being exhibited by the Metropolitan Police.

Amanda glided on to further organisation. Well into her late forties she remained a beautiful woman, hair softly blonde – and helped nowadays only slightly by the colouring skills of an able hairdresser – framing finely chiselled features, the sort that do not readily fall apart with ageing. Unlike her husband, who after all had been born and brought up on Exmoor, she had no natural understanding of West Country ways. To her the people seemed not only slow but also deliberately bloody-minded and awkward half the time. She would never have dared say this to Richard but secretly she thought they were stupid. And the capable Amanda was far too self obsessed ever to grasp the double bluff so effortlessly executed by the people of Exmoor who assumed that most foreigners believed they were stupid and traded on that mercilessly.

The Corrington housekeeper entered carrying a vast bowl of lilies.

'Wonderful, Millie,' Amanda enthused. 'Such a splendid arrangement. You are so clever with flowers! What would we do without you?'

And then, as the beaming woman proceeded toward a window table with her arrangement, 'Oh, but Millie, you couldn't add the weeniest bit of greenery, could you? Just to set off how beautifully you've placed the flowers. You know, the final touch of the magician . . .'

Her teeth flashed a toothpaste commercial smile almost identical to that of her husband. They went to the same Californian dentist after all. Every year. An excuse to use the house in Hollywood. Not much other use for it yet, but she was working on that.

'Of course, Mrs Corrington,' asserted Millie. She called Mr Corrington 'Richard', but always addressed the lady of the house formally. This vaguely irritated Amanda – who suspected that, in a rather perverse way, it was designed to indicate that Millie Brooks actually had considerably more respect for her husband than for her. But Amanda gave no sign of her irritation, nor would she ever.

Amanda actively disliked flowers without greenery. She hated the starkness of naked lilies, loved them nestling softly in a green bed. You'd think that silly cow of a housekeeper would know by now, you really would. Jesus! Did she have to think of everything around here?

And she knew the answer to that, too.

She checked her watch. Richard would probably have finished filming by now. Should she call him at the studio? She thought not. His final day of shooting was always particularly stressful for him – and this time she knew that for various technical reasons the key scene of the final episode had been left until last. Richard would have found that difficult to cope with although she did not doubt that he would have turned in a sterling performance. He knew no other way.

She would never forget the first time she had seen Richard act. It was the moment when she had fallen in love with him – instantly and, as she then thought, irrevocably. Richard was playing Romeo in a drama school production of *Romeo and Juliet*. He and

Amanda had been in the same class for a year, but until she saw him on stage she had barely noticed him. In those days Richard had still been very much a quiet unassuming country boy, and, in spite of his handsomeness, he had virtually no presence at all off stage. He also had little realisation of just how talented he was – something else that had changed with the years. Watching him play Romeo had been a revelation for Amanda. Her rather hard face softened slightly as she recalled the magnetism which had drawn her to him.

He had been so fresh faced and, certainly compared to most of his peers, quite innocent. Choosing him as Romeo had seemed to her to be quite inspired casting – Amanda Lane had never been innocent, possibly not even at birth, but she had had little cynicism then. And when Richard had so eloquently proclaimed Romeo's love for Juliet, Amanda had felt as if he were speaking only to her. It had been an extraordinary experience, and one which had laid the foundations for her entire life. Not only did she quickly become Richard's lover, but also, in spite of being more or less the same age, his mentor. And although Amanda went on to have her own reasonably successful acting career – she was still in demand in the theatre and occasionally made guest appearances on TV – from that moment the bulk of her energies had been dedicated to moulding Richard into the big star she had instantly known that he could be. Her own work always took second place.

Amanda saw Richard immediately for what he was – an extremely promising empty vessel just looking for a pilot. And so she had adroitly steered him through the early days of his career, never doubting for a moment that one day the qualities she had found irresistible would win over millions of others too.

With an effort she pulled herself back to the present. Her thoughts turned to the wrap party. Once upon a time she would have been there at his side.

Amanda had always dreamed of a home somewhere in Britain's answer to Hollywood, along the Thames around Maidenhead; she was after all in no way a country girl. But there were some compensations to being buried in the wilds. At least she didn't have to sit around wondering what time Richard was coming home and in what condition. There was no point, because she knew not to expect him until tomorrow and she also knew he would be in a much better state by then. Strange how geography could make acceptable what would else be an issue. She habitually shut any other considerations out of her mind. It was called survival.

She could not help, however, suddenly remembering again the child she and Richard, particularly Richard, had so longed for. Indeed, the small frail creature she had held in her arms only once was rarely far from her thoughts nowadays. Amanda had wept piteously after the birth, her body racked by agonising sobs, but then she had pushed the damaged baby boy aside. And she had not cried again. The baby had lived just a few days, and his horrendously difficult birth had caused her irreversible damage, leaving her unable to have another child.

Richard had sat in the intensive care unit watching their only son die. He had refused to leave the hospital. He did not sleep throughout the little boy's brief life. But after that one agonising time when she had nursed her baby, and become horribly aware of all

13

that was wrong with him, Amanda had not wanted even to see the child again.

It had been Richard who had named the boy Robert – after his own father. It had been Richard who had arranged the sad little funeral, Richard who, with tears streaming down that handsome face, had carried the tiny white coffin into the church. And it shocked Amanda still to remember that she had only attended the funeral at all because Richard had made her.

Her devastation had been total. Yet at the time she had refused to recognise that feeble misshapen thing she had borne as being any part of her.

The sense of failure had hurt more than the pain she suffered – and had made it impossible for her to grieve properly until years later. Amanda Lane didn't like failure. She wasn't used to it. And so she had blocked out the very existence of her chronically sick child.

She sighed. Richard had been unable to understand her reaction, indeed had been so obsessed with the loss of his son that he had made no effort to do so. He had told her that her attitude disgusted him.

Richard had been different before that, she thought, and so had she. No doubt about that.

She sighed again. She didn't know why, but for the past few days she had been suffering from a feeling of impending doom. She tried to shake it off. Stupid. What could go wrong in such a meticulously orchestrated life?

In a little terraced house in Fulham Joyce Carter, Fleet Street's latest killer interviewer, was stretched on the sofa in front of her gas fuelled imitation coal fire carefully sifting through copies of several years of newspaper and magazine stories on Richard Corrington.

Britain's most successful television actor was about to become her latest interview subject, or victim might be more accurate. In showbusiness circles it was known as being 'Cartered'. Yet she still got the interviews. Sometimes she wondered why, but she knew really. In the first place she worked for the *Dispatch*, the last of the great establishment broadsheet newspapers. And people approached by the *Dispatch*, particularly actors, were inclined to roll over belly up – so flattered were they to feature in such an illustrious paper. Most of them had apparently failed to notice the not so subtle changes in the *Dispatch* over the years.

Secondly, people in the public eye, particularly actors and other showbusiness personalities, were inclined to be incorrigibly vain. They almost all believed that they would be the one about whom Joyce Carter would eulogise. The one she would find irresistibly funny, charming, clever etc. etc.

The thought always made Joyce giggle. Didn't they understand that she was paid not to like them? Would it never occur to them that she earned probably the top non-executive salary in the Street of Shame specifically to execute hatchet jobs which varied only in their degree of viciousness?

Obviously not, she thought to herself for the umpteenth time. And be thankful Joycie, she said out loud.

The doorbell rang, and she consulted her watch. Early tonight. Well, the randy little devil would just have to wait while she finished reading the cuts.

Preparation was the trick of her trade. The interview was scheduled for Saturday, tomorrow she had another job, and for once she was trying to get ahead of the game. Work still ranked ahead of sex. Just. Although since young Jacky Starr had come into her life it was touch and go. Joyce liked sex. She liked it a lot. And at the moment it was about as good as it had ever been . . .

Not all that reluctantly she put down the file of cuttings and went to open the front door. Jacky was twenty-two years old and twenty years her junior. He worked as a stage hand at the National Theatre. He was crude, vulgar, scruffy, smug, streetwise and full of himself. He also had the most perfect body she had ever had the luck to experience. And he couldn't get enough of her.

'I've got a present for you,' he said, as she opened the door. He grasped her wrist and pulled her hand to his crutch. She could feel the bulge there.

His eyes were very dark. She could smell his sweat and there were small beads of it trickling down his forehead. He looked as if he had been running.

'I started to think about it on the tube,' he muttered. 'I ran all the way from the station . . .'

He pulled her tight against him. He was wearing Levi 501s. The buttoned fly stretched tight over his erection and pushed hard and rough into her through the softness of her own clothing. It felt wonderful. He began to simulate intercourse with her through their clothes. Then he walked her backwards, still pressed tightly against him, until they reached the staircase. He pushed her down so that she was sitting on the third stair and knelt across her. His hands began their exploration of her. Everything that he did always seemed so natural and so effortless – even in this awkward location there was a smooth fluency to his lovemaking and his body promised as always to cause her no discomfort whatsoever, merely to give unimaginable pleasure.

There was only one thing to do. She reached for him and unbuttoned his flies.

It seemed that any further study of Richard Corrington would be postponed until the next day after all.

In the stinking darkness of the Waterloo underpass Ruth Macintosh wished she had dodged the traffic at ground level – anything would be better than this. She thought she heard a footstep close behind her and turned to see a rat scurrying into the gloom. She shuddered.

Cardboard city surrounded her. Ruth had known it was there, of course, but had forgotten all about it. She still could not associate this dismal half-underground shanty town with London – the great city she had loved from the moment she landed there from the Scottish highlands almost twenty-five years earlier, just eighteen years old and bursting with enthusiasm and excitement.

Until recently London had only rarely disappointed her. She still believed that the sentiments of Samuel Johnson were every bit as appropriate at the end of the twentieth century as they had been when he first expressed them during the eighteenth century. 'When a man is tired of London he is tired of life. For there is in London all that life can afford.'

She had spent her youth, during the heady seventies, working and living in the heart of London.

Marriage and the birth of two sons interrupted a high-flying secretarial career, but now that her boys were aged thirteen and fourteen, and no longer needed her constant attention, she had returned to a part-time job as a legal secretary in an office in Lincoln's Inn just off Fleet Street.

That night she had stayed much later than usual grappling with a tricky problem. The senior partner had insisted on buying her a glass of champagne in El Vinos, still used by the lawyers but long abandoned by the journalists – now isolated in their ghettos in Wapping and even further east at Canary Wharf – who used to frequent it. She had been fairly easily persuaded as she still thoroughly enjoyed the camaraderie of drinking after work with colleagues. And she retained a lurking affection for the now fairly soulless El Vinos, where she had met her journalist husband, another Scot, all those years ago.

It was well gone eight, a March evening and already dark, when she stepped outside on to the pavement to hail a taxi to Waterloo Station. She rooted around in her handbag for her wallet, which also contained a cash purse. After a minute or two she was forced to accept that it wasn't there. Damn. Had she left it in El Vinos? She remembered with some amusement the days when the place had not allowed women to buy drinks. It now invited women to spend as freely as they wished, but that night her boss had insisted on doing the buying. She had not taken her money out once.

She recalled that as she left the bar a man wearing a dark raincoat had brushed rather heavily against her. And the zip was broken on her bag – she had been meaning to replace it for days. Had the man perhaps taken her wallet? She sighed. More than likely not, she was eternally careless, the wallet was probably sitting on her office desk – and the office was locked now.

She checked the little buttoned pocket at the front of the bag where she always kept her rail tickets. Fortunately her return ticket to Kingston was at least safely where it should be.

She debated what to do next. Her drinking companions had already departed and the doors of El Vinos, which closed at eight, were being locked behind her. There was a public telephone kiosk at the street corner and she wondered if she should call home – but what for? She could hardly ask her husband to drive all the way into central London to pick her up. There was nothing for it, she would have to leg it to Waterloo and serve her right for being so stupid.

Resolved, she strode purposefully along Fleet Street, past the Aldwych, and then turned smartly left on to Waterloo Bridge across the Thames. Once or twice she glanced briefly backwards. She had occasionally over the last week or two had the feeling that someone was following her. There was hardly a soul on the bridge at this hour, and certainly nobody anywhere near her. Of course there wasn't. She was being silly. She began to look around her at the river views she always appreciated – St Paul's over her left shoulder, parliament and Big Ben over her right shoulder, and the South Bank straight ahead; all conspiring as ever to look so much more glamorous and exciting after dark. Actually, now that she had settled into her stride, it was not too bad at all. The evening was mild enough and as she made her way over the bridge she could see the illuminated city reflected diamond bright in the mirror surface of a still river – picture postcard London. She had, in fact, half begun to enjoy the walk until she found herself in the underpass.

Rows of ill-clad feet emerged from cardboard boxes. The stench of urine was overpowering. Somebody was using a broken luggage trolley as a bed. There were signs of considerable initiative – post office sacks apparently made excellent bedding. None the less, the scene was a shocking one to her, and the extreme youth of some of the faces she glimpsed through the increasing gloom added to her sense of sudden despair. Stark, desperate faces. She could not believe that the capital city had come to this. Always in life there are going to be drop-outs, people who cannot cope, men and women at the bottom of the pile – even when she first came to London there were those who slept rough, but nothing like this. The scale of homelessness in the modern capital was suddenly very clear to her and it was utterly shocking. In America, she knew, they had a name for them – the Underclass.

Ruth was quite warm from her brisk walk. None the less she found herself shivering.

As she turned right in the open central section of the underpass below the big roundabout at the south side of Waterloo Bridge her attention was attracted to a young man leaning against the wall at the entrance to the alleyway. His sleeve was rolled up above the elbow of his left arm and he was in the process of injecting something into his body. As he did so his head jerked back against the wall.

Ruth kept walking quickly but found her gaze drawn to the youth. She must have led a sheltered life, she thought to herself. She had never seen anyone shooting up before. She knew all the terminology, didn't everybody? She read newspapers – her husband filled the house with them every day – watched television. But seeing with your own eyes is something else. With a little of the righteous revolutionary fervour of her youth Ruth found herself cursing the Tory government and resolving she would be more active in her local Labour party to get the bastards out at the next election. Surely something could be done, and destroying the last vestiges of Thatcherism had to be a start.

The young drug addict disappeared into the distant gloom as Ruth swung further left into the tunnel leading towards the station. She was surrounded by smelly murkiness. Something moved behind an up-turned iron bedstead obscurely tipped on end against the side of the tunnel. Ruth looked across, unable to see properly. The lights were on, but not all of them were working, and some parts of the tunnel seemed quite dark. Then close behind her she heard a sound. She turned quickly, swinging on her heels, alarmed. But as she did so, peering intently through the gloom, her fearful expression faded. Her lips parted in a tentative smile.

Ten seconds later Ruth Macintosh was dead.

Two

It was the morning after the wrap party. Yet another series of *Sparrow-Hawk* was in the can. Richard Corrington awoke in his London flat feeling dreadful. It was 6 a.m. and there was a brass band playing something unrecognisable inside his head. He had woken before the alarm, a gruelling nine-month shoot did that to you if nothing else. Automatically and in the grip of considerable self-inflicted pain he crawled out of bed. He tried to remember what he had done and where he had been. He had stayed at the party for little more than an hour before calling for a production car to drive him into the heart of Soho where he knew of several clubs and bars in which he could sink into stoned oblivion without being bothered. And the condition he was in indicated that the expedition had been highly successful.

Then he remembered the most important thing of all – and the relief was like the sight of the first daffodil of spring after a particularly vicious winter. It was over – for three wonderful months he would be a free man until the start of the next shoot. He began to savour the prospect of the weeks to come. He could go back to bed for another hour or two if he wished – he had a free day in town before his driver would arrive to whisk him to Paddington Station to catch his favourite 19.35 train west. He smiled at the thought of the beautiful moorland house awaiting him. It would be immaculate and welcoming – you could be sure of that with Amanda. She might have her bad points but when it came to organising a home, or anything else for that matter, Amanda was the tops.

She had always been the organiser. And she had always been the suave sophisticated one. Strange that. Amanda came from a working class East London family and he was the son of a moderately prosperous Exmoor farmer. She had gone to a secondary modern school. He attended a minor West Country public school. And yet she was the one who from the moment of her arrival at RADA played – and very successfully too – at being a grand lady of the theatre. Both of them might have appeared unlikely to win RADA places – certainly neither had any theatrical associations, no well-connected relatives, no strings to pull. But Amanda had been totally stage-struck from childhood and more than anything else it was her single-minded ambition coupled with a self confidence and assurance unusual in one so young that carried her so far from Stepney so fast. In Richard's case it was raw talent which won the day. His ability had been spotted at school by an enlightened teacher who had encouraged and groomed him to study drama. But from the moment he first stepped on to a stage in a school play Richard knew that was where he belonged. He had been an awkward schoolboy, and, although he loved the country, he had never fitted easily into the farming lifestyle. It seemed that it was only when he was pretending to be somebody else that a personality which, certainly as a boy, was lacklustre and unexceptional blossomed into something quite special.

He too remembered that early production of *Romeo*

and Juliet which had won him not only great acclaim, but also, ultimately, a wife. He had been aware almost throughout his performance of the lovely Amanda Lane, whom previously he had considered to be quite out of his reach, gazing at him as if enraptured. And he had indeed felt almost as if he were playing just for her. He had walked off stage every bit as captivated by her as she had been by him. There had been a party afterwards. He was conscious of her presence as soon as he walked in the room. He could feel her eyes fixed upon him. She had stood slightly apart from the rest of the crowd. He knew that she was waiting for him.

It was Richard's night, and a small group of people surrounded him at once. He noticed only Amanda moving nearer, smoothly, steadily, as if gliding across the floor, and it seemed as if the crowd parted for her. Quite suddenly she had been by his side and with the fingertips of one hand she just touched his cheek. It wasn't electricity. It was nuclear fission. His skin burned.

'Congratulations, you were magnificent,' she had murmured. Her eyes shone.

Without warning, she kissed him on the lips, softly, swiftly, longingly. For just a few seconds neither was aware of anyone else in the room. It had seemed to him then the most beautiful and sensual moment of his life. Even now, with all that had happened since, he still felt a stirring inside him when he thought about it.

With what was rare self assertion for him at that age he had shortly afterwards whisked Amanda away to his little bed-sit in Earls Court and they had made love for the first time. There had been no flirtation, no foreplay worth mentioning. They had not been able to wait even to take their clothes off. It was the only time in his life Richard had ever actually ripped a woman's underwear in his haste to get to her.

Since then there had been so many bedfellows, so much energy spent in pursuit of new sensation, so much sadness and so many disappointments. In the beginning sex with Amanda had been good, very good. Yet that was sometimes hard to remember now. But the first kiss, so tender, so intimate in the middle of a students' party, remained as real as if it were yesterday. Without effort, he could still bring the taste back to his lips. He could still feel the tip of her tongue pressing, just a fraction, into his mouth, and the surge of desire that ripped through his body. And he still thought it was the single most erotic moment of his life.

After a bit it became apparent that the need for more sleep, which had become so desperate in recent weeks when he never seemed able to get enough, had departed as the freedom to sleep as much as he wished had arrived. He decided on a knock-your-socks-off super shower instead, and spent a happy half an hour splashing around in the bathroom. With the help of a strong cleansing lotion the dark dye around his temples had been almost all removed, leaving that touch of grey he rather liked. He did not shave. In between filming he often allowed his beard, which still grew a rich dark brown, almost total freedom, and within a couple of weeks or so he would have nearly a full set of whiskers – already there was a heavy smattering of stubble.

The morning passed in rare and pleasant idleness.

Wearing his favourite silk dressing gown, he lingered over the daily papers and lots of black coffee, sitting in the bay window of his embankment apartment. It was a glorious day, the sun high and bright in the sky as he gazed contentedly across the river towards Vauxhall and Southwark.

Just before midday he dressed with his usual care. There was none of the newfangled Italian designer nonsense for Richard Corrington. No Armani suits or Gucci shoes graced his spacious dressing room. He was strictly classic in taste, and had favoured the same small tailor off Savile Row since he was first able to afford a truly decent suit. His shirts were hand made heavy cotton or silk from Jermyn Street, with double cuffs. He liked jackets well shaped at the waist with deep vents at the rear, and winter or summer, he almost always chose to wear a waistcoat – his favourites with collars and of course a pocket for his half-hunter watch. He tied his ties with a Windsor knot and they were all of restrained English design.

Just like Jack Sparrow his trousers boasted button flies instead of zips and he sometimes wondered if there would be anyone in future generations to continue this tradition – except on their Levi 501s, of course. Even his casual dress was strangely formal. If there were anyone else in London who still wore open necked shirts with cravats he would rather like to meet them.

As a final touch he combed his thick brown hair carefully into its distinctive quiff, and attached the famous gold and diamond *Sparrow-Hawk* lapel pin to his jacket. He wore the soaring bird somewhere on his person all the time – on screen and off. It had become his trademark.

Locking the door of his apartment carefully behind him he set out for a gentle stroll to The Ivy, his favourite restaurant, for his annual end of shoot lunch with his agent.

Larry Silver was already seated and waiting for him as Richard had known he would be. Larry had been Richard's agent for twenty-eight years, since the beginning of his career. The man was in love with him and always had been, Richard believed. However, he preferred not to remember nowadays the early affair with Larry which remained Richard's only experiment in homosexuality. The actor was quite capable of rewriting history, and on occasions he chose to blot out the past and even ungenerously dismiss Larry in his mind as a silly old queen. But there was another side to Richard as yet unsullied by all the nonsense of his chosen profession. Somewhere, buried deep, there remained the vestiges of the genuine, good-hearted young man, without edge or malice, who had left his native West Country all those years ago to launch himself into the world of showbusiness.

When Richard arrived at RADA straight out of school at the age of eighteen he had felt totally out of place among his classmates, many of whom came from illustrious acting families. Richard had no dynasty behind him. He knew nobody in London. He had been quite alone. Even his hair and clothes – short back and sides then, flannel trousers worn with sports jackets, sixties fashions having somehow bypassed his part of Somerset – had been conspicuously wrong. And it was not just the dress styles of the swinging sixties that had so far eluded him. He had already discovered sex, he was no longer a virgin, but having grown up on a farm was, unlike most of his

27

generation, under no illusion that he had invented it. He had sampled beer and whisky and actually been drunk once or twice, but he had no idea what marijuana even looked like, let alone cocaine.

His father had been already in his early sixties when Richard was born in 1949, and his mother towards the end of her child-bearing life. The couple had resigned themselves to childlessness and the arrival of their only son was treated as a miracle. Richard had been brought up on a farm in the heart of Lorna Doone country, not far from the tiny village of Oare, a quiet introspective boy who spent much of his childhood wandering alone across Exmoor. Horse-riding over the moors became perhaps his greatest pleasure, and one which had never left him. He also retained a passionate love for nature and for the moors where he had been brought up, and where so much affection had been lavished on him.

When he professed a desire to study drama and become an actor his parents were at first bewildered, and then accepted his chosen career with gentle pride – after all their boy was different. It was only years later that Richard had given a thought to how secretly disappointed his father must have been when he realised his only son would not be taking over the farm which had been his life's work. His father, then nearing ninety, had died when Richard was twenty-five and, at that time, besotted with his new life in London. The farm was sold to provide his mother with an income until she also died several years later.

Richard had changed almost beyond recognition over the years. From those early days at RADA his whole existence had centred around the bitter rivalries and surface-scratching superficiality of the showbusiness world – and it showed. Probably only those who had known him before his transformation into a television star could still be bothered to look for, let alone see, the fundamentally decent man who continued to lurk somewhere beneath the crust of theatrical insincerity which he had grown like a second skin.

It was this side to Richard, as well as his ability to earn a small fortune, that led Larry Silver – who had signed up the then twenty-one-year-old Richard after spotting him in one of RADA's showcase productions performed by final year students especially for agents – to stay with the actor even when he was behaving appallingly. And it was this decent reasonable side to Richard which recognised his agent's worth. The affair which so embarrassed Richard now – although he knew he had experimented enthusiastically enough at the time, before realising that he was not really gay at all – was never mentioned. But beneath all the game-playing Richard had the deepest respect for Larry's professional ability and relied on him absolutely, although he rarely admitted it and certainly not to Larry.

The champagne was on the table. With the manner of long-time associates performing a well tried ritual the two men raised their glasses and clinked them together. Their toast was the same as it always was – to the end of the shoot.

Richard downed his glass almost in one. 'God, I'm knackered,' he said.

'Think of the residuals,' intoned his agent.

Richard worked the room with his eyes, quickly registering who was there and who merited a wave and perhaps even a chat on the way out.

'I've seen a tape of the first couple of episodes,' remarked Larry. 'I think you get better every time, Ricky.'

Larry Silver would never flatter Richard for the sake of it, and they both knew he was merely telling the truth. Richard smiled.

When he looked up he became aware that Larry was studying him very closely. He guessed that the strain was showing.

'It's a long shoot, seventeen episodes, and you do look exceptionally tired, this time,' said his agent with some concern. 'Take it easy, won't you! Have a really good rest.'

'I intend to,' Ricky replied, just as the second bottle of champagne arrived at the table. 'But first I intend to have a really good drink.'

Two hours later, and very slightly tiddly, he strolled back to his apartment. He had long ago learned the knack the famous must always acquire in order to move around in public without being bothered. The golden rule was never ever to meet anybody's eye. Richard walked with his gaze rigidly fixed on the pavement two or three feet in front of him.

Only a couple of people on the busy city streets were even aware of his identity as he made his way home in this manner. One of these, wrapped in a big coat which the weather did not call for and with a baseball cap pulled down over his forehead, walked for quite a while following quietly in the actor's footsteps. Even if Richard had looked up and become conscious of his presence it would neither have interested nor concerned him. It was not unusual for fans who spotted the actor to trail him for a bit. He was used to it.

At 6.45 p.m. precisely his car arrived to take him to Paddington Station.

The journey to Paddington went as smoothly as could be expected on a Friday night, and by 7.10 he was there and could see that the 19.35, although yet unheralded on the station departures board, had arrived as usual. He stopped off at the paper stand outside John Menzies intending to buy an *Evening Standard*, but, glancing at the displayed front page, changed his mind. WOMAN MURDERED IN BRUTAL ATTACK screamed the splash headline. There was a picture of Ruth Macintosh, and another rather moody shot of the Waterloo underpass. Richard decided he did not want to read about anything so unpleasant.

He set off briskly for Platform Four where he boarded his train directly into the dining car.

'Your usual, sir,' said Peter, the chief steward, and a gin and tonic, lots of ice and lemon, was promptly placed before him as Richard shuffled into his regular window seat second table back from the kitchen.

John, the chef, actually christened Gianni and always gallantly trying to produce from a galley the size of a pocket handkerchief dishes worthy of a fine Italian restaurant, appeared briefly in the carriage to give a thumbs up to the steaks and a thumbs down to the pre-cooked vegetarian curry.

It was all terribly reassuring, comforting even. The other Friday night regulars would not be far behind him. For nearly twelve years now Richard had been commuting up and down from his beloved West Country by train. Many of his friends could not understand why he did not prefer to be chauffeur-driven. There were three reasons really, the first being that on a Friday night the journey from London to

Exmoor by car was a nightmare; and during the filming of *Sparrow-Hawk* – they were making seventeen episodes a year now to keep up with the demands of the American network – Richard's gruelling schedule meant he was just like any other commuter, unable to leave town until the end of the working day. Each hour-long episode took eleven days to film and was followed by a three-day break – and so Richard made his trek fortnightly during filming and found the train the only way to get him home fast enough. Secondly, there was habit. He always caught the train. He always sat in the same seat. He always drank the same drink. It was a ritual.

Thirdly, the 19.35 marked a return to about the nearest thing to normality in public that Richard could experience nowadays. He was rarely bothered by fans on this train. In the near seclusion of the first class dining compartment he was, after all, invariably surrounded by the same fellow passengers – and they were thoroughly used to him. He was aware, which he found pleasant, that they rather liked him, and that they probably, after all this time, liked him for himself and not because of who he was. He knew he could be very likeable when he put his mind to it. And at least one of the Friday night set, a highly successful barrister called Paul Newman, was quite convinced – perhaps, who knows, because of his unforgettable name – that he was in any case a much bigger star than any old actor.

Then there was that ridiculous woman journalist they called The Killer Bimbo . . . funny how he didn't dislike her as much as he usually did journalists. Probably she knew how to make herself likeable too. Certainly she had never abused their Friday night journeys, but the cynic might say she had just been leading up to the interview request – which had indeed ultimately been submitted only a couple of weeks earlier. Joyce had very correctly approached Richard's agent Larry Silver who had advised him to turn her down. But, ignoring what was doubtless excellent advice, Richard had agreed a date for lunch. He might have been considerably disconcerted had he known how accurately Joyce had guessed his reasons for agreeing to her request. He was totally sure that he could charm almost any woman into whatever was the appropriate submission – and he certainly did not necessarily mean sexually.

Richard checked his watch. 7.15. Peering out of the window he could see Paul Newman rolling up the platform, all eighteen stone of him. By his side strode the two military members of the 19.35 club, a serving major and a retired naval commander, both of whom made a particular point of pretending to be quite unaware that Richard Corrington was anything other than just another passenger.

Predictably, Joyce Carter flung herself on to the train at the last moment and into the one remaining seat of the double just across the aisle from where Richard sat with his three companions.

Richard glanced at her in some amusement. What did that woman think she looked like? She was short and a bit dumpy although quite curvaceous underneath those ridiculous clothes, he suspected. Joyce only ever wore one thing – layer after layer of black over black; T-shirt, baggy silk shirt, jacket, sometimes a sweater or a waistcoat, all topped by a big floppy black hat. The effect was supposed to be dramatic, Richard guessed, and certainly, with the shock of unruly red hair protruding haphazardly from beneath the black velvet halo of the hat that night, he supposed there was a kind of drama in her appearance.

Joyce's usual Scotch and soda magically appeared. 'God, what a bloody week, Peter,' she muttered, taking a deep drink. The chief steward did his best to look sympathetic but his expression indicated that he secretly thought that she should try being a waiter on wheels for a change and see how she liked that.

Revived by the spirit, Joyce waved across the aisle at the four men. Richard Corrington had moulded himself into his new role. With the country clothes, the greying hair and the five o'clock shadow he was now barely recognisable as Sparrow-Hawk. And the highly theatrical thespian superstar of the afternoon at The Ivy had passed into the mists of London life. He was ready now for a completely different performance.

At Tiverton Parkway his Range Rover was waiting to whisk him off to the moorland mansion. The Killer Bimbo disembarked at the same station en route to her country cottage.

They walked together across the footbridge from the southbound platform. The open fields surrounding the station engulfed them in rural smells and sounds. It was a cold night but clear, and the moon highlighted the dancing white backsides of rabbits, disturbed by the arrival of the London train, running riot in the meadow next to the track. Richard could hear the harsh cry of a distant fox. He breathed in deeply, relishing the sharp country air.

Joyce Carter also seemed to be savouring the moment, and neither spoke until they had reached the car park.

34

'See you tomorrow,' she said then, in farewell, after confirming their lunch date for the next day.

Rather to his surprise Richard found himself almost looking forward to the prospect – she was quite attractive, really, for a hackette, underneath all those layers. And she was certainly a challenge.

Landacre House, curiously the same name as one of Exmoor's favourite beauty spots several miles away and pronounced Lannacker, was, Richard thought, the most beautiful place in all the world. A rambling Georgian mansion set in the heart of woodland just above Porlock, its sweeping views seemed to embrace half the world. On a clear day you could see across the billowing Atlantic to Wales in one direction, and in the other out over Exmoor till the hills blended blue-grey with the sky.

Richard was cosily ensconced now in the front of the Range Rover, his passenger seat fully reclined, as George Brooks, husband of Millie, his gardener, handyman, driver, groom, and almost everything else, purred the big four-wheel-drive homewards.

The actor slumped into contented half wakeful-ness, only jolting properly awake when the Range Rover pulled to a halt outside Landacre's imposing porticoed entrance. The driveway and the front of the house were brilliantly lit, all part of the Corrington's security system. As Richard stepped out of the vehicle, the front door opened and Amanda was framed in an even greater blaze of light. She was in country lady mode – Burberry skirt, cashmere twinset, pearls, hair softly set and becomingly golden. Her arms were outstretched. She puckered her mouth and kissed his cheek, her lips barely touching his flesh.

It was her usual, routine greeting, but if Richard ever cared about, or even noticed, how very different it was to that first wonderful kiss all those years ago he gave no such indication.

'Welcome home, Ricky darling,' she said.

'Thank you my own love,' replied her husband.

Neither of the Corringtons saw George Brooks raise his eyes wearily to heaven as, having carried Richard's bag into the house, he returned to the Range Rover and motored back down the drive to his gatehouse home.

Although still only mid March, there dawned a truly glorious spring morning. And Richard knew exactly how he was going to spend it. At home in Landacre he always slept with his bedroom curtains open – he and Amanda had used separate bedrooms for several years – so that he could be awoken naturally by daylight streaming into the house. His bedroom faced due east and caught the first rays of morning light as the sun rose over the moor. He was fully awake by 6.30 a.m. The room boasted French windows and a small wrought iron-clad balcony. He made a pot of strong tea using the electric kettle, teapot and mugs all left ready on a tray in a corner of his room, and carried them out on to the balcony. It was a chilly morning but he didn't mind. The sky was just starting to turn deep pink, silhouetting the rolling outline of the black moorland hills. Somewhere across the valley a cock crowed, its voice carrying in the dawn stillness.

The sunrise was shaping up gloriously and Richard was prepared. He wore the ankle length quilted dressing gown, richly insulated like a ski suit, which had been specially tailored for him. A silk scarf was loosely knotted around his neck and bootee sheepskin slippers tucked snugly beneath his pyjama bottoms like a pair of extraordinarily thick socks. His hands were clad in woollen mittens and the woollen hat on his head was pulled down over his ears. Sparrow-Hawk fans would not have believed their eyes. More cynical observers may have concluded that the scene merely confirmed a widely accepted theory in show-business circles that all actors were, to some degree or another, mad – or at the very least wildly eccentric.

These early mornings on his dawn-facing balcony were a ritual Richard enjoyed throughout most of the year if the morning was promising enough and his clothing had been acquired to suit his purpose. The cushions for his reclining balcony chair, white plastic but top of the range and wonderfully comfortable, were kept in an oaken box by the window. He put them in place and relaxed back for one of the favourite few moments of his life. There was just one chair on the balcony. Richard had no wish to encourage anyone at all to attempt to share with him this special time of day. The strong brown tea tasted delicious. It was wonderful for him to let nature comfort him again, surround him with its beauty, its promise of everlasting life.

If there was one humble thing about Richard, and indeed there probably was only one, it was that he remained overawed and overwhelmed by the wonders of nature which he still felt to be at their greatest on his native Exmoor.

For almost an hour he sat on his balcony, sipping tea and enjoying the beauty of daybreak. A buzzard wheeled overhead looking for breakfast, soaring and swooping with the currents of air, a magnificent creature built like a glider, barely moving its wings, allowing the natural flow of the air to do its work for it. Suddenly it dived to the ground, disappearing momentarily in distant bracken and rising swiftly in triumph with some unsuspecting prey between its talons.

When, with his first big money, Richard had bought Landacre and returned to the wild country of his roots he remembered telling Larry Silver that he thought there was no more exciting way in the world of spending an evening than watching a pair of buzzards rise and fall before a backdrop of glorious sunset. Larry had laughed.

'Till the novelty wears off,' he had mocked. 'Honestly, Ricky darling, for how long do you think you are going to be amused by the antics of a few hawks, for God's sake? The only hawk that is ever going to matter to you is the one that is making your fortune for you, old love.'

'Buzzards, Larry,' Richard had replied patiently. 'Buzzards . . .'

Amanda, of course, was never a party to his nature vigils. She would merely think he had finally taken leave of his senses. Within their marriage he and Amanda had come a long way since that thrilling beginning. It was certainly no longer a great love affair – but whose marriage was after twenty-five years? The loss of their only son could have brought them closer together, he reflected. Instead it drove a wedge between them.

In the beginning Richard had wanted to comfort Amanda, and more than anything else wanted to share his grief with her. She had shut herself in and refused to let him near. She had refused to talk about her feelings, and there had been times, although he knew better really, when Richard had wondered if she cared at all. Richard remembered his own grief as if it were yesterday, remembered carrying that tiny coffin into the church, and remembered Amanda walking beside him, dry eyed, expressionless. He had been unable to stop crying for days after they buried little Robert, but as far as Richard knew his wife had not shed a single tear. He did not blame her for not giving him the son he so wanted, and was well aware that it was in any case his fault, that he was the one with the genetic problem. But he had never forgiven her for not grieving with him.

None the less, all that was more than twenty years ago, and most of the time Richard considered their marriage to be a satisfactory working relationship. And he knew that he owed Amanda a great deal. But his deep love of the moorland country in which he was born and raised led him to insist that he and Amanda make their principle home there. It was about the only thing he insisted on in their entire marriage, and strangely, Amanda had demurred almost meekly. He knew she would have preferred some home counties pile or even a big London town house instead of the *pied à terre* riverside apartment – but somehow she had known better than to insist on that one.

Quite frankly he did not think he could carry on without Landacre. It was his sanctuary. It was heaven on earth to him. It brought back, just a little, the sense of peace which had been so much a part of his upbringing and which had departed from his life in almost direct relation, it sometimes seemed, to his increasing success as an actor.

He picked up his mobile phone and dialled an

extension which was quickly answered.

'Get the old boy ready, I'll be down in fifteen.'

From his wardrobe he selected a pair of brown corduroy jodhpurs, woollen shirt and yellow roll neck sweater. His Barbour jacket and boots would be waiting by the kitchen door. Humming happily to himself he virtually danced down the back stairs past his wife's bedroom door, where in his opinion, Amanda continued to sleep away the best hours of the day.

He set off for the stables, detouring briefly on the way to peer through the window at the side of the big double garage where he saw, to his satisfaction, that his Triumph Daytona motor cycle was propped gleaming against the wall. He had a long-time enthusiasm for British bikes of which there were very few left in manufacture and this one, a Daytona 750, although no longer made, was in his opinion the best in the range. It had obviously been made ready for him. Good old George, he thought to himself.

Down at the yard Herbert was also standing ready. The actor paused by the gate for a moment admiring the big black gelding. Herbert was tied alongside his stable and was craning his not inconsiderable neck to get at the hay net just inside the stable door. Greedy old beast, thought Richard affectionately. Herbert was still clipped out for hunting and his coat shone the way satin finish gloss paint shines. Every muscle was finely defined, and his mane was hogged close to his neck which suited his fine Roman-nosed head. Herbert was just on sixteen hands but always seemed bigger to Richard. He was a cob, but a particularly handsome one. Some cobs have heads too big for their bodies and bodies too long for their legs. Not Herbert. Every inch of him appeared to have been perfectly fitted together by a master craftsman.

The old horse pricked his ears. He stopped straining for the hay net, turned his head around, and,
spotting Richard, gave a small quiet whinny.

Richard was under no illusion. There were always
Polo mints and sometimes carrots and apples in his
pockets. Any display of affection from Herbert was
far more likely to be cupboard love than anything
else.

He stroked the big animal's neck. Herbert's muzzle
had already achieved the virtually impossible and
squeezed itself inside a pocket. The horse was nib-
bling at the lining with huge yellow teeth. Obediently
Richard removed the packet of mints Herbert was
seeking, unwrapped the silver foil and offered a couple
of the sweets to the horse who sucked them in with
his lips and munched.

Richard pulled off the light rug and stepped back
admiringly. Over his shoulder he glimpsed George
emerging from the tack room. George's father, also
called George, had worked for Richard's father until
he'd been killed in a tractor accident when George
junior was just a boy. It had always been assumed
that young George would take George senior's place
on the Corrington land, which he had ultimately
done.

George was nearly ten years older than Richard,
but had been the nearest the actor ever had to a real
boyhood friend. And with a father already an old man,
George had also been Richard's teacher.

It was George who taught Richard to shoot, and to
ride a horse, who took him ferreting and lamping and
showed him how to tickle a trout. It was George,
white with rage, who had once knocked him to the

ground when Richard, tired and fed up with looking, had ignored all the laws of the countryside and left a badly shot rabbit to die a lingering death in the woods. It was George who had fished him out of Oare Water when Richard had knocked his head and nearly drowned after falling from a sycamore tree in which he had been performing what – until he hit the water and its viciously protruding rocks – he had considered to be an excellent impersonation of Tarzan.

And it was George to whom Richard turned when the desire to spend as much of his life as he could back on Exmoor began to overwhelm him. He doubted if he would have bought a property on the scale of Landacre if George and his wife Millie had not agreed to take care of it for him, and moved into the lodge house. And the debt he felt to George was in no way lessened by knowing how eagerly the other man had left his then employment as a maintenance man at the Butlin's Holiday Camp in nearby Minehead.

Richard beamed his appreciation as George strolled across the yard and came to stand alongside him, hands on hips, ever present pipe sticking out of the side of his mouth.

'Herbert looks magnificent,' Richard said. 'Better every time I see him. Certainly wouldn't take him for eighteen, would you?'

George didn't comment on the amount of work it took to keep the old horse in that condition. Anyway, he didn't care. He loved Herbert as much as Richard did.

'Do you want to see the others?' George asked.

'Of course.' Richard ambled down the row of stables. There were three thoroughbred geldings and a mare in foal.

'How is she?' asked Richard.

''Er'll be fine, built for it that one,' remarked George. 'You want to take any of the others out later?'

'Nope, tomorrow or the day after'll do.' Richard had a stable now of horses far grander and certainly much more valuable than Herbert, but the old cob remained his favourite. Herbert had been his first buy when he returned to the West Country, unsure any more of his riding ability, looking for something steady. Herbert turned out to be not as steady as might have been expected and with a natural penchant for landing everyone who rode him in the muck.

Richard forced his mind back to the rest of the day. 'Anyway, I need you to drive me to Taunton for lunch,' he told George.

'Lunch in Taunton?' replied the older man. 'You've only just bleddy well arrived . . .'

Richard smiled. George was probably the only person in the world who could speak to him like that and know he would get away with it. George was also probably the only person in the world, apart perhaps from Larry Silver, who truly loved the actor for what he was and had always been and not just for what he had become and the power he could wield. Richard knew that too.

'You be at the front of the house with the motor at twelve fifteen,' he grinned. 'Sharp!'

'Hmph,' responded George. 'Must be someone bleddy special to lure you away from yer on your first day 'ome.'

'Nope, just a journalist wanting an interview,' replied Richard, knowing full well the reaction his remark would provoke.

'You must be bleddy mazed,' said George.

'Probably.'

Richard was in a better mood than ever now. He tightened Herbert's girth, pulled down the stirrups and mounted easily from ground level, proud of his agility. The big horse swung around on cue heading for the hunting gate behind the stables. He had been deliberately kept in the day before, and exercised only briefly the day before that, so that he would be fresh and eager for Richard. And he was fresh. Some strange excitement flashed across Herbert's old brain and he skipped smartly to the left and executed a small but deliciously unseating buck. Richard lost a stirrup and a considerable amount of his avuncular aplomb. He kicked Herbert briskly forward into a trot.

'Nearly dumped 'ee again,' George called after him, with some satisfaction.

Richard did not turn around. George had used exactly the same tone in which forty odd years ago, after having saved Richard's life, he had remarked: 'That'll teach 'ee to bleddy well show off.'

He trotted the horse up the lane to the woods, breaking briefly into a canter along the grass verge, then slowed him to a walk through the woodland path littered with stones and broken branches. It was dark and tunnel-like in the woods. At one point something spooked Herbert and he shied nervously. Horses have a more finely attuned sense of such things than humans, but even Herbert's rider was aware of the branches swaying and the crackling under foot. Richard steadied his mount and peered fruitlessly into the dense woodland. It was probably deer, he thought, but he could see nothing.

When they emerged into the brilliant sunshine of

the moorland at the top of the hill the old horse gathered himself together, excited, eager, and pranced sideways along the track. He knew the routine. The little-used path was richly grassed here, and there was a good thick covering of red soil over the rugged sandstone of the moor. Richard gave him his head and urged him into a gallop. Game as ever Herbert threw himself forward and did his best to pretend he was Arkle. Like all horses ever a creature of habit, quick to grasp a routine, Herbert slowed unasked to a trot as he reached the brow of the hill where a rocky outcrop formed a natural platform high above Porlock and the swaying Atlantic ocean.

'Go on then, Herbo,' murmured Richard, and he let the reins fall loose. Herbert trotted easily on to the rocky outcrop and slowed to a halt, again unasked. His ears were pricked forward, head held high, his breath forming a mist in the chilly morning air. He stood still as a statue, blowing through flared nostrils. Richard sat almost still too, gently stroking the horse's great neck. To the observer it might appear that master and horse were both admiring the spectacular view. Certainly Herbert was staring into the distance every bit as intently as his rider. Only Richard and Herbert knew the truth. While the actor was indeed gazing out with joy across the moor to the sea, revelling in the glory of the morning light, Herbert, a grand old hunter, was, of course, looking for the hounds.

The sun was higher in the sky now, over Richard's shoulder, picking out exposed slabs of pale rock on purple slopes and clearly defining the big black burn patches, swaled in the early spring ready for new growth.

The first long hard look at the sea from this special

spot was all part of the ritual, the routine, the rebirth, for Richard. Part of the transition from actor into countryman again. It felt wonderful.

In spite of the chilly start, the day was going to be warm for the time of year and the light was spectacular. The sea was a darkly shining blue grey – the colour and texture of burnished steel.

Once more Richard felt Herbert stiffen beneath him, muscles taut. He followed the old horse's gaze. Something big was moving out there, this time in the bracken on the brow of the hill to his left. It was a stag – a magnificent red deer, the size of a small horse. Herbert's ears were pricked forward, twitching in recognition. The stag stood tall and splendid, silhouetted against the still-rising sun. He had as fine a set of antlers as Richard had ever seen. The great beast was checking out the lie of the land. There would be a herd with him, almost certainly, Richard knew. The stag, serenely untroubled, was looking straight at him and Herbert. It is a strange fact of animal life that when confronted by a man on horseback wild beasts seem to recognise only the larger creature. And so this splendid young stag gazed placidly at Herbert who was no threat at all and remained seemingly unaware of the presence of the man sitting astride him, of deer's only predator. Richard was not surprised. He had experienced this many times before. Thus it is that a quiet horseman can ride straight through a herd of red deer, often exciting no more than curious stares, and pass within inches of a buzzard perched on a fence post, a rabbit crouched by a hedgerow, or even a fox in search of prey.

Gradually several hinds and a smaller lesser stag

46

emerged from their covert to gather around their leader.

Richard sighed his satisfaction. Herbert, old hunter that he was, remained still as the rocks around him. Eventually Richard turned him and kicked him gently on down the hill again. The deer raised their heads attentively. Several backed off slowly, one disappeared, as if by magic, into the bracken from which it had emerged. Horse and horseman moved steadily down the path.

Richard was beginning to feel like a different human being.

Then, just before he entered into the thick of the woodland again, he glimpsed something alien emerging just above the tree-line and steered Herbert to the right for a closer look. The neighbouring property to Landacre, Burrowgate Farm, comprising 200 acres or so, had recently been sold to a new owner from London whom Richard had yet to meet. What he had seen above the tree-line was the top of a huge newly built corrugated iron shed. Richard strained his eyes against the still rising sun. For some reason the shed had been built right on the edge of his neighbour's land, tight up to the woods that divided Burrowgate from Landacre. Richard saw that several trees, including, he was quite sure, at least a couple of grand old oaks, had been felled to make way for the shed which was a couple of hundred yards away from the farmhouse itself.

Richard rode on down the valley to a spot from which he knew he would have the best possible view of Burrowgate. His new neighbour had not wasted a lot of time. Richard was unsure exactly when the farm had been sold following the death of its longtime childless owner, elderly Farmer Sykes, but the shed had sprung up only in the two or three weeks since Richard had last ridden down his favourite moorland path. And the old farmhouse had been given a face-lift. Fresh white paint gleamed starkly in the now bright sunshine.

Anxiously Richard surveyed as much of Burrow-gate as he could for further signs of change. Just across the nearest field he noticed movement, and a dog barked. A strong Somerset voice shouted an instruction. For a brief second it seemed the dog was preparing to make a dash for where Richard and Herbert were only just concealed on the other side of the hedge. The voice called again and a tall burly figure appeared through the gateway just behind the dog. It was Jim Kivel, who for many years had managed Burrowgate for old Farmer Sykes. So he was still there, and there wasn't a better countryman for miles around – apart from George Brooks – Richard knew that. None the less, at the end of the day a farm manager, if that was what Jim Kivel remained, could only do what his boss told him.

The dog barked again. Alert. Hackles up. Richard did not want to be spotted lurking behind hedgerows. He would in any case probably learn more from talking to George Brooks than from any amount of spying. He reined Herbert back a pace or two, swung the old horse around and headed on down through the woods towards the hunting gate that led back into Landacre. The dog turned on its heels and, in sudden obedience, ran to its master's side.

George Brooks was sitting on an old chair smoking his pipe and cleaning a saddle when Richard and Herbert returned to the yard. Richard swung to the ground, his earlier sense of well-being shattered.

'You didn't tell me about that shed,' he said.

George slowly removed his pipe from his mouth. Richard knew only too well that George took the attitude that the countryside was there to be worked. If a farmer wanted to put up a shed, then so be it. Only the new breed of landowners regarded the countryside as their own personal picture window. The man's reaction did not surprise Richard.

'None of my business,' George remarked mildly.

'You didn't think it was just a little on the large side?' Richard's voice was heavy with sarcasm.

George shrugged. 'You can't even see it from Landacre, not through they woods. The only place you can see it from is up on the moor where you was this morning.'

'Yes, well, I don't want to have to look at a sodding great corrugated iron shed when I'm up on the moor.'

The other man raised one eyebrow quizzically. Richard feared that George was about to remind him, as he had frequently done before, that the actor didn't own Exmoor and neither was the moor provided specifically for his pleasure.

'So have you met him yet, the new owner?' Richard snapped quickly. 'What's his name? Parsons, is it?'

'Harry Pearson, Londoner 'e be. See'd 'im the once. Jim Kivel was showing him the wood out the back. Us 'ave got a lot of pheasant nesting this year, you knows . . .'

'Oh for goodness' sake!' Richard interrupted impatiently. 'What did you make of him, George?'

'Same as a lot of 'em, boss, more money than sense, I shouldn't wonder.' George replied levelly, in the manner of one well used to the changing moods of his employer – but the very fact that he called Richard 'boss' subtly indicated his displeasure. Apart from when Richard was entertaining visitors he wanted to impress, George only ever did that if he felt the man he had known for so long was behaving badly. None the less he continued to speak.

'Made 'is pile in the city and knows bugger all about farming, or Exmoor come to that, but 'e's kept Jim Kivel on as manager, and that b'aint daft. Doesn't seem as if 'e be planning to spend a lot of time yer . . .'

George paused, as if he had something else to say and didn't know quite how to say it.

'Yes, go on,' prompted Richard, still irritable.

'Big bloke, 'e is, bald as a coot, too.' George chuckled as if he found baldness amusing.

'And that's it, is it?'

'More or less. I 'ad this feeling I knew him from somewhere, that's all. There's summat familiar about him, but I can't bleddy place it.'

George took Herbert's head. Richard stroked the old horse's neck absently as Herbert strained against his bridle, trying to nuzzle for peppermints again. The sun was soothingly warm now.

Richard's voice was quiet when he spoke again, almost apologetic.

'It's just that I can't stand even the idea of anything happening to spoil Landacre, George.'

George turned and looked at his employer. His face showed both understanding and tolerance.

'The moor's been yer since afore life began, and it'll still be yer after we'm all gone. You, me, and 'e next door . . .'

Richard smiled. George had said that to him a few times, too, and it always cheered him in some strange way. The Landacre-induced sense of well-being began to return.

Then he remembered his lunch date with Joyce Carter in Taunton, which he was suddenly not looking forward to at all. Momentarily he considered cancelling it. But that would not be a good idea, he supposed.

Resignedly he reminded George to have the car ready.

As he walked back to the house his thoughts were fully focused on the forthcoming interview and how he was going to play it. Burrowgate Farm and its new owner were, for the time being, pushed to the very back of his mind.

Three

The Range Rover pulled into the forecourt of The Castle Hotel at almost exactly one o'clock. Joyce Carter was already there, waiting in the bar.

Richard greeted her with a kiss on both cheeks.

Joyce eyed him thoughtfully. He was a handsome beast, no doubt about that, but surely nobody in the world could be more aware of his own presence than this man. Everything about him was so mannered. It was strange how Richard could be so natural as a performer and yet always so unmistakably theatrical off stage.

Joyce Carter wore her usual obligatory layers of black. Almost every layer bore a designer label and cost a small fortune, yet left a combined impression of totally mediocre anonymity. It was her inability to arrange any of the layers satisfactorily which resulted in her looking almost always something of a mess, if indeed a very expensive one. She was herself aware that she never seemed to get it right, never quite achieved the look she wished for, but seemed unable to do anything about it.

'A drink?' she inquired.

'Does the pope wear a frock?'

Good, thought Joyce. He's going to perform for me. He wants me to love him. Bloody typical. Right. Two can play that game.

'How about champagne?' she asked.

'Darling!' he replied, with a very definite exclamation mark. She assumed he meant yes.

It was the beginning of a long and liquid lunch. He was expansive and flamboyant. She was coquettish. She knew he was sitting opposite her convinced that he was charming the living daylights out of her. He would go away from this lunch feeling immensely pleased with himself as was Joyce's intention. Actors were so easy to lull into a false sense of security, so convinced of the power of their own charm that it did not occur to them that anyone else in the world would not be similarly moved.

For Joyce the experience was exactly the way it always was. It was as if she stood outside her own body and mind. Nobody except a journalist ever seemed to understand what hard work interviewing was. The greatest success came with what appeared to be a perfectly natural, animated conversation. But that, of course, was an illusion. Joyce appeared to take part in the conversation as much as her subject, yet was never actually a part of it. Fast as the liquor flowed – there was good claret followed by more champagne with dessert and a pair of large Hine brandies – Joyce did not stop working for a minute. Even those who neither liked nor respected her resolute determination to turn over each interviewee trying so hard to get her to like them, had to admit grudging admiration of her ability to consistently do so.

As she downed the last of her Hine and began to concentrate determinedly on whatever areas of the life and times of Richard Corrington into which she had yet to delve, she became devastatingly certain that the man was going to make a pass at her. She was rarely wrong.

She had in fact slept only twice with actors in her fifteen years of celebrity interviewing, which was mainly because only two of them had ever asked her. Her business was not quite the way it seemed. The truth was that interviewers rarely, and increasingly more rarely as the face of newspapers continued to change and the standing of journalists to plummet, got the chance to get to know their subjects – which in fact made her character-assassination-style interviews all the more absurd, although Joyce would never see it that way. All the honest journalist could do was give a glimpse into a subject's life. With most Hollywood stars a sanitised half an hour in a hotel suite with a publicist on sentry duty was fast becoming the norm.

This lunch with Richard Corrington was not really so very different. They weren't even beginning to get close to each other. The whole thing was a pretence. Joyce did not believe for one moment that Richard really wanted her. What he wanted was to make her love him and he was quite prepared to go to any lengths to do so. If Richard Corrington made a move she would have no doubts at all about his motive. It was probably his final ploy. She suspected that, at this very moment, he was thinking how even Joyce Carter wouldn't rubbish an actor she was sleeping with.

On cue, as if from a long way away, she heard his voice. Low now, intimate. So difficult for an actor with voice projection like Corrington's to make a sexual approach to someone in a public place without sounding as if he was attempting to seduce the whole roomful of people, she thought absurdly.

'Can I take you home?'

She looked at him inquiringly, as wide-eyed and

innocent as she could manage. She wasn't going to help the bugger. No way. Let him spit it out.

She was aware of him taking a deep breath. He was fingering the ever-present *Sparrow-Hawk* lapel pin, a little twitchily, perhaps, she thought.

'I'd like to get to know you better.'

She giggled.

'Right, I'll pay the bill then,' she said.

He didn't offer. Actors, in her experience, either considered that journalists had unlimited expenses, or took it as part of the deal that anyone interviewing them should pick up the tab, or didn't care; or all three. That imminent seduction affected this not a jot was no surprise to her. An actor insisting on paying a bill was also something that had only happened about twice in fifteen years.

'Just tell George the way,' said Richard when they were in the car. And he held her hand lightly and chatted about the countryside they passed through all the way to her cottage in the Blackdown Hills. George the driver, she noticed, looked resolutely ahead.

The glorious spring weather of that morning had changed dramatically by the time they reached the little stone-built Victorian house, known as Beaconview because of its panoramic outlook across a broad valley toward some of the highest points of Devon and Somerset. A strong wind was blowing in typical March bluster, battering the daffodils which sprouted in clusters all over the sloping lawn. A flurry of icy rain, lashing sideways, caught Joyce full in the face as she walked towards the garden gate. Richard climbed out of the car, shoulders hunched against the weather, then turned back briefly.

He appeared to have been giving his driver some instructions, Joyce thought, as she broke into a run up the cobbled path, with Richard right behind her now, equally anxious to avoid a soaking. And she was pretty sure, as they reached the shelter of the porch and she paused to unlock the old oak front door, that she heard the motor start and the Range Rover drive off. Confident bastard, she thought, but she knew it wasn't going to stop her now.

Neither she nor Richard noticed the red van parked in the farm gate just up the lane. George Brooks saw the van but thought nothing of it. He didn't even look to see if there was anyone in the vehicle, and if he had considered the matter at all, he would have expected any occupants to be in the back of the van where they could not be seen. Vehicles parked in strange places in the countryside are commonplace; variously driven by illicit lovers on a tryst, dog owners off walking their pets over someone else's land, fishermen, or men out shooting, sometimes poachers, sometimes not.

OK, Joyce said, when Richard took her in his arms as soon as they walked into the hall of her cottage and told her how much he wanted her. His usually immaculate hair had been left damp and dishevelled – its distinctive quiff flattened by their brief battle with the elements. His cheeks were flushed. He looked surprised, having expected – maybe pleasurably anticipated – a game, having even possibly expected her to say no. Except that she knew it would not occur to him that any woman would ever dream of turning him down.

He wasn't the way she had expected him to be,

however. He was the gentlest, slowest lover she had ever had. She felt as if he had aroused every inch of her body. Yet when he entered her she was aware that he was not fully erect. And it wasn't just that. There was something about him. Something about the way he used her body that made her unable to reach a climax. Eventually he drew away from her, limp, but she was quite sure without having climaxed either. She mumbled obligingly enough that she would help him, do whatever he wanted. He smiled. It was the toothpaste commercial again. And not a lot behind the eyes. He swung his long legs over the bed and stood for a minute or so looking down at her. Strange, the gentleness had slipped away. He had been so completely natural when they were making love. Curiously vulnerable. And so sweet somehow. What on earth was the matter with her? Maybe it was because she was being left unfulfilled, but this man had got to her, no doubt about that.

She watched him dress. Swiftly, gracefully. When he had finished he looked as if he might recently have been sharing afternoon tea with her. His appearance in no way suggested that he had been making love to every inch of her body just moments before. He had such a clever tongue. She felt herself shiver at the thought. He must have brought her to the verge of climax dozens of times and always stopped just before she could become enveloped in the release she so desperately sought. Vaguely the thought occurred to her that it was almost as if that were deliberate. She felt highly aroused still, unsatisfied, and yet unable to move from the bed, to ask for more maybe. His hands, with those long tapering fingers, the immaculate manicure, they would do, they could do the job, if only he would just keep going.

He approached the bed. She knew she was still trembling. He did not seem to notice. He kissed her on the cheek as if she were his sister. 'Gotta go darling,' he said casually. 'I'll let myself out . . .'

She had breathed in the smell of him. He stank of sex. Her sex. Obliquely she wondered what Mrs Perfect, Amanda Lane herself, would make of that . . .

And then he was gone. He had not even muttered the usual niceties about being in touch. With a great effort of will she hoisted herself out of bed and walked uncertainly to the window. She watched him lope down the garden path. If he remained in any way sexually frustrated he had shown no sign whatsoever of it. He disappeared through the garden gate. She couldn't see into the lane at the bottom of her path, but within seconds she heard a motor start. The Range Rover was apparently back, if it had ever left. Maybe she had imagined it.

She felt strange. Uneasy. Certainly not in charge at all. Unlike herself. She checked her watch. It was almost 5.30 p.m. Jacky Starr, working tonight at The National, would be getting the first train in the morning. She had already bought his ticket for him. He didn't like that, independent little sod, but he certainly couldn't afford regular train tickets to the West Country himself, and when he hitch hiked, which he quite perversely seemed to actually enjoy, he sometimes did not arrive much before it was time to leave. As it was, Jacky should be with her shortly after eleven. Not long to wait now.

She fell asleep for a couple of hours, fitfully watched television during the evening, went to bed

58

again at midnight and once again fell into a deep sleep. She woke with a start in what appeared to be the middle of the night . . . There was someone standing by her bed. Involuntarily she cried out, alarmed. Frightened even. Then she realised it was Jacky. She had forgotten that she had even given him a key to the cottage. 'God, what time is it?' she heard herself ask.

'It's about five. I hitched through the night after curtain down. I couldn't wait.'

Her eyes were beginning to acclimatise now. He had not switched on the electric light but there was a nearly full moon. Like Corrington she slept with the curtains open. There was a cold white glow in the room. She saw that he had undressed. He was standing quite naked and quite still, bathed in moonlight, his long hair spread on to his powerful shoulders. He looked like a Greek god and he quite definitely fucked like one. She enjoyed Greek mythology. It was steeped in sex, after all. She particularly liked the story of the god Zeus who appeared in the form of a bull to carry Europa off into the ocean and take her for his own. Seeing her young lover in this light she could drift off into her craziest fantasies, most of which she would never share even with him because his was a completely basic kind of lust in which sex was immediate and straightforward and erotic legend could never play a part.

Jacky Starr's arms and legs were muscled by the manual work that he did and the effect was always somehow quite different from the kind of muscles attained in a gym. He was capable, masculine, and, in Joyce's eyes, quite quite beautiful. He was holding his cock casually in his left hand. It was fully erect.

59

Suddenly he pulled back the bedclothes. She also was naked. He reached between her legs, fingers seeking the essence of her.

'Christ, you're wet, running wet,' he murmured between clenched teeth.

He leaned towards her and kissed her hard on the mouth, drawing back at once.

'You bitch,' he said. 'You stink. You've been fucking somebody else.'

Oh God. She hadn't expected him till morning. She hadn't washed Corrington off her yet.

'Just come to me,' she said huskily.

For a moment he looked as if he might hit her. Instead he leapt on to her. Quite literally leapt. No more foreplay. Nothing. He plunged himself straight into her with all his young strength. It knocked the air from her lungs. She gasped. She could barely breath. It was the first time he had ever hurt her, but the flash of sharp pain transformed itself swiftly into unspeakable pleasure. She climaxed almost at once; instantly, totally, wonderfully. The best thing was that she knew he would not stop. Not now, not for ages. She could come and come until she was completely sated. And she wanted that so much. Needed it. Corrington had left her still gasping for it.

Jacky Starr had hold of her arms at the wrist, pinning them to the bed above her head. Her legs waved ineffectually in the air. She could not move any other part of her body but he was doing all the moving for both of them. He hammered into her more forcefully than ever before.

'I'll teach you to fuck anybody else you slut, you filthy stinking randy slut,' he screamed at her. He was wild. Out of control. Like an animal.

★

The telephone rang at 10.00 a.m. Joyce and Jacky were still in bed. In spite of, or maybe because of Jacky's anger, the night's sex had been quite sensational. He had eventually fallen asleep half on top of her as he often did, with one arm and a leg across her and his face pressed into her breasts. She reached carefully for the phone by the bed. It was Richard Corrington.

'Good morning,' he said cheerily. 'I wondered if you felt like making me a late breakfast . . .'

She felt a hot flush spread through her body, a kind of all over blush. She whispered into the telephone, trying not to wake Jacky.

'I'd love to, but, well, it's a bit difficult,' she heard herself stumble.

Jacky began to stir. She could feel his waking erection pushing into her. The more sex he had during the night the more he seemed to want it when he woke in the morning.

'Oh, that's a pity. I thought we had some unfinished business.' Richard's voice was teasing.

Either Jacky had forgotten his furious jealousy of the night before or he didn't care any more, she thought, but, in a half sleepy way, as if not fully aware of what he was doing, it seemed to Joyce, he began to suck and chew her nipple. His hand pushed her legs open. His fingers sought the parts of her still tender and tingling from his previous attentions. Involuntarily she cried out.

'What's going on?' she heard Richard ask.

'Nothing, nothing at all,' she said hoarsely.

'You've got someone in bed with you, haven't you?'

She did not reply. Jacky rolled on top of her and

eased himself into her. Slowly. The way he liked it in the mornings. If he was even aware that she was speaking on the telephone he gave no sign of it. He seemed huge. She cried out again, she could not help herself. The telephone was still to her mouth.

She tried unsuccessfully to control her breathing.

'I find this rather exciting.' Richard's voice was a husky drawl. 'In fact I just wish I could watch you as well as listen. I'd like that. You won't hang up will you . . .'

And she didn't. She let the phone fall away from her grasp on to the pillow beside her. The session with Jacky went on for a long time, longer than it usually did in the mornings. Even though she had at first felt jaded from the excesses of the night before and disorientated by the phone call from Richard, Jacky successfully brought her to climax more than once before coming himself – rather more noisily than he normally did, it occurred to her only later. And, although she hated to admit it, the thought of Richard Corrington listening to her being so effectively fucked had further added to her arousal.

When he had finished Jacky reached, still breathing heavily, for the telephone receiver and picked it up from the pillow.

'Hope that was good for you too, mate,' he said quietly into the mouthpiece before replacing it on its cradle.

Joyce groaned to herself. Of course the little bastard had known exactly what was going on. What was it about sex which stopped her brain from working?

Jacky swung around on the bed and knelt across her, still naked, as gorgeous as ever, his body shining with health and vitality. Then she saw the look in his eye, and she knew that he was even more angry than he had been the night before.

Without warning he slapped her across the mouth. It made her lips and the surrounding skin sting, but it was not a hard blow. Jacky Starr was an extremely well made young man, a natural athlete. If he had used a quarter of his true strength, even with an open-handed slap, he would have torn her lips to pieces and probably knocked her teeth out, and she knew that. None the less it was the first time he had ever hit her and she was not quite sure what was coming next. She did not speak. She lay very still, watching him. She thought there were tears in his eyes, but she wasn't quite sure.

'You really are evil, Joyce, you know that don't you?' he said. His tone of voice was almost conversational.

Then, as suddenly as he had struck her, he climbed off her, picked up his clothes from where he had thrown them on the floor, and ran downstairs.

She couldn't be certain, but she thought she could hear him sobbing in the kitchen. She sat up in bed fingering her sore face. She was honest enough to reckon that she had probably deserved it although she had always said that no man would *ever* get the chance to hit her twice.

Certainly it seemed that she would either have to start treating young Jacky very differently or else get rid of him quickly. And she couldn't help wondering if she had already pushed him too far.

Four

Jacky intended to walk away and leave her, but by the time he had dressed the will to do so had somehow left him. He sat down at the big kitchen table and rolled himself a joint with trembling fingers. The first deep pull provided an instant surge of soothing numbness. With its help he was able to stem the tears. He cried easily, although hardly anybody knew that. He would always try to run away and hide before breaking down, just as he had done that morning, leaving the bedroom swiftly so that Joyce would not see.

It had begun so simply. She had turned up at the National Theatre to do an interview. Her subject, a much revered theatrical knight, had been late. Stage hand Jacky had been sent with a message to the room where she had been waiting alone, and by chance overheard part of a mobile phone conversation to her office in which she had referred to the man who was usually treated as God at the National in such irreverently derogatory terms that he had burst into nervous laughter. Noticing him standing in the doorway, she had swiftly finished her call and held out both hands in a gesture which eloquently acknowledged that she had been caught out.

'Whoops!' she said.

There was something about her, he was never exactly sure what, which attracted him at once. He did not tell a soul about her indiscretion and contrived to be hanging around in the corridor when the delayed interview eventually ended. He offered to buy her a beer. She accepted without prevarication.

'I'd better, you could blackmail me,' she said, smiling. And he was aware, even then, of her eyes looking him up and down, taking in the width of his shoulders, the flatness of his stomach, his long legs clad in skin-tight jeans and, he was fairly sure, appraising the bulge clearly visible at his crotch. He supposed he had instinctively sensed her extravagant sexuality – that was always what he went for in a woman, not her looks or anything else for that matter. She had responded to him immediately, flirting openly with him.

They stayed in the pub in Stamford Street, just across the road from the theatre, until closing time, and it seemed quite natural that he should then go home with her to her Fulham flat. He had already sensed that she was highly sexed, hungry for new and erotic experiences, but she exceeded his expectations. She was quite rampant. Willing to do and try anything. She was without doubt the best lay he had ever had – and at first that was all there was to it for either of them.

But he had recently been forced to acknowledge that she had become much more than that to him.

Her dismissive behaviour towards him and her cavalier betrayals – Richard Corrington was certainly not the first 'other man' she had strayed with since they had begun their relationship, such as it was, almost a year previously – hurt him deeply. Apart from successive one night stands there was a married lover whom she continued to see regularly and had accompanied a few weeks earlier, without even bothering to lie, on a business trip to New York.

She had been away a week and every day had been torture for Jacky. He had found himself becoming more and more consumed by jealousy. He could no longer abide by the ground rules which Joyce had always made clear – primarily that they would both continue to be free agents, and that theirs would be a no-strings relationship.

In the beginning when they had gone to bed together he encouraged her to share with him the details of her lovemaking with other men, and found it exciting. Once and once only, on her suggestion, he had taken back to her place in Fulham a friend of his from the National, and, inhibitions lulled by some particularly good quality Colombian black, they had embarked on an imaginative and energetic all-night three-in-a-bed session. In the morning Joyce had glowed with pleasure, quite delighted with herself and with him, and remained on a tremendous sexual high for days; but Jacky had felt jaded and a bit ashamed, and resolutely avoided a repeat performance even though she had frequently suggested it. At the time he had found it wonderfully sexy to watch her being fucked, to see her reduced to the most basic animal state. But afterwards the spectacle haunted him, and he realised that he was beginning to care for her a great deal.

Once, in his presence, she had referred to him over the telephone to a friend as 'The Boy'. Her tone of voice had been almost contemptuous. That was the first time he ever wanted to hit her.

But he hadn't. Not then. Not ever before. He was by nature much more gentle than his looks and his behaviour indicated.

He took another deep draw on the joint, thankful that his hands were no longer shaking quite so much. He heard Joyce's footsteps on the stairs. Hastily he wiped the remaining signs of the tears from his face and reached for the dark glasses he often affected, which mercifully were lying on the old pine table. He put them on, leaned back in the chair and swung his cowboy-booted feet on to the table. As she walked through the door he managed to execute an almost perfectly formed smoke ring. He was, in appearance at least, he hoped, Jack the Lad Jacky again. Mr Cool.

She paused, as if uncertain, nervous even, in the doorway. She had on the big towelling dressing gown which she often wore around the cottage. He liked to steal up quietly behind her and slip his hands inside the gown and pull her close to him, feeling the warmth of her, savouring her vitality. His heart lurched as he looked at her. He treasured rare moments like this when she seemed, to him at least, to be vulnerable. He could see the red slap-mark on her face, and he could not quite believe that he had actually hit her.

'I'm sorry,' he said.

'No.' She came and sat down opposite him. 'I asked for it. I'm sorry, I really am.'

He did not think she had ever apologised to him before.

'Look,' she said. 'I know you're hurt and I'll never do that to you again.'

He felt a burst of elation.

'I'm not going to make any promises I can't keep. But I'll make absolutely sure that you're never confronted by anything like this again. Will that help?'

The elation evaporated. It was hopeless. She wasn't

going to change, he should have known that.

'I love you,' he blurted out. He had not actually said the words before.

She shook her head. 'Jacky, I'm old enough to be your mother. We live in different worlds. Can't you just accept what we have and enjoy it, like you used to?'

He looked down at the table, the tears were pricking against his eyelids again.

He could not walk away from her, he really could not. Yet he did not know how much longer he could bear the torment.

Jacky and Joyce returned to London together by train the following day. When they parted company at Paddington Station Joyce found that she was relieved.

Swiftly, as was her habit, her mind switched off him almost as soon as she lost sight of him. In the taxi on the way to her office she began to plan her week ahead and to go over in her mind again her confrontation, both professional and sexual, with Ricky Corrington. All that day in the office she found herself hoping every time the phone rang that it would be him calling. It never was. And by the following weekend he still had not called. Frequently she came close to phoning him, but just managed to stop herself.

Life with Jacky, on the surface at any rate, carried on much as before. She enjoyed several nights during the week with him and, somehow wanting a break from the cottage where so much had happened the previous weekend, spent the weekend in London with him. The sex had been fantastic as usual, and if he was still brooding over her fling with Corrington and suffering the pain of unrequited love, Jacky had said nothing more of it.

Things seemed to have more or less settled back to normal – except that she could not get Richard Corrington out of her mind. Without really doing a great deal he had excited something special in her. He seemed to be dominating her from afar, and she still could not believe that she had allowed him to listen in to her sex session with Jacky. The awareness that it had given her a huge extra kick added to her feeling of humiliation – that and the complete silence which had since followed. One way and another her obsession with him had also made it somehow quite impossible for her to write up the interview with him, even though her editor was waiting for her copy.

The following Monday morning she finally gave in to temptation. She phoned Landacre House. A woman with a strong West Country accent answered, probably a housekeeper Joyce thought. Joyce gave her name and asked to speak to Mr Corrington. The woman asked her to hold the line and disappeared for almost a minute before returning to say that Mr Corrington was not available. Joyce left a message asking for the actor to call her back and hung up feeling even worse than she had before.

She waited all day Monday. There was no return call. Early on Tuesday morning she phoned again and this time only an answering machine responded. She hung up without speaking. On the Tuesday afternoon she made another call and once again got the answer machine. This time she left a message asking Richard to get back to her as soon as possible because she needed to check some facts with him for her article.

There was still no response. She waited until

Wednesday evening. Eventually, and hating herself, she could wait no longer. She phoned Landacre again and a woman with unmistakable theatrical projection answered the phone. She knew at once that it must be Richard's wife, Amanda Lane. Aware that her own voice sounded pathetically tinny in comparison, and just hoping that the note of desperation was in her mind only, Joyce asked to speak to Richard, explaining again that she needed to check some facts for her forthcoming article in the *Dispatch*.

Like the housekeeper two days earlier Amanda Lane asked her to hold on, and it was after an echoing silence that seemed to last for ever that she came back on the line.

'Miss Carter, Ricky says could you possibly call his agent.'

Joyce felt as if she had been kicked in the stomach by a mule.

She heard herself begin to stumble and stammer. 'But, but, it's just a couple of quick queries, I mean, really, I would prefer to speak to him . . .'

She sounded as if she were begging. The voice at the other end of the phone interrupted her. Smooth. Assured. Eloquent. So polite. And so terribly firm.

'I'm afraid he's exhausted after so many months filming the new series. I'm so very sorry, but you'll have to call his agent. Now do you have the number?'

Joyce was not sure whether she replied or not. She replaced the receiver very carefully in its cradle and then threw the whole contraption across the room. To her surprise she found that she was sobbing, and she did not know how much her tears were caused by distress and how much by her fury.

How dare the man treat her like this?

On an impulse she went to her office, switched on the computer and began to write her Richard Corrington interview. Her secretary had already transcribed the tape. Joyce had read through the transcript so many times now she almost knew it by heart. She wrote fluently. The words came easily, for once. By midnight she had finished.

Not giving herself the chance to change her mind she at once transmitted the piece by modem on to the *Dispatch*'s computer system, her face showing her satisfaction. Then she poured herself a large Scotch and went to bed where Jacky Starr already lay, half asleep, half stoned, waiting for her.

Amanda Lane put the phone down, when she'd finished speaking to Joyce Carter, in a cold fury. The call had left her in no doubt at all about what had been going on.

Richard was in the sitting room, lounging on the big sofa, pretending to be quite relaxed and at ease.

'You sad bastard,' she said to him.

He jumped to his feet, immediately on the defensive.

'Look, you've got the wrong idea,' he began.

'Just don't say anything,' she told him. 'I don't want to know. But I'm warning you, Richard. You'd better start cleaning up your act. Because if you ever let me down publicly you'll end up wishing you were dead.'

Then she swung on her heel and left him alone. He supposed it didn't matter all that much in the scheme of things. They had hurt each other so much over the years. But nowadays they existed easily enough together in a courteously distant sort of way, which he had rather got used to and felt comfortable with. When something happened to arouse all the old bitternesses and cause the pain of the past to throb again, he found it quite nerve-racking. He hated it when Amanda displayed open hostility, and it did not help to know that in this case his own foolishness was the cause.

His wife could be cruelly hard. Although God knows he had given her cause. The first time she had caught him out in an affair she had been deeply upset – after that merely angry and contemptuous, or so it seemed.

How different it might have been had their son lived. He had wanted a son so much, just as his own father had before. To have actually been able to reach out and touch his own child, to have been that close, and then to have lost him, was so much worse than never to have been a father at all.

And the final wickedest blow had been when the medical tests had proved that it was something genetic in him which had caused the baby to be so deformed. Amanda could have no more children because of it. So that was his fault too.

In spite of her utter refusal ever to discuss it he felt that she never forgave him, but was aware that the reality was that he never forgave himself.

It was then that he had begun to use drugs regularly. Before that dreadful time he had smoked dope during his student days and experimented with the odd line of cocaine at parties, but nothing more. Before that he had had no fear of anything life could throw at him, and no need of any props to help him cope.

Richard was honest enough with himself to know how easy it is to cast the blame elsewhere for your own failings. But it was only after the death of his son that he became drug-dependent, for many years of his life often relying on cocaine to get him through the day.

All of that was history, now, he told himself. He hadn't sniffed a line of coke for years – his need for anti-depressants on occasions was an entirely different matter. His demons were under control, they had to be. There is a limit to how long a man can grieve for what might have been. He had learned to accept his lot.

But one thing was certain. He had no wish to further antagonise his wife. She was a force to be reckoned with, was Amanda Lane.

Five

The shock was total. Larry called to warn him, and Richard Corrington could not believe it. He continued to only half believe it until George returned to Landacre with a copy of that day's *Dispatch*.

The banner headline set the tone. THE HAWK IS A PAIN, he read. It was a slightly obscure pun on the Ted Hughes poem 'The Hawk in the Rain' which Richard probably rightly assumed would be lost on most of the *Dispatch*'s readers, in spite of the paper's delusions of grandeur. He knew and loved 'The Hawk in the Rain', not because he was particularly well-read, but because he had a passion for Ted Hughes, developed long before the West Country-based poet had become laureate.

Richard closed his eyes. The pun might be obscure but the message was clear enough, and the association with Hughes made it additionally hurtful. He wanted to be on another planet. But there could be no escape. And he had to know the worst. He opened his eyes and read the headline again.

There was also a strap-line, a kind of sub head, incorporating the by-line. 'Ricky Darling thinks charm can conquer all – but not Joyce Carter.'

He continued reading, wishing he could stop.

'The voice is like treacle without the sweetness and so is the man. Sticky, cloying and bland.'

He groaned. How could she do this to him? How

long was it now since that lunch and the afternoon sex session followed by that erotic phone call? Two weeks, more or less. He should have phoned again, or at least taken her calls, he supposed. Was she punishing him for that? Was that what all this was about? Richard sought desperately for reasons. He had been so sure he was going to be different, the exception to the rule. Certainly it had never occurred to him that she would be this vindictive, and he realised now that it should have done.

He had weathered character assassinations before, but never one quite as vicious as this, nor as unexpected.

'Richard Corrington is not only a big star he is a big man. Well over six foot tall, beefy, broad shouldered, powerful. What a pity he doesn't have a brain to match.'

Oh God, thought Richard. He was going to remember this for a long time. He'd sue. That's what he'd do. That stuff about the size of his brain must surely be libellous. And he wasn't beefy, either, he was muscular. He'd sue the two-faced bitch. He reached for the phone and started to dial the number of his lawyer. Then he stopped. He knew that the circulation of the allegedly upmarket *Dispatch* was less than half a million. If he sued his would become yet another celebrity court-case. The *Sun* and all the other tabloids would report every jot of it, gleefully revelling in each embarrassing detail which would then be pored over by half the country instead of half a million. The bitch might well insult his brain but he wasn't stupid enough to go down that road.

Cringing into his chair he read on. The quotes used were one hundred per cent accurate, he noticed. They

would be of course. She was the complete professional, the killer bimbo. No mistakes like that. But
the slant of the quotes, the way in which they were
used, was obviously deliberately and quite brilliantly
crafted to make him look like a prize idiot.

'He is widely known as Ricky Darling and the name
thoroughly suits this ultimate luvvie. Richard Corrington is the kind of actor who consistently performs
better off screen than on. Of course the script might
be sadly lacking. Not surprising since the un-great
man is, in what for him passes for real life, forced to
use his own words.

'Throughout the interview the actor, married to
that alabaster actress Amanda Lane, appeared to be
on the verge of making some kind of pass at me . . .'

Corrington looked up from the page and shut his
eyes yet again. How could she, he wondered. And
how far did she go? He wouldn't be surprised to find
himself accused of date rape. Speedily he began to
read on.

'The man's belief in his own irresistibility shines
from every pore – or would do if they were not
clogged with all that dreadful treaclyness. There was
an offer of a lift home, and an expressed desire to get
to know me better.

'Charitably, I suppose, I could put it down to drink.
But it is well-known that Corrington is no stranger to
alcohol, so he should know how to hold it by now.

'I found him a sad shadow of a man. But then,
perhaps that is all that actors every really can be.'

Richard screwed the newspaper into a tight ball
and threw it across the room.

He was vaguely aware that Amanda had entered
the room. Over the last few days relations between

them had returned, on the surface at least, to the normal distant civility. He had a feeling that situation was about to change for the worse again, and he wasn't wrong.

'I'm just leaving,' she said. He looked at her with unseeing eyes, vaguely he remembered that she was travelling to London that afternoon to go to the theatre and would be staying overnight. 'There's cold pheasant in the fridge or a beef casserole if you prefer . . .'

She broke off, noticing for the first time his distracted expression and the screwed up newspaper on the floor. She shot him a curious look, picked it up, smoothed the pages, recognised the offending article for what it was and gave it little more than a cursory glance.

'Well, what a surprise,' she said. Her voice was heavy with contempt.

Richard struggled to maintain control. One day he was going to hit her. One day he was going to smash his fist into that smug face. And he felt that day approaching. He turned away from her and walked briskly out into the hallway, hoping she would not follow him. He might not be able to contain himself.

In the living room of her cottage Joyce Carter was rereading her work. It was more vicious than anything she could remember writing in a long time – she had been a bit surprised that some of it had got past the subs and the lawyers – and she was already wishing that she had not made the article so extreme. Whatever his reasons for shutting her out of his life, all she had done now was make sure there would never be a way back in.

She was even uncertain of her reasons for being quite so vitriolic. She thought perhaps it was because he was the first actor ever to have broken through her defences. And indeed, the first man to do so in a very long while.

She didn't like that. And she had deliberately set out to prove to herself that she didn't give a damn.

Joyce needed to be in command. And there was another extremely irritating connotation. By putting the boot in the way she had, she had effectively ruled out any further travel in the dining compartment of the Friday night 19.35. It went without saying that she would no longer be welcome. And that was a bloody nuisance. She really had shot herself in the foot in every possible way.

Feeling thoroughly miserable, she poured herself a large whisky and rolled a joint from the lump of hash Jacky had brought with him. It was good dope. The whisky was a fine Islay malt, a fifteen-year-old Laphroaig, with its distinctive peaty taste. She rolled the conflicting flavours around on her tongue.

Then she stretched out on the sofa, trying desperately to put the whole wretched business out of her mind.

Richard retrieved his briefcase from the cupboard where he had stowed it and took out a bottle of pills. His hands were shaking. His much maligned brain was spinning. He looked at the bottle for an instant. Trozactin. Happy pills. The designer drug of the nineties. A new drug for a new sickness. Stress. Previous generations had had no special name for whatever it was that life might throw at them. Richard and his contemporaries were as familiar with 'stress' as with the common cold. And Trozactin was a lot more effective than Lemsip.

It was two weeks since the filming of *Sparrow-Hawk* had ended and that stupid interview, and his even more stupid behaviour. Two weeks in which he had resorted to the pills on only one occasion. And then, realising for once that if he over-indulged the way he usually did the pills would only ultimately make things worse, he had only taken two. It had been a close call another once or twice when he had woken up shivering in the middle of the night, but he had resisted, taken only a couple of long deep swigs of brandy instead, and sweated away the rest of the night. This time he was not going to be able to resist. He could not continue without help. He felt his self control, so fragile at the best of times, crumble.

Fumblingly, he unscrewed the cap to the bottle and emptied half the contents into his left hand. Hesitating only for a few seconds, he placed four pills in his mouth. A bottle of cognac stood on the table by the bay window. He walked across to it, took a deep swig and swallowed. He was incapable of registering anything except his own state of mind. Certainly there was no question of him noticing, through the window, movement near the hedge which bordered his property at the rear, nor the glint of something metallic reflecting the afternoon sunshine.

The liquid burned satisfyingly at the back of his mouth. He took another four pills and again tipped the brandy bottle to his lips. The alcohol was an important part of the process for him. Trozactin, taken correctly, was a safe and effective anti-depressant. Overdosed and washed down with the best part of half a bottle of brandy its consequences were dangerously unpredictable.

The cocktail of pills and alcohol seemed to bring almost instant relief. Certainly they concentrated his mind, giving him a peculiar sense of purpose. He made a snap decision – one which he was instantly sure was correct, and yet, at the same time knew he would never have reached unaffected by the pills.

He would go to see Joyce Carter, and he'd bloody well ask her what she was playing at. He'd confront her, that's what he'd do. He'd make her suffer for what she had done.

He drove his beloved motor bike too fast and was not even aware how lucky he was to get away with it. He should not have been riding a push bike in his condition, but speed always excited him, the motor cycle always exhilarated him. He was lucky also that it had stopped raining earlier that day – a break at last in the weather which had remained wet and windy ever since he had made that first fateful visit to Beaconview two weeks earlier. The roads were mercifully dry, allowing him to get away with taking several corners almost horizontally.

Richard arrived at Joyce Carter's cottage just as furious as when he had left Landacre, but feeling so much stronger, and, strangely, so much more in control.

The door bell rang. Richard stood there, the big leather flyer's jacket with a sheepskin collar that he so often wore for photo sessions somehow, on him, looking not at all out of place on top of a suit. The wind in his face during the bike ride had given his skin a rugged glow. At a glance he looked even more devastatingly attractive than usual. But Joyce could see all too clearly the blind fury in his eyes.

'You'd better come in,' she said.

He followed her into the kitchen, grabbed her by one shoulder and swung her towards him.

'Why?' he asked. His voice sounded quite calm.

'Why what?' she responded, all the time knowing it was far too late to play innocent.

'Don't be a fool, whatever else you are, you're not that.'

Abruptly she sat down on a kitchen chair, releasing his hold on her. In spite of everything, in spite of how impossible she knew she had made it, in spite of the shock of seeing him, in spite of sensing at least some of the depth of his anger, she felt that inexplicable longing for him rise in her again.

And when she spoke she realised she could only say the truth. 'I wanted you . . .' she began.

He did not wait for her to finish speaking.

'And you usually crucify people you "want", do you?' he snapped.

She bowed her head. 'You wouldn't return my calls. You used me. You humiliated me.' She paused.

'Humiliation?' He raised an eyebrow. 'Is that what it was? You seemed to enjoy it. Put on quite a show, I recall.'

She winced. 'That's not what I meant. I really did want you, I don't know why so much.' She looked up. It was suddenly so important to be forgiven. Her eyes implored him. 'I still do want you . . .'

His lips twisted. She was not sure if he was smiling or sneering at her. She was aware that he looked flushed and that his eyes were unnaturally bright. In a curiously detached way she registered that he had probably been taking drugs of some kind, and something much more powerful than the marijuana which was still making it difficult for her to think clearly.

'What do you want exactly?' He made the words sound so unpleasant, so harsh, that she did not reply.

'This? Is this what you want?'

He undid his flies. To her astonishment, remembering the semi-limpness of their previous lovemaking, he was fully erect.

He took hold of her shoulder again and jerked her forwards so that she fell on to her knees before him.

'You like being treated like a slut, don't you? That's what you are, isn't it?'

He pulled her head closer. Obediently, not quite believing what she was doing, she took him in her mouth. With one hand he tore open her dressing gown and reaching down, took a nipple between finger and thumb and squeezed, quite painfully. Curiously at such a moment the thought flashed across Joyce's mind that she had seen him do that often on television in *Sparrow-Hawk*. She could feel him growing more and more excited and as he reached his climax he fixed both hands behind her head and pulled her firmly to him so that she could not move away. She hated what was happening, it was one of the few things about sex she could not stand. Not with anyone. She gagged, almost choking, but he would not let go.

Eventually she felt him relax. He freed his grip on her head, allowing her to move away a little, and began to stroke her hair. Very gently. He was smiling.

'It's been a long time, you wouldn't believe how long,' he said quietly. He sounded absent minded. His voice came from somewhere distant. And for just a moment she thought it was all going to be all right. But it wasn't.

He seemed to shake himself back to reality. Incongruously she noticed that he had not even taken off the flyer's jacket. With one hand he buttoned up his trousers and with the other, quite casually, but with surprising force, he pushed her away from him so violently that she ended up sprawled on the floor.

'I hope you enjoyed that, because it's all you are ever getting from me,' he said. And then she knew that there was no hope, because he only wanted to cause her pain.

Six

Jacky was slightly drunk when he arrived back at Beaconview Cottage. Unsteady on his feet, slow and awkward with his hands. He had been to a football match in Torquay, watching The Arsenal play the home side in a cup game. And he had wriggled out of his normal Saturday night shift at The National, as much because of the big game as because he wanted to spend more time with Joyce. The team was his second great passion.

He used his key with some difficulty to unlock the cottage door and attempted to switch on the lights. Nothing happened. The police discovered later that all the fuses had been removed.

Stumbling uncertainly forwards in the darkness of the hall he tripped over something and fell forwards, face down.

Numbed by the alcohol, it took him several seconds to realise he had fallen across the body of Joyce Carter. She lay spread-eagled on the tiled floor. And she was cold in death.

Jacky's face was actually pressed against her dead face. As his eyes grew accustomed to the blackness he recoiled in revulsion. The towelling robe he always so liked to see her in had fallen apart and she was half naked. Her skin seemed slightly luminous and he could see the bright gleam of her teeth.

The sense of nausea was suddenly overwhelming.

Involuntarily Jacky felt his throat open and was heartily sick. The vomit poured all over Joyce. He rolled off her. He could not even scream. In fact he uttered no sound. He slid around on the floor made slippery by his own vomit. He was disorientated, half out of his head. The vomit no longer seemed to matter. Confused, he reached out for the woman to whom only a few hours previously he had been making passionate love. The woman who had continually betrayed him, and yet whom he adored. In spite of everything, at that moment he felt only terrible sorrow. For a few minutes he held her close to him, nursed her poor bloated face, swollen and discoloured, and wished with all his heart that he could go back in time, at least until that morning.

Eventually he crawled to the phone in the kitchen and dialled 999. In a flat monotone he told the police that Joyce Carter was dead. That he thought she had been strangled.

It was only later when the police asked him how he knew that she had been strangled that he began to think about himself. And by then it was already almost too late.

Detective Chief Inspector Todd Mallett of the Devon and Cornwall Constabulary was the first senior policeman to arrive at Beaconview.

The weather was terrible again. March was nearly over now, but the rain falling heavily had an icy chill to it and gale-force winds were blowing from the Blackdowns right across the valley, giving the old cottage a head-on battering. The windows rattled and a couple of slates had fallen from the roof and lay, broken, on the ground.

The DCI, who had forgotten his raincoat as usual, stepped squarely in a puddle outside the front door in his haste to reach shelter. One of his shoes, which had seen better days, instantly filled with water. He stood for a moment in the porch ineffectually shaking a dripping leg, before struggling into a protective white paper suit and plastic overshoes. His feet still squelched with every step.

Inside, a scene of crime team was already in operation – four of them in all, wearing similar paper suits and surgical gloves. The suits had hoods, the team moved slowly and carefully, their appearance, Todd thought as he always did, lending an eerie unreality to the proceedings.

The Home Office pathologist arrived an hour later, summoned from her Bristol base. A golfing umbrella protected her from the downpour as she made her way up the garden path. She neatly side-stepped the puddle which had trapped Todd Mallett, and slipped into her protective suit with no trouble at all.

Carmen Brown was young for the job, a slightly built woman with an acutely intelligent face but a slightly fragile air about her which she did her best to dispel by always demonstrating a devastating efficiency.

She was able to deduce almost at once that Joyce Carter had had sex shortly before she died.

And there seemed to be signs of Jacky Starr's presence everywhere in the cottage and all over Joyce's body.

'I am fairly sure there are traces of semen both in her vagina and in her mouth,' Dr Brown told the DCI in distinctly matter of fact tones.

Todd Mallett nodded, determined to be as matter

of fact as she was. He had already summarily questioned Jacky Starr and the lad had admitted freely enough that he had made love to Joyce Carter that morning.

'Time of death?' the chief inspector asked.

Carmen Brown paused a moment or two before replying. With all that could be deduced from forensic evidence nowadays, time of death remained a surprisingly inexact science, reliant almost entirely on body temperature. Todd knew that. He also suspected that Carmen Brown would not be all that far out. She never had been before.

'Between three and four o'clock today, as near as I can judge,' the doctor replied. 'Probably closer to four . . .'

Todd nodded again. The body still lay in the position in which it had been found in the hallway. The scene of crime team was still going over the place with a tooth comb, checking for finger prints, and searching for anything that might give a clue to what had happened in Beaconview Cottage earlier that day.

There was no sign of forced entry. At the moment all the circumstantial evidence pointed to Jacky Starr. He had even been sick over the victim's body.

Todd Mallett knew exactly what to do next. This one carried the unmistakable hall-mark of a domestic and the odds were impressive even before the evidence was consolidated. The vast majority of murders are committed by relatives of, lovers of, or someone else very close to, the victim and fall into the category which the police generically label domestic. Todd didn't think they would be looking for anyone else. He planned to concentrate on getting a confession.

Jacky Starr was such an obvious suspect – the bit of rough, young lover of a high flying journalist. The motive had yet to be revealed, but there was plenty to choose from in a situation like this. A drunken row, or wild sex which had gone too far. And, of course, there was always jealousy.

They took Jacky to Exeter's Heavitree Road police station while Carmen Brown and the scene of crime boys were still completing their work. He was more or less sober now. The shock had dulled the effect of the beer, much of which he had in any case disgorged. Yet he remained inarticulate and apparently unaware of the seriousness of his own situation.

His clothes were removed from him for further analysis and he was issued with a disposable paper suit and plastic sandals. He was photographed and examined by a police doctor. Samples of his body tissue were taken for DNA analysis – blood, saliva, pieces of hair, and swabs from his penis.

There were scratches on Jacky Starr's back and remnants of skin had already been found by Carmen Brown beneath the dead woman's fingernails. The DCI and his detective sergeant – Malcolm Pitt, red-headed, freckle-faced, and deceptively boyish looking – took it in turns to interrogate Jacky. They told him they were quite certain that the remnants of skin would prove to have come from him. They were determinedly persistent.

'She scratched me during sex, she often does. I mean did.'

Jacky knew he sounded unconvincing. They asked him repeatedly to account for his movements. He was not even able to do that.

'I was at the football,' he told them. 'People saw me.'

But the game had started at 5.30 – an evening kick off as often arranged to fit in with the seaside-town working lives of the Torquay fans. Jacky Starr claimed he had left Joyce at 2.30. Torquay was less than an hour from her cottage.

'I was hitching,' said Jacky. 'I can't drive. You never know how long it's going to take . . .'

They badgered and bullied him. The sergeant was the worst, Jacky thought. His technique appeared to centre on making unpleasant sexual comments, and it was he who somehow bamboozled Jacky into admitting that he had known Joyce wasn't faithful to him and how much he hated it.

Heads were nodded knowingly. A motive loomed attractively. A quick computer check had already revealed that Jacky had a police record. Seven years earlier, while still at school, he had been charged with causing malicious damage following an outbreak of vandalism. It seems that he had run amok, smashing shop windows and damaging motorcars.

'Got a temper on you, lad, it all fits doesn't it?' Sergeant Pitt remarked menacingly. In spite of his boyish looks Pitt was a very tough interviewer. He was ambitious, and well aware that getting a confession in a murder case would do his career no harm at all.

None the less there were strict rules in modern police procedure – reformulated after the notorious case of the Guildford Four whose unorthodox inter-rogations had led to forced confessions and a national scandal. Jacky had been clearly and methodically informed of his rights by the custody officer, a sergeant, when he arrived at the station. But when he was advised that he might like a solicitor present and that he was entitled to the services of one free of charge, or at least that he may wish to make a phone call, he had barely responded. It took some time for it to dawn on him that he was a suspect, that he was actually under arrest. It was therefore more than an hour after he was taken to the station that he started to think, just a little bit, and asked if he could make that call.

There was only one person in the world he could think of telephoning. Belle – his mother.

He had not seen her for over a year, and even as a child he had spent very little time with her. Jacky had always accepted that he got in the way, that he cramped his mother's style. But the grandmother who had more or less brought him up was now a very old lady. Anyway she wouldn't know what to do. His mother had always seemed to know what to do about most things. That was one of her plus points. And she had always paid the bills. Jacky didn't know a lot about the law, but he was quite sure that justice could be bought. He had been brought up to believe that there was one law for the poor and one for the rich. And nothing had happened yet in his young life to make him think differently. His mother had influence because of who she was. Great influence. He knew that too. And he assumed she had plenty of money. She always had had anyway.

As for his father – his mother had always maintained bluntly that he did not have one. As a boy he had occasionally pestered her for information, but the more he had done so the more his mother had withdrawn into herself. As he grew older Jacky had wondered if his father was a married man with whom his mother had been having an affair. That would have explained a lot. But gradually it dawned on him from all that he learned about his mother's way of life that it was more likely that she simply did not know who his father was, that there had been more than one candidate and none of them seriously part of his mother's life.

He lifted the receiver and dialled his mother's number. He couldn't remember the last time he had called her. Yet it was strange the way he never had to think about the number. For so much of his life it had been his only link with the woman he had never been close to.

Arabella Parker lay in the huge round jacuzzi bath in the master bathroom of her detached mock Tudor house in Essex. The bath was heavily scented, extravagantly bubbly, and fitted with powerful water jets which always made her feel wonderful. She was relishing every minute of it. She might as well, too, because it didn't look as if she was going to own it much longer. Not the bath, not the house, not any of it. The financial chaos that had been mercilessly gathering around her for years had now reached crisis level. The bailiffs, the VAT men and almost everyone else you could think of were all fighting over who should be first in the queue.

Arabella's heyday as an actress was long over, but she had once earned a very great deal of money. She had been queen bee of the British cinema, and when she was everybody's favourite starlet there actually had been a British cinema industry of which to be queen bee. She sighed, and took a deep drink from the pale mauve-tinted tumbler she held rather precariously in her left hand, which contained an extremely large whisky and soda. After the day she had been through she deserved it. The VAT men were creating havoc going through her books, and meanwhile the manager of her mini cab company, which she had set up in a bid to see her through the lean times as an actress, had been beaten up on his way to work that morning. Nobody knew why yet – and she doubted they ever would. The boys had all been in a blind panic as usual when there was trouble, and she'd had to go in to the office to stop the whole shooting match falling apart.

She knew everything was about to go under and there was bugger all she could do about it. A disastrous confrontation with the VAT men had been followed by a last ditch meeting with her accountant. That had been equally fruitless. In her opinion he was at least half responsible for the mess she was in. 'Start a business, Belle, invest your money in something worthwhile,' he had counselled. But he had failed to advise her that it might help if you knew at least something about the business you were launching and do not have to trust other people whose main purpose seemed to be to rip you off.

In the early evening she had had to break off to open a distinctly second division supermarket on the Braintree ring-road. None the less, the day job, such as it was, was about all she had left now. Having completely over-reached herself building a business few, except she and her immediate associates, knew was now sunk, Arabella had recently been desperately trying to worm her way back into the acting world she had more or less given up as a bad job several years before. In the early stages of her career she had made a small fortune. If only she had hung on to it instead of listening to those flash advisers and launching herself into all manner of enterprises she never fully got to grips with.

She sighed again. It was so long since she had made a major film or TV show she could barely remember the last one. She was having to claw her way back with humiliating appearances like the one she'd just made in *Sparrow-Hawk*. And now it seemed pretty certain that whatever she did, nothing in the acting line was likely to bring in a fraction of what she needed to get herself out of trouble.

Arabella was wallowing unashamedly in self pity. None the less she continued to look the part. Her impossibly black hair, inherited from a Greek grandmother, was neatly coiled inside a towelling turban fastened by an ornately bejewelled pin. Her face was still heavily made up. Her lipstick looked as if it had been glued on. Her eyebrows were perfectly plucked above eyes which were surprisingly pale blue and ringed in black liner, and thick layers of mascara coated her false eyelashes. Arabella couldn't enjoy anything really, not even a bath, if she wasn't wearing her war paint, and so skilful was she at both choosing and applying it that even the steam and heat of a frothing jacuzzi did little to shift it. After the bath she would carefully clean her face and, out of long habit, probably apply another light coat before bed, even though she was sleeping alone. A pro from every strand of her thickly lacquered hair to the tip of her vermilion painted toe nails, she never let the act drop.

She didn't cook. Neither did she usually wash up or even load the Miele dishwasher, clean anything, make a bed or switch on the washing machine. It vexed her to think that might all have to change in the forbiddingly near future. Her excellent daily help was a luxury she already could not afford.

Arabella was nearer fifty than forty years old now. Women over forty and under sixty remain largely ignored in film and even in major TV shows. Yet, and rather infuriatingly given her financial circumstances, she remained as famous and popular as ever. Taxi drivers always recognised her and could usually reel off a list of her films from the good old days. It never failed to surprise her really, but she still liked it in spite of the irritation of not earning any money, to speak of, through it any more. After all she had made her first professional stage appearance in pantomime when she was four and had played just about every theatre left in Britain before getting those film breaks in the late sixties and seventies.

Showbusiness was in her blood, as much a part of her as her East End background. She was widely known as Belle, or worse still Belle Girl and in the press Bubbly Belle, all of which she secretly hated, but she was willing to go along with almost anything which helped maintain the myth of her carefully cultivated loveable Cockney persona.

She lowered herself gratefully further into the soothing bubbles and decided not to do any more worrying that day. She would just accept her fate when it reached out and grabbed her in the shape of countless brown envelopes.

She soaped a shapely leg thoughtfully – automatically noting that she could do with a rewaxing and some more of that magic tanning lotion they specialised in at her beauty salon, and that it might be time she had her veins looked at.

It was at that moment the telephone rang. She reached out for the cordless receiver she had automatically taken with her into the bathroom, then for a few seconds considered allowing the answering machine to pick up. She checked her watch. It was gone one o'clock in the morning. A call at this hour was almost certain to be either very good news or very bad. Knowing her run of luck at the moment it was probably very bad. None the less some instinct persuaded her to take the call.

As soon as she heard Jacky's voice she was certain that her worst fears were about to be realised. She was not to be disappointed.

'Hello, Belle, it's me.'

Years ago she had told him to call her Belle. At the time she'd still been trying to pretend she was about ten years younger than she really was. She hadn't wanted a near grown son giving the game away.

'Jacky?' Why had she put the query in her voice. Didn't she know the voice of her own child? Considering how infrequently she talked to him it would actually be quite possible that she didn't know his voice very well. The old guilt consumed her, just like it always did.

This time his voice struck another chord. He did sound strange. She felt nervous, afraid even. She could hear his breathing down the phone. It was uneven, half- strangled.

'What's wrong?' she heard herself asking.

'They've put me in jail,' he half shouted at her. 'They think I've killed Joyce.'

'Who's Joyce?' As she spoke Arabella wondered why she had asked that. Who gave a monkey's who Joyce was anyway?

In any case Jacky didn't answer the question at all. 'They're trying to do me for murder, Mum. They are. Will you help? Will you come . . .'

She wasn't sure, but she thought he was sobbing. Arabella was now sitting bolt upright in the bath. The jacuzzi was still pumping away, powerful jets of air forming a foaming whirlpool. Impatiently she switched the thing off. Frothy bubbles were incongruously running down her breasts and arms.

In spite of the steamy atmosphere and the heat of the water she felt her blood run cold. That had always seemed such a silly expression, and yet that, she discovered, was exactly what happened. Suddenly it felt as if there was ice in her veins.

All the old doubts which plagued their ever strained relationship were suddenly irrelevant. He was her son.

'I'll be with you as soon as I can,' she said. 'Don't worry. And don't say anything more. Don't say anything until I get there.'

She began to pull herself together, recalling dimly the procedural information so readily available from the countless police TV series she'd watched.

'Jacky, this is what you tell them, do you hear me? Tell them you are not answering any more questions until your lawyer gets there. That's your right, OK?'

She remembered she didn't even know where he was. When he told her he was in Exeter she cursed under her breath. It would take her hours to get there and the whole thing was going to be even harder to handle than it would have been in London. None the less, she had to move.

'Just hang on in there,' she instructed.

She switched off the phone, hauled herself out of the bath, flung a towel haphazardly around herself and half ran into the bedroom. She began pulling clothes out of cupboards and drawers and throwing them on the bed. She realised that her body was trembling ferociously and her brain wasn't working at all. With a great effort of will she made herself sit on the bed, just for a moment, quietly, trying to compose herself. She forced herself to think about what Jacky had said and tried to make sense of it. She didn't immediately phone her solicitor. She had a good one. Barney Lee had been more than a lawyer over the years, he had been a friend who had helped her more than anyone else keep her sanity with the odds piled against her. Unfortunately, right now she owed him so much money that, the way things were, she was never likely to be able to repay it. Damn! She cursed herself and everything that was happening in her world. One of the reasons that her son believed so trustingly that money fixed most things was because his mother, born into poverty and knowing from first hand experience the huge difference that wealth could make, believed so too. It was one of the few things she had probably instilled in him. She believed in it irrevocably, and aware that at this moment of greatest need she had no money to mention, Belle felt the old feeling of failure, when it came to her son, flooding back.

Belle clenched her fists and punched the bed on either side of her in frustration. Well, she would merely have to use all she had left. Her fame – or at least the myth. A bit of bluff. She was just going to have to try, wasn't she? Battling Belle – that was another name they called her – and now was her chance to prove that it wasn't for nothing.

She jumped to her feet and began sorting out the

jumble of clothing on the bed, swiftly folding what she felt she needed into a bag. She also plugged in her electric rollers. Belle wore her hair big, like something out of *Dallas*. She was aware that most mothers would probably be paying rather less attention to their hair and their wardrobe at such a moment, but she was Arabella Parker, after all, and she was not about to change her spots.

When she had finished packing she dressed in a simple but beautifully tailored black trouser suit and a pale pink silk shirt. She studied her reflection for a few seconds in the big gilt-framed mirror, and decided that she could only be herself and the image needed a little more attention. She removed the black jacket and the silk shirt and replaced the shirt with a figure hugging shiny gold number boasting a plunging neckline. Then, after skilful use of the electric rollers, she brushed and lacquered her hair into place, cleaned her face and replaced her make-up – not quite as much as usual, but still a pretty thorough application.

She left a note for her daily on the imitation Georgian mantelpiece in her sitting room, picked up her bag and prepared to leave. At the front door she hesitated. She was going to have to ring Barney, there really was no alternative. She used the phone in the hall and dialled his number. An answer machine clicked into action. Damn – but what did she expect at two o'clock in the morning? She left a message as clearly and rationally as she could manage. It was a plea for help. She knew quite enough about police procedure to understand how important it was that Jacky did not get tied up in knots in the early stages. He needed a lawyer with him.

She pushed the button in the hallway that would

automatically unlock and lift her garage door and hurried outside into a cold but dry night. There was a brisk breeze blowing, sending small scudding clouds swiftly on their way. By and large, the sky was clear, and her gold Jaguar car gleamed in the moonlight. Although it was actually almost ten years old, the way things were going this might well be the last journey she would be making in the luxury motor before it went along with everything else.

In spite of its age the Jag's door closed with a satisfyingly precise little clunk, and the leather seats smelt and felt expensively luxurious. When she turned the key in the ignition the motor purred instantly into life. She eased the automatic shift stick into reverse and glided the car backwards. As a matter of habit she switched on the mobile phone followed by the stereo system, then pushed the shift stick into drive, and headed west in the direction of the M4.

It was a long drive. She found her mind drifting back to the birth of a son she had never wanted. She hated admitting that now, but it was the stark truth. Her pregnancy had come as a total shock. She had been taking the pill. She was that one in a thousand statistic, or whatever the risk factor was. Her first reaction when she learned that she was expecting a child had been fury. And her second was to seek to arrange an abortion, but she was already almost five months gone when it eventually dawned on her that she must be pregnant. She had been very stupid, attributing without much thought the disruption in her menstrual cycle to the contraceptive pill.

Belle had been the golden girl then, making hit movie after hit movie, on a roll, on a high, and she had made the most of every minute. It seemed as if every man in London wanted her, and she hadn't been averse to trying them out – particularly as so many of those who pursued her were from the very top drawer. There was not a first night worth mentioning which Belle had not attended with this famous actor, or that wealthy businessman, or maybe a lord or an earl. In those days she had been quite promiscuous, and, in that time before AIDS, protected, as she had thought, by the pill, did not even give her promiscuity a thought – until she became pregnant and realised that she did not even know who the father was. She had narrowed it down to three candidates, but that was the best she could do, and in any case she was not particularly interested in a closer relationship with any of them.

When abortion was ruled out, her next thought had been adoption. It was partly her mother who had talked her out of that, and partly the knowledge that she would never be able to keep it a secret – somehow or other the papers had begun speculating that she might be pregnant at about the same time that she discovered she was. She had known only too well the kind of publicity she would get if she gave her child away. Her mother had promised to play a major part in the upbringing of the child and so Belle had decided to keep it. But even when Jacky was born she had felt none of the rush of maternal love that she was assured would overwhelm her. Instead she could not wait to place him into the care of her mother while she fussed and fretted about getting her figure back in order. She was far too busy and important and famous to be a mother.

There followed one brief marriage – to a handsome wastrel, who, when he tired of basking in her reflected glory, walked out on her without compunction, taking with him an extremely large cheque in exchange for not selling the story of their sorry union to the tabloid press. And during that liaison, blinded at first by her husband's looks and superficial charm, Belle had virtually shut her son out of her life altogether. These were not happy memories. The guilt she felt about the way she treated her only child in his early years seemed to be growing more rather than less lately. At first she had not given it a thought, picking up Jacky from her mother's home and dropping him back when she had had enough of him, with probably slightly less consideration than most people pay their pet dogs. The guilt had only really begun to surface when, in his early teens, Jacky began to display a character that showed just how troubled he really was.

His wayward behaviour was unsurprising. Jacky's upbringing had been curiously discordant. He had lived primarily with his grandmother – his dock-worker grandfather had died of emphysema, the smoker's disease, when Jacky was just a baby – in a terraced house in East London. Odd weekends and occasional holidays were spent with his mother at her big Essex house – but only when she could fit him in. Arabella's idea of fulfilling her parental duties had been to send him to a minor public school. That had been at the height of her fame as the ultimate Cockney pin-up, and Jacky had been teased mercilessly about his parentage and known to everyone at school as The Star. He coped with it all by playing up to it. He kept his Cockney accent resolutely intact and worked hard at appearing rough and uncouth at all times.

He did not shine academically – he was probably of slightly below average intelligence, Belle had once been told to her fury by one of his teachers – but God seemed to have compensated by giving Jacky the body and physical ability of an Adonis. He excelled at almost any sport, yet intensely disliked team games. He told his mother that he could not see the point in chasing balls around. Being something of a natural survivor – it was in his blood, Belle supposed – and aware of the favour he would win, he made half-hearted forays into rugby and soccer – his school played both – often feigning injury to avoid games but usually turning out to help his team win the big ones. Once or twice Belle had found time to watch him play, but had always felt he would rather she were not there because of the attention she attracted.

Young enough to remain fit without effort, Jacky could get away without any training worth mentioning for these pursuits. That would have been asking just too much, because from the age of only thirteen it had seemed to his mother that his greatest interests in life had been sex and the pursuit of physical sensation, and he wasn't all that interested in anything which forced him to divert from that area of activity.

He got away with a lot because of his sporting prowess, always valued absurdly highly by Britain's public schools. A young school matron was sacked after it became known that she had been indulging in regular sex sessions with the fifteen-year-old Starr. But even then the school took the attitude that Jacky was too young to be held responsible and at first no action was taken against him. However Jacky went on a binge of destruction as some kind of demonstration of his loyalty to her. This resulted in a police case against him and the early criminal record which the Devon and Cornwall Constabulary had already unearthed.

It had also led to his being expelled – although the headmaster had confided to Belle that he was secretly rather sorry to see him go. A second school agreed to take Jacky partly because of his mother's fame and partly again because of his sporting ability. But eventually he was expelled again – this time for smoking dope – which had, Belle suspected, more or less been his intention. At sixteen Jacky had had enough of school.

He was still known as The Star – which by then he had rather got to like, and, Belle reflected sadly, he certainly had had no wish to continue to be known as his mother's son. And so it was that he added a second R to his nickname and adopted it as his surname. Jacky Starr was born.

The years since he left school had, his mother knew, passed in a self indulgent haze of dope smoking and sex. But when Belle had once dared to remonstrate with him, Jacky had told her in no uncertain terms that it was a bit late to start playing mummy. That had hurt – although Belle knew it was no more than the truth – and the rift between mother and son grew greater than ever. She wished that she could go back in time and have a second chance at motherhood. She regretted so much the love she had never given Jacky as a child, because now that he was a man she knew she could never build the relationship with him that she had begun to long for.

And now he was facing a murder charge. She found herself wondering if she believed he was capable of murder, if she believed that his temper could take over to such an extent that he might kill someone. She was quite sure that the mess her son was in was somehow her fault.

Seven

Just over four hours later Arabella was in Exeter. In the early Sunday morning half light she coasted to a welcome halt outside the Heavitree Road police station. She had hit the gales sweeping across the West Country at Bristol and driven the last seventy miles or so in torrential rain. For some reason the visitors parking bay immediately in front of the station was coned off, so she stopped on the double yellow line on the opposite side of the semi-circular approach road.

The visibility had been very poor on that final stretch of the motorway. It had been a bit like driving through a giant power shower – and her eyes ached with the strain. Too late to help her journey, the rain had eased now, and slowed to light drizzle. Resolutely she checked her hair and make-up in the driver's mirror, applying another light coat of lipstick, a hint more blush – she seemed to have grown paler on the journey she thought – and a further layer of mascara. She removed her old flat driving shoes and replaced them with a pair of typically Belle Parker stilettos, black suede with lots of gold trim and cripplingly high. Glamorous if you like that sort of thing, but way out of date – only bimbos wore stiletto heels, she had read somewhere recently. At the time the thought had made her smile. Bimbos and those who have made a career out of pretending to be one, she had thought wryly. She stepped out of the Jag just as a young policeman walking along the pavement spotted the car parked on a double yellow right outside his own nick. He approached, looking zealously officious. Arabella drew herself up to her full 5ft 3ins, pushed the car door shut behind her, and flashed him her most studied smile. He recognised her at once, as she had expected him to. She took a step towards him, her shoulders pulled firmly back, her breasts thrust forward in such a way that it was impossible for his gaze not to be drawn to her magnificent cleavage. His jaw shifted a notch or two downwards and whatever words of admonition he had been about to utter seemed to stick in his throat.

'Shan't be a minute, darlin',' she gushed at him, patting him in familiar fashion on his lower arm. She knew she could get away with it, she always had done. She was only behaving in the way that was expected of her. The policeman stood perfectly still looking at her. He remained unable to speak. He could find no words.

Belle was in full flight. 'And I won't need to lock up, parked right outside the cop shop, will I, love?' She treated him to a girlish giggle and trotted up the steps to the station, aware of his astonished eyes fixed on her departing back. Well, he hadn't really expected to bump into Arabella Parker, in full war paint, on the streets of Exeter at 6 a.m. on a Sunday morning. Arabella was well aware of that and determined to make the most of any advantage it gave her. She needed all the help she could get. She was really not sure how well equipped she was to help her son in her present state. But she had no intention of letting anyone else see even a hint of weakness or doubt in her. No way.

At the top of the steps she took a deep breath and positively bounced through the big glass doors into the station front office – a sparse reception area lined with seats from which further, electronically locked, doors led off to the main body of the station. At first sight the place seemed deserted, but when she rang the bell by the inquiries desk a civilian clerk appeared surprisingly promptly. And she was gratified to see the same look of bewildered astonishment manifest itself on his rather world-weary features. While aware that their young murder suspect had called his mother, who was on her way to his side along with a solicitor, the Heavitree Road staff had had no idea who his mother was. They knew now.

Belle, doing her best to appear businesslike and assertive and actually succeeding rather well, explained why she was there and asked to see Jacky. The clerk, a retired police sergeant who did three or four shifts a week only in order to boost his pension, barely reacted. He seemed rooted to the spot. The cleavage, protruding from its glittering encasement and at such an hour on a Sunday morning, was proving impossible for him also to ignore.

'Well then, can I see my son?' asked Belle, winking saucily.

'Just a moment, madam,' managed the man.

There followed rather a lot of scurrying about. A uniformed inspector, young for the job, suave, rather aloof, probably a university entrant Arabella automatically reflected, arrived on the scene. He was determined not to be affected in any way by the sudden materialisation of Arabella Parker. He kept his gaze fixed resolutely above neck level and certainly was not going to be deferential. There would be no favours to the stars in his nick. Consequently he leaned in the other direction. He dealt with Belle in a manner that was abrupt verging on downright rude.

'We have a procedure here and there will be no exceptions,' he said unnecessarily.

Determinedly Belle did not react.

Eventually the paperwork to which there would be no exceptions was completed and she was ushered into an interview room to await her son whom she was told would be collected from the cells and delivered to her. The cells. The thought made her shiver. The same young policeman she had seen in the street outside was now on duty watching over her. He stood just to one side of the door, impassive, staring straight ahead, but slightly flushed none the less.

Belle treated him to one of her saucy winks.

'All right darlin'?' she asked. 'You'll keep an eye on the Jag for me, won't you? Don't want you to have to lock me up too, do I?'

The young constable continued to stare straight ahead. But Arabella noticed with some satisfaction that his cheeks had deepened in colour. She hadn't completely lost her touch, it would appear.

The door burst open, with what seemed to her to be needless commotion, and her son was escorted into the room.

Arabella would never forget the sense of shock and desolation which engulfed her at that moment. She saw the white paper jump suit first, and it stunned her, made her realise more than ever what she was facing. The transformation in her son caused her almost to cry out. She felt as if she had been slapped in the face.

Jacky Starr had always been a cocksure character. Smug. Streetwise. Never vulnerable – or if ever he was, like his mother, he invariably hid it well, even in early childhood. He'd had to hide it, she thought, in order to survive. Now he looked empty, drained of every vestige of strength. He seemed hardly to recognise her.

He sat on the second chair by the table. Arabella found she wanted to reach out and take him into her arms. That had been her first and instant reaction as soon as she saw him – her son accused of murder, but looking so much more like a victim than any kind of criminal. She probably felt greater maternal instincts towards him in those brief shocking first moments than she had since he was born. But of course she did not give in to those instincts. Some things do not change in ten seconds – maybe not even in ten years. There was too much history between mother and son for that. Instead she just sat there looking at him.

From a long way off she heard her own voice. 'Hello Jacky. 'Ow are you then, love?'

A banal beginning. No matter. The boy raised his eyes so that they met hers, and there was a blankness in them. He hadn't shaved for a couple of days and the stubble sprouted in untidy clumps at occasional intervals across his face. Jacky had no beard worth mentioning and probably never would have. She found herself becoming detached from the moment, a kind of defence mechanism locking itself in. She studied her son as if he were a stranger – which in some ways he always had been to her. She noticed the unwashed hair. She looked again at the disposable paper suit, and assessed quite correctly that his own clothes would have been taken away for forensic examination. The suit was brand new and spanking clean, but she became aware that her son smelled. It was the powerful sour clinging stench of vomit. Belle felt nauseous herself. There was a bitter taste at the back of her throat. Involuntarily she leaned back, away from her son, away from the smell, just in time to stop herself gagging.

Overcome by her sense of shock Arabella rounded on the young policeman. She could not help herself. Just for a few seconds she let the act drop.

'For Christ's sake, surely you could have let 'im have a shower,' she snapped.

The constable responded with commendable coolness. 'You'll have to talk to the DCI, madam,' he replied evenly.

Belle surprised herself by reaching across the table to take her son's hand. The stench almost overwhelmed her again, but she steeled herself.

'What's going on Jacky, what on earth has happened, love?' she asked.

As he opened his mouth to speak tears welled up. She did not think she had ever seen him cry before – not since he was maybe three or four years old. She noticed how red-rimmed his eyes were, the lids swollen and sore looking.

When he spoke his voice was just a croak. 'She's dead, Belle, she's dead . . .'

For a few minutes she tried to talk to him, tried to get him to tell her what had happened; to protest his innocence of the crime of which he was being accused. Anything.

Another constable came into the room with mugs of tea and a bowl of sugar. Belle took a mug gratefully and spooned sugar into it. She didn't take sugar in her tea and this brew was much stronger than the way she liked it, but from somewhere in her subconscious came the message that strong sweet tea was good for shock.

Jacky did not touch his mug. He continued to sob uncontrollably. Her efforts to get him to drink went unheeded. She realised that to try to do anything other than give him what comfort she could would be useless. Her son's hand, tightly clasping hers, was icy cold and he was shivering.

'Barney will be here soon,' said Belle. A message left on an answer machine for a lawyer to whom she owed a fortune – that was her only practical contribution to this mess so far.

'Remember Barney, my solicitor? You met him at the Christmas party two years ago.'

The aloof young inspector's head appeared around the door, followed, after a pause, by the rest of his body. He did not speak, but as if on cue the constable stepped forward and placed a hand lightly on Jacky's shoulders, and asked him to go with him back to the cells. Belle said goodbye as fondly and reassuringly as she could manage, and watched as her son meekly complied, without another glance in her direction.

After he had left the room she turned to the young inspector, who told her that Detective Chief Inspector Mallett would see her at 9 a.m. She checked her watch. It was nearly a quarter to seven.

Recovering her composure as best she could, she bounced her way out through the front office into a chilly dampness. The golden Jaguar, its odd rust spot and the general dulling of age sadly more apparent in even rather grey daylight, was still there on the double yellow, untouched and unticketed.

Thankfully she climbed behind the wheel.

She had to find a hotel, fast. She needed a shower, a phone, and a bed, if only for an hour or so. She needed a base. Battling Belle had a campaign to mount.

At Landacre House Richard was beginning to feel the return of the sense of well being which usually enveloped him when he was able to spend time at his beloved home instead of playing Sparrow-Hawk. More Trozactin, washed down with more brandy, had somehow got him through the night in such a way that he woke up feeling much better, which was both unusual and welcome.

It was noon. He had risen later than usual and pottered the morning away. He had at first been a little muzzy headed, and his mouth uncomfortably dry, which he recognised as the usual morning-after symptoms of his drug and alcohol cocktails. But he had recovered fast, and now felt quite relaxed and almost pleased with himself again. He did not, as yet, regret his actions of the afternoon before. He was languidly outstretched on a *chaise longue* at one end of the drawing room. In his hand was a stoneware mug of strong black coffee. The radio played quietly. The gales seemed to be over at last. Even the early rain had stopped now, and a slightly watery sun streamed through the big south-east facing bay window sending hazy beams of light across the glowing Turkish carpet. It was a perfect lazy Sunday.

The second item on the noon news featured the murder of Joyce Carter.

Richard felt his body freeze. Very carefully he sat

upright and put the mug down gently on the marble-topped table at his elbow.

Few details were given except that the police were treating her death as murder and a man was helping them with their inquiries.

Richard sat very still. When the report ended he got up from the *chaise longue*, walked across the room, and switched off the radio. It was then that he noticed his wife standing in the doorway. She was wearing a coat and still clutching her overnight bag, having just returned from London, he presumed. Her manner told him that she had also heard the news item.

She stared at him steadily.

'The world must be full of people who are happy to see that bitch dead,' she remarked evenly. Then she turned and left the room.

Richard sat down again. This time on the piano stool. He opened the lid of the beautiful old grand and played a few chords. Desultory. Unconnected. Then he closed the lid again, and holding on to one side of the piano he leaned back on the velvet-covered stool and began to laugh. He swayed backwards and forwards, powered by the force of it. There was an ache in his stomach but he could not stop. Tears poured down his cheeks.

In the kitchen, pouring herself a large dry sherry from the bottle kept in the fridge, Amanda leaned against the sink listening to the sound of his laughter which was so loud it echoed through the whole of the great house. She uttered not a sound and neither her eyes nor her way of standing gave any real hint of what she was thinking. But her lips were clamped shut in a thin tight line.

★

Todd Mallett was sound asleep when the telephone rang. He had been at the station until the early hours setting up a full murder inquiry unit as well as interrogating Jacky Starr. As a detective chief inspector, Todd was of high enough rank to be appointed the senior investigating officer in overall charge of the entire operation. He had already chosen Detective Inspector David Cutler – a graduate policeman of a distinctly cadaverous appearance whose excellent brain was masked by a permanent hangdog expression – as his office manager whose task it would be to run an incident room equipped with HOLMES (Home Office Large Major Enquiry Systems) computers, linked to other police forces throughout the country. Ten two-men or women action teams, made up principally of detective constables with a smattering of sergeants, were in the process of being set up, each pair to be briefed and debriefed at a daily morning session. Their sole jobs would from now on be to investigate the death of Joyce Carter. And before leaving the station, Todd, by then completely exhausted, had made certain that Cutler – whose only real passion in life was for organisation – was on the case. It would be Cutler's job to ensure that the incident room – already partially in operation in an area of the station reserved for the setting up of major crime investigation – was satisfactorily equipped, and one of his top priorities first thing that morning would be to install extra telephone lines.

It had been one hell of a busy night. Todd felt as if he had slept for about ten minutes and in all reality it was not a great deal longer.

He checked his watch. It was 6.45 a.m. He told the duty sergeant he would see Jacky Starr's mother at nine, an experience he was not looking forward to. Arabella Parker. It was just his luck. When the press found out that his number one suspect was the son of bloody Arabella Parker the whole thing would become a media circus. Todd had very limited experience of showbusiness people, but those he had met he hadn't liked at all. They did not seem part of the real world to him. He and Arabella Parker would be chalk and cheese, he reckoned, little doubt of that.

He hauled himself out of bed, staggered into the bathroom, leaned against the washbasin in front of the window and peered at himself in the magnifying shaving mirror which stood on the window ledge. God, he looked old. He tried to reassure himself that the light was particularly harsh and contemplated moving the mirror – better still getting rid of it all together. What was wrong with a simple job hung on the wall? Did he really need something which so effectively magnified his expanding double chin?

It was no good. Whatever kind of mirror he used the damage was still there, engraved on his features. It was merely a question of how good a look he gave himself. The previous year he had been involved with a case which had seemed to put years on him. And it had obliquely brought about the end of his marriage. A woman he had once loved and had possibly never stopped loving had died, and he still felt in some obscure way that he was to blame.

He was wearing just a pair of old Marks and Spencer jockey shorts, and it seemed to Todd that his belly moved more than the rest of him. With the worries he carried on his shoulders, the stress of the job and all the extra anguish of the last twelve months he might have expected himself to waste away a little bit. There would have been some consolation in that. Instead he had started to blow up like a balloon as soon as he stopped playing sport regularly. His legs looked podgy, he thought. He had always had great strong rugby player's legs. He continued to study himself mournfully. He hadn't felt like playing any kind of sport for a long time, and the way his body was deteriorating he'd soon be totally past it anyway – which might be something of a relief, he thought woefully.

He poured himself a glass of water and dropped an Alka Seltzer in it. He didn't have a hangover – it just felt as if he did. The bubbles hit his nose and he started to sneeze. As soon as he was able he downed the contents of the glass in one.

He took his razor from the pine cabinet on the wall, rubbed the stubble on his chin with soap and prepared to shave.

God, he felt defeated before he had begun. Perhaps it was just weariness. Todd squared his shoulders. He had that uneasy feeling that this case was going to be another nightmare and he was not at all sure he had the strength to deal with it.

He began to scrape the razor across his face, and the familiarity of daily routine started to relax him a little. The hot water with which he had filled the wash basin had caused the mirror to steam up. He could no longer see his face. In some ways he was quite grateful for that, but it did have a down side. Shaving too casually now he nicked himself just below the ear. Perversely this made him smile. Perhaps he should ask for a transfer to traffic he thought to himself wryly.

*

A few hours later, sitting alone in his kitchen morosely scanning the Sunday papers, Bruce Macintosh felt the first spark of real interest he had experienced since the death of his wife just over two weeks earlier.

Ruth Macintosh's husband had been living in an unhappy trance, performing the barest minimum of daily routine. He hadn't bothered to shave for almost a week, which was unlike him. He was still wearing a set of rather grubby pyjamas. His greying hair needed both washing and cutting. These things just did not seem to matter any more. In fact nothing much at all outside his own misery had registered with him until this moment.

With grim fascination he read thoroughly the reports of the murder of Joyce Carter. The news of her death the previous day, and the manner of it, had been released just in time to make the late editions. The stories made no mention of any arrest of a suspect but already included a reference to strangulation and possibly a broken neck.

As a former Fleet Street crime reporter, generally regarded as one of the best there had ever been, it remained habit for Bruce to buy all the newspapers. He knew Joyce Carter from way back. In fact she had come in as a young reporter on the *Daily Chronicle* when Bruce had been a news desk assistant there. He remembered a very keen perky girl who made up for in personality anything she might have lacked in looks, and who as a writer had demonstrated a nice turn of phrase from the beginning. She had also seemed more than a little shy in those days and displayed a rather disarming desire to be liked. A lot of people nowadays would not believe that could be a description of the killer bimbo, Bruce reflected, but that was how he remembered her. And it was those memories which had drawn him to the murder story as soon as he spotted Joyce Carter's name.

Very little else that he had been reading that day had actually penetrated his brain. Bruce was on automatic pilot. The death of his wife had left him in acute shock, and the manner of her death had horrified him. He had also absorbed every possible detail of it, berating police and pathologists for as much information as possible about how his wife had actually died. He wasn't sure if he really wanted to know or if this was merely the old hack in him desperately seeking consolation in the gathering of information.

As a teenager he had studied Shakespeare's *The Winter's Tale* for his A-level GCE and when he became a trainee reporter on a local paper he had remembered the words of Autolycus, the tinker, who described himself as 'a snapper up of unconsidered trifles'.

Just a year or so into his training it occurred to Bruce that the words of Autolycus, more often than not, pretty accurately described the work that he did. Bruce had embarked on his chosen career with a much more high-minded conception of it, but it was a fact of local paper life that he was more likely to be writing about giant marrows and diamond wedding celebrations than reporting on a major crime investigation or uncovering his own regional equivalent of Watergate.

Bruce, in fact, had become an excellent reporter who through the course of his newspaper life did a great deal more than snap up unconsidered trifles. It may have been partly because of his acceptance of trivia as a vital ingredient of almost any newspaper, and the importance of attention to detail, that he became so accomplished. Bruce learned swiftly that to be a good journalist you had to have an instinctive grasp of detail and an ability to explain what lay at the core of any story with absolute simplicity. He was also blessed with a first class memory. He squirrelled away information in the filing cabinet of his head and it often seemed to sally forth, unasked for even, when occasion demanded. He had an instinct for linking together apparently isolated facts and slotting them into an often devastating whole in a way that others did not always seem able to.

He had not thought about his own wife's murder in these terms. How could he? But he had automatically unearthed every detail he could weasel out of the various authorities and equally automatically filed it away in his head. And now that he read about the death of Joyce Carter he was immediately struck by the feeling that these two terrible deaths were in some way connected.

By carefully studying the reports in each of the newspapers he had bought that morning he was able to put together a fuller picture than he would otherwise have been able to, even though these reports were far from complete at this early stage.

Then there was the other murder. The one three years ago in Cornwall, that he had reported on for his newspaper. That victim too had died from a kind of strangulation, and the case had remained unsolved. But he had been unable to convince the police investigating his wife's murder that there might be any connection, and he had to admit it had been little more than a gut feeling. In fact, until confronted now by the murder of Joyce Carter, he had put his theory of a possible connection with that death in Cornwall out of his mind.

He sighed. He knew that his wife's neck had been broken – and according to the police in a quite clinical and efficient manner. Joyce had been attacked in her own home. His wife had been killed in a city subway. While the way in which they died was certainly similar if not identical, the choice of location could not have been more different in style, and one had occurred in London and the other in rural Devon. The earlier murder had also been in the West Country, but in St Ives, a good two and a half to three hours' drive away from Joyce Carter's Blackdown Hills cottage on the Devon–Somerset border.

Bruce had worked on many murder stories including more than one serial killer case, and he knew how murderers liked to stick to their own territories. None the less, there was enough there to disturb him again. It was second nature for Bruce to start to collate information when his interest in a subject was aroused. He carefully cut out all the relevant articles about the death of Joyce Carter, making sure that the name of the publication and the date were included in each cutting, and put them in a cardboard folder along with a few scribbled notes. Then he dug out all his old stories and notes concerning the murder in Cornwall, and the file he had already compiled on his wife's death.

It might be irrational, the police might not listen, but he was becoming increasingly convinced there were links there somewhere.

Eight

Belle drove slowly around until she spotted a big old-fashioned hotel opposite Exeter Central Railway Station, The Rougemont. It had its own small car park which at a glance seemed to be full so she stopped right outside the front door, as was her wont, and looked in vain for a doorman. There wasn't one, at least not at that time on a Sunday morning. She stepped out of the car, slammed the door shut, and with calves tensed above the stilettos, marched purposefully towards reception.

She just hoped that her last remaining credit card still held good – a bouncing credit card really would be the end of what was left of her image. And of a bed for the little that was left of the night.

The porter, who had recognised her, found her a room – a small single was all he had available, he said – handed her the key, and obediently trotted off to sort out her car.

Belle took the lift to her third-floor room, thanked the Lord that she long ago learned to cat nap, set her pocket alarm for 8.30 a.m. and flopped gratefully on to the bed.

She slept soundly for the hour and a half she had allotted herself, and was up, showered, dressed, and fully made up by 8.50.

As she was preparing to leave, her mobile phone rang. It was Barney Lee. He had just picked up her message. She told him all she knew, which was not all that much, while he listened carefully and made no mention of the money she owed him. He really was one of the good guys, she thought, not for the first time, well aware that the one day a week Barney resolutely spent with his family was Sunday. When eventually he spoke he was to the point and practical – as always.

'Even if I dropped everything and came down today, Belle – and I don't want to unless I have to – I couldn't be with you for at least four hours,' he said. 'I'll get on to a local man and have someone you can trust around to the station straight away. These early stages are vital. They can keep Jacky for a maximum of thirty-six hours on various kinds of police authority. That takes us up to tomorrow morning. After that they either have to charge him or get a court warrant for further detention to keep him any longer. If either of those happen, then I'll come, all right?'

It was more than all right. Someone was doing something. And Barney was always so reassuringly sensible.

'Thank you,' Belle said. And she put a lot of meaning into the word.

In spite of the welcome interruption it was nine o'clock sharp when, with warpaint and image well in place and feeling considerably better than she might have expected, Belle Parker parked on the same double yellow and climbed the steps of the Heavitree Road station, just a few minutes' drive from The Rougemont.

She was shown into an interview room to await the DCI. He did not keep her long.

*

Arabella looked up expectantly as the door opened. She saw a middle aged man, tall, slightly portly. He looked a mess. Red-eyed and red-chinned. He had cut himself shaving. No smooth copper this one.

In spite of everything she felt her face break into a smile. She looked into his eyes, and what she saw there surprised her. In fact she didn't need to see anything. She felt it. Clear as could be.

Then she heard his voice.

'I'm sorry we have to meet under these difficult circumstances, Miss Parker.'

He sounded brisk and businesslike. Perfectly normal and straightforward. What was the matter with her? Her imagination was running away with her. She made herself concentrate on the matter in hand. Her son was a murder suspect. How could she even think of anything else?

The policeman was surprisingly forthcoming. She hadn't expected him to be the way he was, not in any sense. She had thought that he would be more secretive. And she was aware that he had no obligation to talk to her, after all her son was twenty-two years old and not a minor.

He explained how Jacky had called the police saying he had found Joyce Carter's body. He told her, although not in all that much detail, how Joyce had died. He said that he hoped this explained why he had to keep Jacky for questioning.

'Are you charging him with . . . with anything?' asked Belle, as calmly as she could. She had expected to feel angry, to lose her temper. In fact this man made her feel calm.

'I can't tell you that yet I'm afraid, Miss Parker.' Todd seemed to be staring at her. 'You may be able to help. Tell me about your son. What sort of lad is he?'

'To be honest, I haven't seen him for over a year.'

Belle saw his surprised reaction and forced herself to concentrate. Her son was in jail. A woman had been murdered. She had to concentrate.

'Look, I am expecting a solicitor at any minute. I don't want to say any more until I've seen him, and until he's talked to Jacky.'

Todd Mallett shrugged his considerable shoulders. He had half-leaned, half-sat on the wooden table, as if determined to appear relaxed and informal. She noticed his hands clasped loosely in his lap. They were big capable hands.

'That's your right – and his,' he said.

'So how long do you intend to keep him?'

'As long as it takes to complete our inquiries concerning him,' replied the policeman.

'He should have had a solicitor before,' she said. It was a statement, not a question.

'He was informed of his rights, we do everything by the book here.'

Belle rose to her feet. 'Could I see my son now?'

'I don't see why not.' Todd buzzed through to the custody officer and asked him to make the necessary arrangements.

'Thank you,' said Belle. She had walked almost to the door now, but she turned back towards Todd and held out her hand. He stood up and took it. His handshake was warm and firm and quite ordinary really. Their eyes were locked together for an instant. He lowered his glance first.

She shook herself, almost angrily, turned on her heel and left the room. She told herself Jacky would be freed in no time, and she would probably never see the DCI again.

Belle spent an awkward few minutes alone with her son. He still seemed disorientated, uncaring. She was disloyally grateful when the Exeter-based solicitor sent by Barney Lee arrived. He was younger than she had expected and disconcertingly enthusiastic. Belle supposed that involvement in a murder case was a rare diversion to a normally much duller routine.

He introduced himself as Mark Crook. In spite of herself Belle felt her face split into a grin.

'I've heard all the jokes,' Mark Crook smiled back.

He then proceeded to take charge, quite impressively, questioning the still largely unresponsive Jacky pointedly and intelligently. And when his manner indicated politely but quite clearly that he had no further use for his client's mother, Belle fairly confidently left her son in his care.

The police were preparing for another interrogation session, but this time Jacky would have a lawyer with him and one who gave the distinct impression that he would let them get away with nothing.

Feeling that she had done all she could for the time being, and with a certain sense of relief at being able to leave the station, she drove back to her hotel.

Jacky Starr was no more articulate than he had been right after his arrest. It was now 11 a.m. on Sunday morning. Jacky had been in custody for little more than twelve hours, but Todd could tell that the lad's brain was just not working properly. Mark Crook, whom Todd was aware had an excellent reputation locally although he knew the solicitor only vaguely by sight, gave the impression that he had not got much more sense out of his client so far than Todd had.

'I didn't do it, I loved her,' was not going to help a great deal.

Todd set out to question Jacky all over again about his relationship with Joyce Carter. The policeman was alternately understanding and provocative.

'What was it about her that attracted you most?' he asked.

'She was different, clever.' Jacky Starr paused. 'A step ahead of all the rest. Different class . . .'

'Yes,' said Todd. 'Different class. A class above you too, aye? Is that what you thought? Was that the problem, Jacky? Was that where it all went wrong?'

Jacky shook his head. His eyes told another story.

'I think so, Jacky, I think she was beginning to want something more than you.'

Todd studied the young man before him. How many times had he sat like that trying to see inside the heads of strangers? Suspects, witnesses, lawyers. On the one hand you had logic and cold, hard, factual evidence. On the other you sought that bit extra, inspiration, the sixth sense, whatever it was.

He stared at Jacky. The boy wriggled uncomfortably.

'You weren't always enough for her were you Jacky?'

Jacky, still trembling slightly, was looking down at his hands.

'I think maybe there were other men sometimes, more sophisticated, educated, intellectual . . .'

He stopped. Jacky was beginning to weep. It couldn't be this easy, this straightforward, could it? The inspector could see Mark Crook stirring in his seat, looking as if he were about to interrupt, and continued swiftly.

'She'd been with somebody else. You couldn't stand it, could you?'

Jacky didn't reply. Todd steeled himself. He hated this approach, but he knew how well it could work. He had tried it the day before without too much success. But if you kept on with the same story, if you niggled and nagged, carried on plugging away; with a bit of luck you wore them down eventually.

'You couldn't stop thinking about it could you? Somebody else doing to her all that you did to her. Somebody else inside her, pushing into her . . .'

This was too much for Mark Crook.

'You're out of order, Chief Inspector,' he cut in, and told his client: 'Don't answer. You don't have to answer.'

But Jacky's sobs were louder now. It was as if he did not hear his solicitor. He looked up at Todd, his face a picture of despair.

'She couldn't stop,' he said. 'She was like a junkie for it. I would have been back with her in only a few hours, but still she went with someone else . . .'

'Don't say any more,' instructed the solicitor. He sounded anxious now.

Todd continued as if nobody else had spoken.

'And so you killed her?'

'No. No. I couldn't ever hurt her.'

The boy was not in a state to deal with his predicament rationally. Todd sighed. He was reminded of the case that had haunted his father for all of his life, and had then risen up to haunt him. A young man frightened out of his wits convicted for the murder of his lover, an older woman too. A man who so long later, after half a lifetime in jail, had been found to be innocent. Was history repeating itself? There were obvious similarities. Todd knew one thing. He was going to be absolutely certain in his own mind that this boy was guilty before he allowed him to stand trial.

'Right then,' he said. 'How do you intend to prove you didn't do it?'

For just a moment Jacky Starr pulled himself together. 'I didn't know I had to,' he said. 'I thought you had to prove that I did. You know, innocent until proven guilty . . .'

Todd smiled quite a sad smile. 'Is that what you thought?' he asked mildly. 'OK. Let's go over it again. Let's see if you can prove you were somewhere else when the murder was committed.'

'I *was* somewhere else,' said Jacky. He almost shouted. 'I was on the road, hitching.'

'Yes. And you were picked up eventually by a lorry, who took you almost to the football ground. Anything else?'

'I know the driver's name.'

'You what?'

'It's John.'

'Terrific. It would be, wouldn't it? What did he look like? How old was he?'

'He was sort of ordinary, middle aged, I don't know. Dark haired I think. Well sort of darkish.'

'And the lorry? Make? Colour?'

'I don't know the make. It was big. And it was green, or maybe blue, I don't know, I'm not sure.'

'So the closest thing you've got to an alibi is an ordinary looking sort of dark haired bloke called John driving a big lorry which was either green or blue, or perhaps neither? Right?'

'Right,' said Jacky, and for the first time he looked Todd directly in the eye.

Proper eye contact came as something of a shock to Todd. He realised, beneath all that hair, the scruffiness and the fear, how much like his mother the young man was – although not in build, the boy towered above her.

In the distance he heard Mark Crook's voice. 'My client has given you all the help he can, I think that's quite enough, Chief Inspector.'

In any case Todd had finished – for the time being.

He went straight to his office and after a few minutes' thought dialled a local number.

'Hello, Mike, you still playing knight of the road with that CB radio of yours, are you?'

'What CB is that then, Todd?'

Mike Hudson sounded as if he were talking with his mouth full. Todd guessed that he had interrupted him in the middle of a big Sunday fry-up. Mike, a little wizened man who resolutely ignored the invention of cholesterol and, rather unfairly Todd thought, never seemed to put on weight, lived almost entirely on a diet of fried foods. He was a doyen of the Citizens' Band radio network, largely supplying information of police speed traps and the like, and still popular among lorry drivers – even in the days of mobile phones because these remained relatively expensive to run and were no good for group chats or homing in on the police network – and usually operated on technically illegal wavebands.

'Come on, Mike, if I'd wanted to get you for that game I could have done it years ago. I need some help, mate, with a murder inquiry.'

Todd could sense Mike tensing at the other end of the phone. Mike was a long distance trucker whose hours spent motoring all over the country and sometimes abroad gave him plenty of time to dwell on boyhood fantasies and let his imagination run riot. Over a few beers one night he had confessed to Todd that he had always dreamed of being a detective or a secret agent, Philip Marlow maybe, or even James Bond. Todd had for years used the trucker as an informant, succeeding – with difficulty sometimes – in not laughing at his fantasies, treating him to countless Greasy Spoon blow-outs, and slipping him a few quid as often as he could. But the policeman was well aware that Mike didn't do it for the money. It gave him a buzz. And it was a secret. Todd knew that Mike liked secrets.

'A murder?'

Mike's voice was pitched higher than usual, the excitement clearly evident. Todd told him as little as he could manage and still hold the other man's interest. He needed to find this truck driver called John fast – if he existed.

'And you want me to put out a call for him over the CB?'

'Knew you'd get it,' said Todd. He was more than happy to allow Mike to appear one jump ahead of him.

It was a long shot, but the Citizens' Band radio network between truckers was legendary. If John existed there had to be a chance. And there weren't too many other leads to chase yet, Todd reflected.

He glanced at his watch. Carmen Brown would have already begun her post mortem examination on Joyce Carter's body, and Todd wanted to hear her report first hand.

He called for Pitt and had the satisfaction of watching the younger man pale. For all his blatant ambition and his tough interrogation technique, Todd knew that Sergeant Pitt remained more than a little squeamish.

The two men stood well back from the examination table in the mortuary of the Royal Devon and Exeter Infirmary while Dr Brown completed her task – but they had a good enough view. Even though the cause of Joyce Carter's death seemed so obvious, the pathologist was taking no chances before giving her formal report. The contents of Joyce's stomach were analysed and her internal organs carefully examined. Her naked body lay sliced open on the slab. It was the smell, Todd thought, that was always the worst thing.

He glanced at Pitt. His sergeant was standing ramrod straight, his face resolutely expressionless, but Todd noticed how clearly Pitt's freckles seemed to be standing out and how his throat kept moving as he swallowed repeatedly. Todd didn't like post mortem examinations either, but he had learned to harden himself over the years, particularly when dealing with a pathologist as mechanically efficient and apparently emotionless as Carmen Brown.

Occasionally the doctor talked into a tape recorder as she worked. It seemed a very long time before she turned away from the body and addressed the two policemen.

'There is no doubt that Joyce Carter was half strangled, you can see that just by looking at her,' she said. 'But, as I suspected, she actually died of a broken neck. Her head has been jerked violently back.'

'How?' asked Todd.

'Hard to tell, but there is some bruising in the small of her back which might indicate that she was pushed in the back, with an arm or a knee perhaps, to give leverage while her head was forced backwards.

'She'd been drinking and had smoked marijuana shortly before she died, by the way, although I can't see that that has any relevance.'

Todd nodded. 'Is there much sign of a struggle?'

'Not a lot. I think she was probably attacked from behind. A pretty clean job.'

'So we're looking for a man who is physically powerful, are we?' asked Todd, thinking of the strongly built Jacky Starr still locked up in the police jail.

'Not necessarily,' replied Carmen Brown. 'This was a precision job. The killer knew what he or she was doing, it wasn't brute force that killed Joyce Carter. I'm choosing my words carefully, Chief Inspector. Joyce could equally well have been killed by a woman in my opinion.'

Todd started. 'Not very likely, surely?'

Carmen Brown smiled with the world weariness of one who has already experienced more than her fair share of the darker side of life. 'I've given up second guessing what's likely, Inspector, haven't you?' she replied.

At Landacre House the tension that had been lurking since the news of Joyce Carter's death broke had built up to an almost unbearable level.

Richard was aware that Amanda, who had said that she was making a salad for lunch, had remained in the kitchen much longer than necessary. He guessed that she was probably knocking back the cooking sherry while desperately trying to pretend to herself – as she always did in troubled times – that everything was normal.

Richard alternately paced around the house and

hammered out tuneless music on the big grand piano. And as Amanda called out that lunch was ready, he realised he could handle his nerves no longer.

He went to his study and removed the bottle of Trozactin which he had earlier locked in a drawer in the desperately futile hope that by doing so he would lessen the temptation to take more of the pills. For a few seconds he stood looking at the bottle. He had already taken half a dozen or so that morning – this time washed down with vodka so that his breath would not smell and hopefully Amanda would not notice what he was up to – and they had seemed to have little or no effect. Or had they? He was no longer quite sure.

He peered at his reflection in the mirror above his desk. It did not give him his usual feeling of self-satisfaction. His face looked drawn. He didn't even seem particularly handsome any more.

Almost angrily he put the bottle of pills back in the drawer. On a pad on top of his desk was a phone number he had scribbled right after hearing the radio news. It was the home number of his Somerset doctor, an old family friend with whom he had gone to school. He sat down on his leather-upholstered revolving desk chair, picked up a pencil and began to doodle around the number. Three times he reached for the phone. The third time he picked up the receiver and punched out the number.

'Jeremy, glad to have caught you.' He did his best, and not a bad job at that, of sounding avuncular and relaxed.

'Old boy.' Jeremy Hunter's drawl rarely failed to irritate Richard. He was a rural GP, quite literally born and bred for the job, who had at first worked with and later taken over from his father in a practice in Porlock. Jeremy was every bit the country gentleman and frequently gave the impression that the one thing he didn't much like about his job was people actually becoming ill.

After a few minutes' obligatory chat about the weather and almost anything else that was of no importance, Richard said with studied casualness: 'I was wondering Jeremy, to tell the truth, if I could pop over for half an hour . . .'

'Love to, old boy, but actually I'm taking the family out for a spot of lunch . . . You only just did catch me, as it happens.'

'Thing is,' said Richard, still doing his best to sound casual, 'thing is, I really need to see you professionally, Jeremy.'

'Can't you come to the surgery tomorrow then?' asked the doctor.

'You *know* I can't come to the surgery, Jeremy. I just can't do things like that any more.'

For a moment or two there was silence, more or less. Richard thought Jeremy may have sighed in rather an exasperated manner, but he wasn't quite sure. Eventually the doctor spoke.

'All right, all right. I'll make you my first house call in the morning, how's that?'

'No!' Richard had given up all pretence now of being casual and virtually shouted his reply. 'I don't want Amanda to know anything about it – anyway it's urgent.'

'Calm down Richard.' Jeremy Hunter had his bed-side voice on. If he was irritated he was no longer letting it show. 'Is this afternoon soon enough for you?'

'Thank you.' The relief poured down the telephone line.

'Four o'clock then. I might even give you a cup of tea.'

Richard replaced the receiver in its cradle and wiped away the sweat which was beginning to form again on his forehead. His fingers were trembling. In the distance he could hear Amanda calling again, very nearly screaming this time, for him to come and eat his lunch.

Breathing with deliberate rhythm he left the study and headed for the dining room, hanging on by just a thread to the remains of his self control.

Had he, on his way, glanced out of the window across the stretch of land leading to the moors beyond, and had he still been able to focus properly, he might even have wondered what, yet again, could be reflecting the bright sunshine so sharply.

As it was, Richard Corrington saw and felt nothing but his own torment.

Nine

The next day Richard woke at dawn as usual. The events of the weekend had overwhelmed him. All he could do now, he thought, was to seek comfort in routine, to hang on to every possible semblance of normality. He made his pot of tea and sat on the balcony to drink it. And little more than an hour later he was steering Herbert through the hunting gate behind the yard and up the lane through the woods to the top of the moor.

Horse and rider paused as usual at their favourite spot above the sweep of the moor leading down to the sea. The weather was much better than it had been through most of March, but it was not a particularly clear day. There was a morning mist swirling about and the pale orb of the sun appeared only intermittently through breaks in low cloud. The yellowish glow in the sky spread in translucent streaks, heavy and menacing, over the sea.

Feeling revived as ever, Richard turned Herbert around and began the ride down the hill. On the way he was once more confronted by his new neighbour's huge corrugated iron shed. The very sight of it upset him all over again. It seemed that everything was going wrong at the moment. Nothing was allowed to give him comfort for long, not even his beloved Exmoor. Somewhat masochistically he manoeuvred Herbert along the edge of the trees to the place from which he could get the best view of the shed. And as he screwed up his eyes against the morning sunlight, straining for sight of any sign of life, he was suddenly aware of the most horrendous roaring rattling noise above his head. Herbert suddenly reared quite spectacularly on his hind legs and, not for the first time in his life, dumped Richard, who had been caught completely unawares, on to the ground. Then, stirrups flying in the air, the old horse set off at a precarious gallop down the hill to his stable in search of more breakfast.

Staggering to his feet Richard called angrily after the horse. A waste of time, and he knew it.

He switched his attentions to the cause of his downfall. It was a helicopter. He couldn't believe it. The chopper had landed now on the flat ground that had been cleared beyond the new shed. He understood suddenly why the trees had been cut down. A tall bald-headed man swung himself, with an easy familiarity, out of the helicopter. Richard could not see his face but assumed from George Brooks' graphic description of his baldness that this must be Harry Pearson, the new owner of Burrowgate. A second man, Jim Kivel, Richard was almost sure, came out of the house and together the two men manoeuvred the aircraft into the big shed.

A fucking helicopter hangar, that's what the thing was, Richard suddenly realised. He was so incensed he was virtually foaming at the mouth. A heliport slap bang on top of his beloved Landacre. Well, it wouldn't be there for long if he had anything to do with it.

Angrily he set off towards the hangar, intending to climb the hedge bordering Burrowgate and tell his new neighbour exactly what he thought of him and his helicopter. After taking a couple of steps he stopped. His left foot had stuck briefly in the stirrup when Herbert threw him and he had twisted his knee. He realised he could only walk with a limp. His fall had thankfully been broken by thick grass and bracken or he would have been more seriously hurt, but his clothes were covered in grass stains. There was a rip in the shoulder of his jacket and he became aware that his face was stinging. He put up a hand to find he was bleeding. He was in no state to confront anyone.

By now quite incandescent with rage he turned on his heel and began the long trudge back down the woodland path, following in the tracks of his rather more fleet footed steed. Half way home he met George Brooks, who had, upon the return of the riderless Herbert, set off on one of the other horses – Dutchy, a fine young chestnut gelding new to the stable – in search of Richard.

'Well what happened this time then?' George asked without a great deal of sympathy or alarm.

Richard was so angry he could hardly speak. 'Did you see that?' he spluttered, waving vaguely at the sky. 'A helicopter, a fucking great helicopter.'

'Ah,' said George. 'I thought that might 'ave been the trouble.'

'And that shed, that ugly great shed. A fucking aircraft hangar, that's what it is.'

'Ah,' said George.

'Well, I'm going to put a stop to it. Right now.'

'Ah,' said George.

'I'm going to phone fucking County Hall and I'm going to let them know exactly who I am and tell them to get their fucking planning people down here pronto.'

'Agricultural building,' said George. 'Farmers don't need plannin' for they, you know that.'

'Bollocks,' said Richard. 'Agricultural building my arse. Now bloody well get off that horse. I'm in a bloody hurry.'

Wordlessly George dismounted. Richard clambered aboard Dutchy and the pair set off down the hill almost as swiftly as had the riderless Herbert earlier.

George's dog, a yellow Labrador bitch, had followed her master up the hill. She stood close now, nuzzling his leg.

Absently George scratched her head.

'I dunno, Flo old girl. 'E can be an arrogant bugger, can't 'e?' he remarked mildly, and began to walk easily back to the yard.

Amanda was having breakfast at the kitchen table when Richard burst in through the back door. She looked up wearily from her wholemeal toast with sugar-free marmalade, taking in the torn and stained clothes and his bloodied face.

'Fallen off again?' she asked in a tired voice.

'Did you hear that helicopter go over right above our bloody heads?' he asked breathlessly, ignoring her question, to which he knew she did not in any case require a reply. He was already leafing through the phone book.

'Yes,' she said.

'And do you know where it was heading?'

'I expect so.'

'It was heading . . .' He stopped, aware suddenly of what she had said.

'What do you mean, "I expect so"?'

'I assume it was going to land next door in Burrow-gate.'

'And why would you assume that?'

She appraised him coolly. He knew that look. It usually meant she was going to do or say something that would hurt him.

'Because when I had dinner with Harry Pearson a couple of weeks ago, while you were in London, he told me all about it.'

Richard was stunned. 'Harry Pearson? The new owner of Burrowgate?'

She nodded curtly.

'You had dinner with him? And you didn't think it was worth mentioning?'

He couldn't stop himself reacting, even though he knew that was exactly what she had wanted.

She took a small neat bite of toast and marmalade, chewed a couple of times, and wiped her lips with a linen napkin before replying.

'I thought you'd find out soon enough, Ricky.'

He scowled at her, replacing the phone book on its shelf. 'So where did this dinner take place? And why?'

'Oh, I don't think you really want to know the details do you Ricky? I certainly don't want to know the details of your dinner dates.' She was mocking him, and he knew it. And every time he opened his mouth he seemed to fall deeper into her trap.

'What are you trying to tell me?' He was aware that he was shouting, but could not stop himself.

'I'm not trying to tell you anything.' Her voice was dangerously calm.

He tried to study her objectively. She could be such a prize cow, but then he supposed that given his own recent behaviour he had asked for it.

139

Know your enemy, he thought to himself.

'What's he like, anyway, this Harry Pearson?' he asked, trying a little late in the day to sound casual.

'Oh you know, rich, clever – made a fortune on the stock exchange – charming. Very charming actually. And, of course, he doesn't have your little problem either.'

Amanda put emphasis on the word little, and swept her gaze down over his crotch. In spite of occasionally still being unable to stop himself from seeking out new conquests, which was probably more habit than anything else, Richard had been unable to sustain a full erection during intercourse for a long time now, and Amanda knew that only too well. She also knew that he could only reach any kind of climax when drugged to the eyeballs, and even that rarely.

Richard winced. He did not try to reply. He forgot about phoning the council. As calmly as he could he got up from the table and left the room. Once again he had to get away from her, because on occasions like this he was becoming increasingly afraid of what he might do to his wife if he stayed a second longer in her company.

For Todd, Monday morning began spectacularly, and that was the key for the next few hours. In his experience police work always was like that. If things began well, they went on like that. And if they began badly, that was how they continued. The depression and lack of self confidence with which the previous day had launched itself was just an unhappy memory now.

Sunday had been messy. All day. Constant questioning of Jacky Starr had continued to lead nowhere worth mentioning. But on Monday he arrived at the station at 8 a.m. feeling considerably better and indeed more able than he had the day before, and his vague feelings of well-being were translated into reality by the two calls he received before 10 a.m.

The first was from Bruce Macintosh. Todd vaguely remembered a Ruth Macintosh who had been killed three weeks or so previously in London. Way out of his patch. He recalled the case but was hazy on it. Bruce Macintosh had talked his way past the station switchboard and onto the DCI's personal line. Todd was not particularly surprised. There was something authoritative in Bruce Macintosh's manner on the telephone, and as the other man explained that he was Ruth Macintosh's husband, Todd began to remember newspaper reports he had seen at the time of her killing. He recalled that the other man was a journalist, and a former crime reporter at that. Working the telephone would be as natural to him as placing one foot in front of the other and walking. Bruce was a man with a lifetime's experience of dealing with busy people in important and powerful positions.

'I have a feeling my wife and Joyce Carter may have been killed by the same person,' he told the policeman.

Bruce spoke calmly and clearly in a voice that held the merest trace of a Scottish accent, but Todd could sense the tension. The policeman was interested, although not overly excited.

'A feeling?'

'Call it an old newspaper man's hunch, if you like.'

It was the first time his caller had mentioned his profession. Todd began to remember more about the Macintosh case as the conversation progressed. Bruce was fifteen or so years older than his wife had been, semi-retired but out of the top drawer.

'I've been studying the reports,' Bruce said. 'At a glance they would seem totally different kinds of cases. But then, when you look at how Ruth died . . .' His voice faltered. 'And now Joyce Carter, well the methods used were so similar. At least that's what I think . . .'

Todd began mentally comparing the Joyce Carter killing with what he could remember of the other case. Off the top of his head he couldn't recall enough to formulate any kind of opinion. He knew one thing though. It was now automatic in any murder for the details to be run through the HOLMES computer system to check for any similarities. If there was a link between these two cases he was going to want to know from his men exactly how they had managed to miss it.

Bruce Macintosh was still talking.

'If you'd see me, I'd drive down to you. I don't know if you can understand, I want to do something. I'm half ways to an idea and I can't get there on what I know. Would you be prepared to help fill in the gaps?'

Todd thought for just a second. The man was a professional journalist and every policeman had a built in wariness of that breed. On the other hand Todd had learned to respect the capabilities of good investigative journalists over the years. Bruce Macintosh sounded highly intelligent, articulate, and sensible – not the sort of man who would put up a theory like that without having thought it through. And he was the husband of a murder victim. Todd made his decision quickly.

'I'll be pleased to see you,' he said. There was a

warmth about Todd which all those years in the job and all the knocks he had suffered had still done little to extinguish.

'I might not be prepared to answer all your questions, I may not even be able to, but I'm happy to cooperate as much as I can,' he added.

As soon as the telephone conversation ended he plugged into HOLMES and meticulously studied the computer files on the earlier murder. He then went over again the more recent data, with which he was already familiar, on the death of Joyce Carter. The man was right, the methods of killing appeared to be identical. Todd called in the detective constable who had executed the original computer check early the previous day. The DC flushed when he was told in no uncertain terms what he might have missed. His excuse was that the circumstances of the two murders were so different, he had not really registered the methods. Also they were so sure the Joyce Carter killing had been a domestic, weren't they?

'And it's all new, boss, this HOLMES TWO. We've never been able to cross check like this before . . .' His voice trailed off.

'Not bloody good enough,' said Todd in a deceptively mild tone.

He had inherited a dedication to old fashioned policing from his father, who had retired from the force many years previously with the rank of superintendent. Nowadays the police used computers every bit as much as professionals in any other walk of life – but as far as Todd was concerned the principle was exactly the same as it had been in his father's day. Method. Attention to detail. Never overlooking anything, however inconsequential, and, above all, never making assumptions without fully investigating every aspect – as the now thoroughly chastened DC had done.

As for the introduction of the advanced HOLMES TWO – well that was designed to make things easier, not more difficult.

When the detective constable, somewhat shame-facedly, had returned to his work station in the outer office, Todd leaned back in his chair, gave in to temptation, and lit his pipe – his first for several weeks. The need for a smoke had suddenly become too great, and there was still some tobacco tucked into the corner of his desk drawer. He did it to calm himself and to help him think. At least, that was his excuse. It was the palaver of lighting the damned thing which did the trick, rather more than actually sucking in the nicotine. As he puffed away and fidgeted, his brain was racing.

He turned his full attention to the keyboard again. This time he printed the details of both deaths and arranged the print-outs on his desk. There was still an enormous amount of work to do but this certainly looked interesting. Todd loved this kind of police-work, and he knew he was good at it.

When the telephone rang again he was vaguely irritated. He didn't want any further interruptions. He felt he was getting somewhere at last.

His irritation faded as soon as his caller spoke.

'My name is John,' said a good strong Devon voice. 'I 'eard you might be looking for me.'

Well I'll be buggered, thought Todd. This looked like the start of a truly triumphant day. Seemed as if Mike Hudson had turned up trumps. The old CB radio network had some uses apart from beating speed traps after all.

'Not a lorry driver by any chance are you?' asked Todd.

'Certainly am. Me truck's not green or blue though. 'Tis brown – with red lettering. The lad's not even close. Glad 'e's not a witness for me . . .'

'The lad?'

'Yep. Silver Fox said you were looking for a trucker called John who picked up a lad hitching on the A38 on Saturday. That's me I reckon.'

'What can you tell me about this lad.'

'Oh, the usual at that age. Told me his name was Jacky . . . I remember it because I thought how it suited him, a right Jack the Lad, he was.'

'Anything else you remember about this hitch-hiker?' Todd asked.

'Yup, he was going to the football. An Arsenal supporter. Even had the scarf on. That's why I picked 'im up really. I've always supported The Arsenal. Well, you might as well have supported a London club where I lived as a boy – not a first division team for miles around . . .'

This man could rabbit for England, Todd thought. Still, there was little doubt about whom he had picked up. The only question was when.

'Oh it was about four o'clock, know for certain almost, because I had the radio on for the news . . .'

Todd's heart sank. If Carmen Brown's assessment of when Joyce Carter died was correct, and he knew she would not be far out, there could still have been time – just – for Jacky to have killed the woman and got to the place where he was picked up by John on the A38 by 4 p.m.

'Sure it couldn't have been any earlier?' he asked.

'No of course it couldn't. I had a load to drop off

at that office block they're building behind the council offices. I'd come from Exeter with it and I had to drop it off first. Desperate for the stuff they were, working all over the weekend to get the place finished. Good money though. Double time for the boys on the site and for me delivering for them, I've got a six-week contract too . . .'

Todd interrupted him.

'What do you mean drop it off first?'

'Well I saw the lad on my way in. I thought if he was still there on my way back I'd pick him up. And he was. You can never get a bleddy lift on a Saturday. I remember that from my hitching days. The pros aren't about you see. The truckers aren't working nor the travelling reps. Civilians next to never pick hitch-hikers up. And 'tis worse nowadays. They'm afraid to. Lucky for him I was doing my bit of overtime . . .'

Todd interrupted again. It was the only way.

'So what time did you see him first?'

'When I passed him on me way in you mean?'

'Yes,' said Todd with more patience in his voice than he felt.

'Oh, it must have been a good hour earlier. Poor lad, standing there like that all that time.'

'As long as that? Are you sure?'

'Oh yes I had to get there and back, and my old truck don't move all that. The unloading took best part of forty minutes. I had a full load of timber aboard you know. And I had to get it all signed for, and nobody could find the foreman. Come to think of it it could have been as much as an hour and a half.'

An hour to an hour and a half. In that case John the trucker must have seen Jacky Starr standing by the roadside hitching a lift at almost exactly the time that Joyce Carter was being strangled to death.

'Bingo!' said Todd. He shouted it actually.

The lorry driver was still talking down the line. He stopped. The policeman's shout had taken him by surprise.

'Pardon?' he said.

'Granted,' said Todd. He felt quite skittish. He should be going strong for a conviction and be pretty peeved that his number one suspect looked to be in the clear. But he wasn't – and he knew exactly why.

For the first time he was able to admit to himself the effect Belle Parker was having on him. She was a potty actress, and she must be forty-five if she was a day – probably more. Yet she had sparked something in him. It was absurd.

Was it lust? Todd wasn't even quite sure. It was so long since he had been with a woman he could barely remember. Amazingly enough the last time had been with his wife, just before they separated six months previously. He couldn't even remember if he had enjoyed it – although he did remember that he was pretty damned sure she hadn't.

Belle Parker was a two bit actress with a faded career. And she wore too much make-up and dressed as if she was a starlet going to a down-market first night instead of a middle-aged mother trying to get her son out of trouble. All that cleavage. The whole thing was ridiculous.

But at least it now looked as if the woman didn't have a murderer for a son.

He forced his attention back to the lorry driver still speaking into a neglected telephone.

'By the way,' he remarked, 'did you say Silver Fox?'

'Yeah, old Mike Hudson's CB handle. Didn't you know?'

'No I didn't,' replied Todd with a laugh. A more unlikely Silver Fox was difficult to imagine. Cheerily now, he made a note of the man's name and address and asked him to come into the station to make a formal statement.

Then he phoned Belle Parker. She picked up the receiver in her hotel room very quickly as if she had been sitting waiting beside it, and it was only when she spoke that he realised how much he had been looking forward to hearing her voice again.

'Your boy's in the clear, I'm almost sure of it,' he told her briskly.

'Of course he bleedin' is, I told you that yesterday.' She was spiky. Very Belle Parker, parodying herself. He had seen her do that on television, in chat shows. None the less he could sense her relief.

'You know we needed proof,' he said mildly.

'So what's brought you all to your senses then?' She was trying to sound blasé, in charge of things.

'We have new evidence . . .'

She interrupted him. She sounded jumpy, suddenly.

'Is Jacky out, have you released him?' Todd picked up the anxiety in her voice, and knew what she really meant.

'I'm about to. I called you first. If you like I'll keep him till you get here. But come right away. I should release him immediately. I have no right to keep him any longer.'

'Ten minutes,' she said.

Todd replaced the receiver feeling ridiculously happy. He reminded himself that he still had a murderer to catch. None the less, after transferring all the information he so far considered relevant into a new file which he saved in his personal data base, he switched off his computer and marched almost jauntily through the connecting security door leading from the station itself into the cell block.

'Right, I'm releasing Jacky Starr,' he announced. 'Get the paper work sorted.'

The custody officer, a sergeant of some seniority, registered surprise at his cheerfulness. He must be up to something, thought the sergeant, always a fly bugger, that one. And he set about doing what he had been told.

Arabella arrived precisely ten minutes after her telephone conversation with Todd had ended. As she bounced through the station door, and she did indeed have an ability to bounce as she walked, Todd checked his watch. She grinned and flashed him a broad wink. He approached her and suggested she might like to wait in his office while Jacky was being processed.

'I don't like the sound of that,' she said.

'We just have to give him back his belongings, get him to check them and sign for them, that sort of thing,' Todd explained, as he sent a constable to fetch coffee.

Todd sat back in his chair. He remembered he was still smoking his pipe. She might not like the smell. He apologised and began to fuss around trying to put it out.

'Bit late for that, isn't it?'

He looked up, startled. She gestured vaguely with one arm, her hand palm upwards. He realised immediately what she meant. The room was already full of smoke and he had not even noticed it. Neither had he noticed that his fumbling attempts to knock out the offending pipe in his ashtray – a heavy brass one made by his father during the war from the bottom of an artillery shell – had merely added to the fug.

'Oh, sorry, I'll open a window.' He began to rise out of his chair and pushed it noisily backwards out of his way. His movements were awkward. Todd was a big man, not built for precision, never neat in anything. But not usually this clumsy.

'It's all right,' she said. 'For goodness' sake, I don't mind. It's only a bit of smoke. Just talk to me. Tell me what's happened.'

Todd filled her in on the events of the morning and she listened in silence.

'Jacky could not possibly have done it whether he had an alibi or not,' she said when he had finished.

She was quick. No doubt about that.

'You are his mother,' Todd said gently. 'It has been known for mothers to be wrong about the saintliness of their offspring.'

'Not this mother,' she responded. 'I'd never say my Jacky was a saint. But I'd stake my own life that he couldn't be a murderer.'

She was being very serious. He knew better than to further question her judgement. He just nodded. Then he said 'Anyway, I can't tell you how glad I am.'

Her whole face changed, it softened, and her manner lightened. 'Why's that then?' she asked. He felt she was teasing him.

'I think you know,' he said.

Belle was a picture of studied innocence. 'I haven't the faintest idea.'

Abruptly he reached out and touched her cheek, then immediately withdrew his hand. He couldn't believe he had done that. And in his office. It was as if his arm had suddenly developed a will of its own.

She did not move. She looked as if she were about to speak and then thought better of it.

Ah well. In for a penny in for a pound, he told himself. Todd Mallett had a penchant for thinking in clichés.

'Would you have dinner with me tonight?'

'I can't. I mean, I have to get Jacky home. He'll want to get back to London, I'm sure. I just want to take him out of this . . .'

Todd kicked himself. 'Of course, stupid of me. Of course you do.'

'Yes. I'm sorry.' She didn't even sound it. Although there was something in her voice. Something special, something he had provoked, he was certain of it. Or was he?

'Will Jacky be ready yet?'

'I expect so. Shall we see?'

Todd rose, walked to the door and held it open for her. He leaned back, careful not to touch her. He did not dare get too close. This really was quite absurd.

'Some other time then?' he said. He did his best to make it sound light.

He followed her as she set off down the corridor to the front office. Today she was wearing a bright red jacket over a matching, figure hugging, mini dress. The neckline was relatively conservative. None the less nothing about her figure was left to the imagination. Her behind wriggled and her high heels clicked on the tiled floor. She was a thing from the past. A throwback. Not his type at all.

'Oh yeah,' she said casually over her shoulder. 'I'm often in Exeter.'

He cringed inside. She was mocking him now. It

was hopeless. He was making a fool of himself. Then she paused in the corridor, turned to him, reached out, and rested her hand lightly on his shoulder.

'Thank you,' she said. And this time there was no doubt that she meant it.

'For what?'

'For everything,' she said. His heart soared.

Jacky was standing by the front desk when Todd escorted Arabella downstairs to meet him. He looked quite forlorn. At once she had no time for anyone but her son. She barely noticed Todd turn tactfully away.

Arabella took her son's hand.

'Thank God,' she said.

The boy shrugged his shoulders. 'For what?' he asked, unwittingly echoing Todd's earlier remark.

'That you're free, of course, you great lummax,' she said.

He turned to look at her properly for the first time. 'It doesn't make a lot of difference though, does it?'

'What do you mean?'

'It can't bring her back?'

'Oh Jacky . . .' she began.

He snatched his hand away from her, then turned back to the front office inquiries clerk, his entire body language dismissive.

'Is that it then?' he asked. He no longer looked beaten. Instead he seemed angry now, but still tired and drawn. He was wearing the new jeans and sweater she had managed to buy at the Sunday market she had found the day before. He had told them they could keep the soiled clothes he had been wearing when he discovered Joyce's body, he never wanted to see them again. The jeans looked stiff and awkward on him. The sweater was too small. Why did she always underestimate his size? It was as if, for her, he had never grown up, after all, she *had* missed most of his growing up.

Jacky's personal effects had just been returned to him: a wallet containing not a lot, a belt, a pen-knife, a packet of Marlboro, and a packet of Rizla cigarette papers. At least when he found Joyce's body he had been fresh out of dope, so there had been no drugs charge.

Without looking at his mother again Jacky swung around on his heels and made his way quickly outside. It was not yet noon, he had been in jail less than thirty-six hours, yet he stood breathing the fresh air in big gulps as if desperate for it.

'Are you all right? Would you like some breakfast? Then if you want, I'll drive you back to London.'

Arabella was fussing, going too fast. She knew both of those things but couldn't stop herself.

'I'm fine, I just want to be left alone,' Jacky said. He still had the brutal honesty of youth about him.

Arabella remained unable to stop. 'I only want to help, would you like some coffee or something? Or shall I book you into a room? I'll bet you could do with some proper sleep.'

'For Chrissake, Belle!' Jacky seemed to be turning his anger on her now. 'Just shut up and leave me alone, I told you.'

So much for their new-found closeness, thought Arabella. Yet again that had never quite got off the ground.

'But you'd like me to drive you home, wouldn't you?' She could hear herself making the offer as if it were a desperate plea.

'No. I wouldn't. How many times do I have to say it? I don't want to talk. I just want to be on my own.'

'Well, I won't talk to you then, really, I won't . . .'

Arabella was also aware that she was wittering. Her son interrupted her.

'Belle, you wouldn't know how to stop,' he said. 'I'll go home on the train.'

She opened her mouth to protest, but this time realised how hopeless it was. She wanted to comfort him, to be there for him, to be a mother to him. It was, she supposed, too late for that. She was aware that she had long ago forfeited any rights she may have had to his affections. It was strange how much she now wanted to be close to him. When he had turned to her at his moment of great need she had been, even through the shock and the horror of it all, quite elated. He had called for her, he had wanted her, he had trusted her to come to his rescue. And she had come, hadn't she, dropped everything and come at once?

He turned his back on her and started to make his way down the steps. She felt the tears prick the back of her eyelids.

On the fourth step he turned back to her.

'Uh, I don't suppose you could let me have the fare, could you?' he asked.

Wordlessly she opened her handbag and pulled out a bundle of twenty-pound notes. She peeled off three and held them out to him. He returned to her side and took two of them.

'I said, the fare,' he told her bluntly. 'You don't always have to try to buy me, you know.'

She flinched. But she knew she had little cause for complaint.

This time when he turned his back on her she could not stop the tears. And it was at that precise moment that two zoom-lensed cameras flashed at mother and son. A good picture sure enough. Grim-faced newly released murder suspect and tearful famous mother.

'Fuck!' said Jacky quite loudly. He bowed his head and took off at a run down the street with what were almost certainly a couple of reporters in hot pursuit.

Arabella cursed herself. Jacky's arrest had been all over the papers – and the information that he was her son given considerable prominence. Somebody some-where had obviously been unable to resist leaking that one. She should have known the snappers would be around. How could she have let herself get caught in a picture set-up like that? Jacky would hate her more than ever when he saw that snap in the papers the next day.

Ten

Shortly after Jacky was released Detective Chief Inspector Todd Mallett received an anonymous call concerning the murder of Joyce Carter.

The caller sounded vaguely mechanical, almost inhuman, and the man, if it was a man – Todd couldn't even be sure of that – did not stay on the line long. He wanted to ask the detective inspector if he knew that Richard Corrington had had a sexual relationship with Joyce Carter.

'Ask his wife,' said the voice. 'She'll tell you all about it.'

The chief inspector had a lot of questions but his caller did not even give him time for one. He hung up immediately.

Todd sat looking at the buzzing receiver in his hand for almost a minute before replacing it in its cradle. He dialled 1471 for a call back. Unsurprisingly the caller had deactivated that facility. It was already too late and the caller had been too fast for a trace.

He picked up the phone and ordered repeat questioning of Joyce Carter's neighbours. He did not at this stage ask his people to specifically mention Richard Corrington. But he instructed them to inquire about anyone at all the neighbours may have recognised visiting Joyce Carter at any time, including well known faces. Todd planned to make absolutely certain that nothing else was missed.

As if on cue DI Cutler, his skeletal features appearing even more care-worn than usual, came into his office with details of the murder in St Ives in Cornwall which Bruce Macintosh had been mulling over the previous day.

'It might just fit some sort of pattern, boss,' said the DI, adding mournfully, 'I'm making damn sure my lot check everything now.'

The victim had been a young woman, just eighteen years old, a children's nanny called Margaret Nance. She'd been Cornish through and through, from a staunch Methodist family, and there had appeared to be no motive for her death. The Truro-based chief inspector who had been in charge of that investigation three years earlier had ultimately accepted that it must quite simply have been the work of a raving lunatic. And those were always the most difficult crimes to solve. The case was now more or less closed.

Margaret had been strangled and her neck then broken. But in spite of the similarity in the murder method, Todd really could not imagine that there was a link with the Joyce Carter killing, although he was not prepared at this stage to dismiss anything out of hand.

DI Cutler had organised teams to dig into every aspect of Joyce Carter's life and compile a complete dossier on her. This included a file of all her writings. Todd had so far taken only a cursory look at Joyce's work, but was aware that there had been a recent Carter interview with Corrington, and of course the man lived locally on Exmoor.

Still half pondering on a possible Cornish connection as well, Todd asked Cutler to dig out the relevant newspaper cutting for him again.

After reading for a minute or two Todd started to laugh. He couldn't help himself.

'She took no prisoners this one,' he murmured aloud.

DI Cutler smiled wanly. His thin lips stretched over his protruding teeth. 'That's what you get when you're a big star; it wouldn't do for me,' he remarked sagely, shaking his big bony head.

Todd looked up into the mournful eyes, and tried to imagine Cutler as a star of stage and screen. It was an entertaining diversion.

He returned his attention to the article from the *Dispatch*. It was brutal. But if being viciously savaged by a journalist was a motive for murder then there would have been a queue to get Carter, he reckoned. Todd could not really seriously consider Richard Corrington as a murder suspect – not yet, at any rate. But he felt that he certainly ought to talk to the actor.

Todd didn't like anonymous tips, never had done. He felt that they left a nasty taste. But you couldn't ignore them. And if it was true not only that Richard Corrington had been knocking off Joyce Carter but also that Mrs Corrington knew about it, then he ought to talk to her too.

He asked for and was given Richard Corrington's telephone number from the local ex-directory list. The telephone was answered by a woman whom Todd assumed was a housekeeper, but Corrington himself was quickly on the line.

The policeman came straight to the point. 'I'm investigating the murder of Joyce Carter,' he said. 'I believe you knew her?'

'Yes, more's the pity.' The actor sounded quite at ease. 'She interviewed me, a couple of weeks ago. It was a hatchet job. Maybe you've seen it?'

'Yes.' Todd did not elaborate. 'I'd like to talk to you, if I could, about Miss Carter. Wondered if you might be free later today, sir? I could come around to the house?'

'Sure.' The actor's voice was relaxed, avuncular, but a little curious perhaps. 'Not that I can tell you anything much, but if you think there's even a chance I could help. Hatchet job or not, it's a dreadful business . . .'

Todd made an arrangement to be at Landacre around two thirty. He replaced the receiver in its cradle and went over the brief conversation for a moment or two in his mind. If Richard Corrington had been having an affair with Joyce Carter he had given not a hint of it. More than likely the man was telling the truth and he wouldn't have anything useful to add.

The phone rang again within minutes. Todd had asked for only calls relevant to the murder inquiry to be put through to him, and for those to be monitored and sifted. He had a lot of thinking to do. He didn't really want to do any more talking for a bit. None the less he picked up the receiver. It was Arabella Parker.

He was already getting used to the affect her voice had on him.

'My son has deserted me,' she said. He thought she was trying to be jokey. It didn't quite work. He could feel an emptiness wafting down the line.

'I offered to drive him back to London, the little bleeder said he wanted to be alone. Maybe he thinks he is Greta Garbo.'

Todd laughed with an easiness he did not feel. He sensed her distress. Also he knew why she had called

– or he hoped he did. She wanted to see him as much as he did her, that must be it. He waited for her to speak. It was her turn to take the lead.

'Anyway, he decided to go back on the train. And I thought I'd stay another night and take in the sights of Exeter.'

She paused. Didn't explain further.

'So I wondered if that supper invitation was still going?'

'I'll pick you up at eight,' said Todd.

The two and a half hours between the detective chief inspector's call and his agreed arrival time seemed much longer than that to Richard Corrington. Immediately after the brief telephone conversation he had set off to walk to Porlock Weir. The excursion had three purposes: he thought the further exercise might clear his head and do him good, it took him away from the disapprovingly prying eyes of his wife, and he wanted to throw his entire supply of Trozactin into the sea. That was the only way he felt that he could ensure he would take no more of them, as he had promised Dr Hunter the previous day – a promise he fully intended to keep because he was now scared rigid.

When he returned to the house there was still almost an hour left before Todd Mallett was expected, and Richard had nothing much to do other than wait and worry. He changed his clothes twice, eventually settling on casual corduroy trousers and a check-patterned woollen shirt.

He paced the house, could not sit still. Amanda even suggested pointedly, knowing that he had already ridden Herbert, that he might like to take one of his other horses out for an hour or so. Richard declined and took the opportunity to tell her what he should have told her earlier – that he was awaiting a visit from the police concerning Joyce Carter.

She looked at him, saying nothing, her expression quite eloquent enough.

'I hardly knew the bloody woman, for Chrissake,' he suddenly exploded.

'Then neither of us have any cause for concern, have we, Ricky darling?' she replied coolly.

God, how much he would like to wipe that smugly composed expression off her face sometimes. She was a woman capable of doing almost anything that she felt was necessary while showing no emotion at all. He was so different. With difficulty he just kept control. He thought maybe a stiff Scotch would make him feel better. Then he thought better of that too. He didn't want to meet the police stinking of booze. He paced the house several times more, meeting Amanda in the hallway, the kitchen, and on the stairs on her way to the bathroom. In that totally infuriating way of hers she treated him with distant politeness, almost as if he were a stranger, and remarked no further on his transparently nervy behaviour – her lack of comment somehow making her icy contempt all the more apparent.

He returned to the drinks cabinet in the drawing room and stood looking at the array of bottles for a few minutes before deciding on a compromise and pouring himself a large vodka on the rocks which he downed in one. He refilled his glass and, sitting on one of the ornately carved high-back chairs in the big bay window, sipped more slowly.

Half a lifetime later a police Rover purred up the

driveway and came to a rather precise halt outside the front door. Richard finished the remains of the second vodka, popped the empty glass into the drinks cabinet out of sight and, just in case, gave his mouth a quick spray of the breath freshener he always kept handy in his trouser pocket.

As the doorbell rang he was already on his way to the front door calling over his shoulder for Millie Brooks not to bother. 'I'll get that.'

Two men stood on the doorstep. The one wearing a slightly crumpled grey suit introduced himself as Detective Chief Inspector Todd Mallett and his freckle-faced companion, somewhat smarter in a well-tailored sports coat, as Detective Sergeant Pitt.

'Come in, come in. Tea? I'm sure you would like some tea? Nothing stronger, eh, on duty, but tea? Surely?' Richard feared he sounded too gushy and swiftly adjusted his performance accordingly.

He composed his features into serious concern as he ordered the tea from his housekeeper. By the time he had turned back to the two policemen his manner was still helpful, but also businesslike and a little puzzled.

'Now, what can I do for you, gentlemen?' he inquired.

'I'd very much like it, sir, if you'd tell me everything about your relationship with Joyce Carter,' said Todd.

Ricky felt his insides turning over. But nobody watching would have had the slightest inkling of how that simple request hit him.

'Hardly a relationship, Chief Inspector,' Richard said lightly. 'But I'll gladly tell you all I can if you really think it will help.'

He began at the beginning with how he had first

met Joyce along with the regular dining car set on the 19.35 Paddington to Plymouth flier. He related how she had ultimately made a formal request for an interview to his agent and how, against his agent's advice, he had decided to risk it – perhaps lulled into a false sense of security by the easy manner of their 19.35 train acquaintanceship – and how he had lived to regret it.

'Couldn't believe it when I read her article,' he said. He hoped he sounded offended but philosophical.

'I gave her every consideration, let her take me for lunch.'

He made that sound like the privilege which, being a celebrity actor, he naturally thought it was.

Again Todd Mallett did not seem to react.

'I did have reason to believe you were a little closer to Miss Carter than that, sir,' the policeman remarked eventually.

Richard had to work to control his breathing. 'What on earth do you mean, Chief Inspector?' he asked. He was relieved that his voice still sounded calm enough.

'We have had reports from witnesses who have seen you coming and going from Miss Carter's cottage,' Todd continued. 'You are frequently recognised, you know sir.'

'Yes, and don't I know it,' smiled Richard.

He was playing for time. What could they really know? The only two people who actually knew what had gone on inside Joyce's cottage were him and Joyce. And she was dead. After that first time George Brooks undoubtedly had a fair idea, but he couldn't know for certain, would probably consider it nobody else's business, and in any case his loyalty went without question. Some nosy neighbour must have tipped off the police, he thought, and a tip like that couldn't amount to much, could it? In any case, he was as sure as it was possible to be that nobody had seen him, not the second time anyway, not the time that mattered. Richard decided to call the DCI's bluff.

'I don't know where your information has come from Chief Inspector, but I can assure you I only ever visited Miss Carter's cottage once, and that was after lunch at The Castle to conclude our interview,' he said coolly.

'And so there was nothing . . .' Todd paused, ' . . . nothing special about your relationship with Miss Carter, sir?'

Richard Corrington raised his eyebrows. 'Are you trying to ask me if I was sleeping with the woman, Chief Inspector?' he inquired in incredulous tones.

'Well yes, sir, I suppose I am.' Richard studied Todd with care. The policeman seemed to be playing Plod, giving the impression of being none too bright. None the less Richard did not feel on safe ground.

'No, I wasn't.' Richard did not reply angrily. Instead he shifted into astonished superiority mode. Todd's behaviour had made that possible for him.

The policeman nodded, as if in instant acceptance, and then said: 'By the way, how did you get that scratch on your face, Mr Corrington?'

The injury was so slight that Richard had forgotten all about it. Nonetheless he involuntarily touched the scratch with his fingertips, in an irritatingly guilty-seeming gesture, he feared, as he explained about falling from his horse on the moor.

'Thank you very much, sir, I'm sure you've given us all the help you can,' the DCI said. His voice was deadpan. He rose from his chair as if preparing to leave.

'Oh, just one more thing, sir, can you tell me what you were doing on Saturday afternoon and evening? Just routine you understand.'

'Yes, Inspector, I was here at home, watching television.'

'And you didn't go out at all, sir?'

'No, not at all.'

'Your wife was with you, I suppose, sir?'

'No, Inspector, as a matter of fact my wife went to London on Saturday and stayed overnight, she misses the theatre, you know.'

'But your housekeeper was here, I suppose, sir, was she?'

'Millie lives in the lodge with George, her husband. She doesn't come up here at all at weekends – unless we're entertaining . . .'

Todd took his time, he seemed to be spelling it out. 'And so you were alone, were you, sir?'

'I suppose so, yes. George and Millie were in the lodge as far as I know, but I don't remember seeing them after lunch at all.'

'That's fine, sir,' said Todd obliquely. 'I'd better have a word with your wife, please, and then I'll be off.'

'My wife?'

'Yes, please, sir.'

'Right.' Richard's heart sank. You never knew how Amanda might play it.

He was about to find out. He opened the drawing room door and called her name. Amanda appeared very quickly, as if she had been waiting nearby.

'Can I help you, Inspector?' she asked.

Richard listened to Todd Mallett explaining the situation. Just routine, needed to check on Amanda's whereabouts on the night of Joyce Carter's murder.

'Good Lord, why on earth would you want to know where I was?'

'Just routine, madam,' Todd repeated.

A tiny smile played around Amanda's lips. She had that look on her face that indicated she might be about to say something vicious. Richard realised he was holding his breath.

'Of course, Chief Inspector. I was staying overnight with a girlfriend in London. Did my husband not tell you that?'

Richard let out his breath carefully. She was going to play it straight. Thank God for that.

'Yes he did Mrs Corrington, but I needed to hear it from you, and I am afraid I'll have to ask you for the lady's name and telephone number. Just in case, you understand.'

Richard thought he saw an expression of concern flit across his wife's face. Anxiety, even. But he couldn't be sure.

'Whatever you say, Chief Inspector.'

Amanda escorted the two policemen to the front door, and Richard watched from the big bay window as they left the house and drove away.

Once the car was out of sight the actor's ramrod straight stance crumpled. He used the back of his right hand to wipe away the sweat forming on his forehead. Strange how when he was concentrating on a performance, on stage or off, he could always keep the sweat at bay, yet once it was over all his weaknesses overwhelmed him. He felt terrible. He was pretty sure he had come across all right, handled the situation capably. But for once in his life he was not certain how long he could keep up the act.

He began to wish more than ever that he had not dumped all those pills so flamboyantly into the sea.

Todd's telephone extension rang almost as soon as he got back to his desk at Heavitree Road – and the caller was Amanda Lane.

'I am afraid I have a confession to make, Chief Inspector.'

Her voice sounded almost playful, yet somehow conspiratorial, as if she were trying to make an ally of him.

'Yes madam.' Todd made himself sound as neutral as possible.

'I did not spend the night with my girlfriend in London, and I thought I'd better tell you that myself before you found out.'

'I see.'

There was a pause. 'Chief Inspector, this is very embarrassing.' She sighed. 'I spent the night with someone, with a man.'

'I need to know who and where, exactly, Mrs Corrington.' Todd spoke very patiently.

'Can I rely on your discretion, Chief Inspector?'

'Mrs Corrington, I am not interested in marital infidelity. I am investigating a murder. I am afraid we are getting to the stage where I need to eliminate you and your husband from my inquiries. Am I making myself clear?'

'Yes, Chief Inspector,' There was another pause. When she spoke again she sounded resigned. 'I spent the night with our neighbour, Harry Pearson, the new owner of Burrowgate Farm.'

What convoluted lives we do lead, thought Todd. When he spoke he still sounded neutral. 'At Burrowgate, would that have been then, madam?'

'Good Lord, no!'

She made it seem as if even the very idea was idiotic, which, within a close knit rural area, Todd admitted to himself, it probably was.

'He rented a holiday cottage for the weekend – not far away actually, but in a very isolated part of the moor.'

'I see madam, and Mr Pearson will confirm this, will he?'

'I imagine so.' She made a rather curious noise, as if clicking her tongue against her teeth. 'At least he hasn't got a wife to worry about.'

'You did the right thing, calling, Mrs Corrington,' said Todd.

'Yes, well, we'll see won't we? My husband is not always faithful to me, Chief Inspector. Just occasionally I like to get my own back . . .'

'You don't have to explain yourself to me, Mrs Corrington. All I'm interested in is finding a murderer.'

'Yes, of course.'

'You might be able to help me a little more though. Could I ask, was your husband unfaithful to you with Joyce Carter?'

This time there was a very long pause. 'I really have absolutely no idea, Chief Inspector.'

Amanda Lane managed to sound aloof and quite self-assured – her usual demeanour Todd suspected. He ended the conversation then and began to think it over. He had a hunch that Amanda Lane was pretty damned sure her husband had slept with Joyce Carter, and that it had made her pretty damned angry.

If he was right that gave Mrs Richard Corrington a motive too. And it called for a visit to Harry Pearson of Burrowgate Farm.

He shouted for Sergeant Pitt.

'Right, get the car round,' he commanded. 'We're off to Porlock again to see the Corrington's next door neighbour.'

'But we've only just got back, guv,' said the sergeant, pointedly looking at his watch. It was a few minutes past four. The journey to Landacre took at least forty-five minutes in a fast car, and like his inspector, Sergeant Pitt had seen little of his bed during the previous night. The red-headed young policeman's tendency to be driven by his ambition seemed to have been momentarily overtaken by the need for sleep.

'Get on with it, Pitt. You're not a blasted civil servant,' snapped Todd.

'You're lucky,' said the tall man. 'I have to be back in London tonight. You just caught me.'

Harry Pearson stood about 6ft 2ins. He looked very lean and fit, although he walked with a slightly awkward stiffness. He had an athletic build, broad shoulders and narrow hips. He seemed to Todd to be aged somewhere in his early fifties but it was difficult to tell. He was completely bald. His face looked naked. Todd couldn't work it out. Then he realised, Harry Pearson had no eyebrows or eyelashes, nor indeed any sign of facial hair.

'Alopecia,' said Pearson. 'No body hair at all. Can look quite startling, I'm told. I used to wear wigs, but they just made it worse somehow.'

The man smiled easily. His eyes were a very pale grey.

Todd was embarrassed. He realised he had been staring. Pearson's easy manner had left him feeling disadvantaged somehow.

'Oh, I'm sorry,' he stumbled.

'It doesn't hurt, Chief Inspector.' The man's eyes twinkled, as if he were amused. He ushered Todd and his sergeant into comfortable chairs at one end of the big farmhouse kitchen. There was a teapot keeping warm on the Aga. Without asking, Pearson poured out three big steaming mugs.

'So what can I do for you, Inspector? I should say I do have some idea.' His smile was quite disarming.

'You do sir?'

'Yes. Mrs Corrington phoned a few minutes ago. I must say, though, I didn't expect a visit as fast as this.'

'We are dealing with murder, sir.'

'Quite. Of course.'

'I simply need to confirm with you, sir, that you spent the night of Saturday March twenty-eighth with Mrs Corrington.'

'I really do not want to cause Amanda any embarrassment, Inspector.'

'You'll be doing her a favour.'

'Maybe. Well anyway. Yes. We spent the night together, and Saturday afternoon too.'

'What time did you meet?'

'We drove to the cottage separately. I got there about one o'clock. She arrived shortly afterwards.'

'And you were together for the rest of the day and all night.'

'Yes.'

'And neither of you left the cottage.'

Pearson affected surprise, raising what would have been eyebrows had he any. 'You have met Mrs Corrington, Inspector? She is a very beautiful woman wouldn't you say?'

'Please answer the question, sir.' Todd had no time for game playing.

'No, neither of us left the cottage. We made the best of the time available to us.'

Todd thought that was an unnecessary remark, and studied the other man carefully. Harry Pearson gave no indication that he had meant any edge.

'Chief Inspector, I understand that Mr Corrington has no knowledge of what went on between his wife and I. Will it be possible to keep it like that?'

Todd looked at him levelly. 'I really have no idea, sir,' he said.

Bruce Macintosh arrived at the station just after five, and was still waiting patiently when Todd and Sergeant Pitt arrived back from Burrowgate Farm just before 6.30 p.m.

Macintosh was slightly taller than average and overly thin, with a haggard look about him which Todd guessed was not his normal appearance, but caused by the tragedy he had experienced. Salt and pepper hair framed an intelligent, sharp-featured face. Even through the thick lenses of the other man's spectacles Todd could see that Bruce Macintosh had exceptionally clever eyes.

The DCI held out his hand in greeting. Bruce's grip was firm, and his slight smile fleetingly transformed the sad weariness of his appearance.

Todd had not really expected him to be there so quickly. He had little idea of both the sense of urgency and new-found purpose which the other man was experiencing.

The events of the day had given the DCI a lot to be thinking about and working on, none the less he gave Bruce more than half an hour of his time and a promise of more the next day. Maybe even a pint or two. It was funny how policemen and journalists almost always liked each other. You would think that they wouldn't get on, and logically both sides had so many reasons not to – yet almost invariably, unless there was some particular personal animosity, they did get on. And Bruce Macintosh, although carrying his grief very obviously on his shoulders, was so patently both sensible and bright. The man's obvious sense of loss made him all the more likeable to Todd. He warmed to people who could not hide their feelings, even though he was himself quite the opposite in his approach to life. He was drawn to those whose true emotions hung before them, invisible of course, yet existing every bit as much as television rays out there in the sky or a fax picture zooming its way down a telephone line. Todd didn't understand it – any more than he understood how a television picture flew through the air or a fax image transmitted itself to the machine on his desk – but he could feel the power of Bruce Macintosh's emotions as clear as he could see the results of either of those phenomena, and he respected the man for it. He feared that most people he had encountered in his life, including his wife, would have considered that he was an un-emotional man. After all he seemed to have spent virtually his entire life concealing his feelings.

Bruce sat in Todd's office and listed the similarities he had noticed in the newspaper reports of the murder of his wife and Joyce Carter.

'There was also this murder in Cornwall in 1993,'

he said. 'I didn't mention it on the phone. I told the London police after Ruth's death and they more or less laughed me out of court. But I was chief crime correspondent for the *Chronicle* then and I covered the case down in St Ives, you see. The victim died the same way. No doubt about it . . .'

Suddenly Todd had no difficulty at all in concentrating on the present.

'Margaret Nance,' he said quietly. He saw Bruce Macintosh jerk upright in his chair.

'You mean, you're looking into that?' Bruce asked eagerly.

Todd decided to keep things low key. 'Not necessarily,' he said. 'It came up on the computer, that's all.'

'Oh.' Bruce seemed disappointed. Todd tried to be as friendly and helpful as he could. He thanked Bruce Macintosh for his help. He agreed that indeed he could see similarities between Mrs Macintosh's murder and that of Joyce Carter, and yes, even with the death of Margaret Nance. But it was far too early to say if they really were linked, and even if they were it might not necessarily be possible for the police to prove it.

He shared with Bruce Macintosh one or two details of the way in which Joyce Carter had died which had not yet been released to the press. He felt he owed him that, and Bruce then became even more sure that the manner of her death was so similar that she and his wife must both have met their end by the same murderer. Todd remained resolutely non-committal.

Much as he liked the journalist in spite of himself, he knew better than to forget what he was dealing with. Something else that journalists and policemen had in common was that they were never really off duty, never retired, never really switched to other jobs or walks of life. To some it might seem surprising that Bruce Macintosh, still a genuinely grief-stricken man, was seeking to actively involve himself in police inquiries of any kind following the death of his wife – but it didn't surprise Todd Mallett.

When Bruce left Heavitree Road police station it was getting on for eight o'clock. He knew that the Granada service station at the Exeter exit from the M5 was also a motel with rooms to rent, and he rather fancied its anonymity. He didn't want to be anywhere with soul. He certainly did not want to be in a place where he might be confronted by people enjoying themselves.

The place suited him fine. He booked in and decided during the night, when he slept little in spite of his exhaustion, what he would do next.

In the morning he looked at a map. He reckoned the Cornish seaside town of St Ives would be little more than two hours' drive away. It was there, at the north end of Porthminster Beach by the putting green, that the body of Margaret Nance had been found early one morning by a man walking his dog. She had been buried in the soft sand, but the tide had washed her partially clear.

Bruce remembered back to the week he had spent in St Ives then. The girl's violent death had sent shock waves through the entire community. Bruce had interviewed her parents several times. Oddly he remembered their bewilderment more than anything else. They could not imagine a reason why anybody should have wanted to harm their much-loved daughter and the concept of a mindless random killing was quite beyond them.

The *Chronicle* had used the Margaret Nance murder as the peg for a major feature on violence against young women. WILL WE NEVER KEEP OUR WOMEN SAFE? the banner headline had screamed. In those days you could get away with a week out of the office on a job like that. Bruce had made a lot of contacts during that time in St Ives.

And he decided that if the police couldn't be bothered to reinvestigate Margaret's murder, then he would do so himself. He wanted to see how much his memory was playing tricks on him. Strangulation is a common murder method, the London detective superintendent in charge of his wife's murder investigation had told him so, quite unimpressed by the added ingredient of the efficiently broken neck. Todd Mallett had at least had the grace to appear more interested, but had ultimately not been particularly encouraging.

Bruce hadn't been eating well since his wife's death. Resolutely that morning he ordered bacon and eggs for breakfast. He knew he needed some fuel. He had already drunk some tea and taken a bite or two, but suddenly he could manage no more. He pushed the food aside, sickened now just by the smell of it. The professional in him was inclined to take over when he started assimilating information, checking facts in his head, making plans. But not entirely.

He had seen his wife after her death, in that cold impersonal morgue. Strangulation is a particularly ugly way to die. And sometimes he could not get the image of her poor distorted face out of his head.

Eleven

Todd walked into the Rougemont Hotel at ten past eight, which was pretty good timing considering the day he had had. After Bruce Macintosh left the station he had moved like the wind. This was the moment he had been waiting for even through all the excitement of the afternoon. He should feel tired, but he didn't. The thought of seeing her again exalted him. He wanted to have a drink so he had grabbed a cab to take him to the hotel and then run the pair of them on to the little French bistro just off the bottom end of the High Street. He could have got himself a lift in a police car, he had the rank for that, but he didn't want anyone at the station knowing that he was seeing Belle Parker.

It was a quiet restaurant where he knew they would not be disturbed.

There was the tiniest buzz of recognition when they arrived. That was to be expected. He was going to have to get used to it, if he really planned to spend any time with her. And, of course, most people in the restaurant would have seen the stories in the papers that morning and known all too well what she was doing in Exeter. Todd rather hoped that there was nobody in the restaurant who would recognise him. In spite of the fact that Arabella's son was now almost certainly in the clear, that could be rather embarrassing.

But as for Arabella herself, he thought as they were shown to a secluded corner table as requested, how could anyone not recognise the woman? There she was in this totally unfashionable out of the way spot looking how TV and film stars are supposed to but, even Todd knew, virtually none of them did any more.

Arabella's hair seemed bigger than ever. She looked as if she had just walked out of the hairdressers. But then, she always looked as if she had just walked out of the hairdressers. Apart from abandoning a much-loved beehive, and that not so very many years ago, Arabella hadn't really changed the way she looked in a long time. She wore plain tailored black trousers and those very high-heeled shoes again, and a glittery silver jacket cut low.

Todd knew that he was staring. He couldn't help it. The strange thing was he didn't even particularly like the way she looked. He didn't go for elaborate hairdos and heavy make-up, he liked simple casual dress, women who dressed down rather than up. Involuntarily he shook his head.

She put down her gin and tonic and smiled at him.

'It's habit,' she said.

'What is?' he asked.

'You know, the way I look.'

Good God. Suddenly he felt very uncomfortable, and also quite transparent. The bloody woman could read his mind. This was absurd.

He didn't say anything. What could he say? He knew that if he lied, if he said that he hadn't been thinking about the way she looked – she would know. And so he sat in silence. Waiting.

'There's a saying in showbusiness,' she said. 'Never let the act drop.'

He found his voice. 'So is that what it is, the hair, the clothes?'

'Even the smile,' she replied, flashing him a broad one.

'How do I know when you are being real?'

She shrugged. 'What can I tell you? I think you do know. Already. But I can't tell you how . . .'

He gazed at her steadily. 'Do you ever switch the act off?'

'I'm not sure any more. I was brought up this way from the moment I first toddled on to a stage. It's like chicken and egg. Me and my image. I don't know which came first.'

She shrugged. 'Can I have another drink?'

He called the waiter over. The man brought the gin in a tall glass full of ice and lemon, and at the table poured in just a splash of the tonic. Already having noticed how she liked her drink, Todd poured the rest of the tonic into the glass for her. He put down the bottle, and as she reached for the glass he put his hand over hers. He felt her start. When they touched something happened. They were both aware of that, he was sure. He increased the pressure on her fingers, enfolding her tiny hand in his big sportsman's grip. She raised her eyes and met his still searching stare.

'You know that I wanted you from the moment I saw you,' he said levelly.

He could not believe that he was actually saying those words. He, Todd Mallett, big, clumsy, man's man Todd – the world's most useless seducer. Whatever was happening to him was happening on auto pilot.

She kept her eyes locked on to his. And then she blushed. Todd could see her fighting it, but it didn't work.

The colour rose from her throat and spread across the whole of her face.

'You look pretty when you blush,' he told her. And then he thought what a damn fool thing that was to say.

His insides felt like jelly. He took his hand away, still looking at her.

He smiled again. 'I'd forgotten what it was like being seventeen.'

'I don't think I ever was seventeen,' she said.

He grinned at her. 'Child star, Rank charm school, no chance, I shouldn't think.'

Todd picked up a menu and passed it to her. 'Let's eat,' he said. 'That's what we came here for, isn't it?'

She giggled. He wanted to know everything about her. But he had a feeling she was uneasy, that she would like him to slow down.

Suddenly she spoke, endorsing the way he was thinking. Lurching them both back to real life, and to the extraordinary events of the last couple of days.

'My solicitor was pleased with you,' she said lightly.

'What, the chap at the station yesterday?'

'No, he was a stand-in. My man, who I've known for years, was going to come down from London today if we'd needed him. We didn't, so someone is happy anyway. I owe him money, too.'

'And Jacky?' Todd asked.

'In a right state. I've never seen him like it before. He loved the woman, he keeps saying, and you guys thought he'd killed her. It's really done him up. And he's taking it out on me at the moment.'

'We didn't have any choice.'

'Maybe. Doesn't help my Jacky though. Or me. So much for the big reunion. We've got a funny relationship, my boy and me. I'll tell you about it one day. Mostly my fault.' She paused, as if struck by a sudden thought. 'Do you have children?'

He nodded. She said nothing, just looked at him. He answered her unspoken question easily.

'But I don't have a wife any more. We're in the middle of a divorce.'

'I'm sorry.' She didn't really sound it, and Todd was rather glad about that.

'I'm not, to be honest, not any more,' he responded. 'My only worry is letting the kids down.'

'You'll never do as badly as I did with my Jacky, that's for sure,' she said. Then she smiled brightly and shrugged her shoulders as if deliberately tossing off a burden.

'Anyway, thank God for that truck driver, I suppose . . .'

'Yes.' Todd thought she was about the spunkiest woman he had ever met. She tore down his defences with her every breath. He shouldn't discuss the Joyce Carter case any further with her really, but he knew he was going to.

'There is a lot more to the story now, another side to it all which also leads away from Jacky,' he continued. 'You always think domestic first. But now we reckon we could be looking for a madman, some kind of pervert. Somebody who gets a kick out of it . . .'

'What makes you think that?'

'Well, partly the way she died. And she wasn't the first woman on our files to have been killed in the same way. There could be a link . . .'

'What, strangled you mean? Is that enough to make you think serial killing? Seems to me, every time I pick up a newspaper there's a story about some poor bleedin' woman who's been strangled . . .'

Todd smiled wryly. 'Not quite, but I know what you mean. And you are right. But well, look, let's just stick to Joyce Carter at the moment. The details haven't been released yet, so keep it to yourself.'

And he explained Carmen Brown's verdict that Joyce had been only half strangled, that the actual cause of death had been a broken neck.

Arabella shuddered. 'Horrible,' she said. 'And she hasn't been the only one?'

'There are two other possible cases, but we do have a lot of investigating to do. We're not jumping to any conclusions. You rarely know for sure, anyway . . .'

Then she paused. She looked startled, alarmed even. 'How were their necks broken?' she asked.

Todd shook his head. 'Look, I've said too much already.' He knew he had been indiscreet. As far as he could remember he had never even talked to his wife that freely about cases he was working on – in fact, perhaps particularly not to Angela, he thought wryly.

'Todd, there's a reason why I want to know, please tell me.' She looked so earnest.

He shrugged. 'The killer jerked their heads back violently. He probably stuck his knee in the small of their backs to give himself leverage. All three had bruising in the lower back area consistent with that theory . . .'

He stopped talking. Arabella's eyes were very wide open. She looked both shocked and excited at the same time.

'What's the matter?' he asked.

'Sparrow-Hawk.' Her voice was little more than a whisper. 'Sparrow-Hawk. That's the way he always kills. I should know, I've had some. But then you must have thought of that? It's so obvious.'

Obvious to her, maybe, but not to a policeman who only saw television on high days and holidays. He had only understood what she meant so quickly because the TV series was already on his mind after the anonymous call suggesting a link between Richard Corrington and Joyce Carter, and because he had interviewed Corrington that afternoon.

'I've never even seen *Sparrow-Hawk* – except maybe the odd few minutes when my sons have been watching,' he said blankly. 'Explain it to me.'

She did so, graphically, telling him also how she was about to be seen on television as one of Jack Sparrow's victims.

'Arrogant bastard, that Ricky Corrington,' she said.

Todd's mind was racing ahead as she talked. Already he was pretty sure that Corrington and Joyce Carter had been having some kind of an affair.

'My God, this is turning into something,' he said eventually.

He couldn't believe that somebody else hadn't picked up on the *Sparrow-Hawk* connection. But it was so often a question of what you were looking for. Only Todd and Detective Sergeant Pitt so far knew about the anonymous phone call concerning Richard Corrington. He had planned to go along to the Corrington household the next afternoon for another little chat. But now he felt the quicker he gave Corrington a thorough third degree, the better.

He took his hands away from his face and gazed at Arabella. There she sat, silly hair do, too much make-up, cheeks still flushed but probably as much from the excitement of what she had just told him as anything else. There was an ache inside him. But he wasn't going to get the chance to even think about satisfying it tonight. Not after what he had just learned.

'Belle . . .' he began, his voice quiet and serious.

'I know,' she said, interrupting him. 'You have work to do.'

He nodded. 'I'm so sorry. You've given me the information. I have to check it out. Now. I really do.'

'Go on,' she said.

He hesitated just for an instant. 'But what about you? Do you want me to take you to the hotel?'

'I've got to eat, you know.'

'Will you be all right on your own?'

'Oh Todd.' A mild admonition.

'I mean, how will you get back?'

'A taxi, perhaps?' He accepted the gentle mockery in her voice.

'I really *am* sorry.'

And how he meant it. In an entire police career of broken dates, abandoned dinners and wrecked evenings of all kinds, Todd Mallett did not think he had ever regretted walking out on anything as much as he did this dinner date with Belle Parker.

None the less he was already half way out of the door as he spoke.

Twelve

Back in his office, Todd sat at his desk rifling through all the papers that he had so far amassed concerning the case. He was killing time really. In spite of the fact that it was already gone nine o'clock in the evening, the ops room was still manned, and he had recalled a further team of two who were currently trying to locate a *Sparrow-Hawk* video tape for him. Try as he may to recollect the programme from the snatches he vaguely remembered seeing, Todd couldn't do so in anything like the necessary degree of detail.

However it was quickly ascertained that the show was available for sale and rent on video and a local shop, fortunately open until 10 p.m., tracked down which had a number of *Sparrow-Hawk* tapes in stock. Within little more than half an hour Todd had a small pile of video tapes on his desk. He instructed his staff that he wanted every single *Sparrow-Hawk* episode ever made, in his office the next morning, and then settled down to some concentrated TV watching.

It soon became apparent that Arabella Parker's thesis was a good one. Todd became increasingly more sure as he watched that the murderer had based his technique on that used by the lead character, Jack Sparrow.

The only difference was that while Jack Sparrow dispatched both men and women who got in his way with calm efficiency – so far, at least, Todd's real-life serial killer, if he existed, appeared to have murdered only women. And while there appeared to be no sexual motive it could be that just killing women gave him a thrill. Todd knew all about cases like that.

Sparrow-Hawk, however, was presented as some kind of grim crusader who did all manner of dreadful things in the name of duty, and who, however many times he killed, was never corrupted by killing. Government-employed vigilante Jack Sparrow was part of a big professional operation, with clean-up operators or sweepers always following at his heels. The bodies of the victims he so effectively dispatched were either never found at all or else their demises disguised in such a way that no hint of there being a professional hit-man generously dispensing rough justice was ever gleaned by Sparrow-Hawk's fictional public.

Todd was captivated by Richard Corrington's performance. He really brought Jack Sparrow to life. No wonder the show was so astoundingly popular.

The policeman started with episode one of the first series, the opening show. It was not until nearly one in the morning and at the end of the third episode that he decided to call it a day, and sat for a few minutes assimilating what he had been watching. Obliquely he wondered what Jack Sparrow's body count must be up to now, after, he had just been told to his amazement, a staggering 176 episodes of *Sparrow-Hawk* including the seventeen yet to be screened – thirteen a year, as is traditional in British TV drama, for seven years and seventeen annually since the American network had taken up the show. Jack Sparrow dispensed of five victims in the first episode alone, just to give the viewers a good early taste of blood, Todd assumed.

Todd vaguely remembered a flurry of press controversy over the show when it first began. To Todd's way of thinking *Sparrow-Hawk* was fiction, and fact was fact – there was no confusion between the two and never would be but it looked as if someone out there might be getting fact and fiction very mixed up indeed.

Todd was both fascinated and disturbed by the realism of the murder scenes. The cameras lingered each time over Jack Sparrow's method of killing – the half strangulation, the knee in the spine, the head jerked violently backwards by hands now raised to the chin. Instant death caused by a broken neck. Brutal. Clinical. Silent. Efficient.

Todd was so hyped up that he thought he would not be able to sleep at all that night, but exhaustion overcame him in the early hours, and when the racket of his alarm clock filled the room at 6 a.m. he was started out of a deep slumber.

He put another episode of *Sparrow-Hawk* on the bedroom video, leaving the bathroom door open and half watching while he showered, shaved and dressed. He was in his office soon after 7.30 a.m. and managed to find someone to bring him coffee and a bacon sandwich from the canteen. The thick coating of mustard he had asked for seemed to awaken his senses as he bit through the rubbery pre-sliced white bread and his taste buds sought for several seconds for the scrap of bacon he presumed must be lurking somewhere.

The forensic science laboratory at Chepstow were now combing over Joyce Carter's body, her clothes, and her belongings. A hair follicle, the smallest drop of blood, saliva, semen; all could give the identity of anyone who had recently been close to Joyce. Criminal investigations have been revolutionised since the discovery of DNA – deoxyribonucleic acid, the substance in the chromosomes of most organisms which stores genetic information – but none the less Todd was not in this case very hopeful.

DNA was likely to point only to poor Jacky Starr again – Starr had lain on top of the woman after her death, coated her body in his own vomit – and he had an alibi.

Todd was also frustrated as ever that it would be at least ten or eleven days before he would know the results of the various forensic tests. This was normal procedure, but he never failed to become impatient.

The policeman's thoughts returned to Richard Corrington. Joyce Carter's home was in an isolated hamlet about nine miles outside Taunton, just over the Devon border. Beaconview Cottage was detached and fairly secluded although slightly overlooked by the bungalow to its left. However every building there used the same access lane and almost any house-holder could have seen visitors coming and going. In addition Joyce and any callers she may have had would have parked their cars in a parking area clearly visible from the lane. So far, though, the team were having no luck tracing the bungalow owners, who appeared to be away on holiday, and inquiries among other neighbours had produced no helpful information. Several people described a young man, quite obviously Jacky Starr, as a regular guest. Nobody knew his name.

His team had reported that there seemed to be a generally apparent, although unspoken, feeling that

Joyce Carter had in some way let down the tone of the place by allowing herself to be murdered. The one remaining hope of anything constructive coming out of this particular line of inquiry lay with the retired couple who lived in the bungalow immediately next door to Joyce. But nobody seemed to know either where they were or when they were returning. In any case, judging by the lack of substance in the responses of the neighbours so far approached, Todd wasn't holding his breath.

He finished his highly unsatisfactory bacon sandwich, and called the entire murder inquiry unit together for a meeting at 8.30 a.m. For the benefit of the majority who had not been at the station the previous night, he explained about the *Sparrow-Hawk* connection. There was a surprised murmur around the room and one or two expressions of self chastisement that they hadn't thought of it themselves.

'Too bloody right,' admonished the DCI, who did not find it necessary to point out that it had taken an actress to bring the possible link with the TV show to *his* attention.

Todd took DI Cutler to one side.

'We need to talk to the producer of *Sparrow-Hawk* and anyone else connected with the show we can get hold of,' he said. 'Put a team on it. I want to know if Corrington or any of them have ever been bothered by some kind of stalker.'

DI Cutler merely nodded, looking as morose as ever, but Todd knew he would have taken everything on board and probably be ahead of him already.

'I reckon we're looking for a copy cat killer, what do you think, Cutler?' Todd asked. He valued his inspector's opinion. Cutler had as incisive a brain as any copper he knew.

'That's got to be the logical answer,' replied Cutler carefully. 'But we need more to go on. We ought to search Joyce Carter's cottage again, boss.'

'Do it!' said Todd. Cutler was right as usual. The Sparrow-Hawk connection just might add a significance to all kinds of things which would previously have seemed to have been of no consequence.

Throughout the morning Todd and his team painstakingly sifted and resifted the little evidence that they had. Todd wanted as much ammunition as possible at his disposal prior to reinterviewing Richard Corrington, but just before lunch he reckoned he should in any case make contact with the actor. It was almost exactly 12.30 p.m. when he once again telephoned Landacre House, and once again the housekeeper answered. But this time Richard was not there. Millie Brooks explained that Mr and Mrs Corrington had already left for the BAFTA Awards in London that night and would be staying in town until the following day. Todd was vaguely irritated, but untroubled. He made a to-be-confirmed arrangement to call around after lunch the next day. At this stage he could see no overriding reason why interviewing the actor shouldn't wait – and meanwhile his team were still desperately seeking that fresh evidence which might in any case help such an interview along.

He made another phone call, this time of a personal nature, which turned out to be equally frustrating. He called The Rougemont and asked to speak to Arabella Parker only to be told that she had already checked out.

'Damn!' he thought, and cursed himself for not having called earlier.

The morning's bacon sandwich still sat heavily in Todd's stomach. He certainly had no desire for lunch. Desperate for action now he called forensic and asked for the name of the scientist in charge of the Joyce Carter case. He was in luck. Peter Conway was one of the Chepstow boys whom Todd had known for years. Just occasionally Conway could be encouraged to take a foray into the world of maybe – not encouraged in his trade – and give Todd an early tip.

Todd considered whether a trip to Chepstow would be worthwhile – a journey of about an hour and a half in each direction. For the time being he could think of nothing better to do. By one o'clock he was on the road to Wales.

It was a dry bright day. Spring seemed to be arriving at last. If he hadn't been so preoccupied with the case Todd would have found the drive pleasant, even along the M5 motorway which had yet to be turned into nightmare road by the annual influx of tourists.

The view from the Severn Bridge out to the estuary was always spectacular. Today the water shone like silver. But Todd didn't even notice as he crossed the river.

He had decided to drive himself, partly to allow Pitt to carry on working with the rest of the team in the incident room, and partly because he liked the idea of some time alone to think. Settled into the plush leather driver's seat of the big Rover, Todd's mind buzzed. This case seemed to be heading in so many directions.

At the Chepstow laboratory, a modern building just

before the racecourse, Todd was shown into a small conference room by a police liaison officer. Minutes later Peter Conway arrived, wearing a white lab coat over collar and tie. He was a big man, taller and broader even than Todd, with a huge broken nose spread across ruddy features.

He looked more like a night club bouncer than a scientist, and the sight of him never failed to cheer Todd. The two men's friendship had begun on the rugby field many years before, although they were almost always in opposing teams, and had flourished in spite of each invariably appearing intent on maiming the other for life whenever given the opportunity.

'Heard you were on your way,' said Peter Conway. His voice was strangely high pitched, the result of a rugby injury to his throat, and always seemed incongruous emitting from such a large frame.

'I need all the help you can give me, and I need it now, Pete,' said Todd.

'So what's new?' responded Pete, doing his best to inject sarcasm into words that were squeaked more than spoken.

'You know, I'd give a lot for just one more chance to rub that smug mug of yours into a very muddy field,' said Todd.

'You'd have to catch me first,' squeaked Pete, prodding a finger at Todd's expanding belly.

The banter was part of it all. But within minutes Peter Conway moved on to the serious business. He told Todd that two minute strands of material, which appeared to have been ripped from a garment, had been found in the catch of Joyce Carter's gold watch strap.

'The material is a top quality wool mix,' said Pete.

'The kind of stuff first-class tailors use for expensive suits.'

'So the strands of wool could well have been torn from a suit worn by Joyce Carter's killer while she was struggling for her life, is that what you're saying?' asked Todd.

'I can only give you the facts.'

Todd pushed the point. You had to with guys like Pete.

'It's likely enough, though, isn't it?'

'Certainly possible,' admitted Pete.

It wasn't much, but it might eventually fit somewhere into the jigsaw puzzle, thought Todd. Certainly it removed any lurking suspicion of Jacky Starr to an even more distant platform. Todd doubted if the boy owned a suit at all, let alone anything remotely resembling the type of garment forensic were suggesting.

He sat in the conference room for a few minutes more with Peter Conway, drinking tea and remembering nights out together drinking much stronger stuff that had often proved more hazardous than anything which occurred on the rugby field.

On the way back to Exeter Todd found that the half an hour or so he had spent with Pete had left him feeling slightly more positive. It was quite a journey for just a short meeting, but none the less he felt the trip to Chepstow had been worthwhile.

By 5 p.m. he was back in his office, contemplating what more he could do that day, when his desk telephone rang bringing news which sent an instant short sharp rush of raw adrenalin to his brain.

'Think you'd better take this one, guv,' said one of the two DIs monitoring all calls to the murder unit.

A Mrs Janice Murdoch was on the line. She and

her husband lived in the bungalow next to Joyce Carter. They had just arrived home from a three-day break in France. They had taken the ferry back from Roscoff to Plymouth that day arriving in the mid afternoon. Aboard ship they had read English newspapers for the first time since setting off the previous Saturday. They had been horrified to read about the murder of their neighbour. And they were even more shocked and astonished when they recalled something they had seen when they had left their home just before four o'clock – about the time that Joyce had been murdered they now knew from the detailed reports all the papers carried – on the Saturday afternoon on their way to Plymouth to catch the evening crossing to France.

As they had driven past Joyce Carter's cottage they saw a man coming out of her garden gate and running down the steps into the lane. They had both noticed that he had seemed to be in a considerable hurry. And Mrs Murdoch, a great *Sparrow-Hawk* fan, had been quite excited.

The man she and her husband had seen leaving Joyce Carter's cottage was Richard Corrington. And, oh yes, Mrs Murdoch was absolutely sure of that. She never missed an episode of *Sparrow-Hawk*.

Todd immediately briefed DI Cutler, told him to put several other officers on stand-by, and asked for Pitt to be sent in.

'You wanted me, boss?'

'Get your jacket, Pitt, we've a job to do,' said Todd, by way of reply.

Mrs Janice Murdoch's white-painted bungalow glowed deep ochre in the evening sunlight. Almost as soon as she opened the front door, with its highly polished brass fittings, it was apparent that Janice Murdoch was excellent witness material. This small, plump woman, hair tightly permed, floral-patterned cotton blouse washing powder commercial crisp, pristine neat in every way, was so obviously straightforward and sensible.

Todd did what he always did, he imagined Mrs Murdoch in Exeter Crown Court, facing some whizz-kid barrister. She'd walk it, he thought. She had honesty and common sense written all over her.

Todd and Sergeant Pitt sat on chintz-covered easy chairs in Mrs Murdoch's over-decorated front room, which was every bit as neat as her appearance, and went over and over with her the details of the incident she had already described briefly on the phone. She did not waver on any point. And nothing either Todd or his sergeant could do or say could in any way shake her total confidence that she had seen Richard Corrington.

'You must understand the importance of what you are telling us, are you absolutely sure without any doubt at all, Mrs Murdoch?' asked Todd for the umpteenth time.

'We saw him bring her home once before, and go into the house – Chief Inspector, if I hadn't been sure I would never have phoned you,' the woman replied. 'Why ever do you keep asking?'

'This is a murder inquiry, Mrs Murdoch, I have to double check everything.'

Mrs Murdoch was not to be shaken. 'It was him I tell you.' The woman was beginning to sound quite cross. 'Just like he is on the telly. Wearing that leather jacket I've seen in so many pictures of him. He came straight out of her garden gate and got on that motor bike of his.

'Such a handsome man . . .' Mrs Murdoch sighed. 'I just can't believe he would be mixed up in anything like this . . .'

She was impressive in her certainty. By seven o'clock that night Todd was quite convinced that he had a first-class murder suspect as well as a first class witness. He knew exactly what he was going to do next, but he needed clearance from above to carry out his intentions. When he and his sergeant left the Murdochs' he went to work at once on his car phone.

Thirteen

Richard Corrington's day had begun when he had woken at six as usual. It was raining. For once he was quite glad. Rain suited his mood.

He thought he might have a cold coming on. That was appropriate too. He didn't even want to be healthy. His head felt thick, as if he had been stoned out of his brains the night before, which really wasn't fair. He had barely had a drink all day – apart from the vodka he downed to calm him while he had waited for the police – and he had not taken any more Trozactin at all since Sunday, which, with the stress he had been under, had proved to be a nightmare. Being no more or less than a good country GP, Jeremy Hunter had not had any suggestions for exactly how Richard was going to cope without the massive doses upon which he had become so dependent. And, in any case, with the last vestiges of misguided pride Richard had vastly understated his dependency on the pills. Both doctor and patient had discussed the matter as if it would be no great problem for Richard to go cold turkey.

In the London circles in which Richard moved such little helpmates were commonplace. Virtually everyone in his business had a tame quack somewhere who would write a prescription on some spurious excuse. If he had fully realised the side effects of his own favourite booster, taken in such large quantities and always accompanied by alcohol, maybe he would never have started on his drug cocktails in the first place, although he was honest enough with himself not to be too sure of that. But with Hunter's explanation of what he had been doing to himself he could not risk it any more.

As if that scenario were not bad enough there was also the memory of yesterday's visit from the police to plunge him into further distress. He still did not know quite what to make of it, nor of the taciturn detective chief inspector whom he somehow suspected was considerably more astute than he seemed. He also suspected that he had not been very wise in his dealings with Todd Mallett so far. And one way or another that interview had dealt the final shattering blow to his frayed nerves.

Then he remembered what day it was and instantly felt even worse.

It was Tuesday, March 31st, 1998, and the BAFTA Awards were to be held that night in The Great Room of London's Grosvenor House Hotel. The British Academy of Film and Television Arts annual bunfight; Britain's answer to the Oscars allegedly, in the film section anyway, although hardly any of the big name Hollywood stars whom the British judges persistently festooned with awards ever bothered to turn up.

Richard Corrington knew that *Sparrow-Hawk* was not only about as good as British TV got in its area, but also in a class of its own worldwide. Usually he loved the recognition his show received and gloried in award nights like this. He already had a cabinet full of BAFTA awards of one kind and another, and, unlike so many actors, he was a dab hand at the speeches. And he knew he was up for a goodie again.

He assumed it was his fourth Best Television Actor award. Nobody had told him so exactly, of course. That was all part of the charade, but he had been tipped the wink. BAFTA wanted their winners there, they needed them. Because so many of the Hollywood victors didn't want to know, home grown stars like Richard were all the more important. And he was certainly not going to allow himself to be humiliated by sitting through four hours of tiresome ceremony, only to be forced to smile for the cameras at the appropriate moment while losing out to some jumped-up competitor.

This particular day, winner or not, he really did not want any part of it. He was afraid of himself and doubly afraid of facing his public – an entirely new experience. For once in his life Richard Corrington did not think there was a performance in him.

With a supreme effort of will, he struggled to gain the composure he knew that he needed to deal with the day. He tried to breath steadily, evenly, using the same technique he had employed on Sunday after making the appointment to see Jeremy Hunter, and gradually his eyes were beginning to focus more normally, or they would have been were it not for his bedroom wallpaper. Richard fairly universally hated all wallpaper – but there were only so many fights with Amanda that he could cope with. Amanda had decided that the bedrooms called for wallpaper – the cosy almost cottagey look. In a mansion like Landacre it had seemed ridiculous to Richard but he had gone along with it for a quiet life. The grim reality of the blue and yellow staccato spots she had chosen for his room struck far too late. The wallpaper turned itself, on bad mornings – and this was a very bad one – into a kind of torture.

If his friends, colleagues or public ever learned of his daily agony and the way in which he meekly put up with it they would have been amazed. Richard Corrington was a famous actor with all the wealth and influence that came along with the deal. So why did he not have his bedroom redecorated and rid himself of his misery instantly?

But anyone who did not understand had never lived with Amanda Lane. Torture by spots was infinitely less painful than torture by his wife's smoothly vitriolic tongue.

They used the Rolls Royce for the journey to London. Richard was never sure how much he liked the damned thing really. It was perhaps a little too ostentatious to be stylish, and maybe in reality not quite as good for his image as might be imagined. But he knew Amanda had no doubts at all about the car. It was the only motor the Corringtons would ever turn up in at a big function. It was Amanda, of course, who had bought the personalised number plate, RICKY I, which Richard secretly hated. However the car was used only for these very public occasions, and he could not deny, as a man whose life was given its most absolute meaning by being the centre of attention, that he rather enjoyed gliding along the roads and watching the reactions of people suddenly realising exactly who and what was passing them by. And Amanda had thought the thing out well. The gleaming gold Roller's windows were made of tinted glass which gave its occupants a privacy within while at the same time they could appreciate any excitement caused without.

Today, though, Richard was able to find nothing

about the car or its stately progress which could give him pleasure. In fact there appeared to be no pleasure left in the world. He was in deep depression. Dressed in country cords and a sweater, he had curled himself into a corner of the back seat. A psychologist might have said that he appeared to be trying to return himself to the womb. His eyes were closed. He was not communicating. He still felt like going back to bed. He just wanted to sleep the rest of his life away. The alternative was a fix. But the drug and alcohol cocktails which had always given him so much relief were no longer on the agenda. And so he sat, wound almost into a ball, as if holding his whole body together with his arms, trembling slightly, sticky with sweat.

At the wheel of the big car, George Brooks could see his employer in the driver's mirror and thought that he looked a right mess. He coasted off the motorway on to the A4 at Chiswick and headed down to The Embankment. The Corringtons were to stop off at their London apartment to change into their finery and compose themselves for yet another big night. Outside the riverside apartment block Amanda was first out of the car. She stood ramrod straight as her husband almost crawled on to the pavement. He looked dejected and round shouldered by her side.

A man who quite obviously recognised Richard came out of the building. He looked the actor up and down curiously. Amanda beamed at the stranger, as if trying to deflect his interest.

'You're letting the act drop, Ricky darling,' she hissed at her husband out of the side of her mouth.

It was, George Brooks knew, the worst censure of all.

Richard squared his shoulders somewhat. But his eyes were red-rimmed, his complexion was grey. No wonder he had attracted a curious look. This was not the Richard Corrington his fans knew, not by a long shot. His gaze was now fixed on Amanda's back.

George, walking alongside, and carefully carrying Amanda's evening gown in a big plastic sack with zip down the front and a hole at the top for the coat hanger, noticed that his boss's fists were tightly clenched. He glanced again at Richard's face.

'If looks could kill,' George thought to himself unoriginally, 'Amanda Lane would be stone dead.'

Exactly two hours later George Brooks was again outside the apartment block as arranged. Richard and Amanda emerged spot on time, and George did a double take.

She looked impossibly glamorous. Smoothly blonde and glittering. But, even after all these years, even knowing all that he did about his employer, George could not believe the change which had occurred in Richard Corrington in the ensuing couple of hours.

This man bore virtually no resemblance to the shambling wreck who had entered the apartment earlier. Richard was, of course, immaculately clad in a beautifully tailored silk dinner suit. His bow tie, hand tied naturally, was perfectly in place. His beard – he had a heavy growth now, already well past the scrubby stage – was immaculately groomed. The scratch on his face was already healing well, and skilfully applied make-up had rendered it practically invisible. His skin looked tanned and healthy, and no one would be likely to guess that its glow was almost exclusively out of a bottle. His eyes seemed clear again without a hint of red. In fact they positively sparkled. There was a bounce in his step. He radiated vitality. One hand was lightly tucked beneath his wife's left arm as he escorted her across the wide pavement to the waiting car. Once again they were the perfect couple, Olivier and Leigh, Burton and Taylor, Branagh and Thompson – and look what happened to all of those, thought George dolefully. Richard flashed his driver one of his best smiles – rehearsing again, considered George who was not in a very charitable mood – and the gleaming capped teeth completed the film star look.

Richard actually felt almost as good as he looked, if only temporarily – which was to be expected, because within the privacy of his apartment he had resorted to another old habit. It had become more and more impossible for him to function for long without an artificial helping hand. No Trozactin, so back to the coke. There had still been a small stash concealed behind the fridge in the kitchen. And Richard's state of mind had been such that the sheer idiocy of substituting cocaine for a prescription anti-depressant did not even occur to him.

So many people of his generation in films and TV had snorted coke for years, in order, initially, to cope with long working hours. Other people in other far more important walks of life, in hospitals and offices, on farms and in factories, worked long hard days without resorting to stuffing chemicals up their noses. But Richard shared the belief common in his profession that his suffering was unique, and that he was more acutely affected by stress than ordinary lesser folk. Also he had risen to a position in which he was largely surrounded by people who relied on his success to provide them with extremely handsome livings, and who were therefore never going to question his behaviour.

Richard Corrington was crammed full of illusions yet he had so many fears as well. He hadn't touched cocaine now for almost a year – but he couldn't do without all his props just like that.

As he climbed into the car he involuntarily sniffed a couple of times. He withdrew a handkerchief from his trouser pocket – not touching, of course, the pristine white silk one so carefully arranged in the breast pocket of his jacket – and dabbed at his nose.

George scrutinised him carefully. It was cocaine that had nearly done for the stupid bugger the last time. And it was a bloody miracle the press had never found out when they'd had to take him off to that clinic in America for nearly a month. Poor Michael Barrymore didn't have his luck. Some charmer blew the whistle on him straight off. Surely Richard had more sense than to get into that nonsense again. But the transformation was too spectacular to have occurred unaided, thought George . . .

He looked across his boss at Amanda Lane, already sitting in the car, long black and silver silken skirts carefully spread around her, diamonds gleaming at throat, wrist, in her ears and on her wedding finger. Her face was set. Her expression was giving nothing away, but then it rarely did. All that woman cared about was appearances. In George's opinion she probably wouldn't care if her husband injected himself full of heroin as long as it meant that he could carry on performing, and continued to bring home the bacon in the manner to which she was accustomed.

George could tell that Amanda knew he was looking at her and was not even going to glance in his direction. She did not regard him as worthy of recognition, and would undoubtedly have liked to have dispensed with his services years ago – but the employment of George Brooks was another of the very few areas in which Amanda knew better than to try to stop her husband having his way.

George had a big soft spot for his boss, flawed though Richard Corrington undoubtedly was, a soft spot going back all those years to their shared youth. And it wasn't often that George could not detect at least some sign of a decent enough bloke still lurking somewhere inside the actor.

But Amanda Lane was one cold fish. Just looking at her sometimes, carved in stone the way she was, could send a shiver down his spine.

As usual on this glittering night Park Lane outside the Grosvenor House Hotel was pandemonium.

In London as in Somerset this was a bright evening, not yet quite dark, and warm for the time of year. The atmosphere was heady. There were paparazzi photographers all over the place, some of them balanced on ladders for a better view of the arrivals, and a battalion or so of fans, many of them dedicated regular celebrity hunters wielding autograph books. Some of the photographers were little more than fans too, getting as much of a thrill through rubbing shoulders with the real paps as they did out of taking snaps of their favourite stars destined only for their own photo albums.

Richard Corrington and Amanda Lane made an impressive couple when they stepped out of their golden Rolls. Richard signed for several of the auto-graph hunters who pushed books and pieces of paper before him, and he beamed obligingly in the direction of as many as possible of the photographers who called out his name. His sparkling smile did not slip and he gave every impression of being open and generous with his time, but in fact his stride barely faltered as he marched purposefully into the hotel. He managed to look gracious while resolutely moving forwards, a guiding hand on his wife's elbow – ever the perfect gentleman.

Inside, the Corringtons were ushered straight into the VIP reception – only the hoi polloi buy their own drinks at BAFTA. Richard and Amanda knew virtually everyone in the VIP room. The *Coronation Street* mob were there again, up for Best Drama for the fourth time. But you knew they weren't going to get it. *EastEnders* had won it the year before while The Street had picked up the prestigious Lew Grade Award, and the famously snobbish BAFTA judges were never going to exalt soaps two years running. Also Granada had only sent their 'B' team – the Street's biggest stars were notably absent, a dead giveaway.

Richard was starting to feel really exceptionally good. He was enjoying the champagne, although vaguely conscious of Amanda giving him a dirty look as he swiftly accepted a second glass. He knew that she had been well aware of what he had been doing for so long in the bathroom at the flat.

It was going to be a long night, the BAFTA Awards always went on for ever. He was already high as a kite. He knew he needed to keep himself in control. Obediently he sipped the second glass slowly.

*

He did win the Best Actor award, as expected, for the fourth time and the second consecutive year, and *Sparrow-Hawk*, also as expected, was voted Best Drama Series for the third time.

His acceptance speech was first class, as usual. Cocaine did not render him forgetful and inarticulate as alcohol would have done. Instead it gave him edge, added sharpness – or so he believed. It always did, until afterwards. He stood with one hand in a trouser pocket. Confident. Composed. So elegant. So relaxed.

'It is true that I have been here before. It is true that I never expected to be here again. It is also true that I could never be here too often.'

Not really a joke – he believed in leaving jokes to professional comedians, particularly in this company – but there was a nice reassuring rumble of mildly amused appreciation around The Great Room.

Richard rocked back on his heels. He had them in the palm of his hand again. It was so easy for him, it always had been. His smile filled the room, took in every table, every glittering guest. His body language switched to sincerity mode.

'Seriously, ladies and gentlemen, this honour never lessens. I am just as overcome by it and by this occasion as I was eleven years ago when I received my very first BAFTA.

'These are the awards given by one's peers. These are the awards all of us in the business lust after . . .'

He could do it blind-folded. In his sleep. And he knew it. He had a marvellous speaking voice, a product of all those drama classes in voice production and his formative years in good old British rep. He was the kind of actor who could make the telephone directory sound like Shakespeare. The Rs rolled off his tongue like caramel, the vowels were as big as London itself and impossibly round.

He carried his trophy back to his table, raising it triumphantly above his head, and the roof of The Great Room was lifted by an adulatory roar.

He placed his trophy in the middle of the table he and Amanda were sharing with the producer, director and other key members of the *Sparrow-Hawk* team. The bosses of production company Wessex TV were their hosts for the night. The entire table, men and women alike, rose, applauding, to their feet as he returned to them. His wife beamed at him, flung her arms around his neck and treated him to a huge kiss. The two tame BAFTA-employed photographers, the only snappers allowed to roam at will around the room during the ceremony, both caught the shot – but then Amanda had made sure that they were appropriately positioned and able so to do before she indulged all that energy on posing.

What neither she nor her husband knew was that events were about to take shape that evening which would wipe all such standard luvvy pictures right off the front pages of tomorrow's papers and straight out of the entire book.

No awards ceremony in history had ever before witnessed scenes like those about to overtake the BAFTA Awards of 1998.

Fourteen

Everyone in the room wanted to shake Richard's hand – or so it seemed to him in his euphoria. The lights were surely more dazzling than they had been earlier in the evening, the smiles all around him were brighter. He picked up a large brandy – which may or may not have actually been his – and downed it in one, ignoring his wife's eternally icy stare. His smile barely shifted as he worked the room. He felt as if he were being wonderfully witty and erudite and simply did not notice that many of his peers, even those who liked and respected him – and, more worryingly, some of the journalists, particularly the *Daily Mail*'s ever-vigilant Baz Bamigboye – were looking at him curiously, surprised by his verbal diarrhoea and the slight glaze in his eye.

Eventually Amanda managed to steer him away.

It was around 12.30 a.m., as they walked together towards the foyer, that Richard Corrington felt a heavy hand on his shoulder.

Todd Mallett had set out to create impact, and could not have asked for greater.

The arrest was a sensation.

'Richard Corrington, I am arresting you on suspicion of murder,' said the DCI in an expressionless voice.

The words wafted over Richard, who stood open-mouthed in horror. He did not speak. He was so astounded he could think of nothing to say. Amanda was shouting and screaming. Richard was vaguely aware of that. Not only had his wife let the act drop in a big way, her accent seemed to have dropped somewhat too. A woman, presumably a female detective, arrived smartly at Amanda's side and tried to calm her down.

For the first minute or two of the nightmare Richard remained curiously detached, as if unable to grasp that it was really happening to him, more aware of the behaviour of others around him than the import of the moment. The cocaine was still in charge of his brain. The false sense of clarity which it brought made him quite curiously aware that this strangely calm detachment might not be such a good thing. Highs and lows were inclined to be greatly exaggerated. And he knew he was heading for an all-time low.

No one apart from Angela seemed to be talking as they hustled him through the hotel. He recognised Detective Chief Inspector Mallett, of course, from their meeting the previous day, and he was being marched out between the DCI, who had now transferred his iron grip to Richard's right arm, and Sergeant Pitt, whom the actor also recognised, who had a lighter grip on his left.

Richard could see his agent, Larry Silver, making an attempt to get to his client by pushing past a now closely bunched group of uniformed police, but he was firmly stopped in his tracks. Everyone seemed to be panicking except Richard. If it had been pandemonium outside the Grosvenor earlier on it was now bedlam. The reporters who had been in The

Great Room, led by Bamigboye whose towering bulk always made him a good man to have at the head of a charge, were trying to get out to see what was going on. Some of the paparazzi from outside had already been let in at the end of the evening as was the custom. They were also pushing and shoving to get out and holding their cameras aloft high above their heads on the half chance of picking up a useable picture that way. The paps still outside – already greatly excited by the arrival of such an unusually big police presence – reached a state of frenzy when they became aware of the extraordinary little procession making its way through the lobby towards them, and were pushing and shoving to get in.

As Richard Corrington, within his small ring of police, was ushered out through the big glass doors on to the street the whole of Park Lane erupted with camera flashes. The blaze of light burned its way straight into Richard's brain. His eyes became locked wide open, pupils dilated. The calm detachment of a moment earlier disappeared almost as if it had been exploded by the bursting brilliance of the flash bulbs. The snappers call it 'getting melted', and that was exactly how it felt to Richard. The actor was suddenly engulfed by overwhelming panic. He could hear people shouting his name from all directions.

'Ricky, Ricky.'

'Over here, Ricky.'

'This way, Ricky, this way!'

His head felt as if it was revolving around without his knowledge. Then Todd Mallett's grip on his right arm slackened somewhat as the DCI was jostled from behind, and Richard reacted instinctively. He was terrified. The last remnants of rational thought evaporated. With a strength born of fear he wrenched his right arm out of the chief inspector's grasp, lashed out wildly with clenched fist at Sergeant Pitt and jerked his left arm free too. Neither of the Devon policemen had expected him to resist arrest in any way, and this sudden break-out caught them both totally by surprise.

For a few seconds they seemed struck motionless as the actor lurched away from them. But he managed just one unhindered step before being smothered in a mêlée of uniforms. More by the force of his own momentum than anything else Richard fell to his knees on the pavement.

The bedlam outside the Grosvenor House now erupted into scenes worthy of a war zone. Excited beyond endurance, the paparazzi surged in all directions in desperate bids to get the angle on this most dramatic of pictures. Several ladders had crashed to the ground, at least one carrying a screaming occupant with it, and further bodies fell over the collapsed ladders. There seemed to be flailing legs and arms everywhere. Cameras were getting smashed, and right across the pavement on to the road spread what looked like an out of control rugby scrum in which fists and boots were flying indiscriminately. But still the flash bulbs blazed. A particularly determined girl reporter very nearly succeeded in crawling through the legs of a battling policeman trying to keep the crowd away from Richard Corrington as he remained slumped at ground level.

Todd Mallett was a quick recoverer. He cut through the crowd like a warm spoon through butter and emerged almost instantaneously with Richard miraculously on his feet again, and the set of handcuffs Todd always kept clipped to his belt now equally miraculously linking him to the actor. Todd's Rover car had been double parked right outside the hotel with a constable in attendance. The rear door on the pavement side was open – waiting. Todd unceremoniously pushed Richard Corrington into the car powering him right across the back seat to make room for himself alongside. Sergeant Pitt had been right behind, helping to keep the crowd at bay, and had read his superior's mind. He was already in the driver's seat behind the wheel when Todd yelled the command. 'Go!'

Pitt switched on the ignition, flashing light and siren, and took off down Park Lane with a squeal of hot rubber. Paparazzi ran, for as long as they could keep up, on either side and behind the car, and one threw himself crazily in front of the vehicle causing Pitt to temporarily slow and then swerve. As if somebody had switched him on again, the stunned Richard Corrington began to put on a parody of a performance. The tumult in the street had reached such a furore that it was sending all kinds of confused messages through the mists of his totally befuddled brain.

Press and fans were baying like a pack of wolves. Wolves. The wolf pack. That's how he thought of the press anyway. But he must smile for the photographers. Always he must smile for the photographers. Never let the act drop, Ricky.

Richard's lips stretched grotesquely across his designer teeth. It was as if he had been programmed. He pulled his lips back so far his mouth hurt. He wished he could think straight, wished he could clear the fog now filling his brain.

As Sergeant Pitt swung the big car around Hyde Park Corner a motor bike roared alongside the Rover and a flash bulb smacked off right at the car window. Several of the paparazzi, originally led by doyen Richard Young, regularly used bikes to get themselves around town quickly through the traffic, and with typical presence of mind and speed of action, Young had taken off in pursuit, with a fellow snapper, the irrepressibly determined Alan Davidson, on his pillion. Involuntarily, Richard Corrington turned towards the flash. He looked like a scared rabbit. His immaculate hair had been transformed into an unruly shock standing almost on end. The wide-open eyes with dilated pupils stared straight into the lens. His lower lip had sagged making him appear vacant while at the same time emphasising his frightened expression. Beads of sweat were standing up on his forehead. Crazily he had tried to raise his handcuffed hand as if to protect himself and this was suspended, clearly displaying the metal bracelet firmly attached to the wrist of DCI Mallett, just below his chin. Richard could hear the whirr of several dozen frames making immortal the full horror of his downfall. No cameraman in the world knew better than Davidson how to make the best of the briefest of opportunities.

Instinctively, Richard Corrington recognised – as a veteran of so many, albeit by comparison very ordinary and harmless, photo opportunities – that this was the picture sure to be carried the next morning in every daily paper in the land; along with whatever could be salvaged from the mayhem when he had tried to break away, fallen down, and been hand-cuffed.

With a thrusting dart of reality, as if understanding

totally for the first time what was happening to him and what it could mean, Richard slumped into his seat and tried to bury his face in his hands.

The car belted down Knightsbridge, roaring past Harrods, heading west for the Chiswick flyover and the M4. The motor-cycling snappers, well-pleased with their result, had retreated into the distance. Todd Mallett sat impassive next to his weeping suspect.

Fifteen

The journey back from London's Grosvenor House Hotel to Heavitree Road – Exeter's premier police station, built in the modern style virtually adjoining the regional magistrates' court, Exeter and Wonford, and linked to it by a connecting tunnel – took just under three hours. With lights flashing and sirens blazing Sergeant Pitt had broken every speed limit. That too was designed to weaken the prisoner's defences, and in addition Pitt was very eager to be allowed to go home to bed. Neither policeman spoke to their prisoner throughout the drive except to inform him that he would be formally interviewed when he reached Exeter, and however much he blubbered and begged – as the cocaine wore off Richard was even more adversely affected by the circumstances in which he found himself than he would otherwise have been – he was given no further information.

At Heavitree Road the custody officer told Richard to empty his pockets and checked through the contents of his wallet. The small packet of cocaine thus discovered gave Todd considerable satisfaction, all the more so because this was not only a bonus but could quite easily have been dumped by the actor in the Park Lane mêlée, had he shown the presence of mind to do so. If all else failed now, Todd could keep his suspect on a drugs charge. And if he was able to get him on the charge he was really looking for, the fact that he was, as Todd saw it, obviously some sort of junkie, could only work in the favour of the prosecution.

Richard Corrington was given no chance to sleep before the interrogation began, although he had of course been informed of his rights and invited to contact a solicitor. Fleetingly he thought of Amanda, upon whose strength, in spite of the way he often felt about her, he so relied. But she had seemed to fall apart back at the Grosvenor House. He did not know where she was or if she was capable of helping him. For the time being at any rate, he was on his own, and, a little late in the night, he battled desperately to regain some of his self assurance. In a rather theatrical final bluff, he declined legal advice.

'I am an innocent man, a wronged man,' he proclaimed, suddenly, after all that blubbing in the car on the drive down, starting to act again and letting forth as if he were playing Hamlet at the very least.

'I have no need of lawyers. The truth will out.'

Sergeant Pitt shook his head sorrowfully. 'Barking mad,' he whispered conspiratorially to the inquiries clerk, as Richard was ushered into an interview room by the DCI himself. Todd glanced back impatiently, unwilling to waste a minute.

'Come *on* Pitt,' he bellowed over his shoulder.

'Still on duty then,' said the clerk to Pitt's retreating back.

'Don't push your luck, mate,' muttered Pitt.

'Todd was already timing the start of the interview at 3.50 a.m. when Pitt entered the room. Richard had only been in the station for fifteen minutes, but in that time had been photographed and issued with the standard paper suit in exchange for his clothes and personal effects. This sent the actor reeling, and it did not even occur to him that the removal of his clothes was chiefly a psychological ploy as there was little likelihood that his dinner jacket would provide any clues. The speed with which the interview began was also designed to prevent him from having too much time to collect his thoughts, and he was in far too much of a state to recognise that this was quite deliberate too.

The DCI opened a manila folder on the desk before him and removed three pictures which he slapped face up in front of the actor. Richard started. The photographs were of the dead bodies of three women. The pictures were not a pretty sight. The manner of the death of the three women meant that their faces, clearly featured in the photographs, had been cruelly distorted. Richard could not keep his eyes off them. He felt as if he was locked on to the images before him.

In the distance he could hear Detective Chief Inspector Todd Mallett's expressionless monotone methodically relating the names of each murdered woman – Margaret Nance, Ruth Macintosh, and Joyce Carter – the time, date and place of each death, and the exact way in which they had been killed.

'Just the way you do it in the programme, Richard. You don't mind me calling you Richard, do you? Or Ricky? Isn't that what they call you? Do you prefer that?'

The actor stayed slumped in his chair, his eyes no longer focusing.

'Or is it Sparrow, Jack Sparrow?' continued the DCI relentlessly. 'Each of these women died the way Sparrow-Hawk kills his victims. Exactly the same.

And you were in the right place when each woman was murdered. Quite a coincidence, aye, Ricky?'

This Richard Corrington did understand. It was exactly what he had feared. He did not respond mainly because he had no idea what to say. He knew about these three women, all right. He knew exactly how they had died. He knew all about the Sparrow-Hawk killings. And he had so hoped that nobody else would ever know.

The policeman was carrying on as if he had not really expected the actor to say anything at that point. As if it were not really his intention that he should say anything.

'So what I want to know from you, Richard, is exactly where you were, what you were doing and who you were with when each of these women died.'

The actor continued to stare at him in silence.

The DCI passed him a piece of paper. On it were printed the details of time and place that he had just recited, and an explicit reminder of the murder method in each case.

'Will that make it easier for you?'

'It makes no difference.' Richard spoke at last. He sighed. He no longer seemed on the one hand distant and bewildered or on the other as if he were still trying to play a part. His voice was a strange croaky thing, a million octaves away from the professional resonance of just a few hours before.

'I don't need to be reminded. I know exactly when they died, and how.'

Todd Mallett was right on the edge of his seat now, leaning forward, encouraging.

'Of course you do, Ricky,' he said quietly. 'I know that.'

The words were a caress. Only when there was no further response from the actor did Todd speak again.

'Why don't you tell me about it?' he asked, his voice little more than a whisper.

Richard Corrington shrugged. 'Tell you what? There is nothing I can tell you.'

'I am going to ask you again, Ricky, where were you and what were you doing when each of these women was murdered?'

The actor slumped further in his seat.

'Take your time, Ricky. You want to tell me, don't you? You want to get it off your chest, don't you?'

Richard buried his head in his hands.

In the distance he could hear Todd Mallett's voice. Twice more, methodically, calmly, relentlessly, the detective inspector repeated his question.

Finally Richard Corrington dropped his hands away from his face and gave his answer. His voice was stronger than before, but still sounded as if it belonged to somebody else.

'Chief Inspector, I do not know where I was when any of the women were murdered. I have not the faintest idea where I was, who I was with, or what I was doing.'

Todd felt a tremor of excitement race through his veins. He studied the actor carefully. The strained and drawn face, the strangled voice, the words forced out as if by a huge effort of will. Todd's gut reaction was that Richard Corrington was, to the best of his ability at that moment, being totally honest.

A couple of times already during the interview he had suspected that he was on the edge of a break-through. Now he was almost sure of it. He wasn't often wrong. He decided to go for broke.

'Did you kill these three women, Ricky?' he asked. His voice was still low and soothing. The message behind the words was trust me, tell me.

The actor did not drop his gaze. The strained eyes were still locked on to Todd's.

'I don't know,' said Richard Corrington softly. 'The truth is I don't know whether I did or not.'

He let out a big burst of breath as if he had been holding air in his lungs ready for this moment. He relaxed. A look of relief spread over his face, the look people get when they have decided to come clean about something, to share a secret.

Todd had worked on the principle that Richard Corrington was bearing a dreadful burden of guilt. He had first played on this and then given his man the opportunity to lighten the burden. It was always what lay behind confession. Todd knew all about that, and not only from the experience of his police work. His estranged wife was a Catholic, and the Catholic church had an entire ecclesiastical system aimed at getting rid of guilt through confession.

There was total silence in the little interview room. Todd realised that the next step was crucial. But he never had the chance to take it. To his intense irritation he was interrupted by the custody officer.

Richard Corrington might not have been able to see the necessity of summoning a lawyer and getting his back covered, but others working on his behalf had sprung into action the moment he was arrested, in the way that they are inclined when wealthy and powerful men find themselves in trouble.

In Larry Silver, Richard had one hell of an agent. Silver's responsibility to and for his clients was total, and contacting arguably the top criminal lawyer currently operating in Britain had been just one stage in the damage limitation operation which the agent had launched immediately after Richard's arrest.

John Nemrac arrived at Heavitree Road only an hour or so behind the arrested actor and his police escort, having high-tailed it down the motorway through the night – his fleetness of travel encouraged by the assurance not only of a huge cheque to be supplied by clients for whom the sky was the limit when it came to bank balances, but also by the promise of the most high profile case in even his illustrious career.

And the first thing John Nemrac did upon arrival was to insist that his client was given the opportunity to rest, and that there would be no more interrogation until morning, and no more, naturally, without his presence.

Todd was frustrated, but aware that the night had already provided far more progress than he had imagined possible. This one was turning into a corker . . .

Richard was escorted to the cell block medical room where samples of body tissue were taken by a police doctor. As with Jacky Starr earlier, the doctor removed samples of hair, saliva, and blood, and also took a swab from Richard's penis.

The actor felt totally degraded. But the greatest shock of all came when they locked him up.

They led him into a bare cell, around eight foot by six, with grubby cream walls, old graffiti half scrubbed out, and a concrete floor. A single light bulb hung untidily from the ceiling. The only furniture took the form of a thin plastic mattress laid on a narrow concrete platform. He was handed a single blanket. No pillow.

There was a lavatory pan set into a recessed area to one side of the cell. The pan had no seat. The recessed area no door. Prisoners do not get privacy. The whole cell, including the lavatory, could be easily viewed from the little panel with sliding shutter set into the cell's heavy metal door.

Richard was still taking all this in when he heard the door crash shut behind him. He swung around, feeling suddenly trapped. An animal in a cage. The metal shutter in the viewing panel was open. For a few seconds a pair of eyes stared straight at him. Then the eyes disappeared and the shutter slammed closed.

He heard the unmistakable sound of retreating footsteps.

Involuntarily he cried out. 'Don't go! Don't leave me here! I can't stand it . . .'

The cell was quite cool but Richard was sweating. The paper suit stuck to his skin when he sat down and the clammy plastic of the mattress stuck to the paper suit.

He wondered if anyone would come in answer to his call. Nobody did. He sat quite still, staring dully ahead, for fully half an hour before he heard footsteps approaching again. The shutter in the door was pulled to one side and a pair of eyes appeared once more in the little window. He stared back uncomprehendingly. Then the shutter was closed again and the footsteps retreated.

If Richard had previously experienced any difficulty in grasping the grim reality of his situation it now overwhelmed him.

He looked around him again. He had seen photographs of police cells and watched endless TV dramas in which they had been quite accurately recreated. He had even acted the role of a prisoner before.

But nothing had prepared him for the stark horror of being locked up in this horrible little room in the bowels of Heavitree Road police station.

He began to sob, then reached for the single blanket and wrapped not only his body but also his head in it before curling up in as much of a ball as he could manage on the narrow bunk.

Sixteen

Larry Silver's disproportionately large head held a brain of such exceptional capacity that it may indeed have required an unusually sized cranium to contain it. He had long ago been nicknamed Quick-Silver because of his speed as well as his enviable shrewdness in making deals, and the way in which he set his damage limitation operation into motion was predictably formidable.

Larry took charge at once when confronted with the unprecedented events at the BAFTA Awards. And his doing so, under such extraordinary circumstances, was a measure of the importance Larry attached to his leading client as well as to his own daunting professionalism. There was also the question of habit: Larry was the kind of man who always did take charge – it was second nature to him. And, of course, his personal feelings naturally influenced his behaviour and encouraged the alacrity with which he swung into action. Richard Corrington's own somewhat arrogant certainty that his agent was in love with him, and always had been, was not quite so. But certainly Larry had great admiration and fondness for his number one client, in spite of the off-hand manner with which Richard often treated him. And it was true that Larry had once, many years before, been quite head over heels in love with the actor. However, the way in which Richard had eventually made fun of this, his mockery verging on downright cruelty in the end, had considerable bearing on the fact that it was not the case any more.

Richard had, of course, earned Larry a great deal of money over the years. None the less, whatever his motivation, Larry's conduct on the night of Richard Corrington's arrest was such that the actor, had he been in a place or a condition to know what was going on, should have been blessing the day more than twenty-five years earlier when Larry Silver, albeit impressed as much by Richard's physical attractiveness as by his acting ability, had taken him on his books.

Larry's first move was to get Amanda Lane away from the Grosvenor House. The woman had lost it, completely – not like her at all, but there it was. And she could only do harm to her husband by remaining publicly visible. Amanda had stayed in the foyer of the hotel throughout the pavement skirmish – partly because she had been unable to get out for the crush of people, and partly because she was being restrained and resolutely calmed by a WDC from the Met. Larry, making soothing noises and smoothly thanking the nursemaid WDC at the same time, had taken Amanda by the arm, steered her smartly through the Grosvenor's big glass doors and hurried her across the pavement into the back of the still waiting Rolls where an astonished George Brooks was gazing open-mouthed after the departing police car containing his boss. The paps had still been running down Park Lane following the retreating police Rover, which allowed Larry to at least achieve one result. Amanda Lane was in no state to be photographed, and by moving so fast Larry had managed to remove Amanda from the scene without a single snap being snatched of her, because the press were still all too busy chasing Britain's top television actor.

Throughout the three and a half hour journey down to Porlock, Larry worked on the mobile phone, checking notes with other mobile users from the *Sparrow-Hawk* team who had been at the Grosvenor, waking up any of the Corrington entourage who were not at the awards, alerting an impressive network of friends and contacts. He contacted not just the legal experts on the Corrington payroll but also accountants, bank managers, all the people who were important to the actor and who should not be allowed to learn about the scandal from the television or their daily newspapers the following morning. Most were at first irritated to be woken in the middle of the night, but then, in spite of undoubted shock, enjoyed a certain vicarious thrill and sense of self importance at being involved so swiftly in such high drama.

Larry did virtually everything possible to contain an impossible situation. He had realised at once that he must warn Millie Brooks, whom he knew always stayed in the big house at Landacre when the Corringtons were away overnight, before the first press calls started coming through, and he had been well aware that they would begin almost instantly. Larry had in his day cursed the British press, particularly the tabloid sector, as roundly as anyone in showbusiness circles – but he retained a sneaking admiration for the speed and slickness with which they operated. Indeed Larry got his call through to Landacre only just in time, he later learned. A stunned Millie had listened to, without fully comprehending, his calm and brief account of what had happened and had gratefully obeyed his instruction to switch on and hide behind the telephone answering machine, which duly fielded the first press call only seconds after Silver had rung off. It had been from the *Sun*, almost always the first off the mark, Larry knew. The *Star*, its highly professional news operation often underestimated, had been second in line with the others not far behind.

It was still dark when the Rolls swung into the drive of Landacre House just after four in the morning, George Brooks operating by remote control the big iron gate. Larry had not been surprised to find that a couple of hapless stringers, rudely awakened by their London news desks, were already on doorstep duty, shoulders hunched against a chill wind blowing in over Porlock from the sea. He told George not to slow, and the final camera flash of the night focused only on the retreating rear end of a Rolls Royce whose occupants were effectively protected by tinted windows. Larry did not notice, however, that one of the cars he had, at a glance in the dark, taken to belong to the stringers was in fact a police car.

Within the welcome seclusion of Landacre's extensive grounds Larry gently woke Amanda who had, to the agent's relief, fallen asleep on the journey. It was as if the shock and her near hysterical reaction had been too much for her body to cope with and she had slumped into welcome oblivion. Her face was tear-stained, eye make-up had run down her cheeks, she was trembling and her eyes did not seem to be focusing properly. Her evening gown was now a crumpled mess.

Her distress and lack of control were clearly apparent, and the motherly Millie Brooks instinctively put her arm around her. But even in this condition the lady of the house had not had a character transplant. Suddenly aware of what was happening she angrily shook off Millie's kindly attentions. The woman took a step backwards, unsure of what to say or what to do.

The intercom bell on the iron gate rang at 6 a.m., less than an hour and a half after Amanda, followed within minutes by Larry, had retired to bed. It was answered by Millie, who had been sitting fully dressed in the kitchen clutching her umpteenth cup of tea. George Brooks, exhausted by hours of driving, had also gone gratefully to bed as soon as he was able, but his wife had known she would in any case get no more sleep that night and had settled by the Aga with the teapot.

It was the one call Millie could not ignore.

The police have power according to the Police and Criminal Evidence Act, known as PACE, to search the property of a suspect under arrest without a warrant, and Todd had considered sending a team to descend on the Corrington mansion simultaneous to the arrest of Richard Corrington. But he had wanted to oversee the operation himself, he always preferred to execute a search in daylight if at all possible, and also, the danger of any evidence being destroyed before his arrival was minimal, he felt, because the only person likely, or indeed probably even able, to do so was safely behind bars at Heavitree Road nick. He had, however, stationed a police car outside Landacre on a watching brief.

The duty call for the team he needed had been at 5 a.m. Todd had released a grateful Sergeant Pitt, all ambition temporarily forgotten in his desire to see his bed, who left for home announcing that he needed to sleep for a month. Curiously the DCI barely felt tired although he had endured a completely sleepless and highly charged night. Adrenalin, he surmised. And his sense of excitement was somehow heightened when he and his team arrived at Landacre just as a glorious dawn was breaking. It was April 1st, and Exmoor was giving the new month a splendid welcome. The wind had dropped and the air was quite still. The sky was vermilion, a pair of early flying wild duck suspended in silhouette. There had been a heavy dew and the lawns of Landacre shimmered, almost as if they were covered in frost.

Millie Brooks, looking fraught and close to tears, flung open the door to the house before Todd needed to use the ornate lion's head brass knocker. There were seven police in all standing outside. Almost involuntarily she allowed them into the hallway. As she did so, somewhere in the house a telephone rang – four rings and then silence. Todd immediately guessed correctly that it had rung more or less ceaselessly since the early hours and that an answer machine was in action – and how the Corrington household must at least be blessing that bit of modern technology, he thought. Politely he asked if Mrs Corrington was at home, although he knew, of course, from his watchdogs by the gate, that she was.

As if on cue the lady of the house appeared at the top of the stairs. She was wearing nightclothes and a dressing gown which appeared to be made of a silk brocade. They were expensive glamorous garments, totally out of place on this morning of crisis, and somehow contrived to add to the crazed, manic look she had about her. The act had not so much dropped as detonated itself.

'What do you want? What are you doing in my house?' she shouted. She was on the edge, her voice shrill and uncontrolled. There was none of the usual icy cool about her.

Todd explained with further courtesy that he intended to search the house.

Amanda Lane's face, already flushed, turned crimson. Her fine-drawn features seemed to have collapsed overnight. Her eyes were angry slits. Her hair hung in lank strands. She was a woman who normally took as much care in removing her make-up as she did in putting it on, but last night's mascara remained still smeared in congealed rivulets down over her cheeks, like the remains of dirty rain on a window pane.

She yelled desperately for Larry who, in fact, had appeared at the top of the stairs only a couple of minutes behind her. He was dressed in the trousers of last night's dinner suit with the belt still loose and frilly white shirt undone, both garments obviously hastily pulled on.

The police took the place apart. Todd knew that if he was to stand a chance of a successful prosecution with a man like Corrington in the dock his case had to be flawless. The main purpose of the search, following the discovery of the threads of material caught in Joyce Carter's watchstrap, was to examine Richard Corrington's clothes. He did not know quite what else he was looking for but a packet of cocaine had, after all, already been found on Richard's person. The DCI sifted through the actor's dressing room himself, and, as he had expected, within Richard Corrington's extensive range of fitted wardrobes were several jackets and suits from which the tiny strands of material might have been torn. The clothes all seemed immaculate and there were no visible signs of any damage except that a sleeve button on one dark brown worsted was loose. Todd studied the jacket carefully. Was it his imagination, or was the cuff very slightly frayed? He made a mental note to put that suit top of the list of those that he intended to send to forensic.

No stashes of drugs were revealed. Todd could not have known, but he would never have found illegal drugs at Landacre because Corrington had always somehow managed to keep himself clean of cocaine there, even when he was hitting the stuff heavily; and the destructive little white pills, which were in any case available on prescription, were by now fully dissolved in the Atlantic Ocean.

However Todd was not displeased with the results he had achieved. He had a feeling about that suit . . .

Seventeen

Amanda Lane arrived at Heavitree Road police station at 10 a.m., just two hours after Todd Mallett had returned there. Police officers were still searching her home when she left, but she had not been detained.

She looked a million dollars. The transformation from the woman Todd Mallett had last seen as a screaming hysterical wreck at Landacre was quite staggering. And unlike her husband Amanda Lane had not needed cocaine or any other drug of that nature to assist in the metamorphosis. It was true that she had, largely on the advice of Larry Silver, swallowed a couple of Valium, but mostly the change in her was down to her own natural determination. The old Amanda had reasserted herself in fighting form.

Together Larry Silver and Amanda Lane had nurtured the Richard Corrington myth for many years, and together they must maintain it – Larry had reminded her. Strangely the final indignity of the dawn police search had taken Amanda beyond shock, and made it easier for her to accept the fact that her back was firmly against a wall that she could only claw her way off.

Amanda Lane was not going to allow herself to be beaten that easily. A sordid little murder was not going to rob her or her husband of all that they had achieved, was it? The answer was no. The sniping between her and Richard, the playing away from home, none of that affected one jot how much Amanda Lane valued her marriage. And if she was to stand a hope of keeping her status and her lifestyle she had to be prepared to fight for it.

She had shut herself in the bathroom with her make-up and her hairdryer and gone to work on her appearance. As with Arabella Parker, her looks were her instinctive first defence and a well-proven weapon. When she had restored her face and hair and dressed herself in a style that was classic elegance on legs, she immediately felt better able to do battle.

With her initial terrible panic finally under control, she rode the press gambit with her usual aplomb. It was entirely her decision to ask George Brooks, summoned from his bed to drive her, to stop outside the gates to Landacre. She stepped out of the Range Rover, greeted the by now quite large throng gathered there graciously and, although apologetically declining to comment, treated them to a beautifully formulated pose which would present just the right image in tomorrow's papers.

When confronted by the press outside Heavitree Road, Amanda Lane behaved with a style and aplomb that, if anything, surpassed even her leaving of Landacre. Still she would make no comment, for which she again apologised, but she posed easily and with apparent unconcern for a second photograph; thus already presenting picture editors with a choice for the following morning and so much more clever than trying to dodge the cameras and ending up, looking ridiculous and as if you had something to hide, in a smudged snatch shot. Amanda knew all about that kind of thing, and she oozed self assurance. The photographers and reporters jostling on the steps were every bit as impressed as Larry Silver had been at Landacre.

'Smooth as a pint of Murphy's,' remarked one snapper. And that was about the finest compliment he could pay anyone.

Amanda Lane was a vision in Chanel, her smile firmly in place. She could have been walking into a smart restaurant for lunch instead of a police station to visit her jailed husband.

Todd Mallett, summoned by the inquiries clerk on duty in the front office, had to work hard not to show his amazement at her changed appearance. He swiftly gave his permission for her to see her husband, and then retreated home to grab a few hours', by then desperately needed, sleep. He could not fail to notice, however, the hard glint in Amanda Lane's eye as, with the barrister John Nemrac by her side, she strode down the police station corridor on her way to see her husband for the first time since his arrest.

Because of the serious nature of the charges Richard Corrington faced, his meeting with his wife and barrister took place in the only interview room within the station cell block – grim, grey, smelling of disinfectant, and almost as much of a culture shock to the likes of Amanda Lane as a medieval dungeon must have been in ages past. But if she was affected in any way she gave no indication. She sat down on an upright chair in the small claustrophobic room – fully sound-proofed, with double security doors, itself like some kind of padded cell – with as much grace and ease as if she were settling into a sofa in her own drawing room.

John Nemrac, an imposing looking man in his early

fifties running slightly to fat due to an unfashionable fondness for good lunches, observed her admiringly. During the few minutes he was able to spend alone with her, the barrister had felt the need to say little to Amanda. She had several questions for him, points to clarify, and he did his best to do so; but other than that he was more than happy to let her play it her way.

Nemrac was a man unused to failure, and he specialised in high profile cases – particularly murders. He suspected that his client was going to be a rather different man after seeing his wife. The ice lady was back in business.

When Richard Corrington was escorted into the room to meet her, Amanda was shocked, although she still managed to conceal her reaction. She had not expected the white paper jump suit. He looked quite pathetic, she thought. And more than anything else she had to overcome an overwhelming feeling of contempt. She hated weakness, loathed it probably more than anything else in the world. Indeed the thought of her collapse into unthinking hysteria earlier that morning made her even angrier now than she might otherwise have been.

With a considerable effort of will Amanda composed her features into something resembling affectionate reassurance. Her husband stood before her looking a complete wreck. His hair and beard were greasy and unkempt. The cell block was cool, yet he had been sweating profusely, and you could already see a grimy tide mark around the neck of his paper suit. It was his eyes which told the story. More than anything else they indicated a dull acceptance of his fate.

Amanda did not like the look of that at all – and she moved fast. She stepped forward and took him in her arms, aware that she couldn't even remember when she had last done that.

'Ricky darling,' she cooed. 'What have they done to you, my love?'

She touched his face, and he gave a small resigned smile. His breath smelt. Last night's booze and un-brushed teeth, she thought, yuk.

'My darling,' she continued. 'Larry and John say it's sure to be all a dreadful mistake and we'll have you out of here in no time.'

The actor raised his eyebrows. His expression clearly said 'that's what you think'.

With an even greater exertion of will she continued to maintain her façade of cheery optimism.

'Anyway, no wonder you feel so awful, darling. Such a shock. And that dreadful paper suit . . .' She paused.

It had occurred to her even before she left Land-acre that Richard would need fresh clothes, but she had not been allowed to take anything from the house. Any of his clothes could become evidence . . .

She shivered. 'I'll send George off to buy you something nice and new to wear, darling. Although I'm sure you won't be here long. You are, after all, innocent.'

The final sentence was more of a command than anything else.

Richard remained silent.

'You'll soon be freed. John will see to that.'

Richard sat down suddenly. Then, with a jolt, he leaned forward in his chair, eyes bright, lips trembling as he at last began to talk. His voice was high pitched, he spoke uncertainly and yet with a kind of suppressed anger.

'You don't know anything about it, Amanda, not the first thing, the agonies I have been through, none of it . . .'

She interrupted him, suddenly even more aware than she had been throughout their meeting of the policeman standing silently in the corner of the room.

'Ricky darling, you don't have to tell me anything. I know all I need. You are innocent.'

'You don't know a damned thing Amanda.'

Amanda again interrupted him swiftly.

'You don't have to say any more, my darling. We will all cope. Whatever happens you must just remember that you did not do these terrible things, you would be quite incapable.'

She leaned across the table and fixed him with an earnest stare. 'I have plenty of fight for both of us,' she said. 'I am not going to let you lose all that you have worked for all these years. I am not going to let us lose it.'

She grasped him by the shoulders, one strong long-fingered hand on each side of him, her salon-sharpened crimson talons digging through the flimsy suit.

'Don't let the act drop, darling . . .'

It sounded more like a threat than reassurance.

Eighteen

Later that same cool but bright morning Bruce Macintosh visited Margaret Nance's parents in St Ives. He had yet to learn of Richard Corrington's arrest – the events at the BAFTA Awards had happened too late to make the Cornish editions of the national press, and Bruce had been too preoccupied to tune in either to radio or television.

David and Bridget Nance – who had also yet to hear any news bulletins – seemed almost pleased to see him at first.

David Nance, typically Cornish in build, short and stocky, had been a fisherman once, until government regulations and diminishing stocks of fish made it impossible for him to continue earning a living. He and his wife now ran a souvenir shop in St Ives, and when Bruce arrived they had put a 'closed' sign on the glass-panelled front door and taken him into the little back room.

'There's no business worth mentioning anyway,' said Bridget Nance, a small pretty woman who had aged dramatically in the three years since Bruce had last seen her. She had lost weight and he was shocked, although unsurprised, by her haggard appearance.

''Tis only the first of April, after all, and Easter still nearly two weeks away. Hardly anybody else is open yet, but well, we've nought else to do . . .'

Her voice trailed off.

Bruce apologised for bothering them, for reminding them of their terrible tragedy.

'As if we needed reminding.' David Nance had very clear blue eyes, and the pain in them was bleakly evident.

'We never mind talking about her, it makes it seem as if she is still with us, you see . . . the memories are that vivid. 'And if there's aught we can do to bring the bastard who killed her to justice, well, we'd do anything.'

Bruce explained his serial killer theory, how he believed that Margaret, Joyce Carter, and his own wife Ruth had all been killed by the same man.

David Nance reached out and clasped his hand – an unexpected gesture.

'I read about that murder in London, so that was your missus.' The blue eyes filled with tears.

'You know then, you know what it feels like.'

Bruce nodded, overwhelmed for a moment by his own pain and the depth of sympathy and understanding he was feeling from these people. He feared that he must have seemed very brash and superficial to them when he had investigated their daughter's murder, long before he was to share the agony of a similar violent loss.

'People say you'll get over it in time, them as don't know,' said David Nance. 'You never get over it, but you learn to live with it, that's the only comfort I can give you.' He drew away, straightened in his chair. 'Right, what do you want to know.'

They went over it all again. From the dreadful moment when the police arrived with the news of a body found on the beach, two days after Margaret had gone missing, to the time when they learned that inquiries had been more or less dropped. And in spite of David Nance's assurance that he and his wife were happy to talk about Margaret's death, Bridget Nance began to weep quite openly.

'I can still see her, you know, lying in the mortuary, her poor face twisted and swollen,' she said. 'That was the worst of all – the identification . . .'

Her voice trailed off.

Bruce leaned towards her and touched her shoulder, starkly aware that it would never have occurred to him to make such a gesture three years earlier.

'Have the police been back?' he asked after a moment. 'I know they are looking into a possible connection with Ruth's murder and the other recent one.'

'No, they've not been back, and if they had, I don't know what we could tell 'em,' said David Nance.

'Are you quite sure you can think of no connection between Margaret and either Ruth or Joyce?'

David Nance shrugged. 'Why does there have to be a connection?' he asked. 'The police reckoned Margaret's killing was a random murder by some psychopathic lunatic. Even if the same man did for the three of them, couldn't that still be the case?'

'You're probably right,' said Bruce wearily, although he actually thought it was pretty shabby police-work that they hadn't been re-questioned.

Bridget Nance was still crying when he let himself out through the shop door, shutting it firmly behind him and obeying David Nance's instruction to leave the 'closed' sign in place.

Around mid afternoon just before Todd Mallett returned to Exeter's Heavitree Road police station following his all-too-brief sleep, came the little bit extra that the DCI had been hoping for. On the sleeve button of one of Richard's suits, the very button which Todd had noticed was loose, a gratifyingly clear thumb print had been discovered – it belonged to Joyce Carter. And the suit in question was also the one with the very slightly frayed cuff which Todd had spotted. Loose buttons and frayed cuffs were not a common sight in the actor's immaculate wardrobe, and, later backed by the off-the-record tip from Pete Conway at forensic, had led Todd to believe from the beginning that this was the suit from which the threads caught in Joyce Carter's watch strap had most likely been torn. Although it would still be ten days before he received the official forensic report which he hoped would give him confirmation of that, Todd felt confident now that he had enough evidence to charge the actor with the murder of Joyce Carter.

In addition, a team at Landacre that morning had interviewed George and Millie Brooks about the whereabouts of Richard Corrington on the afternoon of the murder. Somewhat to the devotedly loyal George's obvious annoyance, the two detective constables noticed, Mrs Millie Brooks had admitted that although they knew Mr Corrington had been at home that afternoon and it was unlikely that he could have left the premises by the main gate without their noticing, there was the hunting gate behind the stables through which he sometimes came and went on his motor bike; and indeed although she had not heard the bike leave, as far as she could remember – but then, she would only expect to hear it were she in the kitchen at the rear of the gatehouse – she had heard it return while she was washing up the tea things. And that established the time – it would have been just before five o'clock.

The evidence of the thumb print on the sleeve button and the frayed cuff led to the assumption that when attacked by her murderer Joyce had frantically grasped at his arms, trying to pull away the deadly hands around her throat. Her watch strap had caught in the material of her assailant's jacket during the struggle and she had left a thumb print behind.

It was a pretty devastating piece of evidence, strong enough to give even John Nemrac, expert that he was at manipulating the law, cause for concern.

Certainly this new evidence coupled with witness reports meant that Nemrac knew his client had no chance at all of avoiding the murder charge – and the police indicated that further charges might follow. Although he had now begun to believe that Richard Corrington had also been responsible for the deaths of Margaret Nance and Ruth Macintosh, DCI Mallett knew that it was unlikely that he would ever unearth enough evidence to charge the actor with either of those two murders. Better to stick to one strong case. Richard was also charged with the possession of an illegal drug, namely cocaine, but not wanting to bog down their main case the police asked the magistrates for that charge to remain on file.

When Richard was confronted with the thumb print evidence, he shrugged his shoulders, almost as if accepting the inevitable.

'What happens now?'

John Nemrac explained that it was a matter of record that Richard had met and been interviewed by Joyce Carter. His job would be to make the court believe that the evidence of the thumb print and the torn threads, if indeed they were from Richard's jacket, had come from that meeting.

'She grasped my wrist and caught my jacket in her watch strap while we were chatting about the latest series of my show – very bloody likely,' mocked Richard. He did not even seem to want to hear anything positive.

'It will be by the time I've finished,' remarked Britain's leading barrister casually.

Meanwhile the force of Amanda's personality continued to engulf Richard, and, as ever, he had no choice in the end but to do her bidding. On this occasion that meant going to court and performing according to instructions. There was to be no hiding his head beneath a blanket for Richard Corrington as he arrived to be formally charged at Exeter and Wonford Magistrates Court right next door to the police station. That old blanket trick just gives an instant impression of guilt, his barrister told him firmly. The connecting tunnel between police station and court was closed for repairs, so Richard would be transported the short distance from the cells in the old-fashioned way – by van. And Nemrac and Amanda – both confident of Richard's ability to play to the gallery, not to mention the press cameramen they all knew would be in mass attendance, once he had been suitably motivated – agreed that this could work in his favour.

At six o'clock on the evening of Wednesday, April 1st, 1998 – just eighteen hours after his arrest at the Grosvenor House, and four days after Joyce Carter's death – Richard Corrington was charged by the police with Joyce's murder. His formal court appearance was scheduled for late the following morning. That gave him time to rehearse, time to utilise his every advantage – because ultimately Richard merely pretended to himself that he was playing a scene for television, in common with almost every actor in the world he had done that often enough in the past. Weddings, funerals, award ceremonies, after-dinner speeches.

Amanda had furnished Richard with a formal pin-striped suit. His hair was freshly washed, his beard neatly trimmed. He looked the usual handsome Richard Corrington. He had asked for and been given temporary use of a mirror in his cell.

He played around with his reflection until he reckoned he had found just the right look – humble yet dignified, hurt, yet slightly indignant. As long as nobody looked too closely into his eyes, he thought, he could get away with it. Just.

For most of the early morning before they called him for the court appearance he sat with his head in his hands and considered the evidence against him. How on earth was even John Nemrac going to wriggle him out of it? And there would be more. The DNA evidence had yet to come. Ten days at least, standard procedure, Nemrac had informed him, which had been both a surprise and a relief, even if only delaying the inevitable, because only Richard knew how anxious he was about that.

Just another performance, he told himself as the police van arrived at the courthouse – even though it was next door to the station the police were not going to walk a murder suspect along the road, particularly one as well known as Richard Corrington. He would woo them in the aisles, he would pretend to himself that he were on the West End stage, that he was making a Hollywood movie, that he was collecting another BAFTA – no, better still, an Oscar. He would imagine anything other than live through the truth. He would transport his mind and body somewhere else, on to another planet, into the London Palladium, the Old Vic, the National Theatre, the Albert Hall of the sky – anything other than live out the grim reality of pleading not guilty to a murder charge in Exeter Magistrates Court.

It began on the steps to the courthouse. Richard found the sight of hordes of reporters and photographers curiously reassuring. At least he knew what to do. He pulled his shoulders back, walked straight, and looked as dignified and untroubled as could ever be possible while at the same time remaining hand-cuffed between a pair of large policemen. He even managed a small polite smile in the direction of the biggest bunch of cameras.

By the time he came to step into the dock to make his plea he had created just the kind of early impression his barrister and his wife had been hoping for.

'Not guilty, your honour,' he said gravely. Just like at the BAFTA Awards, his voice turned each word into a symphony.

After he had spoken he glanced towards the public gallery, his body language honesty on legs, and was rewarded by several cries of 'Hear, hear!' and even a gentle rumble of applause.

The magistrate called for order. Richard was remanded in custody, and that meant at least six or seven months in jail waiting for his case to come to trial at Crown Court. But this was no surprise – he had already been warned that a successful application for bail in a murder charge was virtually unheard of, and particularly so when the accused man had been stupid enough to try to make a run for it when he was arrested.

In stark contrast to that early display of wild panic, he left the court with equal dignity to that with which he had made his arrival. The words he had spoken, his whole demeanour, radiated innocence.

In St Ives, Bruce Macintosh sat in his room at the Porthminster Hotel, overlooking the beach where the body of Margaret Nance had been found, and watched the TV coverage of Richard Corrington being charged on the one o'clock news.

He was angry with himself. Having studied to the best of his ability the way in which the three murdered women had been killed he had completely failed to make the quantum leap to the *Sparrow-Hawk* connection. Mind you, like Todd Mallett and his team, Bruce's work had over the years given him little time for television.

When the news item was over Bruce switched off the TV and contemplated his detective work so far. The reality was that he had achieved next to nothing, and upon reflection, he was not even sure what he had expected to achieve.

Margaret Nance had been murdered in the open air by a coolly professional killer who had left no clues. There was apparently no motive.

In addition to talking to Margaret's parents, Bruce had talked again to the local police, to the man who found the body, and to Margaret's employers, both at the time of her death and before.

He had learned little new, except that *Sparrow-*

Hawk had been on location near St Ives at the time of the murder, but that would have meant nothing to him three years earlier. And in any case, he had also learned that every last detail on file locally concerning the murder of Margaret Nance had been supplied to DCI Mallett in Exeter.

The policeman had obviously done his best to cement a link between the two deaths and Bruce knew the Exeter DCI had been reinvestigating his own wife's death too. But Todd Mallett must so far have failed, because, significantly, Richard Corrington had been charged with only one murder.

Bruce had twice tried to call Todd, and left messages, since learning the previous evening of Richard Corrington's arrest. So far his calls had not been returned, which he supposed was not surprising considering the pressure Todd Mallett must be working under.

As he was contemplating this the telephone rang. It was Todd Mallett at last.

'Been a bit busy, I'm afraid,' the DCI said by way of greeting. Followed swiftly by: 'And what the bloody hell are you doing in St Ives, anyway?'

'I had this feeling the key to it all might be down here . . .' Bruce began haltingly.

'God save me from gifted amateurs,' boomed Todd, who gave the impression that he was in fine humour now that his prime suspect was safely charged. 'And have you found the magic key then?'

Bruce sighed wearily. He had nothing to be in good humour about. He had lost a wife he had loved very much and now it seemed likely that the man guilty of her murder might never even stand trial for it.

'No,' he said morosely. 'I found bugger all – except

that *Sparrow-Hawk* was being filmed here when Margaret Nance died, and I expect you know that already.'

At the other end of the phone Todd grunted his assent. When he spoke again his tone was quieter and more considerate, as if he had just remembered how Bruce must be feeling.

'We are looking into every possible aspect, I promise you, Bruce,' said the DCI. The two men had swiftly reached Christian name terms.

'But nobody has even talked to Margaret Nance's parents again . . .'

'Bruce,' Todd sounded very patient, 'I have in front of me now their statements taken at the time of their daughter's death. I do not see how they can possibly add anything. I will talk to them again if I have something constructive to ask them, but other than that I saw no reason to rake up their distress by raising a possibility for which I have no proof.'

'Oh, Christ,' said Bruce, thinking of how he had the previous morning left Mrs Nance in tears.

'Do I take it that you have already done that?' asked Todd.

'Yes. And you're right. It got me nowhere.'

'Well don't worry about it. They were going to have to face it sooner or later, anyway.' Todd was really being very understanding.

Resolutely Bruce put his misery to the back of his mind.

'Todd, what I want to know more than anything else is, do you really think Richard Corrington is guilty?' he asked.

'Of course I do, I wouldn't have charged him else.'

Bruce paused, took a deep breath. 'I'm sorry. I

don't just mean of the murder of Joyce Carter. I mean, do you believe he also killed Ruth and Margaret Nance.'

There was a long silence down the line. 'I guess I do,' replied Todd eventually. 'But unless a miracle comes my way I don't think I've got a cat in hell's chance of proving it.'

'But he'll go down for Joyce Carter, are you sure of that?'

Todd gave a brief hollow laugh. 'You're a crime reporter, have you ever been able to be sure of anything in a court of law?' He continued more solemnly. 'I am as sure as I have ever been, Bruce. I've got a damn good case and it's getting stronger by the minute, I promise you.'

'I see,' said Bruce, and added almost plaintively, 'is there anything at all I can do to help?'

'If there was something that might connect Ruth with *Sparrow-Hawk*, or Margaret, come to that, that would help,' said Todd. 'That would help a lot. Do you know of anything?'

'I don't know. Ruth was a fan, I think, but there are millions of those . . .'

'Well, maybe you could try your wife's friends and family. Go back a long way. I just need a link.'

Bruce said he certainly would try, but he felt heavy of heart. Beaten.

After the conversation had ended, he phoned down to reception to ask them to prepare his bill. The best you could ever hope of justice was a decent compromise, he had learned that long ago, but sometimes reality was hard to face.

Only later did he remember that there was something he had forgotten to tell Todd. But, although it was a niggle that had always bugged him, he had never been able to work out any relevance to Margaret Nance's murder. And it certainly was not important enough for him to try to call Todd back.

In Exeter the hard slog of police work continued as Todd, driving his team relentlessly, strove to fulfil his pledge to Bruce Macintosh and come up with an even better and more watertight case.

Three days after the actor was charged, his doctor came forward. Richard Corrington had visited him on the day after Joyce Carter had been murdered, explained Jeremy Hunter on the telephone. Normally he would never reveal the details of a doctor–patient consultation – which was why he had not contacted the police earlier – and it still went against the grain. But he had talked the matter over with his wife and had eventually decided that he could not withhold what might be vital evidence. This was murder, after all.

Todd and Sergeant Pitt drove at once to Hunter's Porlock surgery, where they were greeted by the country doctor in unusually anxious mood.

'I just can't believe any of this is really happening,' he said at once. 'I've known Ricky Corrington for years, you see, we were boys together, and his father, a respected farmer around these parts, you know . . .'

The DCI interrupted him. 'Why don't you simply tell us exactly what happened when Mr Corrington visited you, sir. Start at the beginning . . .'

Hunter did just that, explaining first of all how the actor had called him and absolutely insisted that he must see him that day, Sunday or not.

'I reckoned he must have been thinking he had a

brain tumour at the very least,' said the doctor with a nervous laugh. 'But it was nothing like that, or at least, not really, I mean it was his brain he was worried about, I suppose, in a way . . .' His voice trailed off.

Todd tried not to sound impatient. 'So tell us *exactly* what he was worried about, will you, please, sir?' he said as encouragingly as he could manage.

'Yes, well, he was worried about drugs and what he was afraid they had done to him. He'd been taking Trozactin for years – but huge doses of it and always washed down with huge amounts of alcohol.

'Richard had a doctor in London who gave him all the supplies he asked for and he was popping them like smarties.

'I told him he was doing his head in, and must stop at once. There's also an accumulative effect, you know, when you misuse drugs the way he had. He assured me he would stop, however hard it was, and I think he meant it. He seemed quite frightened.'

'So he was worried about brain damage, is that what you are saying, Dr Hunter?' asked Todd.

'Well yes, but more specific than that. Richard wanted to know if the combination of drugs and alcohol that he had been knocking back could cause temporary amnesia. The answer was, yes, of course. Any anti-depressant taken in the quantities he was swallowing and washed down by half a bottle or more of spirit would have that effect.

'The loss of memory would be temporary, but very acute, and possibly grow more extreme the more regularly and for the longer period of time that you take the pills.

'Several hours or even a whole day could be a complete blank – an absolute wipe out.

'The thing that Richard wanted to know about most was how well it would be possible for him to function in this state. And of course, the more regularly you misuse any drug the less dramatic its effect seems to be. I reckoned that even after quite large doses combined with alcohol, Richard would seem almost normal, a bit flushed perhaps, a little strange, but could travel from A to B, carry on a conversation, even drive a car and quite probably get away with it.

'He could do almost anything, but not remember a thing about it the next day, sometimes not even where he was during the wipe-out period. He could easily commit a . . .'

Jeremy Hunter's voice trailed off again.

Todd felt quietly triumphant.

About a week later, forensic came up trumps and confirmed that the strands of material found in Joyce Carter's watch strap had indeed come from the suspect Richard Corrington suit.

Peter Conway called Todd as soon as he was certain of the news.

'The official report's on its way,' he said. 'That's another night out you owe me.'

A couple of days after that came the most devastating evidence of all. The DNA report showed that Joyce Carter had actually had sex with two men not long before she died. The first was Jacky Starr, as had been expected. The second had been Richard Corrington. The semen found in her mouth matched up with the samples of body tissue taken from the actor after his arrest.

'Bingo!' said Todd. And he punched the air triumphantly.

The next day John Nemrac visited his client in Exeter prison where he was being remanded in custody. Richard Corrington had been in jail for less than a fortnight but already seemed institutionalised. This was not unusual. John Nemrac had long since ceased to be surprised by how quickly people became immersed in the daily routine of prison life. Mealtimes and exercise sessions provided the only breaks in the monotony. Survival was all. Every prisoner developed his own defence mechanisms, his own way of dealing with it. Richard seemed to be coping by withdrawing into a world inside his head.

This was dangerous and annoying. As his barrister he was allowed to see Richard in private, without a police presence. The lawyer was about as close as he ever came to losing his cool.

'Why the hell didn't you tell me?' he asked his client. 'You've heard of DNA, haven't you? You can't fuck somebody and then claim you've not been near them.'

Richard Corrington had that glazed look in his eye again. 'I left her alive.' He spoke very quietly.

'Yes,' said his barrister.

'I left her two or three hours before she died.' He paused. 'At least, I think I did.'

'You don't think in this game, Richard. You have to know.'

'OK. I left her at least two or three hours before she died. She was alive when I left. I should have told you before. I'm sorry. But that's the truth.'

The actor sounded as if he were reciting something.

Nemrac sighed. 'It's not me you have to convince, Richard. It's the jury.'

'Isn't that your job?' Richard sounded petulant.

Nemrac frowned. 'One day I'm going to run out of miracles,' he said, more to himself than to his client.

'Your wife's outside. She doesn't know about this latest little bombshell yet. I thought *you* ought to tell her.'

Richard's face dropped. Nemrac found himself rather enjoying this bit. 'I'm not telling her. I don't want to see her.'

'She has to know. You need her even more than before. The jury has to see her standing by you – even though you've been unfaithful.'

'Jesus Christ,' said Richard. He buried his face in his hands.

John Nemrac resigned himself to the inevitable.

'I'll tell her,' he said.

He took Amanda for an early evening drink to the bar of the Rougemont Hotel and there, as they settled in a corner as far away as possible from a group of loud-talking businessmen reliving a sales conference, ordered a bottle of champagne.

'God knows why, though,' he said. 'We're not exactly celebrating.'

Her gaze did not falter when he told her. Although she did have trouble stopping herself from wincing when he related quite clinically how traces of Richard's semen had been found in the dead woman's mouth.

'I'm sorry,' he said.

'No need to be,' she responded brusquely. 'I've never been under any illusions about Richard's extra marital activities. It's the thrill of the chase, you know – he usually doesn't quite know what to do with them once he's got them.'

She laughed harshly.

Nemrac shifted in his seat.

'So where does that leave us?' she asked.

'In the shit, but we may still be able to wriggle out of it. The murder happened two or three hours after Richard left her. That's what I'm going to have to prove.'

'But didn't that bloody woman who lives next door say that she saw him leave the house at four o'clock, around the time Joyce Carter was supposed to have died?'

'I'm working on that.'

Amanda noticed that John Nemrac was studying her closely. She realised that he had been wondering whether she would want to continue with the fight, to carry on in her support for Richard.

The man did not understand yet, she thought. Richard might be a pathetic excuse for a husband, but that was not the point. There was nothing pathetic about the life they had created together, not in her opinion anyway, and that was what she was fighting for.

Amanda returned his gaze, almost challengingly. She was wearing a short straight dress which had ridden up over her thighs when she sat down. She was well aware of this and of the effect her long elegant legs, which she now crossed provocatively, were inclined to have on men. For an instant she wondered disloyally how her life would have been had she married a man like John Nemrac. What a team they'd have made.

She cursed her husband's weakness. It was a reflex action, really, for Amanda to stand by him. She had not even fully considered the position she and Richard would be in even if he were cleared. There would be a shadow over them for the rest of their lives, she knew that. And it had already occurred to her that the knighthood she had dreamed of for Richard, and indeed more or less expected sooner or later, would now never be any more than that – just a dream. But she had not dared consider the further consequences.

John Nemrac was smiling at her. Invitingly, she thought.

He touched her hair, fleetingly.

'You're some woman,' he said.

She smiled back. Lips slightly parted.

'More champagne?' he asked.

She considered. He was not particularly physically attractive, he was definitely overweight, but there was something quite charismatic about him. She felt his eyes all over her, appraising, interested. She knew he had a room upstairs.

'No thank you,' she said. 'We both have work to do, don't we.'

On the way home she went over in her mind the interlude with John Nemrac and what he had told her about Richard. She was actually more upset by it than she had let on, which was one of the reasons why she could not have stayed with Nemrac, she didn't think, even if he had asked her. In any case George Brooks was driving her, and she knew he had a low enough opinion of her already.

At Landacre all was quiet. She unlocked the front door and slammed it shut behind her.

He was waiting for her in the kitchen, methodically tipping backwards and forwards in the old rocking chair. He was playing with a ball of kitchen string, tossing it casually from one hand to the other.

'Why have you been avoiding me?' he asked. 'Why didn't you answer my calls?'

She was startled. 'How did you get in?'

'The door at the back was open. You really should be more security conscious.'

He smiled at her. The hairs on the back of her neck bristled. She remembered vividly the last time, the only time, they had been together. Harry Pearson was a rare man. He understood what she needed sexually, which Richard never had. Maybe no other man ever had.

She struggled for control.

'I haven't got time for this now, I have to concentrate on Richard. I have to.'

Harry stood up and walked across the room to her. Without warning he kissed her very hard on the lips. He used his teeth, biting the soft inner flesh of her mouth. The pain was sharp and acute. She tasted the saltiness of her own blood. A gasp rose in her throat.

He stood back and looked at her. She could already see the triumph in him. His voice was husky when he spoke again.

'You can still feel it, can't you?' he asked.

'I don't know what you're talking about,' she said.

He reached out with both hands and caught hold of the sleeves of her dress. Tensing the muscles in his shoulders he wrenched the flimsy material apart. The dress split right down the front. Then he tore her underwear off her so fast she would not have had time to protest even if she had wanted to.

Roughly he pushed her on to the kitchen table. She felt his teeth on her breasts, his finger nails dig into her buttocks. With the pain came the pleasure.

He understood the balance. That was what she had been remembering, he was right about that. She was excited from her confrontation with John Nemrac. She was both wearied and disgusted by her husband. She could not control what was happening inside her.

She began to move with him. She wrapped her hands around his neck, her fingers digging into him, ripping his flesh.

He slapped her face twice. Light but stinging blows. Then he caught hold of her wrists one by one and tied them with the kitchen string to the legs of the table. She did not protest. Only when she was quite securely bound, lying spread-eagled, did he continue. And it was more spectacular even than before. With this man she could totally let go.

In the distance she heard herself screaming. And the more she came the more she screamed.

When they had both finished he stood looking down at her, elated as if in victory.

'Do you really need him, now that you can have me?' he asked. And he didn't seem to notice the change in her expression.

'Untie me,' she instructed. He did so. Roughly.

'Why don't you forget about that apology for a husband?'

He ran a finger nail tantalisingly across her naked belly, scratching just enough to leave behind a fine red line. She shivered with pleasure.

None the less, Harry Pearson had just made a big mistake.

'I value my marriage,' she said coolly. 'Nothing between you and me has any bearing on my relationship with Richard.'

'Let him rot in jail. And every night I'll come to

you and take you to a kind of heaven.'

'You're talking nonsense, Harry,' she responded. She had needed the frenetic excitement he so ably aroused in her, she had needed the release of orgasm, something she was finding increasingly difficult to achieve, but that was over now. She was the ice maiden once more.

'I don't think we'd better do this again,' she said sweetly.

He did not answer. Silently he fastened his trousers, which he had not bothered to remove, picked up his jacket and left the house.

Nineteen

By early May the bleakness of the moorland around Landacre had burst into life. The gorse had blossomed into its full iron-yellow splendour already and mingled with freshly blooming wild flowers to give brilliant colour to the rolling hills. Fox cubs, deceptively cuddly, were opening their eyes to a bright new world, the rigours of winter and the blind fear of the hunt both unknown things a joyous lifetime ahead. The red deer were also bearing their young and the great Exmoor stags proudly marshalled their growing herds. The migrating birds were back. The ponies, some with recently arrived foals teetering alongside on spindly legs, were beginning to shed their rough winter fur in favour of a glossy summer coat. The grass was growing. There was food again. The moors would soon be a larder of fruit and vegetation and, of course, meat. The hedgehogs and dormice, and all the creatures that seek to sleep the winter away, were coming out of hibernation.

This was the time of rebirth, every countryman's favourite season. Richard Corrington, however, was not free to enjoy it. He remained locked up in Exeter jail, the small window of his cell looking ominously across to the towering old castle which housed the Crown Court where he would eventually stand trial for murder.

The police case against him was a devastatingly

simple one. It was also quite extraordinary. Backed up by considerable incriminating evidence they sought to prove that Richard Corrington was guilty of murder, having slipped into the personality of his television hit man Jack Sparrow.

And from the moment the concept began to form itself in his mind, Todd Mallett realised that it was beyond his powers of reason to accept that anyone could portray through 176 hours of television a character as clinically brutal and as prolific in dispensing death as Sparrow without being affected by it.

It was now his job to convince a court of law of that. The forensic evidence which now proved beyond doubt that Richard had been at Joyce Carter's house not long before she died, and that he had had sex with her, was particularly strong.

One way and another Todd had every reason to be confident that Richard Corrington would be successfully tried and found guilty of Joyce's murder

Certainly the committal proceedings at least – at Exeter and Wonford Magistrates Court, where the bench was asked to send Richard for trial by jury as the law required with a crime as serious as murder – were, as had been expected, a brief formality because the defence accepted that there was a case to answer.

There was, however, something happening many miles away, and in no way directly relating to the Corrington case, which threatened to tip the balance in the actor's favour.

On Wednesday May 6th, on a blazing spring afternoon exactly six weeks after the actor was charged and just the day after he was committed for trial, parliament prepared to vote on a Private Member's

Bill which would change the entire face of British justice.

The Bill called for England and Wales to follow America's example and allow, for a provisional period of twelve months, live television coverage of court proceedings.

The matter had been the subject of deliberation for years – there had been an earlier Private Members' Bill which had run out of parliamentary time in 1991 – and there were strong feelings on both sides.

But, not for the first time in its history, parliament took a course of action which was largely unexpected and certainly did not reflect the wishes of most of the people whom it would directly concern.

The Private Members' Bill was passed by a small but adequate majority. And the act allowing television coverage of court proceedings would come into force just before the start of the trial of Richard Corrington, which was scheduled for mid October 1998.

The actor's trial would almost certainly be the first to be broadcast live from a British court, which was certain to transform the proceedings into even more of a media circus than it was already destined to be. In fact it would surely be a television spectacular on a Hollywood scale.

Richard's barrister had been in his office half listening to the debate on the radio while sorting through various papers. John Nemrac was interested only in the result, and could barely resist a small whoop of satisfaction when the vote was announced.

Ever the showman, he rather looked forward to the television experience, not only in this trial but for the rest of his career. But, most importantly at present, he was quite sure that the chances of success in his current major trial had been suddenly increased dramatically. Every TV station on air would want to cover the case of Richard Corrington superstar on a murder charge – and in the opinion of John Nemrac nothing would suit his client better than the sight of a TV camera in the courtroom.

In his bed-sit just off the Old Kent Road, Jacky Starr had also heard the news about the change in the law. And that night he watched a documentary which discussed the difference allowing cameras into courtrooms would make and how this would almost certainly work to the advantage of celebrities on trial – as it undoubtedly had in America in the case of O. J. Simpson. The programme also speculated that the Richard Corrington trial would be one of the first to be televised in the UK, and concluded that the accused actor could only benefit from this.

Jacky Starr had watched every minute that he could of the O. J. Simpson trial. He had been fascinated by it. He had also formulated his own idea on whether or not O. J. was guilty and the effect of the TV cameras on the case.

He felt that he knew exactly what would happen to Richard Corrington. He had no doubt about the actor's guilt – it all fitted in so neatly with what he himself knew about Joyce's activities during the last days of her life. And the man who murdered Joyce was not going to get a proper trial now, Jacky was sure of it. The bastard was going to walk free.

Jacky switched off the television. There was no other light on in the room. He sat quietly in silence for several minutes. Joyce's death and the manner of it had left him emotionally vulnerable. Unstable almost. He knew that, but his reactions were somehow beyond his control.

In the six weeks since her death he had lived in a dream world. He had continued to work in his usual spasmodically frenzied fashion. Indeed the sheer physical effort of his job at the National was the one activity which seemed to give him solace, take his mind off what had happened – that and the dope he was smoking more and more of. He was aware that he was overdoing it, but he didn't really care.

He had not seen his mother since his release from jail, and although he knew he had been a bit harsh with her in Exeter – after all she had come to his aid when he had so desperately needed her – had not felt he could cope with her. Their relationship was so strained, so steeped in its own sorry history. She had written and phoned several times. He had ignored her letters and her messages and had once even put the phone down on her.

But the news he had heard that night had made him suddenly very emotional. He hated Richard Corrington. He grieved for Joyce. And in the depths of his misery there lurked a need for some warmth, maybe even some love. He realised he did not want any more sorrow and bitterness in his life. He thought the time had maybe come to make his peace with Belle. He switched on the lights, picked up the phone and began to dial her number, but then half way through replaced the receiver in its cradle.

It was still too soon.

Todd Mallett's reaction to the televising of court cases had been just as desolate as Jacky Starr's. He couldn't believe his luck. Bad enough that it was being allowed at all, but the real kick in the teeth was that the Richard Corrington murder case seemed set to be the first on the new television courtroom schedule.

Todd had been studying the actor and his wife for weeks now. He had seen their shock reactions on the night of the arrest. He had watched Amanda Lane throw a fit of hysterics in the hallway of Landacre when he had turned up there with his dawn search party. And just four hours later she had arrived at Heavitree Road – in complete control. Her husband's recovery took a little longer. But by the time he had appeared in court to make his plea all except the very closest observer would have considered him a man remarkably at ease in appalling circumstances.

There was no doubt about it. The Corringtons were wonderful performers and they were going to be sheer magic on the box. He on the other hand would seem wooden and dull and keep saying the wrong thing. He had watched himself on television before. It was not a pleasant experience, and one which he did his best to repeat as infrequently as possible. Now he was threatened by hour after hour of it. Like a lot of the best cops he had never been all that comfortable giving evidence – his skills were in the field tracking down criminals and putting a case together – and the thought of having to do so with a TV camera directed at him sent a shiver down his spine.

He also considered the spectacle of the Crown prosecution counsel up against the practised show-manship of John Nemrac. Nemrac was in another class, a man who worked a courtroom like the theatre he obviously half considered it to be. Todd reckoned Nemrac was going to just love playing to a wider audience. And the *Daily Telegraph* had that morning predicted that if the Richard Corrington trial was the first to be televised, as expected, it would rake in audiences of around 25 million in Britain alone – far bigger than the *Sparrow-Hawk* series itself.

Todd sighed. He imagined dolefully that John Nemrac was probably already rehearsing – and he wasn't far wrong.

Twenty

It had to happen. He had to come to her in the end.

She picked him up at the little suburban station half a mile from her home. He had told her on the phone that he was going to be in London for a couple of days making further investigations into the Ruth Macintosh murder, and had asked if they could meet up. She had offered him a bed for the night – in her spare room of course – and although he had accepted readily she had afterwards feared that she may have seemed too eager.

As he walked towards her she could see little beads of sweat gleaming on his forehead. It was a warm and sultry June evening and he was wearing an unseasonably heavy tweed jacket over dark grey flannels. None the less, she wondered if it was only the heat of the day that was making him sweat, or if he felt as nervous and yet as expectant as she did.

He was carrying a brown leather briefcase with a broken handle in one hand and an overnight bag in the other. He looked even bigger and more solid than she had remembered. He might just as well be in uniform. Todd Mallett could never be anything other than a policeman, not in a million years. The sight of him made Arabella chuckle. He really was not going to be good for her image, this man – and yet she knew her pulse was racing.

He stood before her now, beaming, put down bag

and briefcase, and looked for a moment as if he were going to envelop her in a big bear hug. At the last second he let his hands hang loosely by his side, leaned forward and kissed her lightly on one cheek.

'Good to see you, so good . . .' He sounded quite shy.

On his instructions she had booked a local restaurant, an Italian, for dinner. It was, he insisted, his treat. And the evening began brilliantly. Todd was warm and witty and had considerable natural charm, which seemed to her to be almost enhanced by his slight clumsiness.

'God, I've been looking forward to this,' he said.

She could hear the excitement in his voice and was aware that he took every opportunity to touch her, his knee casually resting against hers beneath the table, his hand brushing hers as he poured the wine.

She began to feel more and more aroused by him. They drank a lot of Chianti and then started on the grappa. She was not sure if it was the nervousness, or even because she was beginning to feel so sexy, but she was downing the grappa too fast. She knew it, yet didn't seem able to stop. She was also talking too much. And she couldn't stop that either.

It was probably inevitable that they should stray on to the subject of the Richard Corrington murder case.

'You know,' she said eventually, 'I can't believe Ricky did it, Todd, I really can't.'

Todd had explained to her his thesis on the *Sparrow-Hawk* killings, and Arabella could not imagine any actor taking on the persona of a character he portrayed, let alone one so violent as Jack Sparrow. She failed to see that it was what she had spent her entire life doing

– although, indeed, in her case it was rather more the other way around, because the characters she played were invariably just extensions of her own personality.

'Really.'

If it hadn't been for the excess of grappa, Arabella might have noticed the sudden coolness in Todd's voice, and been warned off. As it was she guilelessly continued.

'If actors went out killing people in real life just because they do it on film there'd be an awful lot of murders about,' she rattled on. "'E's a berk, that Ricky Corrington – but 'e's no killer . . .'

It occurred to her that if Todd was as affected by the grappa as she was, he was giving little sign of it.

There was a chilling pause. 'We do have some evidence as well, Arabella,' said Todd.

Now she could not help but be aware of the sudden coldness in his voice and the use of her full name instead of the familiar, and somehow so much more friendly, Belle. But not being able to shut up had always been one of her failings.

'It's somebody copying Sparrow-Hawk, it's got to be, it's some kind of stalker . . . I mean, what hard evidence have you got on Richard, then?'

'I am sorry, I really can't discuss this with you any more, Arabella. I've said far too much already. A man has been charged with murder.'

'I know, but surely you can tell me . . .'

His leg was no longer resting against hers. The big hands were in his lap, no longer seeking to touch her.

She tried to put it right. 'I'm sorry, Todd. Really. You're the expert. I've always had a big mouth.'

She touched his shoulder. Seeking a return to the intimacy of a few moments earlier.

He smiled, a bit forced though, she thought.

'I'm sorry too,' he said. 'You put everything into a murder inquiry, you know. You get a bit touchy when someone tells you you've got it all wrong.'

'Put it down to the grappa.' She hadn't even wanted to talk about Richard Corrington in the first place. All she really wanted was to get close to this big, comforting man, to feel his arms around her.

'Let's get you home,' he said, as if reading her mind.

They took a taxi back to her house. She led him into the sitting room and made him coffee. He refused another drink. She sat down by his side on the sofa, aware of the tension remaining in him.

'Can we just concentrate on us?' she said.

'I was hoping so.'

He kissed her. Properly this time. Full on the lips. He had smoked his pipe after dinner, confessing that, hard as he had fought against it, he had fallen totally back into the habit. He tasted of tobacco, which normally she hated. With him it was somehow all right.

She tried to relax as his tongue tentatively began to explore her mouth, but she too was not finding it easy. She attempted to remember when she had last been with a man and realised it was more than a year earlier. One extreme to another, bloody typical, Belle, she thought to herself, reflecting briefly on the excesses of her younger days.

She felt his hands move lightly over her body, his fingers beginning to explore her breasts. He sighed involuntarily and she moved her head away slightly so that she could look at him. His eyes were shut. She wondered what he was thinking. He was very gentle. Surprisingly so for such a big man.

'Am I really sleeping in the spare room?' he asked suddenly.

She giggled. 'Is there somewhere else you'd rather sleep?' she asked.

By answer he kissed her again, slowly, longingly. Her body was beginning to remember what to do. The kiss went on for a very long time, his arms clasped tightly around her and his hands quite still now, holding her. She loosened his tie and began to unbutton his shirt. She really wanted him now. Her fingers sought him out, reaching for the zip to his trousers.

Very slightly he drew away. 'Let's take our time,' he murmured.

Once more he started to kiss her, to stroke her. She unbuttoned her own blouse, felt for the catch of her bra. And, just as she had hoped, he dropped his lips to her breasts. The roughness of his chin added to her excitement. When he covered her nipples with his mouth her desire for him became out of control.

It had been so long. She could not restrain herself. Her need to touch him was suddenly urgent. She tore at his trousers, blurted out what she wanted him to do to her, her voice husky and demanding.

But almost abruptly he pushed her away and stood up.

'I'm sorry, it doesn't feel right,' he said. He spoke gently, but he sounded firm, as if he had made a very definite decision.

She sat panting, half naked to the waist, bewildered.

'What's wrong?' she asked.

'I'm sorry,' he said again. 'It's my fault. I thought I could, but I can't.'

Feeling suddenly ridiculous, that she had made a

fool of herself, Belle scrabbled to button up her blouse.

'It's OK, I understand,' she said, in a voice which clearly indicated that she didn't.

She wished fervently now that she had not drunk so much grappa. She wasn't able to think clearly.

Todd looked uncertain what to do or say next. 'Well, I've got an early start, so I'll see you in the morning,' he said eventually.

She watched him leave the room, and wondered if there was ever a time in life when rejection became any easier or any more comprehensible. It had all been so lovely, so warm, so sexy. She wondered also if her remarks in the restaurant were still offending him, although he had seemed eager enough when he had first kissed her.

It was several minutes before she followed him into the hall and up the stairs. There was a light on in the guest room. The door was firmly shut. She took a step towards it, her hand almost reaching the handle. Then she stopped.

For a few seconds she stood looking at the closed door, but she could not take any more humiliation. She made her way forlornly to her own room, and went to bed. Alone.

Todd left Arabella's house at 6 a.m., while she was still in bed. He had not slept well. He felt drained. He still longed for her. He wished he hadn't behaved so stupidly.

More than anything in the world the previous night he had wanted to make love to Belle. Yet the more willing and eager she had become the less he had seemed able to respond. She had overwhelmed him.

In his mind he had wanted her so much, and yet he had become starkly aware that his body was going to let him down. He had not felt even the stirring of an erection, and that was something that had never happened to him before, not even with his wife long after he had ceased to have any true sexual desire for her.

Todd was an old-fashioned macho man. It was totally against his nature to allow Arabella to become aware of the problem, and he had feared that if he had let things go any further between them he would just have ended up being horribly humiliated. And so he had backed off, unthinking of the humiliation his apparent rejection of her would cause Belle. Absurd, he supposed, and probably quite incomprehensible to her.

As he walked towards the station on an already bright and sunny morning he could not believe that he hadn't simply told her the truth. For whatever complex reasons he had known he was not going to be able to perform, but she would have understood, he was sure of that. Their relationship, whatever was left of it, was not based on his having to prove that he was some kind of superstud, he knew that. And by behaving in the way that he had, he had merely left her hurt and confused, he assumed. There had been magic between them again, and he had destroyed it with his own idiocy.

He had scribbled an inadequate note which he had left on the table in the hall. 'I'll call you. Thanks for the bed.'

Now all he had to do was to put her and everything about her out of his mind, because he did not see how he could hope to resurrect the flame between them after the way he had behaved to her.

However, when he switched his attentions to the case in hand, it was Belle's instinctive belief in Corrington's innocence which dominated his thinking. And he realised for the first time that there was just the smallest element of doubt nagging away within him.

He spent the day at West End Central where, although even more zealous than usual in his endeavours, he unearthed nothing that took his case any further. Todd talked at length to the London DCI in charge of the Ruth Macintosh case, going over every possible point, trying desperately to come up with something which might help, which was maybe not included in the information he already had.

His lack of progress depressed him. He still felt uneasy on his return to Exeter, and was well aware that a lot of this was down to Arabella Parker.

At Heavitree Road first thing the following morning he talked to DI Cutler.

'We have thoroughly checked the stalker angle, haven't we?' he asked.

'Of course, boss,' replied the inspector, looking surprised. 'We've had three teams on it ever since the *Sparrow-Hawk* business first came to light. Nobody knows of anything like that, not for years and years anyway. Not since that actor who caused a bit of bother in the very beginning. I told you about him.'

'Tell me again,' instructed Todd.

Cutler, as Todd had hoped, was able to do so off the top of his head, reciting the information in his precise deadpan way. 'His name was Martin Viner and he starred in an ill-fated pilot of *Sparrow-Hawk* which was made almost five years before the series was eventually launched. It was never shown – some say because the script was lousy and the character not properly developed and others that Viner made a balls of it. Either way, the ITV network wouldn't screen it.

'When they resurrected the show with Corrington and it was such a huge hit, Viner took umbrage and launched a campaign. He turned up at the studio to protest and even tried to take legal action, but, of course, the TV company had its contracts well sorted and he didn't have a leg to stand on. He gave it all up fairly quickly.

'Anyway, he's dead, boss, if you remember. Quite a story. He'd been a stunt man first, and after *Sparrow-Hawk* went wrong for him he went back to it. Couldn't seem to get any more acting work. There was an accident on a film set, a stunt that went wrong, he was crippled, and had to go into a nursing home. Then there was a fire in the home. He died along with several others. Tragic. But no doubt about it.'

Todd grunted his acknowledgement. 'And there is nothing else at all? I want to be really sure nothing turns around and bites us on this one.'

'Nothing, boss. We are still working on it, and we even have a team going through all the *Sparrow-Hawk* and Richard Corrington fan mail – but so far there has been nothing out of the ordinary.'

Todd grunted again and dismissed the inspector. He checked his messages. Bruce Macintosh had called to say he had now contacted everyone he could think of who had been close to his wife – and none of them knew of anything which might connect her with Richard Corrington or with the *Sparrow-Hawk* programme.

Well, that had always been a long shot. Todd's head ached. He told himself there was nothing wrong with his case, it was just the prospect of Court TV that was bugging him.

He decided that what he needed was an extremely large drink. In fact a succession of extremely large drinks. He packed away his papers, locked his desk, and left the station at the unprecedentedly early hour, for him, of just on five o'clock. He had made a quite calculated decision to drown his sorrows in alcohol. It was not something he often did, but when he did do it, he did the job thoroughly. For a start he always went on a bender the serious way – alone – and he kept drinking until he virtually could not stand any more. On this occasion the more he drank the angrier he became. He was hoping at least that the hangover he was sure to suffer the following morning would be so acute that it would keep any other pain at bay, but at the moment he had merely reached the stage where he was beside himself with rage. Never mind the alcohol, he knew he did not think well when he lost his temper but he couldn't help it. Honest men often can't. He had painstakingly built a case which he considered to be good and strong, but now, with the Crown Court trial set for mid October, he feared that all the hard work he and his people had put in might be to no avail. This trial was going to be all about showmanship, and that was not one of Todd Mallett's strengths.

'Justice my left fuckin' foot,' he muttered to himself out loud, fortunately in a voice so distorted that nobody else could understand a word he was saying.

'There he is, the biggest effin' star on TV, and TV is his effin' judge and jury. 'Why do I effin' bother?'

He was slumped over the bar in a pub he had never before been in, and had no intention of ever revisiting. He was, after all, a detective chief inspector. He did not want to meet anyone he knew, and this dismal bar, with its damaged furniture covered in greasy-looking dark red plastic, was an understandably unpopular place, inhabited only by sad drunks. Like me, he thought to himself morosely. The pub was called The Merry Ploughman although it seemed unlikely that much merriment had occurred there for many years or any ploughing for that matter, Todd thought obscurely, as the pub was situated in a distinctly urban Exeter backstreet. One way and another the noticeably un-Merry Ploughman thoroughly suited his mood.

Todd sighed heavily into his beer. He was drinking pints of bitter with whisky chasers, a potent mixture. The glum thought crossed the haziness of his mind that he had better make the most of it, because his chances of getting blind drunk unnoticed in any bar after The Trial of the Century began and his reluctant features had been emblazoned across TV screens throughout the nation, seemed pretty slim.

The story was so juicy that already the newspapers were playing every game they could possibly get away with; and it seemed to Todd at that moment, as he gazed gloomily at his bleary-eyed reflection in the mirror running along the back of the bar, that he and his team were probably the only people in the world who believed Richard Corrington was guilty. Even Belle Parker thought he was wrong. And that had been a real slap in the face.

In spite of all his good intentions he was not able to put her out of his mind.

*

He held back for two weeks before he phoned her, his desire to speak to her again ultimately overcoming his embarrassment. She had not called him, which he thought was hardly surprising. She was friendly enough at first, and had responded quite eagerly when he opened the conversation with the topic which he had partially used as an excuse to himself for calling. She was, after all, an actress who had been in the business a long time, so it was worth a try.

'Did you ever know an actor called Martin Viner?' he asked.

'Oh yeah, Mad Martin we used to call him, quite barking,' she replied.

He smiled. 'Madder than actors usually are?'

'Much. I suppose you want to know about him because of that ill-fated *Sparrow-Hawk* pilot, which was actually the ultimate example of how crazy he was.

'He lived and breathed it, he was obsessed with Sparrow. He was ex-army, trained in unarmed combat by the SAS, he claimed. Obsessed with that, he was. He started in the business as a stunt man so he was always telling the stunt guys on the show what to do.

'He was another arrogant bastard. I did a TV chat show with him once when he decided for some reason to try to make the interviewer look a fool. He had this thing that he was the only real professional in the business – problem was, he ended up making himself look a fool.

'It was being dropped as Sparrow-Hawk that sent him right over the top, of course, but then I assume you know about that.'

Todd confirmed that he did.

'Bet you didn't know that I played his wife in the pilot?'

Todd was intrigued. 'No, I didn't,' he said.

'Yep. And after it went wrong the big-headed bleeder made it quite clear that he considered it to be all my fault. In a funny way he may have been half right, actually, because Jack Sparrow should never have been given a wife. It was ridiculous.'

Todd remained silent, thoughtful.

'I can guess what you're thinking, but he's dead. A fire. I remember reading about it at the time.'

'I know,' said Todd.

'Anyway, I thought you were absolutely sure about Ricky.'

'I am.'

'Well, there you are then.'

'But you don't agree, do you?'

'I am not privy to your evidence,' she said, obliquely reminding him of his curtness when they had been together in London.

He changed the subject. The sound of her voice brought back all the memories, the promise there had been between them. He had told himself that he quite obviously could not cope with a woman like Belle Parker right now. He was under too much pressure, he was still an emotional mess – and a physical one too, it seemed – and in any case she probably wanted nothing more to do with him. But none of this could stop him. Suddenly he heard himself ask her if he should try to visit her again, or perhaps she would like to visit him?

'I've got a few problems at the moment, Todd, love,' she said. 'Let's leave it for a bit, shall we . . .'

The easy friendliness had gone. She sounded

distant, almost aloof. He assumed he had offended her much more than he had realised when he had stayed with her in Essex and that she was putting him off. The disappointment was a leaden weight inside him.

He did not call her any more. He could not face the rejection. And again she made no attempt to contact him.

It was not until a month before the trial that he picked up the *Sun* to be confronted by a story which made him realise she may have had her own reasons all along for not wanting to see him.

Belle Parker had been sued for bankruptcy.

At once he tried to phone her, but the Essex number was unobtainable. Quite possibly she had been forced to move out. There must have been numerous ways he could have got in touch with her, found her again, but somehow he had not had the energy. And he was still frightened of a rebuff.

As the Richard Corrington trial approached Todd became more and more overwhelmed by nervous tension. He had an impending sense of doom about it all, and about his apparently now stagnant relationship with Belle. It seemed to him that every part of his life was suddenly a disaster area.

Twenty-One

The trial of Richard Corrington, due to start on October 19th, 1998, was set to be the biggest event in British media history. Two weeks before, Jacky Starr sat alone and only very slightly stoned in his Kennington bed-sit contemplating the part he had to play.

Jacky, as the finder of the body, had been called as a material witness at the trial. He was not looking forward to it. He still did not believe he would see justice done, although he was beginning to be more philosophical about it. Time was just beginning to heal his hurt. None the less, and in spite of the cavalier way in which she had so often behaved towards him, Joyce's death had left a bigger hole in his life than he would ever have dreamed possible. He continued to fill it, in as much as he could, by working more shifts than usual at the National Theatre and indulging in all the one night sexual stands which came his way. His need for sex – as raunchy as you like, and he had always found it exciting to wake in the morning alongside a woman whose name he could not quite remember – had not abated a jot, but he had no desire at all for any kind of relationship.

Flushed with his expanded wages he had a few weeks earlier called his mother and arranged to visit her to pay her back the money he had borrowed for his train fare from Exeter all those months previously. She had sounded surprised. Jacky had surprised himself a bit too. It wasn't just that he wanted to pay her back, he also found that he rather wanted to see her again. He had at last felt ready for her.

'Come on over, love,' his mother had invited, adding, rather curiously it seemed to him then, 'after all, it might be your last chance . . .'

And when he had returned her £40 she had used the occasion as an opportunity to explain that she faced a bankruptcy order and to turn it into as much of a joke as she could possibly muster.

'I'm grateful for this, Jacky love, might keep me off the street for another day or two after all . . .'

Jacky, who had always considered his mother to be totally invulnerable, was astonished.

'You're really going to have to lose this place?' he asked incredulously.

She nodded.

'Where will you go?'

'Well,' she looked at him quizzically, 'there's this little flat in docklands. Limehouse. It's in your name, actually.'

He was even more astonished.

'I bought it in the good times and I was going to give it you for your twenty-first, but I got selfish – I already suspected I was probably going to need it. It's yours really. You can kick me out if you want.' She said it lightly, as if it were another joke, but perhaps nervously too. 'Or come and live there too, if you like.'

Jacky declined both options. The concept of kicking anybody out of a property he had not until a few minutes ago even known that he owned was beyond his comprehension – but living with his mother was going too far.

Yet he now felt a certain warmth for her, at least

greater than ever before. So it was not quite so unexpected as it might otherwise have been that when he learned that he had to appear in court, and realised how uneasy he felt about it, it was his mother again to whom he turned.

'Of course, I'll come to Exeter with you,' she had responded delightedly when he phoned.

She sounded so enthusiastic. 'Steady on,' he said. 'It mightn't be that much fun . . .'

She was immediately apologetic. 'God, I'm behaving as if you were taking me on a bleedin' seaside outing,' she said. But she was still bubbling over.

'It's just that I can't ever remember you asking me to go anywhere with you before, Jacky, love. We'll book into a hotel, somewhere modest I'm afraid, will that be OK?'

He replied that it would be quite OK, and she was to remember that he would be on Crown expenses.

She had laughed.

'Do you want me to drive us?' she asked.

'Have you still got the Jag then?'

'To be parked only in hidden places,' she said.

She put the phone down, smiling, then immediately picked up the receiver again and began dialling the number of Heavitree Road police station. Her thoughts had instantly turned to Todd. She had not allowed herself to contact him since their last rather unsatisfactory telephone conversation, partly because she did not want to inflict her own dire financial situation on anybody else – preferring as ever to keep her worries to herself – and partly because of what had happened between her and Todd when they had been together at her home.

Now she told herself that this was fate. After all she was going to Exeter with her son. But as the number began to ring the doubt and uncertainty came flooding back. Abruptly she disconnected the line.

Her gut feeling was that Todd Mallett considered it to be pure folly to continue his relationship with her. She knew he was greatly attracted to her, but she suspected that he was fighting it as hard as he could. It was obvious that he had grave misgivings about Jacky, and about her too, no doubt.

She still hoped that one day she and Todd would get together. Something had passed between them from that very first meeting which was too rare and special to ignore, but she felt that the timing remained wrong for them.

Everything that there had been between them had in some way been intrinsically linked to the murder of Joyce Carter and the trial of Richard Corrington.

And Belle suddenly realised with total clarity that there could be nothing further between her and Todd until that trial was over and the file on the murder finally closed.

Then? She sat down in a particularly comfortable chair, closed her eyes, and let her imagination run riot . . .

On the very eve of the court case Amanda Lane was enjoying an American-style power shower, letting the jets of water engulf her, preparing for the day to follow.

When she stepped out of the shower Harry Pearson was standing there. She was startled. None the less the now familiar tingling sensation began immediately at the base of her spine. She had been with him only twice, she really had not intended to see him again after she had dismissed him so abruptly the last time, more than six months ago – and yet her body had badly missed his particular attentions.

On two or three occasions since she had given in to temptation and tried to contact him. But it had been his turn to ignore her calls . . .

'Hello Harry,' she said. She made no attempt to cover her nakedness, or to dry herself. She noticed that he had one hand inside his trousers and was breathing heavily, and she realised that he must have been watching her through the glass door of the shower compartment.

'How did you get in . . .' she began.

She was dripping wet and slippery from the shower, but he grabbed her firmly around the waist and threw her face down over the edge of the cast iron Victorian-style bath. The ridged edge dug into her belly. He used one hand to jerk her legs apart and, without even bothering to speak, thrust himself violently into her.

It was over quickly. She had no chance at all of reaching an orgasm.

He withdrew from her as carelessly as he had entered her, zipped up his trousers, and leaned against the bathroom wall watching, as, with some difficulty, she hoisted herself upright.

There were red marks across her stomach. This time it had been all pain, there had been no time for the pleasure. And yet it had made her want him so much.

He still had not spoken. Half smiling he turned his back on her as if he were going to leave.

'Don't go,' she begged him. 'I want . . . I want more . . .'

He laughed, reached out and drew her to him roughly, squeezing her far too tightly. She gasped.

'You like danger, don't you?' he murmured.

'I need you. I'm sorry about before . . .' she said.

'Damn right you need me. If you upset me again, I'll tell . . .'

He began to use his fingers on her. The excitement was beginning to overwhelm her.

'Tell what?' she asked, none the less.

'Tell how you asked me to lie for you about the afternoon Joyce Carter was killed, to lie that we met four hours before we really did.'

His eyes bore into her. With his free hand he pushed her left arm behind her back, wrenching it upwards so that her whole body jack-knifed. She cried out.

'It just seemed easier . . .' she said.

He leaned forward and bit her neck. Hard. She suspected he had drawn blood. Obscurely the thought crossed her mind that she would have to wear a high-necked blouse in court the next day.

'You're just going to have to do everything that I want now,' he whispered in her ear, taking the lobe between his teeth. 'Everything . . .'

He hooked one leg behind her knees and she fell heavily backwards on to the tiled floor. She cracked an elbow. Her back hurt.

He lowered himself on top of her, pressing his mouth on to hers, using his teeth again. She tasted her own blood. His weight was crushing her. She could feel that he was already erect once more.

This time she climaxed as soon as he entered her.

PART TWO

Ricky Darling

Dance your dance
Ricky darling,
Let's see you prance
Ricky darling.

You may ache
You may weep
You may be
In a deep sleep,
Your brain may shake,
Your heart may break,
You may cry to be free.
But never
As long as you have breath,
Never
Until stopped short by death,
Never ever
Will you let the act drop,
Ricky darling.

Twenty-Two

If the setting for England's first televised court case had been hand-picked, it could not have been better chosen. Exeter Crown Court, built within the great walls of Exeter Castle which dates back to Roman times, is spectacularly atmospheric.

The castle is set on a hill top, once known as Ruge Mont and after which the nearby Rougemont Hotel is named, and its sole approach is from a narrow city street leading steeply upwards to a forbidding iron portcullis, which forms the only entrance. Within the crumbling red-brown walls, virtually all that remains of the original fortification, is a courtyard area now used as a car park and vaguely reminiscent – somewhat appropriately in its new role as a TV location – of a Roman amphitheatre.

It was here, on a windswept autumn day, that, locked in a sealed vehicle accompanied, as usual nowadays, by private agency security staff, Richard Corrington was brought to stand trial for murder. His prosecution was, by now, huge international news, and press photographers from all over the world lined the approach road – somewhat irritated at being kept outside the portcullis even though the remote control cameras of the newly formed Court TV UK were set up ready for operation inside the court.

When he clambered out of the van Richard – again handcuffed to a guard – could not help remembering the history of the place as related to him endlessly by the jail's resident scholar while he had been held on remand in Devon County Prison. In medieval times the courtyard had contained a pit in which prisoners were held until they stood trial, women to one side and men to the other. The bodies of those who were hanged, which was most of them in an age when even minor theft was a capital offence, were buried to the left of the courtyard as you face away from the portcullis – all around the spot where a statue of a famous Lord Lieutenant of Devon, Hugh Earl Fortescue, now stood. Richard shuddered involuntarily, his brief reverie intruded upon by the resounding chorus of shouts from the cameramen outside the gates, and some, he noticed, who had climbed on top of the ancient walls.

'Ricky, Ricky!'

'Over here, Ricky!'

'Look this way, Ricky!'

Richard squared his shoulders and set his chin – he was clean shaven again now, his barrister having explained that he wanted to make the most of his television superstar image, the trial was going to be a TV show after all. This, Richard knew, was where the performance must begin.

An assault force of 500-millimetre and even some giant 1,000 mm. lenses, set up on monopod supports, were wielded expertly by masters in their craft, bringing him sharply into close focus. The metallic hum of a multitude of motor drives, capturing a staggering six frames a second, merged into a throbbing cacophony known in the trade as The Nikon Choir. And as he disappeared inside the courthouse Richard left behind the pandemonium of excited snappers, almost all armed with portable computerised picture-wiring machines, rushing to send their photographs throughout the world.

Richard was escorted to the jail in the basement of the building from which he could then be taken directly up the flight of stairs into the central dock of Number Two Court. This was the court where all Exeter's major trials were held, an awe-inspiring room, which somehow seemed to retain in its polished wood panelling and lofty ceiling all the high drama it had witnessed since its construction more than two centuries ago.

'It's like the Bailey, even the air's different in there,' Richard's jail historian had somewhat gleefully informed him. And, indeed, the actor, used to playing the world's most alarming theatres, was surprised at just how daunted he felt when he emerged into the ominous legal solemnity of Court Two.

'RIGHT AND WRONG – between whose endless jar justice resides' read the inscription facing Richard on the wall opposite the dock.

Court Two was a brightly lit room, its ceiling fitted with squares of electrically-powered illumination, giving the effect of a patchwork of skylights, and Richard emerged from the darker area below blinking slightly as his eyes adjusted to the glare. His counsel, John Nemrac, clad in traditional black gown and horse-hair wig, sat before him facing the judge's bench; the jury bench was to his right. The judge, Mr Justice Sinclair, resplendent in the red robes and white sash of the High Court, immediately and irresistibly drew Richard's attention. At the same time the actor, as was second nature to him, checked out the positioning of the remote-control operated cameras.

There were three of them, one pointing more or less straight at him in the dock, one directed at the witness box, and one pointed at the judge – all three set on pivots so that they could also focus on other areas of the court. The jury, of course, was out of bounds. Richard recalled that an early inadvertent and clearly identifiable shot of a juror during the O. J. Simpson trial had led to proceedings being temporarily halted.

He studied the judge. Mr Justice Sinclair was a man in his early sixties with, in view of the old judge's nickname of The Beak, an extremely appropriate nose. Upon this formidable projectile balanced an impressive pair of black horn-rimmed spectacles through which his eyes gleamed unforgivingly. His lips formed a thin stern line above a firmly set jaw. His head seemed rather small compared with his considerable bulk, to which the heavy red robes added even more substance, but balance was partially re-dressed by his wig, set square above a sprouting of wispy grey hair. He was in his natural element, this was his court, he exuded easy arrogance and every-thing about him led Richard to the conclusion that Mr Justice Sinclair regarded conducting England's first televised court case as the high-spot of his career. His demeanour also indicated that he considered there to be only one star of the show – himself.

Well, we'll see about that, sunshine, thought the actor who, although rather disconcerted by the judge's appearance and manner which he assumed was His Lordship's intention, was recalling John Nemrac's advice to always concentrate on the jury.

Richard made another quick check of the camera positions. He had actually been rather disappointed to learn that the proceedings would be shot by remote control – with director and production team safely isolated in a control room elsewhere in the building. The idea of a Timberland-booted film crew trundling all over the courtroom had rather appealed to him; not least because he was every bit as adept at handling and manipulating cameramen – who, with clever timing and the right angle, could make you look as good or as bad as the mood took them – as he was at handling and manipulating an audience.

From somewhere in the distance he became aware of John Nemrac looking around at him. The barrister gave a friendly reassuring wink and smile of greeting. 'Act One, Scene One,' he whispered. And when the clerk read the charge Richard had to make a conscious effort not to be still smiling as, with his usual dignified resonance, he pleaded 'Not Guilty'. John Nemrac was going to be a worthy and impressive co-star, thought the actor.

The trial lasted eleven working days, and did ample justice to its advance publicity.

The prosecution put its case fully and with care. Richard Corrington, crazed into believing that he had become his television creation Sparrow-Hawk, had killed Joyce Carter because she had set out to harm the show and its star with her vitriolic writing. There had also been an unsavoury sexual liaison between the two, which had added to Corrington's sense of betrayal.

The forensic and eye-witness evidence was meticulously set out.

It appeared to be a pretty good case. But John Nemrac was brilliantly cool. He had an answer to everything. Allegations he could not actually fully refute he made light of, and when he knew he had a strong response he laboured the point, making the most of every possible angle. Todd, giving the police evidence, as clearly and as succinctly as he could, while trying desperately to forget the TV camera pointing menacingly at him, had been the first victim of the barrister's incisive cross examination technique.

'So, Detective Chief Inspector, you are suggesting to this court that my client made a confession to murder, are you?' John Nemrac's voice was packed full of incredulity.

'Well, very nearly, sir,' Todd had replied, thinking that if the barrister had not turned up at Heavitree Road when he had, there might not have been any doubt about it.

'Very nearly,' repeated Nemrac with careful annunciation, turning theatrically for a moment toward the jury. He reverted his attentions abruptly to Todd Mallett.

'Very nearly what, exactly, Detective Chief Inspector? Very nearly a confession, or very nearly a murder?'

Several members of the jury tittered. Even the judge's lips twitched into the ghost of a smile. Todd groaned inwardly. He didn't stand a chance with this man, and he knew it.

'Very nearly a confession, sir,' said Todd, trying to sound calm and controlled.

'Really, Chief Inspector, well I put it to you that a man so publicly arrested, dragged half way across the country and interrogated in the middle of the night would "very nearly" not know what he was saying. Do you agree with that?'

'Yes' was obviously the wrong answer. 'No' was asking to be torn to shreds. He settled for: 'I really wouldn't know, sir.'

Unsurprisingly, that turned out to be very wrong.

'You really wouldn't know, Chief Inspector, and yet you have submitted a statement obtained under these circumstances to this court?'

'Yes sir.' Todd wished the floor beneath the witness stand would open and swallow him up.

'Well, it will be my submission to the jury that they should disregard a statement procured in such a manner, does that surprise you?'

It didn't surprise Todd one bit. He mumbled and stumbled some kind of reply. By the time he had finished Nemrac had moved smoothly on to his next point, turning his attention more than a little contemptuously to the whole crux of the prosecution's case.

'And do you really think, Chief Inspector, that an actor of Richard Corrington's standing is likely to be so taken over by a role he plays that he turns into a murderer?'

There was only one answer. 'Yes, I do, sir.' How pathetic it was all beginning to sound. Todd sought to add substance to his reply.

'I have watched dozens of episodes of *Sparrow-Hawk* now, sir, and quite frankly I have never before seen such gratuitous violence. Jack Sparrow is an extremely brutal anti-hero and I'd say it is quite reasonable to expect the person who portrays him to be affected by doing so.'

'Would you indeed, Mr Mallett? So, I take it you do not much like the *Sparrow-Hawk* TV series.'

'Not a lot, sir, no.'

'And you'd like it taken off the air would you?'

'I suppose I would sir, yes.' Afterwards Todd could not understand what had made him say it. He sounded stuffy, petulant and small-minded.

'I am quite sure that the members of the jury are fascinated by your views, Chief Inspector.'

The man managed to sound both sarcastic and dismissive at the same time. Todd glanced sideways at the jury – *Sparrow-Hawk* fans to a man and a woman, he expected. Well done, Todd, he thought to himself. He was cross-examined for little more than half an hour – John Nemrac always knew when to stop and never allowed a jury to become bored – but it felt like half a lifetime.

The nightmare continued after he returned to his seat. Nemrac proceeded to systematically decimate much of the key evidence for the prosecution. He had just one question for the expert witness giving the forensic evidence, the scientist Peter Conway, Todd's friend from Chepstow.

'Is it not possible that the thumb print could have been left, and the strands of material torn out from Mr Corrington's jacket during a normal physical exchange, even perhaps when he had lunch with Joyce Carter? And certainly during a sexual encounter?'

Pete Conway made no better job of his time in the witness box than had Todd. Being an expert in a given field, and Pete Conway really did know his stuff, can sometimes make people seem over-confident – patronising even. Todd had seen that happen before. Certainly Pete allowed himself to be rubbed up the wrong way by the smooth John Nemrac, and from the beginning had an unfortunate look in his eye which said quite clearly that he had seen it all before and certainly wasn't going to be bullied by the likes of Nemrac. He also made the mistake of trying to be glib.

'What, with his suit jacket on?'

Nemrac remained expressionless. 'Indeed.'

Pete made things worse by at first bristling and then rather pompously attempting to explain how improbable he thought the barrister's theory to be. His squeaky voice did not help, particularly when so starkly contrasted with Nemrac's perfect speech pattern.

John Nemrac was relentless. 'I am not asking you to gauge probability, I am asking you if what I have suggested to you is possible?'

In the end Peter Conway could only agree lamely that, yes, it was possible. And he grimaced in resigned apology at Todd as he left the witness box.

Meanwhile Nemrac gave Richard another wink, as aware of the camera angles as his client and careful not to be in shot.

The evidence of Dr Jeremy Hunter was made to appear highly questionable. The barrister simply encouraged him to agree that he was indeed a country doctor with no specialist knowledge of drugs at all – and later Nemrac's own expert witness for the defence expounded at some length on the positive qualities of Trozactin while obligingly glossing over the consequences of knocking back huge amounts of the stuff washed down by similar quantities of alcohol.

The former director of *Sparrow-Hawk* was simply asked if it was true that he had been sacked from the show for incompetence – and when he admitted, after some prevarication, that it was true, more or less, Nemrac said he had no further questions. Then it was Millie Brooks' turn.

'You say you heard my client's motor cycle returning through the hunting gate into the stable yard on the afternoon in question, Mrs Brooks, can you tell me what kind of motor cycle it is?'

'Uhm, it's a black one,' stumbled Millie.

'A black one!' John Nemrac gave it exactly the same emphasis as did Dame Edith Evans to the famous Lady Bracknell line 'A handbag?' in *The Importance of Being Earnest.* He was rewarded by a rumble of amusement around the court.

'Do I take it you are not an expert on motor cycles, Mrs Brooks?'

Millie Brooks was forced to admit that she was not an expert on motor bikes, that she had not actually seen the bike nor its rider, and indeed she could not say for certain that it had been Richard Corrington's machine nor him aboard it . . .

'But who else's would it have been, coming through that little hunting gate, nobody else uses it,' she did manage to remark rather courageously.

'Let's stick to the facts, shall we, Mrs Brooks,' the barrister responded sternly.

It was poor Mrs Murdoch, Joyce's neighbour, on whom the prosecution had so much relied, who was on the receiving end of the most devastating display of John Nemrac's skills. Mrs Murdoch was the witness he had been most looking forward to cross examining. The barrister had noticed something crucial about her written statement of evidence which had failed to occur to DCI Mallett and his team.

'Mrs Murdoch,' he began, 'you are absolutely sure that the man you saw leaving Miss Carter's home was the defendant?'

'Absolutely sure, sir,' replied the woman. At first she gave exactly the impression of self-assurance and honest reliability that Todd had hoped for. 'I never miss *Sparrow-Hawk*. I'd recognise Richard Corrington anywhere.'

'Indeed. And you are absolutely sure that it was at four o'clock that you saw the defendant.'

'Oh yes, sir, that's when we left for the ferry, you see.'

'So it could not have been two hours earlier, as my client claims?'

'No. It had to be four o'clock.' The woman was adamant.

Nemrac nodded. 'And you would recognise Richard Corrington anywhere.' He repeated her earlier words.

'Yes, I would.'

'In fact you have already stated that he looked "just like he does on the telly"; is that not right?'

'Oh yes, sir, just like he does on the telly.'

'And is Jack Sparrow clean shaven on TV, or does he have a beard?'

'He's clean shaven, sir, of course.'

'I see, and so, was Richard Corrington clean shaven when you saw him on the day of the murder?'

'Yes, sir, he was, I keep saying, just like on the telly.'

'And when you picked Mr Corrington out of an identity parade three and a half days later, was he clean shaven then?'

'Oh no sir, he had a full beard, but I recognised him all right because I've seen lots of pictures of him with a beard . . .'

The woman stopped abruptly, sensing danger too late.

'So when you saw the defendant leaving the victim's house, as you claim you did, he was clean shaven, and when you formally identified him three and a half days later he had what you describe as a "full beard". Is that what you are telling me, Mrs Murdoch?'

She looked frantically around the courtroom, as if seeking an escape route. There was none. The trap had been adroitly laid and she was enmeshed.

'Well, I know what you mean . . . I can't explain it, just can't explain it . . .' She was rambling now. The judge interrupted imperiously, looking down on her from the commanding position of his elevated platform.

'Just answer the question, Mrs Murdoch.'

'Yes sir,' the witness replied plaintively. She looked back at John Nemrac. 'Yes sir, what you say is right, sir.'

'So how can we explain this, do you think perhaps that the police allowed a suspect held in custody to don a false beard for the identification parade?'

'No sir, of course not.' Janice Murdoch gave the impression she would agree to anything now just to make him stop.

John Nemrac knew how to milk an advantage to the full. He would not let up until even the dimmest juror had the scenario indelibly fixed in his mind.

'But in your opinion, Mrs Murdoch, how long would it take an average man to grow a set of whiskers as full as those boasted by my client when you formally identified him?'

'Well, I don't know, sir . . .'

'Come now, Mrs Murdoch, you are a married woman with grown sons, I believe. You must have some idea. A month? Two weeks? Even with heavy growth, surely not less than two weeks?'

Mrs Murdoch sighed. She was confused, bewildered, and thoroughly beaten.

'No, not less than two weeks, it couldn't be less

than two weeks . . .' she replied in a very small voice, so small that Mr Justice Sinclair did not fully hear her. Or at least he said that he didn't.

'Could you please repeat your answer and would you speak up so that the court can hear you properly,' he instructed.

Visibly trembling now, Mrs Murdoch did so.

'I see. So, Mrs Murdoch, now we come to the time when you claim you saw a clean shaven Richard Corrington leave Miss Carter's house. Do you still say it was four o'clock?'

'Well y-yes sir.' The woman had even developed a stammer.

'Are you not so sure of yourself now, Mrs Murdoch?'

'Well, I thought I was, but . . .'

John Nemrac interrupted swiftly. 'You *thought* you were sure? Well that's not good enough, Mrs Murdoch. Thank you very much. I have no further questions.'

The barrister swung on his heels and paused at just the right moment so that the camera with its red action light glowing caught a good long full frontal of his almost professorially solemn look. Then he returned to his table in front of Richard Corrington and immediately wrote a brief note which he passed to his client.

It consisted of one bastardised word. ''Owzat?'

Richard flicked his eyes downward and almost imperceptibly bowed his head – one master professional acknowledging the deadly talent of another.

As they left the court after the fourth day's proceedings at the end of what was supposed to be the case for the prosecution, Todd Mallett had sunk even deeper into pessimistic depression. How on earth had he and his team missed that business of the beard, he wondered. He had watched the jury's reaction. They had thoroughly enjoyed the destruction of poor Mrs Murdoch. When Nemrac had started to ask about how long it took to grow a beard, one or two of them had been unable to stop themselves chuckling knowingly – just as they had tittered over all that 'very nearly a murder' stuff.

He winced at the memory. Wondering whether he dared go on an almighty bender again he swiftly descended the steps outside the court. He bumped straight into Jacky Starr, who, as a material witness quite free to do so, had stayed on to watch the proceedings after giving his evidence.

'I didn't expect you still to be here,' he greeted the young man.

'I want to watch that bastard go down,' said Jacky. He did not seem particularly pleased to see Todd, which the policeman thought was fair enough considering the circumstances under which they had last met. He also noticed that Jacky still looked distressed and under strain. His eyes were bloodshot and swollen.

'You're not going to do anything barmy if he doesn't, I hope.'

Todd's manner was almost threatening, Jacky's reply correspondingly belligerent.

'Like what?'

'Like anything that might hurt your mother.'

Jacky grinned knowingly. It was almost a leer. 'So that's it,' he said. 'I thought as much.'

Todd felt himself flush. He had been both clumsy and obvious, and he should remember that Jacky wasn't always quite as thick as he sometimes seemed. On the other hand he might as well carry on now.

'So how is your mother?' he asked as casually as he could.

Jacky shrugged. 'She's lost her house, she's broke, but, you know Belle, she's keeping her end up. And she's here with me. She wouldn't come to court though – said she'd only add to the circus . . .'

That stopped Todd in his tracks. The last thing he had expected was for Belle Parker to be back in Exeter. For a start she had given him the distinct impression that she and her son were not very close at all.

And she had been quite right in her assessment of Todd's feelings for her, he was still not yet ready for her. But the thought of her being so close stirred him, his pulse quickened. He could feel the excitement rising in him in spite of his better judgement.

Jacky had volunteered that he and his mother were staying at a place called Light Hall, which Todd knew to be a not very prepossessing block of inexpensive holiday flats on the edge of town. As he watched Jacky set off at a trot down the hill to the town he began to ponder whether or not he should call Belle. What he would say to her. Would she still want to see him?

Bruce Macintosh had also turned up for the trial. Todd found it hard to understand why anyone who didn't have to be there would want to be, but looking at Bruce's face he could see still that need to be doing something, to be in some way involved, that he had noticed all those months ago. That was the thing about murder. It wasn't just the death of the victims, so many connected lives were destroyed and turned upside down.

Bruce had been hovering nearby while Todd talked to Jacky, waiting to approach the DCI. Now he fell into step alongside Todd and walked across the car park with him. Although they had actually met only a couple of times, the two men were easy together.

'You don't think he's going to get away with this one too, do you, Todd?' Bruce asked, referring obliquely to the murders – including that of his wife – with which the police had been unable to charge Richard Corrington. He sounded bitter and disillusioned.

Todd gave a wry smile. 'We're not doing very well, I'm afraid.'

The other man grunted. 'Tell me, do you still believe in justice?' he asked glumly.

Todd had been slightly bent over unlocking the door of his car. He stood up straight and directly faced Bruce. He waved an arm impatiently at the courthouse and then at the vehicle, parked alongside his, with Court TV UK emblazoned colourfully on its side.

'Yes, I believe in justice,' he said quietly. 'It's the damned law I don't believe in any more.'

He climbed into the car, started the motor, and turned on the lights. It was gone five and heavy cloud had already turned the sky dark as he steered out through the portcullis and down the castle approach road. It was scarcely possible to make normal progress through the heaving mass of people. The world's press had by now been joined by hundreds of *Sparrow-Hawk* fans and others who were attracted, by some morbid fascination, to the spectacle. On the first day of the trial 27 million people in Britain alone had tuned in on television.

Vaguely Todd thought that the public hangings of another age must have been a bit like this.

At the bottom of the hill, where the crowd thinned out a little, he spotted Jacky Starr threading his way through the remaining onlookers. It had just started to drizzle and he was wearing a denim cap and had his coat collar turned up. He seemed to have miraculously passed through the ranks of the press without being bothered – he was, after all, the toyboy lover of the murder victim, thought Todd, slipping easily inside his head into tabloid speak. But Jacky was fleet of foot, and the press were really only interested now in the star of the show, Richard Corrington.

Todd made a spur of the moment decision. He slowed the car and unwound the driver's window. 'Want a lift?' he called.

Jacky looked startled, and none too welcoming. At first he made a move that suggested he was going to turn the offer down. As well he might, reflected Todd.

Then he looked up at the sky, the rain was beginning to fall more heavily. 'OK,' he said gruffly.

Once settled in the passenger seat he made no further attempt at conversation. Todd didn't particularly want to talk either. He was lost in his own thoughts. Neither he nor Jacky noticed the red van which remained about 100 yards behind them throughout the journey.

When they reached Light Hall Jacky glanced at Todd and remarked casually: 'I suppose you'll be wanting to see Belle.'

Todd took it as an invitation, followed Jacky into the building and puffed his way up three flights of stairs to the top flat. Arabella might have fallen on hard times but she continued to look the part, complete with salon hair-do, immaculate make-up and tight black sweater over leopard skin-patterned leggings. And if she was surprised or embarrassed by seeing him she did not show it. She was warm and welcoming.

'Afraid I don't run to The Rougemont any more,' she remarked ruefully. 'However, I've discovered that off season holiday flats are a bargain.'

Todd smiled. 'How long are you staying?'

'For the duration. We had to take this place for a fortnight anyway – but it's peanuts. Jacky wants to see justice being done. Any chance?'

'Depends from where you are standing,' said Todd, and immediately regretted it. He saw the hurt fleetingly but unmistakably cross her face.

'Todd, you've no idea how much I wish I'd never said anything . . .'

'Don't be daft,' he interrupted her, kicking himself. 'I didn't mean to bring all that up again.'

He wondered if the court case would ever stop coming between them. He had no desire even to speak about it. He wanted only to talk about Arabella Parker. As soon as he had seen her again he had longed to take her in his arms, just like before.

He stood awkwardly, his big hands hanging at his sides, not knowing what to say or do. Jacky had sat down at the table in the corner and picked up a newspaper, but to Todd he seemed to be dominating the room, making it impossible for him to concentrate on Belle.

She seemed to read his mind, as she had before. 'Come and see the view,' she said, and led him out through French windows on to a tiny balcony. The rain had suddenly stopped and the sky cleared to give a glimpse of a late October sunset that was unseasonably stunning. The main road lay directly in front of the block of flats, but beyond it, glowing in amber light, Devon rolled endlessly glorious, culminating in the rugged purple hills of Dartmoor in the distance.

'Great, isn't it?' she remarked.

'I thought you were a city girl,' he said.

'Oh, I like the countryside well enough as long as I can look at it from somewhere civilised,' she replied.

'Like an air-conditioned Jaguar?' he suggested.

'Absolutely!' she said.

He thought, not for the first time, how plucky she was, she seemed so remarkably untroubled by her sudden change in circumstances.

'I'm sorry about your money troubles,' he said.

She shrugged, and nodded her head in the direction of the living room, in which Jacky remained sitting at the table. 'Funny thing, I lost my son because all I wanted was my career and the rewards it brought. Now I seem to have lost all that, but I may be getting him back. I'm not so unhappy, actually.'

They continued to chat for a while, but he did not seem able to take the conversation beyond rather stilted small talk. He realised he wanted to be properly alone with her, to take her into his own territory. On impulse he reached out and clasped her hand in his, oblivious, suddenly, of anything in the world except her and his quite unaccountable feelings for her.

'How about another dinner date?' he asked, surprising himself. 'Tonight, if you like, and I'll try to do better than before.'

What an awkward, clumsy invitation, he thought.

But it probably would have made no difference however he had phrased it.

'You did fine,' she replied quickly.

'It's just that I'm not very good at saying what I feel . . .' he tried to explain.

'I know, it's OK. Very British. Stiff upper lip and all that.'

He smiled wanly. 'Yes, well that was about all that was stiff the last time, you see . . .'

She interrupted him, wonderingly, as if understanding at last. 'Was that why you backed off the way you did?'

He nodded.

'You big fool,' she said, but the words were not harsh. She sounded reproachful yet hugely affectionate, and most of all relieved.

He flushed. 'Well, it's never happened to me before, and I didn't, couldn't . . .'

She interrupted him again. 'So that was all, and there was I thinking you'd gone off me.'

She was smiling and her tone was bantering now. She went on, more softly, more gently, 'Didn't you know it would have been enough to lie in your arms?'

He thought his heart was going to burst, and yet he still did not know what to say. He could be such a blundering oaf. Never again would he lose the magic.

'So what about dinner then?' He tried to keep his voice light, it was the best he could do.

She was still smiling at him, but then she turned his invitation down. 'I'm sorry, Todd, love. I'm cooking supper for Jacky . . .'

Todd nodded, accepting it, trying to keep up the lightness.

'You once told me you didn't cook,' he said.

'Times have changed,' she said.

She paused and then added: 'You can stay, if you'd like.'

Todd shook his head. He didn't think so. He wasn't sure that he could trust himself. 'I've got work to do later, anyway,' he said, which was only half an excuse.

She nodded. 'Another time, then.'

It was all they ever seemed to say to each other, he thought.

She was still talking. 'That might be for the best. I have this idea that things will never be right for us until this case is over, until the file is closed.'

He felt that already familiar sense of accord pass between them.

'I know exactly how you feel,' he said.

'Yes, I think you do,' she said. And she touched his cheek with her free hand.

Suddenly he was assertive. 'So how about making a date for the last night of the trial, it'll be one day next week?'

'Mightn't that be too soon?'

'Not for me, it won't,' he said, and at that moment he really meant it. He could think only of those very special words – it would have been enough to lie in his arms she had said. Now that was magic, wasn't it?

As if she could read his thoughts she stretched upwards, wrapping her hand around the back of his neck, and kissed him very slowly and very gently full on the lips.

He left her, then, feeling more cheerful than he had in ages, certainly far more cheerful than he had since the start of the whole awful courtroom extravaganza in which he was grimly aware he was such an outclassed player.

It was an extremely cheerful John Nemrac who took Amanda back to the Rougemont that same evening. Again he ordered champagne, as he had done all those months ago when they had just received the bad news about Richard's DNA.

'This time we might have something to celebrate,' he remarked as they raised their glasses.

Amanda regarded him carefully. He had had an excellent day and was flushed with his own success. He was a very powerful man. People said that power was the greatest aphrodisiac of all, greater even than money. Certainly at that moment it seemed so to Amanda. She was one of those women who could go without sex for months on end and not miss it, but when she did have sex which excited her she wanted more of it soon. Yet she didn't dare try to contact Harry Pearson again. He had indicated that he wanted her all to himself – whereas not only was John Nemrac a quite exceptional man, it also seemed that he was about to save her husband. And that meant saving her entire way of life.

The irony of her train of thought totally failed to occur to Amanda.

This time when Nemrac suggested a second bottle she agreed. He was being extremely attentive. She had no doubts at all as to his intentions. They had both been tempted on the previous occasion, and it was perhaps only through lack of an appropriate opportunity that they had not got together properly before now. Certainly neither of them had any moral qualms, she was quite sure of that. They were two of a kind. And when he suggested that they enjoy the second bottle in the privacy of his suite upstairs, she swiftly agreed to that too.

'I think we could be more comfortable together there,' he said.

He gestured her to the little modern sofa, sat opposite her too far away to touch, and made small talk until the champagne was safely delivered, then he stood up and walked behind her. He leaned over her and brushed his lips lightly against her hair. His hands were already on her breasts, feeling her through the soft material of her blouse.

'Wouldn't you prefer to have the champagne afterwards,' he suggested.

'It would be nice to be asked first,' she responded. Coquettish. Trying to pretend she was still playing a game. But she was already breathing quickly, her body beginning to take on a will of its own. She wasn't going to refuse him, and he knew that well enough.

'Amanda Lane, I would very much like to make love to you,' he whispered.

'Isn't there any code of conduct about lawyers screwing their client's wives?' she asked, still pretending.

'Ah,' he said. 'So you want to be screwed do you, that's what it is.'

He took her almost as roughly as Harry Pearson had so recently done, although without as much invention. He pushed her sideways on to the sofa and thrust himself into her without bothering at first to properly undress either himself or her.

When he eventually saw the bite marks still evident on her neck he tightened his grip on her body.

'Is that what you like?' he asked. Then he buried his face in her breasts and used his teeth on her nipples until she cried out with the pain.

Afterwards he poured the champagne meticulously

311

into the two flute glasses, careful not to spill a drop. Then he let just a little from the bottle drip on to her sore nipples. The liquid stung sharply. He used his mouth on her again. Her body continued to respond even though she began to find that she no longer particularly wanted it to.

'I'm sorry this will have to be the only time,' he said when he had quite finished.

But she didn't think he was really sorry at all. She suspected he was never very interested in sleeping with the same woman twice. She thought that he had at least one thing in common with Richard, only the conquest mattered to him. She was quite sure of that.

He had excited her – although not as much as Harry Pearson, whom she also knew she really must never see again. But she actually wished she had not given in to the temptation to sleep with John Nemrac. On balance she rather preferred the myth to the man.

The case for the defence began on Friday, October 23rd, the fifth day of the trial. It was superbly presented, as Todd had expected it to be. The actor's agent, Larry Silver, the current *Sparrow-Hawk* director, and Richard's wife, Amanda Lane – still wearing a high-necked blouse – were among those called as character witnesses giving evidence of Richard Corrington's undoubted sanity and exemplary conduct.

Difficult to work with? 'Not a bit of it,' asserted Larry and the director. Erratic behaviour, impossible to live with? Complete rubbish, responded Amanda.

'There is absolutely no way he would be capable of anything like this,' she gushed. 'I know my husband. He is a gentle, sensitive man.'

She remained a picture of elegance, a paragon of

reason, the ultimate caring and supportive wife. No-body in the courtroom could ever have guessed at the violent sexual excesses in which she had so enthusiastically taken part over the previous few days. And anyone observing that her lips looked a little fuller than usual would probably have assumed that she had indulged in the fashion for collagen injections, rather than that they were swollen because they had been chewed until they bled.

Todd – unaware, of course, of any of this – was reminded of the famous Jeffrey Archer libel case won without doubt from the moment the judge had memorably described Archer's wife as 'fragrant'.

Amanda Lane was most definitely fragrant of appearance, and the transparently captivated Mr Justice Sinclair indeed looked as if he were quite capable of publicly describing her as such.

But the moment the court, the whole country, and at times it seemed, half the world, had been waiting for came when – after the testimonies of Nemrac's expert witnesses, the drug doctor and finger print and DNA specialists pouring further scorn on the police evidence and the psychiatrist avowing to the defendant's perfectly normal mental state – counsel for the defence called his client to the stand on the afternoon of the seventh day of the trial. Richard Corrington was his own trump card.

Richard had worn a different suit each day. For the day when he was to give evidence he had chosen a very formal city suit, a navy and black pin-stripe, beautifully cut and flattering to his figure. His shirt was heavy cream silk, his tie navy and black with occasional flashes of deep red, his shoes gleaming black Church's brogues.

He stood very straight in the witness box. Millions of eyes were fixed upon him – and, in direct contrast to poor Todd Mallett, this brought out the best in him.

Carefully Nemrac took Richard through the circumstances of his arrest at the BAFTA Awards, and his experiences at Heavitree Road police station afterwards.

'It was impossible for me to think clearly, I felt under the most terrible pressure. I could not believe I was being suspected of such a terrible thing. And I was tired, so very tired . . .'

It was not so much what he said as the way he said it. He humbly admitted that he had over the years overdosed on disorientating cocktails of prescription drugs and alcohol, and on the night of his arrest had taken cocaine to calm his nerves, which had ultimately made him less able than he would otherwise have been to withstand the police barrage. He deeply regretted his misuse of drugs which had been partially responsible for a succession of dreadful misunderstandings leading to this court case.

He also deeply regretted his infidelity with Joyce Carter, which he knew had caused such pain to his loyal and supportive wife.

As instructed by John Nemrac he did his best to appear to be directly addressing the jury, whose attention was riveted. But when he mentioned his wife he had glanced briefly and proudly towards the public gallery where Amanda Lane sat, her demeanour as ever giving no clue to her nocturnal activities, and somehow managing to wear an expression which contrived to be both long suffering and loving.

'But, I have to take responsibility for my actions,

because never, at any time in my life, have I been so under the influence of any substance that I have not known what I have been doing,' he said. 'Never.'

John Nemrac asked the question designed to lead Richard into the climax of his performance. 'And what about the police suggestion that you have taken on the persona of Jack Sparrow?'

Richard smiled slightly. 'I am an actor,' he said, and the jury appeared to be treating every word he spoke as if it were a precious pearl of wisdom. 'Actors act the characters we portray, we do not become them. I have played Othello and Macbeth, I have become neither a Moor driven mad by jealousy nor a megalomaniac Scottish king. I have played a surgeon in a television soap, but I think it would be unwise for me to operate. In various films and TV shows I have played an airline pilot, a university lecturer in ancient Greek, an architect, a racing car driver, an Olympic athlete and a stonemason. I have taken on neither the characteristics nor the attributes of any of these characters. My ancient Greek, in particular, remained at the same zero level throughout the making of a two-hour feature film . . .'

The jury were laughing aloud now. Richard turned to face the judge.

'M'lud,' he said. 'My name is Richard Corrington and I am an actor. I am not Jack Sparrow.'

The verdict was a foregone conclusion.

The closing speeches of counsels for the prosecution and for the defence, and even the judge's summing up, were mere formalities.

The jury found Richard Corrington not guilty.

Todd Mallett felt utterly defeated. He telephoned

Belle to cancel their dinner date, unable to remember, in the depths of his depression and when he had already suspected what the result would be, why on earth he should ever have suggested a date for the last night of the trial.

He went to an off licence and bought two bottles of whisky – one might not be enough. Tomorrow he had work to do all over again. If Richard Corrington was not guilty of murder, then who the hell was? One way or another the killer was still at large.

Trial by television be damned, nobody could stop him getting blind drunk in the privacy of his own home.

Twenty-Three

It seemed like half the world was camped outside Exeter Crown Court.

Richard Corrington stood ten foot tall on the top of the steps. He was beaming. Seven months on prison fare had made him just a little leaner. His cheek bones were more finely defined, the breadth of his shoulders enhanced by a slimmer waist. He looked even more handsome than before. The crowd roared its appreciation, the adulation of his fans heightened rather than lessened by the charges their hero had faced and ultimately conquered.

Amongst them stood a strangely quiet man wearing a baseball cap pulled down over much of his face. From beneath the peak little could be seen other than a pair of dark glasses, in no way necessitated by the day's weather, and a full grey beard. He would have attracted little enough attention even if anyone had been looking at him particularly, but in fact nobody was interested in an anonymous man in a baseball cap. Nobody was interested in anyone except the star of the show.

All eyes and all cameras were on Richard Corrington, and the actor responded magnificently. He posed for photographs and motioned for silence so that he could speak. TV and radio microphones were thrust in his face. Richard was not in the slightest bit phased. He was, of course, in his natural element.

When he spoke, the hullabaloo subsided and the assembled crowd waited in eager anticipation, hanging on his every breath. A reporter turned a page of his notebook in order to have a clear sheet before him and you could hear the paper rustle – so much so that one or two of his colleagues turned to glare at him.

'Ladies and gentlemen,' Richard began. 'Justice has been done today. The people of Britain can walk tall. I am an innocent man, and I thank God that in this country I was able to stand before a jury of my peers and rely on the judgement of the people. And the people have spoken!'

He gave the last sentence full projection. The assorted microphones fairly shuddered with the power of his delivery. He thrust one arm triumphantly in the air, remembering, of course, not to clench his fist. That always gave the wrong impression, as Neil Kinnock found out to his cost in 1992.

Brushing aside further questions with an imperious wave softened only by his most charming smile, Richard, with his wife just a step or two behind him, was then escorted swiftly by aides through the pulsating throng to his waiting Range Rover and the faithful George Brooks.

Coincidentally he passed right by a man wearing a baseball hat, who, watchfully silent, stood out somewhat in the noisy crowd. In fact, he almost bumped into him.

But Richard did not notice the man any more than he would have noticed Salman Rushdie or Princess Diana in the frantic throng. Indeed, such was the commotion surrounding his freeing, it was even possible that nobody would have noticed Princess Diana.

*

The man in the baseball cap acknowledged grudging admiration.

Richard Corrington had turned his statement into exquisite high drama worthy of any stage in the world. The man bet himself silently that the words had been written for the actor and carefully rehearsed in anticipation of this moment. An actor always needs his lines.

With eyes narrowed behind the concealing sunglasses he watched the car draw away, Corrington turning to look through the back window and execute one last imperious wave.

The man knew a fine performance when he saw one, but beyond that he felt only anger. Richard Corrington was going to get away with it again. That was the way the man saw it. And he did not like that one little bit.

The Dom Perignon was already being poured by the time Larry Silver, the last of the Corrington entourage, arrived at Landacre. A fire roared in the Adam fireplace and Richard and John Nemrac were leaning on either side of the grand white marble mantelpiece clutching fine crystal glasses. They were laughing loudly at some shared joke, or perhaps just with pleasure. Both looked radiant. Amanda stood by the corner table, smiling a welcome, champagne bottle at the ready. Larry approached her and gave her a kiss on each cheek. Her smile widened, but she appeared coolly controlled, showing little of the excitement being exhibited both by her husband and his lawyer. Planning her next move, Larry reckoned, just as he was. It was hard even to remember how broken up she had been on the night of Richard's arrest.

'We all owe you a great thank you, my dear,' Larry said to her.

Amanda was almost arch in her reply. 'What on earth for?'

Larry leaned forward and gave her a third kiss, and then spoke again, this time almost into her ear, his voice little more than a whisper.

'You know what for,' he said.

He stepped back and looked into her eyes, but she lowered her lashes briefly. For once there seemed to be no affectation in her. She uttered a small, almost inaudible sigh.

'We got through it, Larry, didn't we?' she asked. 'We did it, Quick Silver. You and me.'

'Yes, my dear, we did it,' replied the agent.

'Do you still love him?' Amanda asked, very very quietly. Larry studied her without alarm or surprise.

Larry had always assumed that Amanda had known about his affair with Richard, which had not ended until after the Corrington marriage – an affair Richard would now deny every bit as vociferously as he had eventually denied his murder charge.

'No,' he said evenly. 'I don't love him any more.'

He paused, then not knowing quite why, he said: 'He was never really gay, you know. Our liaison meant nothing to him.'

She raised one elegant eyebrow. 'I know that. As it happens, his affairs have never been about love, or sex, for that matter – just ego.'

Larry couldn't help laughing. She was some woman, and she was right, of course.

He looked deeper into her eyes. Her expression was unreadable.

'Do *you* still love him?' he asked finally.

320

She smiled the ice smile. 'No,' she said. 'But he is mine. I made him, and I wasn't going to lose him.'

Larry took her hand and squeezed it between both of his, affectionate, familiar, admiring. Then he swung about and raised his glass to his client, still raucously cheerful by the fireplace.

'Here's to you, superstar,' he said.

Richard beamed. 'I think we should drink a toast to John, myself. Here's to the world's greatest barrister.'

John Nemrac was a picture of triumph, he radiated victory. Understandable enough, Larry supposed, although, while he respected the lawyer's talent he did not much like the man. And he could not help noticing the quick, almost gloating, look the somewhat flushed Nemrac, his brow beaded in sweat, shot across the room at Amanda. There was triumph in that too. Larry had already suspected that there might be something between the two, and he certainly would not blame Amanda if there were. Rather, as he observed the self-assured arrogance of the portly legal wizard, he almost pitied her.

Quite oblivious to any of this, Richard in turn raised his glass, downed the entire contents in one, and gestured loftily for a refill. Amanda obediently obliged. She had apparently lost all interest in John Nemrac, Larry thought, if indeed she had held any real interest in him in the first place. She was concentrating on Richard now. And her expression indicated that she knew there was no point in arguing or trying to reason with her husband on this of all days. None the less Larry saw the anxiety in her eyes.

It was not until lawyer and agent had departed, both heading back to London, that the trouble started.

Three bottles of champagne had already been swiftly demolished – and at least half of each by Richard himself. And right after his guests left Richard opened a fourth bottle of Dom Perignon which Amanda somewhat frostily declined to share with him.

Idly he began to read some of the cards and letters from well-wishers which had already been delivered to the house. His *bonhomie* was disappearing fast to be replaced by the morose surliness she had become more and more accustomed to in the weeks before his arrest.

Amanda decided to leave him to his own devices in the living room and settled herself in the kitchen, sitting in one of the pair of Victorian rocking chairs on either side of the Aga. She had no wish to watch him make an exhibition of himself. She knew he was going to get even more maudlin, and she had no time for that either. She already wanted to start rebuilding, and she was afraid Richard was going to rake up the past in a way she wished to be no part of.

Her husband had downed another three glasses of champagne and was clutching the glass and the already half-empty bottle in one hand and a piece of notepaper in the other when he somewhat unsteadily entered the kitchen. He kicked the door shut behind him, his drink-induced clumsiness causing him to stagger even more dangerously as he approached his wife.

He tossed the sheet of paper at her.

'What the fuck is this about?' he asked.

With a sinking heart she realised that it was a letter was from Harry Pearson. 'Just a note to welcome you home,' she read. 'Congratulations on your release . . .'

'It's just what it seems to be, Ricky,' she said.

'Is it? I think he sent this to mock me. You've been fucking him while I've been inside, haven't you?'

'Would you care?' Suddenly Amanda reached breaking point with her husband. Her control snapped without warning. His casual adultery had almost brought about their downfall. How dare he be sanctimonious.

'I don't like being made a total fool of, that's all.'

With an awkward bump he sat down opposite her on the second wooden rocking chair.

'There's something you need to know,' he told her. His voice held defiance, the words only very slightly slurred by alcohol. His attitude was devil may care, Errol Flynn on a bad day. He was going to cause damage, and he didn't give a damn.

Amanda spoke quickly. 'There is nothing I need to know. I've told you that before.'

He laughed, and the laughter contained none of his earlier good humour. It sounded harsh, cruel almost.

'Listen to me,' he said. 'I'm a killer. Watch my lips. *I killed Joyce Carter*. And she wasn't the only one . . .'

'Don't be ridiculous, Richard.' Amanda was shouting now. 'You're mad. You don't know what you're saying. You're mad.'

'I know,' he said. 'That is what I am trying to tell you, you stupid bitch. I am mad! And I killed them. All three of them.'

Amanda began to cry. Except in the hysteria of the night of Richard's arrest she could not remember when she had last cried, probably not since the death of their child. And even then there had been just the one awful outburst of desperate sobbing tears, followed by nothing. Yet the loss of the little boy, and

323

the manner of it, had changed her, hardened her beyond recognition, she knew. Now she recognised the defeat in her husband, in spite of his hollow victory, saw the crazy gleam in his eye, and for once, after so long of being the crutch at his elbow, she could not cope.

But Richard wouldn't let go. He wouldn't, or couldn't, stop.

'I did it, I can't pretend any more. Can't kid myself any more, let alone you.'

He hurled his champagne glass at the floor. It smashed to pieces on the Delabole slate tiles, the little champagne left in the bottom of the glass splashing over the slate, forming tiny glistening spots. He threw back his head, tipped the neck of the bottle into his mouth and drank long and deep. His cheeks were flushed now and he was dribbling the liquid before he could swallow it properly. He swilled the stuff like beer, twenty or so quids' worth of Dom Perignon emptied down his throat in one gulp.

Amanda felt the familiar surge of disgust, loathing almost, begin to overwhelm her.

'You're married to a fucking serial killer, my dear, so how do you like that?'

It was too much. He was taunting her with their own destruction, she who had done everything to hold his pathetic life together. For the first time ever she let her true feelings run riot. She began to scream at him, horrible insults, obscenities, turns of phrase and expressions of ugliness from her rough and ready past that she hadn't used in decades.

She rose to her feet, filling her lungs to capacity in great belts, the better to give power to her raving demolition job.

'Without me you'd be floundering in a filthy gutter somewhere, and don't you forget it. You can't even fuck properly, and you never could. You're just an inadequate wretch, a pathetic worm.'

She thought she would tame him with the force of her fury. And that was to be the biggest mistake of her marriage.

Unthinking in her rage, she stormed on, incapable now of stopping. She heard the final words that she yelled at him almost as if someone else had shouted them.

'I gave birth to a deformed freak because of you . . .'

Richard stood up and faced her. He rocked back on to his heels and gathered up all of his still considerable strength. He tucked the elbow of his right arm in close to his waist and drew it back, with muscles tensed, every sinew tightened ready for release, taut as a medieval crossbow. He drew in his breath, paced himself, and let rip.

This time she had gone too far. She should not have said it. That was his son, his poor dead son, she was talking about.

His arm shot out as if jet-propelled and even before the punch landed he could feel the immensely satisfying sensation of his clenched fist smashing into Amanda's face. He could already hear the crunch as his knuckles crushed her nose. He could see the torrent of blood bursting from her shattered features and drenching him in its warm sticky wetness.

Yet at the very last moment something stopped him. He swerved to one side and opened his hand. In the end he caught her with little more than a glancing slap on the cheek with his palm. But she had drawn back, physically alarmed by him for the first time in their life together, putting herself off balance, and the force remaining in the blow was enough to cause her to fall, which she did awkwardly.

Her head cracked against the unforgiving slate floor, and bounced just once. She gave a little grunt. Unsteadily he leaned over her, staring at her. Her eyes were shut. He leaned closer, saying her name, suddenly afraid of what he had done. He still had the bottle of champagne in his left hand, some of it dribbled on to her face. With his right hand he reached out and very cautiously touched her.

She opened her eyes. They were as clear and icy as ever. His face was just inches from hers and his sour drink sodden breath was all over her. Even through the alcoholic haze he was starkly aware of the way in which she was looking at him. He thought he had never seen such hatred.

Twenty-Four

It was dawn when he woke up, November 3rd, and unusually bright for the time of year. The clocks had just gone back and the early sun streamed in through the great east-facing window and bathed the room in orange light. He was in his bed wearing his silk pyjamas. The curtains were open as usual and he blinked painfully in the morning glare. Everything seemed normal, although he realised he had no memory of going to bed. All he desired in the world was to return to his usual beloved routine. He wanted to sit on the wrought iron terrace clutching a mug of tea and gaze out over the moors, and yet, even before the numbing ache in his head allowed him any memory of the previous evening, a voice told him that would not be possible.

His head really hurt. An empty Laphroaig bottle was on the floor by the bed. Had he drunk all of that, and on top of the champagne he remembered downing after his release? There was a medicine phial on the dressing table. He peered at it, bleary eyed. It was empty. The label indicated that it had contained Valium. He groaned. He must have raided Amanda's medicine cabinet. She would be furious.

No wonder the previous evening was a disjointed blur. He remembered again what Jeremy Hunter had told him about the combined effect of drugs and alcohol. He had vowed never to take the risk again.

But all those months in jail without any props at all had taken their toll. He had exerted every last ounce of his strength, summoned up every last vestige of will power. His performance had impressed even Amanda.

Oh God, Amanda, that was it. He swung his legs out over the bed and sat there for a moment, feeling giddy. He almost wished he were back in jail. At least he was safe there. At least he could not harm anyone there. He shut his aching eyes and tried to think. How badly had he hurt her?

Across the room his clothes were neatly folded on the bedroom chair, trousers in the trouser press he could see through the open door of his dressing room. He was always meticulous with his clothes, but pretty sure he could not have managed that last night. Amanda must have helped him to bed, surely – she had done it often enough in the past.

Amanda's casually vicious remark about their dead child, he remembered that all right, had taken him over the edge, and the alcohol had made everything so much more extreme – but the true wretchedness was inside him, at the very core of him.

Amanda had not understood the rage welling up inside him the previous night. She had no way of knowing that the not guilty verdict, hard as he had worked for it, had been perhaps even more devastating to him than a conviction would have been. She had absolutely no appreciation of the precipice upon which his state of mind balanced, of the way in which he felt the last threads of his sanity were stretched to the edge of endurance.

He realised now, that as a man cleared of all charges in a court of law, he had to live alone with his abiding sense of guilt and that this might prove to be beyond him.

He felt terrible, as if he were groping around in a pea souper of a fog – only it was all happening within his head. And he still had the terrible lurking fear that somewhere in that fog lay some fuzzy knowledge of events that would finally destroy him.

On auto pilot, he stumbled to his feet and used his bedroom electric kettle to make the tea. Then, clutching a steaming mug of tea he went into the bathroom adjoining his bedroom. Methodically he brushed his teeth and shaved, seeking reassurance in routine. Finally he put on his silk dressing gown over his pyjamas and very slowly went down the stairs to the kitchen.

What he saw there shocked him rigid but did not surprise him. He stood silently for a moment surveying the scene. He knew exactly the meaning of it. It had, he supposed, been inevitable. The miracle perhaps was that it had not happened before.

Carefully he put the still half-full tea mug down on the work top. He thought that if he tried to drink any more of it he would be sick. Quietly he moved into his study where he sat for several minutes at his writing desk.

Then he went upstairs to his bedroom again and changed into his riding clothes. Any other man might not have bothered with the breeches and tweed coat and roll neck sweater, might have considered that any old clothing would do on such a morning, but Richard was not any other man. He stood before the full-length mirror studying his reflection. The handsome face, eyes deceptively clear, the gleaming head of hair, the athletic sweep of his broad shoulders, all meant nothing now. Instead he saw straight through the handsome face to the grim emptiness within.

The clarity of his eyes did not disguise their awful blankness as he pulled on his brown leather riding boots, left the house and strode purposefully down to stables.

Richard had not seen Herbert for seven long months, yet the horse whinnied softly as his master approached, and Richard rubbed his muzzle affectionately, enjoying the warmth of the horse's breath and the musky stable smell. In spite of everything he felt momentarily lulled, strangely relaxed. He went to the feed bins behind the looseboxes and prepared the horse's morning feed. In a bucket he mixed presoaked sugar beet, oats, nuts, barley and a couple of handfuls of roughly chopped carrots, before tipping the mess into Herbert's black rubber feeding bowl. Standing back to admire his handiwork he had second thoughts and added another scoop of oats and a few more carrots. He wanted Herbert to have a particularly good breakfast.

Then he pottered about, picking up this, putting down that, giving Herbert a few minutes for his stomach to settle before beginning to tack up.

It was such a long time since he had ridden, yet he mounted easily from ground level – after all, he had always promised himself he would give up riding when he was no longer able to do that. He squeezed Herbert forward and steered the horse out of the yard through the hunting gate behind the stables and on to the path that led to his favourite moorland route.

It was a particularly beautiful morning, and Richard was immensely glad of that. The sun was well up in the sky now but its light still glowed amber. So far the weather had been extremely mild, and there had yet to be a proper frost, or even any really severe winds, to cause the leaves to drop massively from the trees and bushes blazing with the glory of autumn colour. The sea, when Richard began to glimpse it through foliage growing more sparse as horse and rider climbed higher and higher, was a glittering gleaming mirror far beneath.

At the top, as the pair emerged from the woods of the lower slopes on to the bright open moorland, the joy of the turf beneath his feet and the sharp cool Exmoor air caused Herbert to break unasked into a trot and then a canter. Richard gave him his head. He had genuinely only intended to walk the horse, but he loved it when Herbert was sprightly and full of himself like this. Equally unasked, as ever, Herbert veered off the main track on to the jutting outcrop of grass-covered rock which formed such a spectacular viewing platform of the ocean and had for so long been the favourite vantage point of horse and master. As usual he stopped at the very edge of it and stood still as a glorious black marble statue, muscles tensed, ears pricked, staring down across the sweeping miles of moor, over Porlock, and way out to sea.

Richard was overcome by the beauty of the moment more than ever before.

He felt the tears prick against his eyelids and ultimately could no longer prevent them from falling. Great drops trickled down his cheeks and his shoulders began to heave with massive sobs.

After a while he dismounted, still weeping, but gently now. He walked around to the front of Herbert and stood facing the horse, his face pressed close to Herbert's muzzle.

'You're a beaut, a beautiful great beast and I love you to pieces,' he told the horse. His voice seemed to come from a long way away and cracked as he spoke.

He stroked the big neck, and spoke quietly into a twitching ear. 'I can't do it without you, old boy,' he said.

The horse was so calm, so splendid. For a moment Richard felt he could not go through with it. But he had made his decision, the only choice.

From out of the woods he came silently. The sound of the gunfire still echoed in the hills and a small pall of smoke drifted lazily skywards above the bodies of man and horse.

He walked right up to them and stood looking down at the carnage. His eyes were very pale grey like the sea in the early morning, and they shone bright as the white orb of the sun in the October sky.

The man drew back his lips in a humourless grin. He leaned forward, took the *Sparrow-Hawk* gold pin from Richard Corrington's jacket and very carefully attached it to his own lapel.

Neither the sight of an animal nor of a human being with their heads blown off lying in a pool of blood and gore seemed to move him at all. He was, by now, beyond normal human emotion.

Twenty-Five

It was the daily cleaning woman arriving at 9 a.m. who found her. The woman's screaming, they claimed later, could be heard right down at Porlock Weir, although that was probably an exaggeration. Certainly George Brooks, in the stables seeing to his charges, heard her clear enough and set off for the big house at a run.

Amanda Lane lay sprawled across the kitchen floor, still clad in the cream Chanel suit she had worn to court the previous day. She was lying on her back, legs and arms spread-eagled, her face discoloured and swollen, eyes wide open and sightless.

The daily remained looking down at her employer as if unable to move. George took the woman by the arm and led her out of the kitchen, closing the door behind them. He escorted her into the drawing room, sat her down on an armchair and used the drawing room phone extension to call the police and to ask for an ambulance, although it was quite patently obvious that the latter was a merely academic request. Then he called his wife at the gatehouse lodge, told her, with as little drama as possible, what had happened, and asked her to come up to the big house. He had a feeling the daily help was about to lurch into an attack of hysterics and he was not sure that he could cope on his own. He had never been very good with hysteria, which was one

333

of the reasons he had married the woman he did.

'The police should be yer any minute – I've got to find the boss,' he told her urgently.

His wife was ahead of him, reading his mind.

'George, don't you,' she instructed. 'Wait for the police, I wish you would.'

''E's got 'Erbert up on the moor,' George said by way of reply, as if that explained everything.

He was at the door already. He looked back over his shoulder at her.

'I'll be back before you've blinked.'

It took him just a couple of minutes to dash back to the stable yard. No warning bells had rung that morning when he had arrived there to find Herbert missing. It was not unusual for his employer to take out the old horse so early, and on this particular morning, Richard Corrington's first day out of jail and first opportunity to ride his beloved Herbert after so long – and such a sparkling bright autumn morning too – it had seemed totally to be expected. Nothing in the stable had been out of order either.

Until the body of Amanda Lane had been discovered there was no earthly reason why George should have been alarmed.

Now, though, he almost took a running dive at the security cabinet concealed in a corner of the backroom, fumbling the combination lock in his haste. Quickly checking the contents, his worst fears were realised. Two twelve-bore shotguns and a .22 rifle lived in the steel cabinet along with a stack of ammunition. One of the twelve-bores was missing, a box of cartridges had been newly opened and several removed.

George swore roundly under his breath. Then he

grabbed the saddle and bridle belonging to the fastest horse in the stable – the new chestnut, Dutchy – tacked up and swung himself aboard the handsome young gelding in little more than a minute. He knew of no faster way to get to the top of the moor.

At a spanking trot he rode Dutchy across the yard and around the back of the stables through the hunting gate on to the track which led up through the woods to the moor. It took him just over ten minutes to reach the rocky outcrop.

He pulled Dutchy to a halt. The horse was on his toes, frothy white with sweat and dancing around, not just because of the excited exertion of the gallop. The creature was afraid and trembling now. His nostrils had been filled with the stench of blood.

A nightmare scene lay before horse and rider.

George half fell out of the saddle, and, not really knowing he was doing it, began to shout out loud at the already cold, nearly headless, corpse of Richard Corrington.

'You bastard, you mad mad bastard,' he yelled. 'Why the fuck did yer have to take 'Erbert with yer, you mad bastard?'

The hills had no answer. A breeze blowing up from the sea caused the bits of Richard Corrington's hair still sprouting, uncongealed with blood, from the small part of his head which remained intact, to flutter about.

The local police from Minehead were on the scene within fifteen minutes. Todd Mallett and Sergeant Pitt arrived from Exeter little more than half an hour later. Under normal circumstances a crime at Landacre would have been the responsibility only of the Avon and Somerset force – but anything connected with Richard Corrington was Todd Mallett's domain. He was, after all, the policeman who had charged the actor with murder. And Pitt – an advanced police driver transferred the previous year from the Regional Crime Squad – had again driven like the rally driver he had once dreamed of becoming.

Amanda Lane still lay across her kitchen floor with her head at an impossible angle. Todd could see at a glance from her distorted and discoloured features that she had been half-strangled, but he suspected that she had died from a broken neck, and that the manner of her death would fit the pattern of the murder for which Richard Corrington had stood trial and the two previous murders for which Todd had believed he should also have stood trial. Indeed, Home Office pathologist Carmen Brown, who arrived within the hour, confirmed his analysis.

'It's just too much of a coincidence,' said the small, intelligent-faced doctor, provoked by the unique circumstances she faced into being far more speculative than usual.

'If Richard Corrington has killed his wife, then he really must have killed Joyce Carter too.'

Todd and Carmen Brown used a four-wheel drive to travel up the hillside to the top of the moor where a scene of crime team had already set up camp around the body of Richard Corrington and his horse. All three deaths seemed straightforward.

'Classic shotgun suicide,' said Dr Brown, looking down at Richard's gruesomely displayed corpse, and sounding more matter of fact than ever.

Meanwhile Todd tried desperately to maintain the

illusion that the sight of a decapitated man and a horse with a bloody great hole in its head had no effect on him at all.

When he returned to the house Todd learned that on the desk in Richard Corrington's study was a sealed envelope addressed to Larry Silver. Todd did not hesitate. This was a murder inquiry. Carefully, and still wearing the paper suit and surgeon's gloves with which he had been issued on arrival at the scene, he opened the envelope and removed from it a sheet of headed notepaper on which was handwritten in black ink, by fountain pen Todd thought, a letter to Larry signed by Richard Corrington.

'I cannot explain why I have done the things that I have done,' it began. 'I did not mean to kill Amanda. I did not love her, sometimes I even thought that I hated her, but I did not mean to hurt her.

'The terrible truth is that as I write this I have no memory of killing her. What they said in court was true, perhaps you knew that? I think Amanda did, although she was not afraid of me. I believe that the drugs combined with alcohol which I have O. D.'d on for so long have dangerously distorted my mind, and I have feared for some time now that I have driven myself mad.

'I have to accept that I am either mad or unimaginably evil, and I prefer to think that I am mad. Either way, I can no longer pretend to myself, as well as to everyone else, that I have not done these terrible things.

'I am a murderer, and I cannot live with my guilt.

'The act is over, Larry. You have been good to me always, better often than I deserved.

'I can think of nothing more to say, except goodbye.

'With love, and sorrow.

'Ricky.'

Silently Todd passed the letter to DS Pitt. The other man read it swiftly.

'Well that's that then, boss,' he said. 'You were right all along. Guilty as hell and nutty as a fruitcake.'

'Yes,' replied Todd.

He felt no sense of triumph, it was already too late for that. If there had not been that TV show farce of a trial, if Richard Corrington had been found guilty and put away for life, then there would have been one murder less. Amanda Lane would not be dead.

Anyway, it was finally all over. Done and dusted. And Todd just could not understand why he continued to feel so uneasy.

Twenty-Six

Unaware of the high drama that had already occurred at Landacre, Arabella Parker and her son Jacky left Light Hall soon after midday on the day after the trial. Belle still had money matters to sort out, and in any case she couldn't bear the idea of waiting around in Exeter for Todd to call.

Jacky was unusually quiet, and while Belle had relished the chance to spend time with him – to her shame she was not sure if they had ever spent almost a fortnight under the same roof together before – and delighted in the change in his attitude to her – he was so much warmer, warmer probably than she deserved – she continued to be concerned about him. She knew how depressed he remained, and the Corrington verdict had not helped one bit, although he had appeared to take it quite philosophically – he had been expecting it, he said – and she still secretly suspected it was probably the right verdict. Also she wished Jacky didn't hit the dope so heavily. She had said nothing, she had relinquished that right in his childhood, and in any case realised he would find it pretty hypocritical coming from her, with the amount of booze she'd put away in her life. She just hoped to God he was sticking to dope.

Jacky quickly fell asleep beside her in the front passenger seat, and, coasting along the motorway with no one to talk to, she became aware of a motor bike which seemed to be keeping speed with her consistently, even when she slowed to fiddle with the car radio. The bike became the focus of her attention for some time until she was suddenly jerked out of her absorption by the lead item on the two o'clock news. The bodies of Richard Corrington and Amanda Lane had been found at or near their Exmoor home. The former had died of shotgun wounds and the latter from a broken neck. The police were not looking for anyone else in connection with the incident.

Involuntarily she cried out. Jacky woke at once. Together they listened to the rest of the report, much of which was speculation and conjecture concerning the trial of Richard Corrington for the *Sparrow-Hawk* killings and his subsequent clearing.

'So the bastard did kill my Joyce then, didn't he, Belle? That's for certain, now, isn't it?'

Yes, Belle agreed. There couldn't be any doubt any more.

At the right moment, for once, she passed a sign telling her that there was a motorway service station approaching. She indicated left, then put a hand affectionately on Jacky's arm.

'Time for a cup of tea, love,' she said. 'And I couldn't 'alf do with one . . .'

She had completely forgotten about the motor bike and did not even notice whether or not it pulled off the motorway into the service station behind her. Such was her preoccupation with the dramatic radio news bulletin that neither did she check for the presence of the bike during any of the remainder of her journey home to London.

She dropped Jacky at his Kennington bed-sit where, in the spirit of their new mother–son relationship, she had given him a key to the dockland flat, which was technically his after all, before driving on there. In spite of the impact of the latest and presumably final development in the Corrington case, she spent a pleasantly peaceful evening watching a curiously reassuring rerun of *The Man From UNCLE*, on TNT cable, in between the TV news bulletins that she could not resist tuning into. And the next morning she woke feeling really quite happy under the circumstances and went over in her mind the state of her life.

She was broke but, more by luck than judgement because when she had bought the Limehouse flat in Jacky's name it had not even remotely occurred to her that she might end up living in it herself, she had somehow retained a decent enough place to live and even the aged Jag – for the time being at any rate. A letter from her agent had awaited her, telling her that she was up for a tasty role in what promised to be a thoroughly decent little Channel Four film, and the director had already confided that she really did think Belle was right for the part.

When Todd Mallett had cancelled their end-of-trial dinner date, which had not offended her as much as it might otherwise have done because she had understood, he had, even in what appeared to be a state of abject misery, still asked if he could perhaps visit her in London as soon as he had cleared everything up concerning the case. That might take longer now with what had happened the previous day, but she hoped he had really meant it, and found herself looking forward, almost indecently, to such a meeting.

Most important of all she really did seem to have discovered that she had a son, and, rather more remarkably, he seemed to have started to accept her as his mother.

Ever the fighter, ever willing and eager to find the best in any situation, Belle really felt quite chirpy – until she went to the bathroom and happened to glance out of the little window, the only one in the riverside apartment which looked on to the street.

There was a man standing across the road. He was leaning against the wall of the old warehouse opposite and he appeared to be staring quite intently up at her apartment. He was wearing motor bike leathers topped by a flyer's jacket with its sheepskin collar turned up, and his head was encased in one of those helmets that covered virtually the whole of his face, even though there was no motor bike anywhere in sight as far as Belle could see. She watched him for several minutes. He did not move. There was something about him which was familiar, yet she could not for the life of her think what it was or who, even in the helmet, he reminded her of. She told herself she was being neurotic in thinking he was watching her flat, there was nothing much to watch for a start with almost all the windows looking towards the river, and she couldn't see his eyes although his head was pointed towards her apartment block.

Eventually, always a practical and unusually down-to-earth sort of person for an actress, she admonished herself sharply for being silly and returned to the living room where she had earlier started to respond to her accumulated mail and the various messages left on her telephone answering-machine – many of them concerning her financial dilemma and quite unwelcome, but none the less demanding attention. She wished she had stuck to showbusiness, although for so many years chance would have been a fine thing.

She sighed. After half an hour or so she could no longer concentrate and returned to the bathroom for another look out of the window – just in case. The man was still there. Damn! She watched him for a few minutes more, the feelings of anxiety fully returning now in spite of her attempts to quell them, but was just about to make herself turn away and ignore his presence – he could be there for so many reasons, she told herself – when the man removed his motor bike crash helmet.

She could see his face clearly and he did indeed seem to be staring directly at her, although she knew that he could not see her through the mottled glass of the bathroom window.

Recognition came swift and sharp as the thrust of a knife to the heart. The hair, with its idiosyncratic quiff, was so distinctive. And the leathers, that flyer's jacket – of course! She had many times seen photographs of him wearing those, with that blessed bike of his.

It was Richard Corrington. He was dead. And yet he was alive and watching her.

She shook her head as if she mistrusted her own vision, then she pushed her face against the window, screwing up her eyes to get a better look and ensure she had made no mistake. She remembered the binoculars she always kept by the balcony window, in order to be able to study the river, and ran to fetch them, but the man replaced his helmet just before she had managed to focus properly.

She craned her neck and peered up and down the street, and then she saw it, its front wheel and part of the handlebars just sticking out of the alleyway close to the river – a black motor bike. She recalled from the court case that the bike Richard Corrington rode was a black Triumph Daytona. She wouldn't know a Daytona from a skateboard – but it was a black motor cycle out there, sure enough.

Involuntarily she shivered.

Shaken beyond measure she returned to the living room and half fell on to the big squashy sofa. Pulling herself partially together with a huge effort of will she reached for the telephone and dialled the number of Exeter's Heavitree Road police station.

In Exeter Todd was enjoying a rather better day than he had experienced in a long time. He had spent most of the previous afternoon and that morning running the gauntlet of the press, but it was not proving to be that unpleasant an experience, as they seemed to want to turn him into some kind of hero. The cop who was right all along. Everybody wanted to talk to him, and a lot of people, including some of his superiors, wanted to congratulate him. He had got the result in the end. It was not in the way that Todd would have wished, certainly not with two more deaths to take into account, albeit one of them the murderer himself, but, in the police force, as in any other line of work in the modern competitive world, it is ultimately only results that count.

The murder of Amanda Lane followed by the written confession and suicide of Richard Corrington seemed to prove the case for the prosecution – which in court, amid all the showmanship of a TV spectacular played out to the biggest public gallery in the history of the British legal system, had failed to convince a jury that the actor was guilty – beyond any doubt at all.

Todd was pleased, of course. He could not help but reflect that he was almost certain now to walk the promotion he was up for that winter. And he was in the middle of this thoroughly satisfying thought when his direct line rang. He picked up the receiver and heard the voice of Belle Parker.

'Todd, he's not dead, he's here outside my flat.'

Her voice was high pitched, verging on hysteria, he thought. In spite of his strong feelings for her he did not know her all that well, none the less he did not think she was a woman who would often lose control.

'What are you talking about, Belle?' he asked.

'Ricky Corrington.' She was shouting into the phone now. 'It's Ricky Corrington. He's outside my flat. He followed me all the way from Devon on his motor bike, I'm sure of it.'

Todd groaned. Don't say Belle was going to turn out to be a complete nutter, too.

'Belle, listen to me very carefully.' He was aware that he was being patronising, but he couldn't help it. This was one of the good days. There hadn't been too many of them lately, and he didn't want it ruined by a load of hysterical nonsense.

'Richard Corrington is quite definitely dead. I went to Landacre yesterday morning and I saw the bodies of both Amanda and Richard Corrington. He'd shot himself through the mouth with a twelve-bore and damn near blown his head off. Not a pretty sight.'

Belle was quick. 'If he'd blown his head off then you couldn't see his face, could you?'

Todd sighed. Why was he always attracted to difficult women?

'No, I couldn't see his face, but there is absolutely no doubt that Richard Corrington killed himself yesterday and that I saw his body and his poor bloody dead horse beside him. I also saw the suicide note he wrote in his own handwriting.'

'And what the fuck does a suicide note prove?'

She sounded very angry and Todd was taken by surprise. He had not heard her swear before. When he spoke again he had changed the tone of his voice.

'Look Belle, Richard Corrington is dead, but if there's some kind of a prowler watching your flat, call your local nick.'

'You're not bleedin' listening to me, are you?' she still sounded angry.

He sighed. They'd really got off on the wrong foot this time.

'Call your local nick,' he said again. 'There's nothing I can do from here.'

'Thanks very much,' she responded. The phone went dead.

He sat for a few seconds looking at the humming receiver he still held in his hand. Finally he replaced it, and made himself return to the pile of paperwork concerning the case which he had been trying to plough through.

After a few minutes he gave in, sat back in his chair and buzzed for Sergeant Pitt. 'Has Corrington's body been formally identified yet?' he asked.

'Well, no boss, it's a bit difficult when he's got no head left worth mentioning, but we've got George Brooks coming in this afternoon to keep the book straight.'

'Right, I want a finger print check on the body, and I want it fast,' said the DCI.

Pitt looked surprised. 'But there's no doubt, boss, there can't be.' He said it as a statement but with a note of wondering none the less.

'Just do it, Pitt,' snapped Todd.

When the man had retreated he picked up his phone and contacted the London police station covering the area where Arabella Parker lived. He told them they may or may not receive a call from the actress concerning a prowler which could be connected with the Corrington murder inquiry, and either way, he would appreciate a thorough check around her dockland home.

Belle, by now very anxious, did call her local police. They turned up at the apartment in comforting strength and were indeed reassuringly thorough, although obviously quite bemused by her repeated claims that she was being watched by a dead man.

There was no sign of any prowler in the vicinity. The uniformed sergeant in charge, who looked about twenty years old to Belle, assured her that he would have someone regularly patrol the area for a bit, and then left. It was already early evening. She poured herself a large gin and tonic and tried to think of something else.

She dug out a favourite old video and watched it resolutely. Eventually she decided to indulge in a spot of comfort eating and phoned for a takeaway pizza.

Was it possible that she had been mistaken? She knew she hadn't been, really. Disconsolately she wandered into the bathroom and peered out through the window. It was dark, but the street outside was well-lit, and there was no sign of a lurking motor cyclist, or anybody at all lurking, come to that. Just as she was turning away a police car obligingly drove past, very slowly, its two occupants obviously carefully scrutinising the street. Somewhat cheered by this, she accepted delivery of the pizza – none the less checking carefully through the spy hole in her front door before opening it – and uncorked a bottle of Chianti. She drank the lot, and this further cheered her. She even managed a little half joke to herself. Perhaps she had seen a ghost.

The finger print check was a disaster.

'What do you mean, they've been destroyed?' stormed Todd.

'Once someone has been acquitted of an offence we have no right to keep his prints, boss,' Pitt explained early the next morning. 'They wouldn't normally be wiped as quick as this – but you know Nemrac, he was on to it straight away.'

Dental records were a non starter. The corpse had virtually no head left let alone teeth. Todd was beginning to get a very bad feeling about all of this. He called Belle Parker. Her answering machine replied. He did not leave a message. He told himself that he was in danger of becoming as hysterical as he had judged her to be – and that he must not let his personal feelings influence him. Richard Corrington was dead, and that was that.

Minutes later came a telephone call that really set him thinking. It was from Bruce Macintosh. Todd assumed the man just wanted to talk about Corrington's death, to be reassured again of Todd's belief that the actor had also killed Ruth Macintosh, to be able to believe perhaps that it really was all over. The policeman could not have been more wrong.

'I've just had a phone call from one of the women Ruth shared a flat with in London before we married.' Bruce sounded breathless. 'There is a connection between Ruth and *Sparrow-Hawk*, would you believe. About a year before I met her – around seventeen or eighteen years ago it would have been – Ruth had an affair with the actor who first played Jack Sparrow, in a pilot that never got shown or something. His name was Martin Viner.'

Todd sat up very straight trying to take in what he had been told.

'The woman who called me is a nurse, I knew about her but I hadn't been able to find her. She's been with the Red Cross in a remote part of Africa for almost a year. I wrote to her at the last address Ruth had for her, but she didn't get the letter until she returned to England yesterday.

'She said Ruth met Viner when she worked for his solicitor, and she saw him for several months around the time he made the *Sparrow-Hawk* film. He was a real looker of course, flavour of the month, and all that, but apparently Ruth was always a bit afraid of him. He had a terrible temper. And she chucked him after he lost the *Sparrow-Hawk* role.'

'Because of his temper?'

'It was more than that. Ruth told her friend that she reckoned losing *Sparrow-Hawk* sent Viner right over the top. She couldn't cope with his behaviour any more. He was desperately possessive and always in a rage.'

Bruce broke off from the narrative. 'I don't know what this means, Todd, maybe it's just a coincidence . . . I mean what do you think?'

Todd didn't respond. 'Is there anything else?' he asked.

'Well, apparently he wouldn't take no for an answer. He kept following her around and writing her letters. Although, whatever happened, by the time I met her he had given up and it was all history.'

'And you never knew anything about the affair?'

'No. We had a pact never to discuss our previous relationships.'

'I'm surprised none of the other people you contacted earlier knew anything about it, though.'

'He was a married man, Todd. It was all a secret, but I suppose Ruth needed to talk to someone, and it seems that she confided in just this one friend.

'And she tells me Viner kicked up a real stink with the TV company, too, when he was dropped,' Bruce went on. 'I would've expected you guys to have found out about him earlier, I mean, I'd have thought he would have been an obvious suspect once you had the *Sparrow-Hawk* link . . .'

'We did find out about him, Bruce.' Todd cut him short. 'He died three years ago.'

'Are you sure?'

'Of course I'm sure.' Todd snapped his reply.

The truth was he was beginning not to be sure of anything any more. Life and death at least were normally straightforward enough, weren't they, whatever Belle Parker and Bruce Macintosh might think?

He forced himself to calm down. 'Viner died in a fire in a nursing home, he'd had a terrible accident and was confined to a wheel chair, he had no chance.' Todd could not resist getting his own back a little. 'I'm surprised a journalist like yourself didn't know that . . .'

'I haven't checked cuts yet, I came straight on to you. But in any case he wasn't that well known, was he?'

'No, you're right. I was just winding you up. The pilot was never shown, he'd done bugger all else, nobody really knew or cared who he was. There was little or no publicity about him when he died.'

'I didn't think so, but wait a minute.' Todd could hear Bruce gasping at the other end of the phone. 'You said he died in a fire in a nursing home, didn't you?'

'That's right.'

'Do you know where?'

'Yep. It was here in Devon. Place called Craddack, just outside Plymouth.'

'The Oceanview.' Bruce said the name very slowly and deliberately.

'How do you know that?'

'Todd, I meant to tell you when Corrington was arrested, but I couldn't see how it fitted anyway . . .'

'What?'

'Margaret Nance was an auxiliary nurse at the Oceanview.'

Todd stiffened. 'But she worked as a children's nanny in Truro.'

'Only after Oceanview burned down.'

'There's damn near a whole county between Craddack and her home . . .'

'Todd, if you live in Cornwall you go where the work is, there's not much of it down there – you know that. Her family home was in St Ives but she used to travel to Devon every week and live-in at Oceanview when she was working.

'The fire happened just a couple of months before

she died. She was one of the lucky ones. Off duty.'

'Dear God!' Todd turned the two words into a cry of anguish.

Bruce Macintosh was still talking. 'Are you absolutely sure he is dead, Todd?' he asked.

'Of course we bloody are. Do you think we didn't check it? I had a team on it. There was an autopsy. An inquest. But I didn't know Margaret Nance worked at Oceanview – I don't even remember it being in her file.' Todd took a deep breath and started again. 'Bruce, I don't know what to think, mate, any more. But thanks anyway.'

He finished the conversation as quickly as he could and then called in Sergeant Pitt.

'Martin Viner,' he said simply. 'I want all we've got on him on my desk – now – and I want everybody we've got looking into his history.'

'But he's dead, boss.'

'For Christ's sake, Pitt, do you have to question everything?' Todd was a lot more ruffled than he liked to admit to himself. 'When we talked to Viner's wife, she didn't have any doubts about him being dead, did she?'

'Good Lord, no, boss. And she was glad to see the back of him, made no bones about it. I reckon he used to knock her about, until he was crocked, that is. She said he had a vicious temper and put it about a bit, but fortunately that kept him out of her way a lot of the time. Quite open about it all, she was.

'They'd been separated for years but never got a divorce. So when he snuffed it, she got the life insurance. Happy woman.'

Todd thumped the top of his desk with a clenched fist.

'There's something not right, Pitt. I want the investigation into Viner opened up. And I want Mrs Viner's phone number.'

Anxiously Todd called the number in Richmond, Surrey. There was a quick reply, and fortunately it was Mrs Susan Viner at the other end of the phone and not a dreaded answering-machine.

As calmly as he could, Todd apologised for bothering the woman again, muttered something about 'one or two gaps in our inquiries', and began to ask Mrs Viner about her husband and his death.

'I wonder if you could tell me what kind of man your husband was, Mrs Viner?' he asked evenly.

'I've already told you all about it, he was barking mad and he had a vicious streak running right through him,' she responded.

Pitt was certainly right. There was no love lost there, Todd thought. 'But people say things like that about actors, don't they? You know, actors are all mad?'

He was coaxing her almost, he wanted her to talk freely to him, although he was becoming more and more afraid of what she was going to say.

'Detective Chief Inspector, when I said that my husband was mad that is exactly what I mean. His father was a violent schizophrenic who took his own life. His only brother was a diagnosed psychotic schizophrenic who died in his teens. There was a sister who died as a baby – a cot death allegedly although there were those who suspected differently, I later learned . . .'

Susan Viner's voice sounded shaky. 'I didn't find out about Martin's background until about four years after we married. He always claimed he had avoided any mental illness, but he would never go near a doctor, and the more I lived with him the less sure I became of that. As time went by the more relieved I became that we never had children.'

Todd could feel the ground being pulled away from beneath his feet. 'Mrs Viner, why didn't you tell my officers about all this in the beginning?'

'My husband is dead, Chief Inspector. I got to the stage where I believed him to be capable of almost anything, but he couldn't be involved in your inquiries. He died three years ago, you know that. And there's no point in raking up a very painful past.'

'Mrs Viner, how did your husband respond when he was dropped as Sparrow-Hawk?'

'It took him right over the edge. It was the accident which really broke him, though. Do you know about that?'

'Yes of course, but I'd like to hear it from you.'

'Martin was a brilliant stuntman, Mr Mallett – because he was crazy, I always said. He had no fear. Even after the *Sparrow-Hawk* fiasco he had his stunt work. He was particularly talented as a pilot, but he always pushed everything to the limit. There were a number of producers and directors who would not work with him because they did not think he was safe. He was being filmed flying a helicopter under a low bridge when apparently he misjudged by inches and crashed. He was lucky, although he never saw it that way, to come out alive.

'His legs and his pelvis were shattered, and he never walked again. But because of his reputation he didn't even get damages. The director claimed he had been asked to fly just over the bridge, not beneath it. It was typical of Martin to go a step further . . .'

The woman paused. She sounded weary. 'And of course he took the attitude that if he hadn't been dropped as Jack Sparrow he would still have had the use of his legs because he would not have had to go back to stunt work . . .'

Todd interrupted. His imagination was getting the better of him. 'Mrs Viner, did you ever see your husband's body?'

'No Chief Inspector. He was burned to a cinder. There wouldn't have been much to see.'

'Mrs Viner, do you think there is the slightest possibility that your husband could have survived the blaze and started a new life for himself, taken on another identity?'

'My husband couldn't walk.' Mrs Viner enunciated as if she were talking to an idiot. 'He could barely move unaided. He could never have survived. He was burned to death in his bed. And in any case there was an autopsy, you know . . .'

Desperately Todd tried to work it out.

He called Belle Parker's number again. He checked his watch. It was almost midday. There was still only the answering-machine in attendance. He cursed silently and this time left a message for her to call him urgently. God knows who was standing outside Belle's flat. He kicked himself for not taking her more seriously. He had been revelling in smug euphoria, and that was the kind of luxury a good policeman could not allow himself.

Under the circumstances Belle had had a pretty good day, even though during the brief amount of time she spent in her flat she had been unable to stop herself frequently glancing through the bathroom window.

Outside there had been no sign of a motor cyclist or any other kind of prowler, and once more she had seen a police car driving slowly by – the local nick were proving as good as their word and were obviously keeping an eye on her. She had begun to work really hard at convincing herself that she was mistaken, that Richard Corrington had not been lurking outside her home, and, perhaps, Todd's opinion that she was being hysterical – so clearly indicated by his patronising attitude – had been justified.

She had been shopping that morning and picked up his message when she returned briefly at lunchtime before dashing off to a meeting at Channel Four with her agent. She had not really had time to return his call, and in any case, although it pleased her considerably that he was concerned about her, she had not quite forgiven him for being so patronising during their earlier conversation. She thought it would do him no harm to be kept waiting for a while before she called back.

Grateful for the underground garage – in addition to keeping the Jag out of the sight of anyone who might be inclined to remove it from her, the garage could be approached directly from within the building and there was a complex security card system controlling access from outside – she took the lift downstairs and collected her car. As she swept through the garage doors in the big motor she slowed down and carefully surveyed the street to either side of her. It was a typically dull early November day. There was nobody suspicious around, in fact, nobody at all. Limehouse Mews was a quiet cul-de-sac constructed only to give access to the homes built as part of the development around Limehouse Basin – which in prouder days had linked the River Thames with Britain's foremost canal, the Grand Union, and had been the dock where cargoes were transferred from sea-going vessels on to canal barges.

She drove slowly up the mews on to the main drag heading for the City and throughout the journey to Channel Four's Victoria HQ – in an area where it was mercifully still just about possible to park, Belle, always unhappy when separated from the Jag, liked to drive everywhere if she could – she checked frequently in her mirror to see if there was any sign of being followed.

The meeting went well. The station's new chief executive had asked that she pop into his office for a chat; and every indication was, that as long as the film went ahead as planned, the part would be Belle's if she wanted it. So when Belle and her agent left the futuristic metal and glass building they both considered that a small celebration was in order and found a nearby wine bar where they treated themselves to a bottle of champagne.

'Here's to the future.' Belle proposed the toast with feeling, and her agent happily drank to it.

But when the bottle was empty Belle reluctantly declined the offer of a second one.

'I'm sorely tempted, I reckon I could do with a really good drink, but I've got the motor,' she offered by way of excuse.

On the way home she hit the full force of the evening rush hour. The journey back to Limehouse was mind-bogglingly slow, taking more than an hour.

She finally unlocked the door to her apartment at 8 p.m. And as she stepped gratefully into the hallway, she considered that she might console herself by

357

cracking that bottle of rather good champagne she knew she still had in the fridge and drinking it all on her own.

The frustrations of driving under such conditions, and the excitement of the prospect of quality work again, so occupied Belle's mind that she barely gave a thought to her mystery motor cyclist.

Twenty-Seven

Todd had a photograph of Martin Viner on his desk. He was a handsome man with a strong, chisel-jawed face framed by a shock of blonde curls which would now be considered unfashionably long. His eyes were striking. Pale grey and, even in a photograph, somehow penetrating. The picture had been taken around the time that Viner made the *Sparrow-Hawk* pilot, seventeen years earlier, and was the latest photo it had so far been possible to obtain.

The policeman stared long and hard. There was something familiar about Viner. Todd had the distinct feeling that he knew the man from somewhere.

'Well, I don't know, boss, maybe he's just got one of those sort of faces,' said Sergeant Pitt unhelpfully. 'And he did an awful lot of telly once, didn't he? Small parts, maybe, but all over the place he was . . .'

Todd put the photograph in his briefcase. Pitt was probably right. In any case he had no intention of wasting any more time.

Abruptly he rose to his feet.

'We're going to Plymouth, Pitt, and I want you to imagine you're driving in Le Mans,' Todd commanded.

The high-powered police Rover roared through the gates of Heavitree Road police station as if it were about to take off and fly, which was more or less Sergeant Pitt's intention.

'What I want to know first,' said Todd, 'is if there is any chance at all that Martin Viner could still be alive. And I don't trust any other bugger on this one.'

En route Todd worked on his mobile phone. First he called Plymouth's premier police station, Charles Cross, where the duty inspector, who introduced himself as Jim Pendennis, promised to have all the files on the nursing home fire ready for Todd's arrival. Then he contacted the fire brigade and talked to the chief fire officer.

'All three residents who died were wheel chair cases and they didn't stand a chance,' reported the man. 'The nurse who tried to help them went with them. It was the worst case I have ever dealt with. The screams were terrible. They didn't die at once, you see, and the fire erupted so suddenly they didn't have the mercy of being asphyxiated by smoke.

'They were in rooms on the second floor. The lifts went down straight away, and within minutes the staircase collapsed. Those who could walk were able to get out straight away, but the wheel chair cases were trapped. They couldn't get out and we couldn't get to them. Their rooms had fire doors and window seals. If the doors had been shut the people inside should have been reasonably safe for an hour – that's the regulation now with nursing and old people's homes – but the doors had been left open. So bloody stupid – it happens again and again.

'I'll never forget that night as long as I live. Half my men were weeping as they worked.'

The fire chief had a quiet, matter of fact way of talking. Todd found himself imagining the scene vividly. He shuddered.

'I'm trying to find out if there is any chance at all

that one of the wheel chair cases, a man called Martin Viner, may have secretly escaped.'

A hollow laugh came down the air waves.

'You should have been there – you wouldn't even ask.'

Was he on completely the wrong track? Todd didn't know. All he could do was to carry on digging.

Pitt touched almost 120 on the motorway-standard A38 between Exeter and Plymouth. Even though he had torrential rain to contend with for most of the way, the journey was covered at the highest possible speed with blue light flashing and siren wailing, and took just on half an hour. They arrived shortly before 1 p. m.

Sergeant Pitt looked as if he was on a high, driving fast excited him.

'Well done Pitt,' said Todd. 'Eat your heart out Damon Hill.'

The sergeant was beaming as the two men, heads bowed against the still heavy rain, walked briskly into Charles Cross police station. But Todd could not help his attention being drawn to the ruined church, bombed during the Second World War, which had been preserved as a memorial in the middle of the roundabout in front of the station.

He turned to look at it, as he had so many times, today a starkly dark shape, strangely featureless, shrouded in a veil of rainfall. He barely noticed the stream of traffic roaring around it. Todd always remembered his mother talking of the wartime night when Plymouth burned and the red glow in the sky could be seen in his North Devon home town seventy miles away. The city, its entire centre destroyed, had suffered a blitz every bit as devastating as London.

Todd shivered. To him Plymouth would always be a town of ghosts.

Inside the police station he focused his concentration on to more recent tragedy. The files on the Oceanview fire were filled with chilling photographs of burning rubble, and of the remains of the victims. Remains was the accurate word.

'A lot of petrol went up, and there's nothing quite as devastating as a petrol explosion,' said Inspector Pendennis by way of explanation.

'Petrol?' Todd was puzzled. 'In a nursing home?'

The inspector shook his head. 'The boat work shop next door. I say next door, you know Craddack, don't you? It's an overgrown fishing village, attracts the tourist trade in spades now. In the heart of Craddack everything is back to back, on top of everything else. That's where Oceanview was – not the usual location for a nursing home, because it was part of a terrace – but it was a huge building on several storeys with fabulous sea views on every floor, and they'd installed lifts of course. It was also damn near on top of Ely Trevilian's boat workshop.

'And he had the place stashed full of petrol. He worked on power boats, the kind you use for water skiing, and they usually run on petrol. A couple of them went up too.

'Funny really if it wasn't so tragic. All the safety regulations there are if you run a nursing home, and yet neither the fire people nor us have any jurisdiction at all over the property next door.

'Old Ely was damn lucky not to go to jail for manslaughter. He was actually prosecuted for misuse of premises and he got a suspended sentence. It was probably his age that saved him.

'He'd broken every rule in the book. Mind you, I reckon they all do . . .'

Todd's luck was in. Jim Pendennis, every bit as Cornish as his name suggested, was a long-serving officer in the Devon and Cornwall Constabulary and had been stationed in the Plymouth area for almost twenty years. He knew his manor and its history backwards.

'So what actually caused the blaze?' asked the DCI.

'An electrical fault in the workshop. Old Ely again. He'd wired half the place up himself and a right botch up, it was.'

'I'd like to talk to this Ely.'

'You can try, but you'll be lucky to get any sense out of him. He's more Cornish than a tiddy oggie and he doesn't trust foreigners. He's always been a bit eccentric, Ely, and since the fire he's gone right off his rocker, if you ask me. But he's supposed to have been a superb natural engineer in his time, worked in Devonport Docks, which is what brought him up this way . . .'

Todd told Pendennis about the Martin Viner connection, but the policeman merely reiterated the verdict of the local fire chief. Martin Viner was dead, all right, along with the other wheel chair cases.

The DCI picked up a photograph of Margaret Nance.

'She worked at the nursing home. There are all these threads, Inspector. Too many coincidences . . .'

Jim Pendennis took the photograph from Todd. 'I come from Hayle, you know, just this side of St Ives; went to school with the poor maid's father.'

He sighed. 'It was two months after the fire that

she was murdered. How can it be anything other than a tragic coincidence?'

'I don't know, Inspector, but if there is a link then I'm damn well going to find it.' Todd was brisk again. Business-like.

'Is there anybody else I should talk to?' he asked.

'Well, there's Dr McTavish. He ran Oceanview. A bit of a character around these parts, but the fire destroyed him. He's a broken man, really. There was some criticism of the way he ran the place, bound to be. He must be well into his seventies now. People say he was too old to be in charge of a nursing home.'

'McTavish? He's not local then?'

'From Glasgow. Came to Craddack on holiday thirty years ago and never went home.'

John Pendennis walked over to the open window and took a big breath of fresh air. Beyond him through the window Todd could see the shell of the church again. Pendennis was staring at it, as if he were seeing much more than a carefully preserved ruin.

The Plymouth policeman's voice was sad when he spoke again. 'It's not just the dead and injured who are the casualties . . .'

Ely Trevilian was not quite what Todd expected. The old man had a leathery weather-worn face and impossibly black hair which Todd thought must surely be dyed. In different circumstances Todd would have found it difficult to keep a straight face.

Ely lived alone in an old coastguard cottage on the edge of Craddack, a little white-painted place which seemed to be almost precariously balanced on the cliff side. A sea breeze turned the rain to salt and Todd could feel his skin stinging as the wind lashed his face.

He hammered for some minutes on the front door, causing fragments of peeling blue paint to fall to the ground, before Ely eventually emerged. And, as Jim Pendennis had predicted, he was not best pleased to see his visitors.

'Questions, questions and more bleddy questions – for three bleddy years,' he grumbled.

If the old man felt any remorse or even responsibility for the terrible fire which started in his workshop, he certainly wasn't showing it. He was, in fact, openly belligerent.

'They'm be putting the blame on me and tidn't right,' he said. ''Tis a bleddy load of nonsense. There weren't nothing wrong with me electrics.'

'But Mr Trevilian, you had wired the place yourself. Didn't it occur to you to bring in a professional electrician, at least to have it checked?'

'A professional? I can do a better job with electrics then any so-called professional. I always 'ad a way with electrics.'

He looked pleased with himself. His eyes shone unnaturally. Jim Pendennis was probably right, thought Todd. Off his rocker.

'Mr Trevilian,' he persisted, 'your workshop was full of petrol. Didn't it occur to you that was dangerous?'

'Pah.' The old man oozed contempt from every pore. 'You'm never worked in an engine room when yer ship is under fire then? More'n fifty years ago 'twas, and I can still taste the fear. Seven attacks I survived, what be the odds on that? That be danger, I tell 'ee.

'There weren't nowt dangerous in my workshop. I don't care what thigee rule book says – I knows 'ow to keep petrol safe enough.'

'Mr Trevilian, your stash of petrol exploded and caused a terrible fire. How do you explain that?'

'Some bugger tampered with me electrics, I told em all that. Never took no bleddy notice.'

'A team of fire experts went through what was left of your premises with a tooth comb. There was absolutely no indication that anything had been tampered with. They concluded that the fault was in your wiring which could have self ignited at any time.'

Ely Trevilian was not impressed.

'Pah,' he said again. 'Bleddy experts. Brains in thigee backsides. What do they bleddy know?'

Todd was smiling in spite of himself as he and Pitt left the old man in his little cottage.

'Now you know why we won the war, Pitt,' he said.

Dr Iain McTavish was a rather different proposition. His thin, acutely intelligent face clouded over when Todd explained who he was and what he wanted to talk about. Dr McTavish was a tall man with a slight stoop. Deep lines of sorrow were etched on pale parchment skin. His eyes had a permanently haunted look in them.

He lived in the Barbican now, the touristy part of Plymouth full of cobbled streets and curio shops, surrounding the famous old harbour from which sailed the Pilgrim Fathers' ship, *The Mayflower*. Dr McTavish's small neat flat was tucked away at the top end of an insignificant little lane, far too narrow for a car to manoeuvre. It was almost as if the doctor were deliberately hiding, and in some ways he was. Certainly he confided straight away that he could no longer bear to even visit Craddack.

'You were cleared of all blame,' said Todd.

The older man smiled wanly. 'Not possible,' he said. 'I shall carry the burden to my grave. Those people were in my care and I failed them.'

'I want to talk to you about Martin Viner,' said Todd. 'What can you remember about him?'

Todd was aware of the doctor almost physically pulling himself together.

'A difficult patient, a difficult man, really. But then he had a lot to put up with. Terrible thing for such an active person, a man who made a living out of performing stunts. You know all about the helicopter crash, I presume?'

Todd nodded. 'And Viner never walked again. Is that correct?'

'Absolutely. His legs and pelvis were smashed to pieces. He suffered terrible pain.'

'And there was nothing that could be done about it?'

'Well, no . . .' The doctor hesitated.

'Dr McTavish was there any chance at all that Martin Viner would ever have been able to walk again?'

'Well, there's been extraordinary progress in that area in recent years. Hip replacement. That kind of thing. There are surgeons who can virtually rebuild a person's legs. But Martin's case was extreme. He'd had surgery, of course, but it had not been successful.'

'How long was he with you, doctor?'

'About a year. His accident happened a year before that and he had been in hospital before coming to us.'

'And was he regularly medically examined?'

'Not in the way that you mean. He hated being "messed about with", he called it, and there wasn't

367

much point, so we held off. I wanted him to have psychiatric help, for his depression, you know. But he wouldn't. Went quite white with anger when I suggested it, I remember . . .'

'Dr McTavish, is there any way Martin Viner could have regained the use of his legs without you knowing about it?'

The doctor ran his fingers through his sparse grey hair. 'I suppose there is. He had his own room. But why would anyone keep something like that a secret?'

'What if he wanted to disappear, to create a new identity for himself?'

Iain McTavish looked startled. 'And deliberately cause the death of severely disabled people? Even if it were possible, Chief Inspector, nobody could be that evil, could they?'

Todd looked at the other man. You could almost reach out and touch the gentleness in him.

'I wouldn't be too sure of that, Doctor,' he said quietly.

McTavish shook his head. His eyes were troubled.

'You know once, at night, when everyone was in bed, I thought I heard footsteps from Martin Viner's room. Up and down, as if someone was pacing the room. I went to investigate, and the door was locked. Now that was never allowed for safety reasons.'

He paused, and for a moment Todd thought he was going to break down. 'Safety! What a joke that seems, now, Inspector, aye? There shouldn't even have been a key, God knows where Martin got it from.'

The doctor continued as if there had been no interruption in his narrative.

'Eventually Martin came to the door, in his wheel

chair. I said I thought I'd heard footsteps. He looked down at his legs, and then just laughed at me. Rather unpleasantly I recall. He gave me the key meekly enough when I insisted, although I remember that he seemed terribly angry. But then, he was almost always angry.'

Todd was riveted. He felt that burst of adrenalin he always got when he knew he was making some progress at last. Even his anxiety for Arabella's safety had been banished firmly to the back of his mind.

'Dr McTavish, was there any link at all between Martin Viner and the girl who worked at your home who was later murdered – Margaret Nance?'

The expression 'jumped out of his skin' flitted across Todd's mind as he watched the doctor's alarmed reaction.

'Why on earth do you ask that?'

'Will you just answer me, doctor.'

'Inspector, you are beginning to frighten me. There was something between them, yes. You see, I started to keep an eye on Martin after the incident of the key, and one day, well, I caught Margaret in his bed.'

It was Todd's turn to jump.

'So what did you do about it?'

'My first reaction was to sack her, but I've never been very good at sacking people.'

Iain McTavish sighed. 'She broke down in tears and begged me not to tell anyone. Said it would never happen again and she was only comforting him because she felt so sorry for him. A man struck down in his prime, she said.

'In the end I just gave her a severe warning. I spoke to Martin pretty sharply though, told him he might be disabled but that didn't excuse his behaviour. I mean, Margaret was only eighteen, and he was almost three times her age. I told him that if anything like it ever happened again he would have to leave.

'He apologised. But he gave no appearance of being at all sorry. In fact I remember thinking that he seemed quite smug . . .'

Todd could feel his fingers tingling with excitement.

'Can I ask, in the condition he was allegedly in, would he have been capable of full sexual relations?'

'Of course, Chief Inspector. Just about every bone in his lower body had been broken, but he wasn't paralysed. And anyway, even in cases of paralysis sex is frequently possible . . .'

'Dr McTavish, did you tell anybody about this when Margaret Nance was killed?'

The doctor shook his head. 'No, Chief Inspector, I didn't. Her family had enough grief to cope with. Martin was dead. There seemed no point. Not then.'

He looked directly at Todd. 'I see what you are driving at very clearly. I don't know if I can believe it . . .'

Todd shrugged. 'I don't know either. But it's beginning to fit. A patient who is not as disabled as he pretends to be seduces a young girl. She is under his spell. She provides him with the key you discovered. Maybe she also provided him with the key to Ely Trevilian's workshop, maybe he needed tools and she got those for him. Transport too.'

Todd was warming to his theme. 'But unlike our man she has a conscience. It probably had not occurred to her that people would have to die. She shares a terrible secret with Viner and he doesn't trust her. He fears she is going to break and give him away. So he kills her . . . What do you think, Doctor?'

Iain McTavish looked stunned. He did not speak.

'If Martin Viner had been able to walk,' Todd continued, 'would he have been able to come and go quite easily from Oceanview, at night, say?'

'Well yes. We didn't run a prison. The front door had an ordinary Yale lock.'

There was bitter irony in the doctor's voice when he added: 'And, of course, there was a fire escape . . .'

'So,' Todd seemed to be talking to himself now, 'if Martin Viner did fake his death and take on a new identity, where is he now? And who is he now?'

Uneasily Todd found himself thinking about Belle and her prowler again.

'You haven't got a more up to date photograph of Viner, have you, Doctor?' Todd asked. 'The only stuff we could find was donkeys' years old.'

McTavish shook his head. 'That was another of Martin's phobias. He would never let a camera near him. Mind you, I suppose you could understand it . . .'

Todd's antennae started to waggle again. 'Why? Was he scarred? Nobody told me?'

'No, nothing like that. He had no facial scars at all. But he suffered all kinds of psychological reaction to the accident. The most dramatic thing was that he lost all his body hair. He had alopecia . . .'

Todd felt the blood rise in him. He looked at Sergeant Pitt. The younger policeman was already on his feet. The two of them bolted out the door and ran down the cobbled street towards their parked car like a pair of sprinters.

Twenty-Eight

He came at her like Jonah Lomu. His bulk propelled itself through the doorway as if catapulted, smashing into the small of her back. She had not had a chance to turn and lock the door behind her.

Arabella was already falling forwards, the breath forced out of her body, when he wrapped his arms around her legs, whipping her feet off the ground. She crashed heavily to the floor, somehow managing to twist herself around so that she was looking up at him. She had to see his face.

He stood above her staring down at her with contempt, not even bothering to hold on to her. He knew that she was completely in his power. With one leg he kicked backwards slamming the door shut. She was trapped in the apartment with him, and she thought crazily that the slam of the door had sounded like the lid of a coffin being closed.

She could see his face quite clearly now. It was like a death mask. Cold. Merciless.

He was wearing beautifully cut country tweeds and highly polished brown leather boots, and he was smiling as if already pleased with what he had done. Almost dispassionately she realised she probably had only minutes to live, possibly only seconds. She felt unable to move, frozen in a pain-racked heap on the ground, almost beyond fear, resigned to the inevitable. She could not take her eyes off him, although she had been stunned by the fall and her vision was slightly off key. She took in the thick dark hair in its distinctive quiff, the famous *Sparrow-Hawk* lapel pin. She was not sure if she could speak, but somehow the words came.

'Hello, Ricky,' she said.

The contempt in his chilling stare increased. 'What did you call me?' He just breathed the words, his voice a menacing whisper.

She didn't know what she was supposed to say but suspected it would make little difference.

'Ricky.' Perhaps he did not like the diminutive. 'Uh, R-R-Richard,' she stumbled uncertainly, staring at him, suddenly acutely aware that she was seeing only what she had by then expected to see.

He took a step to one side and kicked her viciously in the ribs. It felt as if the polished leather boot concealed a metal tip and she cried out with pain as his foot crunched into flesh and bone. There was a definite cracking sound. She was sure that at least a couple of her ribs had been broken, and she seemed to have no breath left at all. He pulled back his foot and lashed out a second time. This time the lethal toe made devastating contact with her wrist as she ineffectually stretched out a hand to defend herself. The pain was overwhelming. She no longer had the strength to plead for him to stop as she lay gasping on the ground completely at his mercy. Only with her eyes, full of pain as they were, could she beg for her life.

He had no pity in him.

'My name is Jack Sparrow,' he said.

And it was then that she knew who he was . . .

*

'Burrowgate Farm?' Pitt had asked as he threw himself into the big Rover.

'How did you guess?' responded his superior, who within seconds was on the phone talking to DI Cutler.

'I want a team at Burrowgate right away, and I want the place turned over.'

There was some crackling interference.

'What? What are you saying?' yelled Todd. 'I don't care how you get a soddin' search warrant, just get it. And if you have a problem, go, go, without. Do you hear me?'

DI Cutler indicated in his customary expressionless monotone that he heard well enough.

'Right. And I want the Met round at Belle Parker's again. I have reason to believe she is in grave danger. Move! Then get back to me.'

Within half an hour, great organiser that he was, Cutler called to say that a team of officers, including forensic, were on their way to Burrowgate.

'Right,' said Todd. 'Now – get me an order to have Martin Viner's body exhumed, wherever it is. Also, I want all his medical records. I want to know exactly where he was and what happened to him during the year between his helicopter accident and his arrival at Oceanview. And find out if any middle-aged men disappeared from the Plymouth area around the time of the Oceanview fire.

'One more thing. Any news from London about Belle Parker?'

'The local nick will send a couple of chaps around as soon as they can, boss.'

'What! Nobody's on their way?'

'Unsavoury characters lurking outside people's homes are two a penny up there, I gather, boss.

And they have been keeping an eye . . .'

'Get back to them and put a rocket up their arses, Cutler!'

Todd's every nerve seemed to be standing on end. He tried Belle Parker's phone for the umpteenth time. Still there was only the answering-machine.

The scene at Burrowgate Farm was chaotic. Mercifully the rain had stopped, but the ground was still sodden underfoot.

There were police all over the place, dogs barking, Jim Kivel demanding over and over again to be told what the hell was going on and his wife in floods of tears.

Thanks again to Sergeant Pitt's extraordinary driving skills Todd arrived only twenty minutes or so after the team from Exeter. And as he picked his way across a farmyard awash with vibrantly aromatic slush he wondered fleetingly just how many years he would have to work as a rural policeman before he remembered never ever to go anywhere without a pair of Wellington boots.

'Nothing yet boss,' said the sergeant whom Cutler had put in charge of the operation. 'We've had at least a quick look everywhere. There's a big red van in the helicopter hangar, the back of it's sealed up and there are black-out curtains across the rear windows, so you can't see into it at all. It's locked up, and I'm waiting for a PNC check on it before we go any further . . .'

On cue the sergeant's radio bleeped.

He listened for a bit and then, looking rather puzzled, turned to Todd.

'The van is registered to one Jack Sparrow,

Wellington Mansions, Wellington Square, Fulham,' he began.

Todd went white.

'Search it, now!' he ordered, and began to run across the muddy field towards the hangar, no longer even remembering his unsuitable footwear.

'It's locked, sir,' said the sergeant again, trotting behind him.

'I want the thing broken into, fast!'

Todd was shouting at the top of his voice.

It was Pitt who produced a crow bar from nowhere. First he tried to wrench the rear doors open. They were extremely well secured.

'Get on with it, man, smash the damned window,' yelled Todd.

Pitt did his best to comply. It took several almighty blows. The van had been fitted with toughened glass.

Finally Pitt broke through. He tapped out the remaining splinters, and leaning inside the van, managed finally to prise the doors apart.

The interior of the red van resembled a detective's dream of Aladdin's Cave. There was a small bunk bed, a sleeping bag and pillows, a rack of the kind used to carry motor cycles during transit, a selection of stylish suits and country clothes suspended from a rail fastened to the roof, an assortment of false beards, some theatrical make-up, several pairs of dark glasses, a couple of baseball caps, a pair of powerful binoculars, a stack of *Sparrow-Hawk* videos and a selection of posters and photographs from the TV show.

Probably the most chilling discovery of all was a wallet bearing a label with a name and address on it. The name was Ruth Macintosh. Todd felt a tremor run up and down his spine. But there was yet more.

Pitt had also found a surgeon's rubber apron and cap and a box containing surgical gloves

'No stray fibres, no DNA, clever bastard,' thought Todd, and out loud he said: 'Bingo. Now all we've got to do is find the sod.'

His nearly-new suede shoes were wet through and oozing mud and slime. Todd didn't care that they were almost certainly ruined, but became suddenly acutely aware that his feet were icy cold. And as his thoughts once again turned to Belle Parker he felt a raw numbness spread throughout his body.

For the umpteenth time he reached for his telephone and dialled her number. This time there was no reply at all.

Twenty-Nine

The pain in Arabella's ribs was such that she thought her body was going to break in two when he hauled her roughly to her feet. The phone began to ring as he was dragging her upright and he pulled her across the hall to the main telephone point and casually ripped the wires out with one hand.

Then he swung her around, wrapped his hands around her neck, lodged his knee in the small of her back and began to squeeze with strong, expert fingers.

He was concentrating so hard that he was not aware of the door to the spare bedroom opening to his left and very slightly behind him. Jacky stood there, rubbing his eyes with his hands, as if half-asleep or half-drugged or both, struggling to take in the scene before him. The mists cleared suddenly. He picked up the big Chinese vase by the front door, took a step forward, and just as his mother's assailant became aware of movement behind him, smashed him over the head with it.

The man rocked on his feet but did not go down. He was big and powerful. He let go of Belle, though, pushing her away from him so that she dropped to the floor again, a gasping wheezing wreck.

The attacker knew better than to waste energy on words. He let fly with a powerful punch which, even though Jacky had ducked away from the worst of it, caught him a glancing but effective blow on the side of the head. Jacky reeled, collected himself and hit back. He was young, heavily muscled and very strong. But he wasn't a fighter, he'd been on one hell of a bender that afternoon, and his opponent had been trained in how to kill and inflict pain. The viciously booted foot which had already caused his mother so much damage shot out skilfully, like a professional kick box. Jacky, naturally so athletic, dodged the first kick but took a second one full in the stomach. He doubled up, dropping to his knees, and felt a numbing karate chop slice into one shoulder. Jesus! If that had been to his neck he'd probably be dead already. He tried to get to his feet, aware that another blow was about to land. Then the doorbell rang.

The shrill tone just tipped his assailant off balance, Jacky managed to avoid the next brutal chop and flung himself backwards at the front door, fumbling for the lock, thankfully taking in that neither the security chain nor the bolt at the bottom of the door had been slotted into place. His shoulder, the already injured one, had been grasped in a vice-like grip which was sending agonising messages direct to the core of his nervous system, and he felt himself being bodily lifted away from the front door. He gave the lever on the Balham lock a final desperate twist and, just as he was hoisted away from it, the door swung slowly open behind him.

Standing in the doorway, confronted with probably the most extraordinary scene of their careers stood two young uniformed police constables from Limehouse nick.

Belle was still flat out on the floor whimpering to herself and watching with horror as the Sparrow-Hawk attacker, completely ignoring the two policemen, aimed another karate chop at her son.

'What the bleedin' 'ell is going on?' asked the smaller of the two policemen, presumably not really expecting a reply. The other, a keen amateur boxer with the build of a budding Bruno, decided to act first and talk later. He grabbed the raised arm of the attacking man, wrenching it to one side and backwards at an impossible angle. The man screamed and let go of Jacky whom he had still been grasping by the shoulder with his other hand.

'Would you like me to break this arm for you, sir, or are you going to calm down now?' asked the powerfully-built constable conversationally. His colleague took advantage of the moment to grab the other arm of the man who called himself Jack Sparrow, and together the two policemen managed to successfully lock him into a pair of handcuffs.

Studying him as they did so, the second policeman's face was a picture of open amazement. He took in the distinctive head of thick dark hair, the characteristically tailored clothes, and the gold sparrow-hawk pinned to the lapel.

'You're dead,' he said. 'You're that Ricky Corrington.'

'Oh no he bleedin' isn't,' said a weak voice in the corner. Belle, still breathing with difficulty had dragged herself into a sitting position.

'That's Martin Viner you've got there, the mad bastard.'

Viner turned and looked at her. She cringed away from his steady gaze. There was death in his pale grey eyes. She had no doubt that if he could break free he would still finish the job he had begun on her, even with two policemen in the room. He thought he was invincible. The TV hero who must win through to fight again next week. The evil madness was clear in him now.

'I am Jack Sparrow,' he said again. And his delivery was just perfect.

Back in Exeter DI Cutler was on overdrive. He was in his element. Information was coming at him from all directions, and that was just the way he liked it. He was about as near as it was possible for him to get to happiness.

Within minutes of receiving Todd's second lot of instructions the computer search he had ordered revealed that a fifty-one-year-old man had disappeared from Plymouth two days before the Oceanview fire. The man, Peter Nash, had last been seen at midnight leaving a particularly disreputable Union Street strip club where it was well known that the artistically described 'exotic dancers' also provided an imaginative variety of additional services for the right price. And although Peter Nash's wife had claimed her husband would never willingly leave home, police inquiries had revealed that Nash was a regular of the sleaziest joints the notorious Union Street could offer, and, unsurprisingly enough, had a history of marital troubles. He was listed as a vulnerable missing person, but only limited inquiries were undertaken.

'Clever sod,' said Todd when DI Cutler radioed him the news. 'Watch for some sad-looking character leaving a knocking shop and then whack him. Chances are the police won't even think murder. Blokes like Nash do disappearing acts all the time . . .'

Cutler had relaunched investigations into every aspect of Martin Viner. There were still so many unanswered questions. The detective inspector learned that there seemed to be an unaccounted six months in Viner's life following his medical treatment immediately after the helicopter crash. He had, in fact, been released from the London hospital – where he had indeed undergone extensive surgery which had not resulted in him being able to walk again – six months before he went to Oceanview.

Reports indicated that the London hospital had believed that they could do more for him, but Viner had declined. Although British doctors pioneered hip replacement surgery and are probably the best in the world at rebuilding shattered legs, Viner apparently had a fixation with American medicine.

DI Cutler instructed a team to contact America's leading orthopaedic specialists. The DI now thought it likely that Viner had spent the missing six months undergoing surgery and rehabilitation in the States. Then, determined to seek revenge against those he felt had destroyed his life, he returned to England and hatched an elaborate plot to stage his own death and reinvent himself as the only person he had ever wanted to be. Jack Sparrow.

But the DI realised that if this theory were correct, Martin Viner would have needed to be a very rich man. Without money – a very great deal of money – he could not have gone to America for medical treatment, he could not have bought Burrowgate, he could not have acquired a helicopter. And yet Viner had allegedly been near enough penniless after his helicopter crash.

The team Cutler had ordered to look again at the accident provided the solution to that one. The film director who claimed that he had asked Viner to fly just over the low bridge and not beneath it had originally lied. Overcome with guilt and remorse he had confessed to his deception a few months after the crash. As a result, the film company, one of the American giants able and willing to spend almost anything to avoid a major scandal, proposed an out of court settlement. They made Martin Viner a damages offer of Hollywood proportions – in excess of two million pounds. There had been only one condition. Total secrecy.

Cutler whistled out loud when he heard the news.

'And he did keep it secret too,' he muttered to himself. 'Even from his wife . . .'

The autopsy report was the clincher. In Cutler's opinion it had not been conclusive at all.

It noted that the body of the man believed to be Martin Viner had been so badly burned that the only way of identifying him was through dental records. Teeth survive a blaze beyond any other part of the human body – but there had been no dental records available for Martin Viner. He had apparently not been to his dentist for eleven or twelve years and his records had been either lost or discarded.

However a heavy gold ring which Viner always wore on the index finger of his left hand had been found among the remains along with a gold sovereign he wore on a chain around his neck. His charred wheel chair and other belongings were also found among the ashes. The remains had been removed from Viner's room. There had been absolutely no reason for forensic to suspect that they could be dealing with anything other than Martin Viner's remains. And so his identity had been verified, based on a considerable amount of assumption, and a death certificate issued.

Todd Mallett was in the car being driven by Pitt back to Heavitree Road when Cutler contacted him for the third time.

'Any news from Limehouse?' the DCI asked at once.

'Two blokes have definitely gone round to her place now – nothing more yet.'

Cutler had a suspicion that his chief was showing more than professional concern, but he passed no further comment before informing his boss of the news of the autopsy report, the question mark over Viner's true medical condition, and the fresh information on his financial situation.

Cutler was just finishing a phone call when Todd walked into the Heavitree Road Ops Room. He looked slightly flushed.

'You were right, boss. Belle Parker's been attacked. And it looks like it was our man . . .'

To Todd it seemed as if the world had jolted to a halt on its axis. He could no longer hear the police station hubbub. He felt as if he was in a vacuum. Every second seemed like a day. His voice, when he eventually found it, sounded as if it belonged to somebody else.

'Belle?' he stumbled.

'He gave her a right going over . . .'

'Cutler!' Todd stepped forward, grabbing the inspector by one arm. 'Is she alive, man?' This time his voice was stronger but curiously high pitched. Vaguely he registered that he sounded hysterical.

'Oh yes, boss, she's alive. Knocked about a bit, but she'll get over it. 'They've got the bastard, too, boss. Pair of young bobbies walked right in on it . . .'

DI Cutler was still talking. Todd was no longer listening.

He felt his legs go weak. Abruptly he sat on DI Cutler's desk and buried his head in his hands. The relief of the news he had just been given was totally physical. For just a minute or two he was unable to function.

'Thank God,' he said quietly.

It was some time before he became aware of DI Cutler studying him in open-mouthed surprise.

Todd came to pick her up when she was allowed to leave hospital two days later, just as he had said he would.

He had driven to London on the morning after Belle was attacked to liaise with the Met and take part in the interrogation of Martin Viner. He also wanted, more than he could remember wanting anything in his life, to see Belle Parker.

He felt terribly guilty about her ordeal – he really should have both thought and moved faster. And he should never have failed to take her seriously.

Her appearance was a shock. She looked pale and wan and was transparently still in pain. She walked stiffly, four ribs had actually been broken, and her fractured wrist was encased in plaster and carried in a sling held around her neck. But she was coping with the horror and the shock of being so brutally attacked far better than Todd could have imagined possible.

And she was still Belle Parker. She wore a big fluffy coat over a black mini dress brought to the hospital on her instructions by Jacky, who had appeared battered but clearly more chirpy than he had been since Joyce Carter's death.

It was difficult to show off her cleavage in the condition she was in, so she had settled for showing off her legs, which were encased in the kind of fishnet stockings nobody wore any more, except Belle Parker of course, and displayed to their best advantage with the help of her usual stilettoes. A hairdresser had visited her in the ward that morning and her hair was a sculpture of big black curls. And although the strain of her ordeal showed in her face on close examination, she was made-up as if she was setting off for a party.

Todd thought she was magnificent. And so did the snappers gathered outside the hospital – tipped off that she was about to be released by Belle's agent who hadn't thought the publicity would do his client any harm at all, particularly with a new film in the offing. Did she know how to play to this kind of gallery or what, thought Todd admiringly.

Having faced quite enough publicity for one lifetime he kept as much as possible out of the way of the lenses. Jacky Starr, whom Todd felt more able to cope with now that the case really was solved, offered to be driver for the day.

'Thought you couldn't drive,' said Todd.

'I've learned, gone right off hitching.'

Todd grunted. 'Just do us a favour then, don't drink or smoke anything,' the policeman instructed grumpily, but he had agreed readily enough to the proposition. After all, Jacky had come good in the end. He had saved his mother's life.

And so Jacky, using Belle's Jag, had picked up his mother at the front of the hospital after she had been photographed and then whisked her around to the back where Todd waited, before driving the pair of them to her home.

At Limehouse Jacky had told his mother that he wouldn't be coming into the flat.

'I'll be off back to my place,' he said. 'I reckon you'll be in safe hands. Well, sort of safe . . .'

Jacky had grinned broadly. Todd realised suddenly that he had never seen the lad smile properly before. He had his mother's smile.

Todd grinned back. 'You did a good job, boy,' he said.

'Well, she is me mum,' replied Jacky.

Todd felt Belle stand two inches taller beside him.

'Goodbye, son, and thank you,' she said. There were tears in her eyes.

Once inside the apartment she slumped on to the big squashy sofa clutching a mug of instant coffee made by Todd.

'It's good to see you,' she said. 'And I've got so much to ask you . . .'

'I know,' he put a reassuring arm around her, and it was he who asked the first question. 'When did you know it was Viner?'

'It was his voice first of all. Then there were the eyes. He was staring at me with those grey eyes, cold as steel, and although I wasn't functioning properly I suddenly remembered that Richard Corrington had brown eyes – 'aven't you seen all those stories about his blessed come-to-bed brown eyes? I had to look into them enough when I made that episode of *Sparrow-Hawk* with him.

'Then I realised his face, close up – and 'e was bleedin' close – wasn't Ricky's face at all. Ricky's hair, Ricky's eyebrows, Ricky's colouring. But not Ricky. The teeth clinched it.'

'His teeth?'

'Yeah. Ricky Corrington had designer molars – a Hollywood capping job. That bleeder Viner's got 'orrible teeth.'

Todd could not help laughing.

'But the really crazy thing is, why was I so easily convinced that he was Ricky?' Belle continued.

She leaned back against Todd's arm as he started to reply.

'The man was an actor who did everything in his power to make you believe he was someone else. It's association too: the hair, the clothes, the famous *Sparrow-Hawk* lapel brooch, false eyebrows identical to Ricky's, same skin colouring, thanks to make-up. Quite a package. And even the motor bike.

'Also their height and build were much the same and facially they really were quite alike. Same basic bone structure. I suppose the *Sparrow-Hawk* producers had a particular look in mind when they were casting their show, and when it didn't work out with Viner subconsciously they sought out someone of similar appearance.

'When Viner had all those blonde curls you'd never have thought about the similarities, and of course his colouring is naturally very pale and Richard was dark to the point of being swarthy.

'When I met him as Harry Pearson, he was completely bald, his paleness was all the more apparent, and of course the baldness changed the way he looked completely. His face became an empty canvas – I think that's the way he saw it too. The alopecia was almost a bonus.'

Arabella clasped Todd's free hand with one of hers.

' "I am Jack Sparrow." That's what he said, Todd.'

He was aware of a shiver running through her body.

She had used her actress's voice and he had a feeling it was a pretty close impersonation of the way Viner had spoken. He found it quite chilling.

'I thought I was going to die, Todd,' she said. 'In fact I knew I was going to die.'

He squeezed her hand. 'Bloody lucky Jacky was here. Why was he here anyway?'

'Little bugger had been on the piss all afternoon, pub crawling around the East End, and been indulging in all sorts of other things you don't tell policemen about, I shouldn't wonder. They finished up in a boozer just around the corner from my gaff and he staggered around to bum a cab fare home – spent out as usual. When he found I wasn't there he decided to wait and crashed out in the spare room to sleep it off. I think Viner was probably following me all day – so he wouldn't have known Jacky was here.'

She looked at him. 'Todd, it's just ridiculous. How did he do it, how did he convince everyone he was dead?'

He told her all about it, everything she did not already know, and saw the shock in her eyes.

'I spent all day yesterday at your local nick,' he said. 'Our friend is singing like a bird. It's as if he is proud of himself. The only thing you have to remember is to call him Jack all the time. You were right about him being barking, you and his missus. Call him Martin or Mr Viner and he throws a major wobbler.

'We guessed that he probably went to the States to have advanced surgery on his legs and he confirmed that. It actually worked better than even the doctors had expected – come to think of it he still limps but it's little more than an awkward stiffness – and that was when he began to hatch his revenge plot.'

'But why did he have to stage his own death, kill all those innocent people?'

'They didn't come into the equation. They were in Jack Sparrow's way. He didn't want to be Martin Viner any more, he wanted to be Jack Sparrow, the mad bastard. You mistook him for Richard Corrington – but he didn't see himself as impersonating Corrington at all. He saw himself as taking on the persona of Jack Sparrow.

'It would be almost sad if he hadn't done so much bloody evil.

'His ultimate aim was to destroy Richard Corrington, but he couldn't kill him. In Viner's convoluted mind Corrington was an imposter but none the less he was also Sparrow-Hawk. He could not face him directly and murder him. I think he also thought that would be too easy, the twisted sod. He planned an extraordinary frame-up, the key of which was to make Corrington believe *he* could be a murderer.

'Viner stalked him relentlessly for the three years he was on the loose after the fire, spying on him through binoculars, planning and scheming. He knew everything the poor bloody man was up to, he knew about the drugs, he knew when Corrington was out of his mind with them – which was when the murders were always committed and was inclined to be towards the end of a *Sparrow-Hawk* shoot when Corrington would be at his lowest ebb.

'He got right inside Ricky's head. You could say his aim was to drive Richard Corrington as mad as he was himself. Even the helicopter he took down to Landacre and the hangar that he built were designed to send Richard potty.

'Along the way he killed with seeming abandon. Although in his mind it wasn't like that. Ruth Macintosh and Joyce Carter had both wronged him or wronged Jack Sparrow – and he, of course, *was* Jack Sparrow. Poor Margaret Nance became a threat to Sparrow-Hawk. The others, Peter Nash, the man in Plymouth whose body he substituted for his own, and the nurse and two invalids who died in the fire, were deaths necessary to his cause.

'His wife believes, incidentally, that he always hated women. Apparently his mother walked out when Martin was a toddler – not surprising with their family history. They were all half-mad. You were a bonus, by the way...'

'What do you mean?'

'Well he was out to get Joyce Carter anyway, after the hatchet job, and he said he knew Corrington had knocked her off, but when he found out who Jacky was he saw that as fate. Indirectly it was all going to cause you trouble and he still blamed you for losing him *Sparrow-Hawk*. He hadn't foreseen Jacky being arrested, but it didn't affect his end game. The sod followed me when I came to see you during the trial, I'm afraid, and saw us kissing on the balcony. His attempting to kill you was also partly my fault, because he then reckoned that would hurt me.

'I had admitted in court that I hated *Sparrow-Hawk*, you see, and that I'd like to see it scrapped – and I had failed to make Ricky Corrington's charge stick.

'He was appalled when Ricky was freed, of course, and killing Amanda Lane so that Richard would get the blame was his last ploy. He had slept with her, you know – that was all part of the game too. But he had no compunction about murdering her when it suited his purpose.

'It went like a dream, that too – with Richard getting out of his brains on his very first night after jail and finally going right over the edge – and Viner might well have got away with it. But by the time he attacked you he thought he was immortal, and I don't think he could stop . . .'

Belle shivered again. 'And all the time he really believed he was Jack Sparrow?'

'Absolutely. It was schizophrenic delusion. His vehicles were registered in the name of J. Sparrow, he rented his London flat as J. Sparrow – he was even on the electoral register as Jack Sparrow. Amazing, isn't it?

'Only in Somerset was he Harry Pearson. Even Viner was just sane enough, unfortunately, to realise that if he had bought the house next door to Ricky Corrington as Jack Sparrow there may have been a few questions asked.'

Belle was fascinated. 'But didn't anybody in London suspect anything, didn't anybody here think Jack Sparrow was an odd name?'

Todd smiled. 'Why should they? There are nearly 150 Sparrows in the London area phone books alone and over thirty J. Sparrows. We checked.

'He had it all worked out. As well as being part of the revenge campaign, his affair with Amanda Lane gave him access to Landacre. He admits that he took Richard Corrington's suit – the one we found the thumb print on and which the strands of material in Joyce Carter's watch came from – and then planted it back in Richard's wardrobe.'

Belle gave a little snort. 'Pity he didn't put his

inventive brain to better use,' she said. 'You couldn't fault the maniac on initiative, could you?'

Todd smiled his agreement.

'What will happen to him?' she asked.

'He'll stand trial, probably at the Old Bailey, two of his crimes were committed in London, the murder of Ruth Macintosh and the attack on you, and he was arrested here. He'll plead insanity, which nobody's going to argue with. He's a psychotic, and he is congenitally schizophrenic. What a mixture. He'll be sent to Broadmoor, more than likely.'

Belle studied the policeman carefully. 'I have one more question,' she said. 'What about us?'

Gently, he drew her closer to him.

'We had to wait until it was all over, really and truly over. We both knew that, didn't we?'

She nodded. 'And now?' she asked.

'Well, if I can get it together . . .' he shifted uncomfortably in his seat.

'Don't be a prat,' she said. 'Less booze, a bit more time, and some peace of mind, that's all you ever needed.'

'OK, woman,' he said, deepening his voice, playing at being masterful. 'In that case, we are going to get to know each other very, very well indeed . . .'

'But not today we're bleedin' not, with me in this condition,' she told him, suddenly sparky. She waved her injured wrist at him, which proved to be a mistake and caused her to wince with pain.

'Serves you right for presuming . . .' he replied, enjoying the banter now.

With her good hand she touched his lips. 'Just you wait, Detective Chief Inspector Mallett,' she said. 'Just you bleedin' wait.'

'That's all I ever seem to do,' he responded.

She grinned, yet could not help her thoughts returning to the grim events of the past few months.

'At least we are able to wait,' she said quietly.

He knew what she meant. 'Nine victims: the three at the home whose names I do not even remember, Peter Nash, Margaret Nance, Ruth Macintosh, Joyce Carter, Amanda Lane, and Richard Corrington.'

He spoke solemnly, as if reciting names on a roll of honour.

When he stopped speaking she remained silent. He thought that suddenly she seemed very small and vulnerable and overwhelmingly sad. Typical Belle Parker, probably much more affected by it all than she was ever going to reveal.

He smiled at her wryly. 'And you were right about Richard Corrington. He was just an averagely mad actor. No more or less bonkers than all the rest – including you.'

It was an attempt to lighten the moment which did not work all that well. She looked at him with eyes full of sorrow.

'Poor old Ricky darling,' she said.